BELL
BOOK
AND
KEY

ALSO BY RYSA WALKER

THE DELPHI TRILOGY

NOVELS
The Delphi Effect
The Delphi Resistance
The Delphi Revolution

NOVELLA
The Abandoned

ENTER HADDONWOOD

As the Crow Flies (with Caleb Amsel)
When the Cat's Away (with Caleb Amsel)

BELL BOOK AND KEY

CHRONOS ORIGINS ⧗ BOOK THREE

RYSA WALKER

47NORTH

Text copyright © 2021 by Rysa Walker

Published by 47North, Seattle

www.apub.com

Amazon, the Amazon logo, and 47North are trademarks of Amazon.com, Inc., or its affiliates.

ISBN-13: 9781542019576
ISBN-10: 1542019575

Cover design by M. S. Corley

Printed in the United States of America

*For Pete, who always helps when time travel
breaks my brain.
Also for Griffin, who keeps me company while I
write the night shift . . . and who would probably
prefer another cookie instead.*

Part One

En Prise

En prise [from French, "in a position to be taken"]: describes a piece or pawn exposed to a capture by the opponent.

FROM "ABRAHAM DAVENPORT"
BY JOHN GREENLEAF WHITTIER
(1867)

'Twas on a May-day of the far old year
Seventeen hundred eighty, that there fell
Over the bloom and sweet life of the Spring
Over the fresh earth and the heaven of noon,
A horror of great darkness, like the night
In day of which the Norland sagas tell,
The Twilight of the Gods.

FROM "SOME CONSIDERATIONS, PROPOUNDED TO THE SEVERAL SORTS AND SECTS" BY PUBLICK UNIVERSAL FRIEND (1779)

While Abel lived in you, Cain could not rise up
in his dominions; but now the right seed is
slain, the murdering nature appears.
But why should we wonder at these things?
There is no new thing under the sun. The
state of the world is just as it always was.

∞ 1 ∞

The proprietor of the Little Rest Inn slides a large copper mug of cider and a shallow wooden plate in front of me. He places a second, considerably smaller mug in front of Clio and says he'll return shortly with her food.

Clio tosses back most of her cider as soon as it hits the table. I do the same. The closest stable point was several blocks away, and it's unseasonably warm for late spring in New England. A passing carriage raised a cloud of dust just before we reached the inn, and while we managed to get most of it off in our room before coming back down to the tavern, my throat still feels like I've been eating sand.

"Now we know why he charges half price for women's room and board," Clio says, giving the tiny mug a foul look.

The innkeeper returns with a plate of something called *pandowdy*. It looks good. Smells good, too, with hints of apples and cinnamon.

I stare down at the massive blob of cold pastry in the center of my own plate. It's pork pie, apparently—something I ordered only because I recognized the words *pork* and *pie* on the bill of fare posted behind the bar, and it sounded less gross than boiled fish or calves' head soup. I have no idea what the other option, cock-a-leeky, even is, but I know I'm not eating it.

"Are ye certain yer missus wouldn't rather take her meal into the ladies' parlor?" the innkeeper says, still holding Clio's plate.

It's the third time he's asked this. We seem to be violating some sort of norm, which is something I'd prefer to avoid when jumping to a strange time and place. But we wouldn't be able to see the dining room from the windowless, oversized closet he showed us when we checked in a few minutes earlier. And splitting up worries me more than offending this guy's sensibilities.

"We thank thee for the kind offer," I say, "but this table will do nicely. My wife likes having a view."

"Good thing your wife's not particular," the man says with a snort as he heads back to the bar. "'Tain't much of a view."

He has a point. The window near our table looks out on a dreary street with a smattering of foot traffic and the occasional carriage headed for the Kings County courthouse. According to the research Jarvis pulled up for this trip, Rhode Island delegates will assemble in that building a little less than ten years from now to reject the newly minted US Constitution for the eleventh time. *Exactly* ten years from this day, the new Congress of the United States will respond by passing legislation banning the states from commerce with this lone holdout that preferred to stick with the Articles of Confederation. Faced with the prospect of being the sole entity outside the new union, the "Rogue Island" delegates will grudgingly agree to ratify a few weeks later. And even then, they'll send back a whole shopping list of proposed amendments along with the signed document.

"'Tain't much of a day, neither," adds a man two tables over. "Can barely make out the sun through those clouds. Mebbe Judge Potter's prophet is right." He stares around the room, somberly adjusting his glasses on his rather large nose as the rest of the tavern looks on. Then he slaps his palm against the wooden table and bursts out laughing. The two other men at his table join him, as does the innkeeper and several of the patrons seated at the bar.

"Far more likely we're going to get a bit of rain," another man at the table says. "God knows the fields could use it."

I exchange a look with Clio, who is clearly wondering the same thing I am. Will any of these men be among the crowd storming Judge Potter's farm tomorrow afternoon when the sky above Little Rest, and indeed, above all of New England, begins to go black? A massive forest fire currently raging in Ontario is the reason, but that won't be discovered for several centuries. The majority of people here in Little Rest will, like many others, assume it's a harbinger of the end times. This exact sign was, in fact, predicted by the prophet that the joker at the next table just mentioned. Born Jemima Wilkinson, the minister now goes by the name of the Publick Universal Friend, the genderless embodiment of Christ. Or at least that's the claim.

We have three different descriptions of how the events of the next two days will unfold. Only Katherine remembers learning about the first, in which little mention is made of the Dark Day, aside from the fact that the event occurred at the same time Susannah Potter, the judge's daughter, died. Wilkinson attempted to resurrect her. When the attempt failed, Wilkinson blamed it on the lack of faith among the group. Apparently, there were no hard feelings on the matter. Most of them followed Wilkinson to upstate New York where they founded a community called the Society of Universal Friends, which lasted well into the 19th century.

The second version of upcoming history is detailed in one of the books protected by a CHRONOS field in Madi's library in Bethesda. Katherine also remembers that version because she watched the events unfold during one of her first jumps as Saul Rand's partner. That time, Wilkinson predicted the Dark Day in vague terms, saying it would happen sometime during the month of May, and the judge's daughter lived.

Now we have a third version, based on the history Jarvis pulled up for this timeline. This time, Wilkinson predicts the Dark Day will happen tomorrow, preceded by a red moon tonight. When these predictions come true, a mob will reward accuracy with fire, torching Wilkinson, an unspecified number of followers, and Judge Potter's farm, chanting that witches must die. The Dark Day massacre will launch a new round of witch hunts in New England nearly a century after the first wave died out. This twist, combined with the reference to the Dark Day that Saul's splinter whispered to Katherine just before dying and the changes in the Austrian legend of the Zaubererjackl, suggest that whatever Saul is planning involves witches. And so we're here, trying to get a head start before he makes the move that finally flips the timeline.

The chatter in the tavern has turned to other topics, so we focus on our food for a bit. The pork pie might have been decent if they served it hot, but the crust is soggy, and the filling is sort of congealed. While I don't doubt it's pork, I have serious questions about which bits of pig were used. I'm not a picky eater by any means, but I have my limits. Clio clearly made the better choice.

Between bites, she sneaks glances at the door. I'd love to have taken her seat. I'm never entirely at ease unless I'm facing the entrance. But despite the fake braid running down my back and the stupid blue lenses in my eyes, there's a risk Katherine or Saul might recognize my face. Not a major risk, given that I was two years behind Katherine at CHRONOS. She was eighteen when this jump happened, which means I'd have been sixteen, probably before my final growth spurt. That's also one reason Clio is with me on this jump, rather than Rich. He was in the same class as Katherine, and they've been friends since they were ten. Even five-years-younger Katherine would recognize him.

Clio tucks a stray dark curl under her white bonnet and then checks the time with her key again. It emits a faint purple glow under the table.

"Stop giving me the evil eye," she whispers as she slips the key back into its pouch. "No one is looking. And even if they were, they couldn't see the light."

"True," I admit. "But Katherine and Saul—"

"Would have been here twenty minutes ago if they were coming. And that's using the *outside* estimate Katherine gave us."

I look around, worried someone might be wondering why we're talking so low. But the men at the next table are lost in their own conversation. And I guess a young couple whispering across the table is a common enough sight in any century. "Katherine admitted she wasn't certain of the time."

"Oh, come on, Tyson. You read the entry. It was one of her first jumps. She was meticulous about recording every little thing she did."

I break off another bit of crust from the pork pie and pop it into my mouth, mostly to avoid responding. The diary was typical Katherine, detailed and precise. For her to have been off by even five minutes seems out of character, and the diary entry said she and Saul checked in at the inn at twelve fifty in the afternoon on May 18th, had lunch, and then hiked up North Road to Potter's farm.

"Alex was right," Clio says. "Katherine's trip doesn't happen."

I sigh and push my plate away. CHRONOS apparently exists in this timeline, but not in the sense that Rich, Katherine, and I knew it. Alex, our resident temporal physicist, is convinced some sort of rudimentary organization is there based on his bubble grid, which measures chronotron pulses in the past and, through extrapolation, the future. He's still picking up chronotrons from CHRONOS HQ in the decades before 2305, just much fainter, similar to the ones he's isolated at Madi's place when we use the diaries. It's a definite improvement over the timeline before this, where the US never entered World War II. In that reality, there were no pulses emanating from CHRONOS. The equipment picked up some jumps that would have happened around the time of the first training cohort, but nothing during the time any of us were employed there. Alex's best guess is that they abandoned the program. Richard, who understands more about the mechanics of time travel than Katherine and I combined, agrees with Alex.

And so does everyone else, apparently.

From a standpoint of pure logic, I'd be inclined to agree, too. Before Team Viper screwed with the timeline, Alex was able to isolate the exact geographic location of the jump room, based on those pulses alone, even though he's never been to CHRONOS HQ or to any year beyond 2136. The jump room was inside a building that houses some sort of museum. Or technically, it was located two non-existent stories *above* that museum, since the CHRONOS campus that will be built there over a century later is a much taller building. All of our previous trips to the past began in the jump room, so if Alex isn't picking up a regular barrage of chronotron pulses in 2305, the blank square we've seen on our keys each time we've tried to go home is probably correct, and there's no active time-travel program. If that's the case, the odds are exceptionally strong that none of us with the gene exists outside of a CHRONOS field.

Trouble is, I know from personal experience it's not that simple. Alex's system is either wrong or there are exceptions to the rule, because one of those exceptions nearly got me killed in an alley behind a nightclub in 1939 New York.

Clio nudges her plate toward me. "Trade you this for some of your cider. It's hot out there, especially in this black dress, and unless they walk in the door in the next minute or two, we're about to go on a hike."

"You're not hungry?"

"Not especially. I know Madi's food unit is crap, and I generally avoid gambling on historical cuisine. So I ate before I left Skaneateles."

Her mouth tightens slightly as she speaks. I'm sure there's been some tension with her parents. They'd almost certainly prefer that she stay out of this. I can't say I blame them. Kate and Kiernan Dunne have memories of a timeline where getting involved went very badly for their daughter. Clio doesn't seem like she's ready to talk about it, though, so I change the subject.

"Did you know this was pie or did you just get lucky?"

She raises an eyebrow. "I'd say it's more of a cobbler, but sure. It's better with ice cream but . . . I doubt our host could accommodate a request for à la mode. My mom makes pandowdy, although this one is better, to be honest."

Well, I *thought* I'd changed the subject, but apparently not. And since Clio pulls Katherine's diary out of her bag and starts thumbing through it, my guess that she's not ready to talk about the situation in 1940 Skaneateles is probably dead-on.

I drag out the last few bites until even I have to admit it's bordering on the ridiculous. We're coming up on two o'clock, which is when the tavern stops serving lunch, or *dinner* as they seem to call the midday meal here and now. And Clio, who has put the diary away, is drumming her fingers on the table, clearly restless and ready to get on with it.

"Fine. Alex was right. You're right. Everyone was right. Let's just go."

I take a deep breath once we're outside and instantly regret it. The air seems to be laced with smoke as well as dust. But that could be partly my imagination, since I know the odd haze settling over the town is due to the distant fire.

As we cross the street, I glance back over my shoulder at the tavern. Just in case.

Clio shakes her head and tugs at my arm. "They're not coming, Tyson. I understand why that bugs you. I've got a whole set of memories from my jumps with Simon that one half of my mind remembers vividly, and the other . . ." She shrugs. "The other insists the jumps never happened at all. That Simon never even existed. Which is probably a point in favor of this timeline over the one I remember. It still messes with my head, though."

"But that's just it. You remember those things because you're wearing a CHRONOS key. Lawrence Dennis wasn't wearing a key. And yet, when I spoke to him in that alleyway in 1939, despite a time shift that should have meant I was dealing with an entirely different version of Lawrence Dennis, he *still* remembered me showing up at his book talk. Still remembered my little dig about his career shift from child evangelist to cheerleader for fascism. He even remembered seeing me blink out in an alley. That's why none of this makes a damn bit of sense to me. If that jump happened, I can't see why this one didn't."

"That was in the previous timeline, though."

"Right . . . but that really doesn't make the situation any clearer. CHRONOS didn't exist at all in that timeline. The building was gone, so we *know* CHRONOS was erased. We saw Angelo just . . . vanish. Add all that together and the whole thing with Dennis bugs the holy crap out of me. It doesn't fit."

"You could check. Watch the stable point and see if you ever jump in." When I don't respond, she gives me an annoyed look. "You already did. And?"

"And I didn't see myself jump in. That's not conclusive proof, though. Maybe something changed. Maybe I used one of the other New York stable points. There are a lot of them, as I'm sure you know. Or maybe I went to a different event he held for that book. CHRONOS might exist, in some form, just not in DC. The bottom line is that I *must* have made some sort of jump or Dennis couldn't have remembered seeing me. Couldn't have seen me blink out."

What I really want is to change the subject, because I get an odd, almost painful sensation when I think about that trip. It's a bit like a double memory, but not quite. It's the same feeling I've gotten when I thought too much about CHRONOS this week. Thoughts about my training, the people I work with, even my family, trigger the same gut-clenching sensation. But it's not like there's another memory competing with it. More of a black void. And I have no point of comparison to know if that's my mind trying to balance this reality with one in which I never existed or the ordinary grief anyone would feel when almost everything and everyone they've ever known is gone.

"Leaving the thing with Lawrence Dennis aside," I say, "we *do* know Saul visits this time and place at some point. Otherwise, the people back there in the tavern wouldn't have been talking about Wilkinson's prophecy that the sky will go dark. Katherine seems convinced that the prophecy was one of Saul's little tests to see how much he could change without CHRONOS security catching on."

"It's still unlikely Saul is here *now*," Clio says, although I notice that she glances over her shoulder as she says it. "Katherine also thinks he did something to cure the judge's daughter of typhoid on their jump, and no one saves her in this timeline. One of the eyewitness accounts noted that they were in the process of burying her when the mob approached the farm."

Susannah Potter's survival was something Katherine initially assumed was her fault. Saul apparently encouraged that assumption, but it seemed reasonable, since Katherine watched over the girl briefly and Saul swore he was never in the same room with her. Now, of course, Katherine is far less certain. She had been relieved to return to CHRONOS after that trip and find that the small changes didn't affect the timeline, possibly because the judge's daughter died during childbirth a few years later. Wilkinson's fame grew slightly, due in part to her prediction but also due to the healing of Susannah. In the end, however, the trajectory of the religious community was pretty much the same. The group outlasted their prophet by a few decades and then disbanded. And that's probably what would have happened in this timeline, too, if the prophecy hadn't been so eerily accurate that it triggered accusations of witchcraft.

"Wilkinson made the prophecy weeks ago," Clio says. "So Saul must have come and gone. That's a good thing in more ways than one. I'd be way too tempted to pull that little ray gun out of my pocket and shoot the rat bastard as soon as we spotted him."

"Which would run the risk of you getting torched along with Jemima's followers if anyone saw you."

"True," she admits as we turn onto North Road. "And knowing my luck, if I managed to kill him, we'd find out it wasn't him at all, but another one of his splinters. Maybe we'll get lucky, and it will be a case of us or him."

I know she's joking. Neither of us wants to be in a situation where our lives are in danger. But it's the only circumstance under which the group has agreed we'd have to risk killing the son of a bitch in front of witnesses. Saul killing other people is something we can undo. If he manages to take our group out of the equation, however, there are no do-overs.

The bigger question is whether we can risk *erasing* him. Katherine said that erasing him was the only way to be certain he'd never be a problem again. But Madi says even that's not a guarantee. According to Kate Pierce-Keller's diary, Saul's key was pulled once before. As long as they continue creating the technology that eventually leads to CHRONOS, there's a risk that we'll end up with Saul or someone very much like him again. Alex described it as a perverse sort of time loop. The only way to break it is to not create the technology . . . but then you face the reality that the technology has already been created in other timelines. If Alex could send out a cross-timeline cease-and-desist order to all conceivable versions of himself, it would be a start . . . but then all of those Alexes would have to wage a crusade to convince other temporal physicists around the world to halt the development of time travel. He might be able to delay it for a while, but prevent it? No way.

Another complicating factor is the role that Saul played in helping us evict the time tourists six days ago. As much as I hate to admit it, we'd have lost without his help. Would erasing Saul completely undo that victory? Would it give those of us unlucky enough to know him for the past eight years or so double memories? We don't really know the answer to those questions, and they're kind of important.

It seems the best we can do is fix *this* timeline. Even then, Alex says we're really only creating a new version. The other one goes on without us, with the occupants blissfully unaware that anything changed.

I'm normally not the nihilistic type, but his assessment has me wondering what's the fucking point of any of this. On the other hand, we can't just sit by and let Saul Rand kill anyone he wants to simply because this isn't our original universe. Ethical issues aside, that could mean we're constantly jumping from one reality to the next. We become his playthings. And so do all of the other people in this timeline . . . whether they know it or not.

"I think not being able to take him out is what pisses me off most about all of this," I say. "It was difficult enough watching the Klan threaten the livelihood of a family I knew in South Carolina. Not sure I can stand by and do nothing when I know a mob is about to kill innocent people."

Clio gives me a skeptical look, which is fair. It *shouldn't* bug me. I mean, it should bug anyone on a moral level, but I should be used to it by now. These are pretty much the exact same guidelines Rich, Katherine, and I—and yes, Saul, too—operated under at CHRONOS.

We went into the field to observe. To learn history by living history, so we could fill in all of the context the historical record was missing. Correct the things conventional historians just plain got wrong. And there were plenty of them.

The cardinal rule, however, was that we did not *change* our history. CHRONOS put in place a ton of safeguards designed to prevent that from happening. For nearly six decades, the restrictions worked. Until someone on the genetic-design team was apparently asleep at the controls and gave a sociopath the ability to time travel.

"Yeah, yeah," I tell Clio. "I get the irony. But that was history that had already happened. Where anyone who died was supposed to die. This is a history where Saul Rand has set himself up as judge, jury, and executioner."

"We won't be *leaving* these people dead, though. At some point, we'll fix it." The words are true enough, but I'm guessing she knows they'll be cold comfort in the moment. "At least we don't have to worry about avoiding Katherine and Saul. And we know their cover story should get us in to talk with Wilkinson."

I'm less certain on that point. We know Katherine and Saul posed as a newlywed couple seeking advice from the Publick Universal Friend on the issue of celibacy. Wilkinson encouraged, but did not require, followers to be celibate. Hopefully, we won't get to the point of actually having that long of a conversation, because I'm not exactly equipped for it. Katherine and Saul were much more accustomed to the norms and the language of this era. In Katherine's case, she'd spent several months in a Quaker community during her training. Clio and I only had a couple of days to do a crash course, and this is well over a century before my earliest jump with CHRONOS. It's nearly two centuries before the mid-1960s that I specialized in. Clio will have the advantage of being able to play timid. Quaker women are far more outspoken than most during the Revolutionary era, but even so, it's common enough for the wife to let the husband do the talking. It's not exactly Clio's nature to take a back seat, but it will give her a chance to wander around a bit and set stable points while I talk with the Friend or whoever is willing to give me a couple of minutes of their time.

"I'm not sure how much of their success with that cover story was due to Saul's previous conversations with Wilkinson," I say. "The family may be a lot less welcoming of us, especially with illness in the house. And it's not like it instantly opened doors, anyway. Katherine said the P.U.F. kept them waiting for over an hour."

"Do they really use the initials?" she asks, wrinkling her nose.

"At some point, yes. The Friend will eventually have someone paint *P.U.F.* on the side of the wagon used in the ministry."

Clio laughs. She has a very nice laugh. "I wonder if they abbreviated to conserve paint or were just lazy?"

A wagon passes us, heading toward town. We cover our mouths and noses, and squint to ward off the worst of the dust kicked up by the hooves and wheels. North Road stretches out in an almost perfectly straight line in front of us. There are trees on either side here, but up ahead, it's straight farmland as far as the eye can see. Not that my eyes can see very well right now through lenses that feel like they're made of sandpaper.

I take advantage of the last bit of tree cover to step off the road and set a stable point, just in case we need to jump back in where we won't be observed. While I'm out of sight, I pull out the tiny bottle of lens cleaner I keep in my bag. Not exactly sanitary conditions, but at least the lenses are clear enough that I can see again.

Two men on horseback pass us on the left as we continue up the road. I nod at them, and then Clio and I walk along quietly for a few minutes in what I assume is a comfortable silence, until I glance over and realize something is bothering her.

Before I can ask what's up, she says, "Do you think there will still *be* a Madi's house when we get back? The waiting is making me crazy.

I almost wish the timeline would flip already and get it over with so we'll know what we're facing."

She's right. Things could change at any minute. We might not feel it this far back in time, depending on when Saul makes his next little tweak to history, but it's possible that we get back to 2136 and find ourselves in a new reality in which there's not only no CHRONOS, but also no base of operations in Bethesda. And I'm sure Clio is also worried about her family. Unlike virtually everyone else in the world, her parents are under a CHRONOS key. Depending on when in time it happens, they may not feel the actual impact, either, but they'll eventually realize that reality has shifted beneath their feet.

So far, the changes Saul has made haven't been massive enough to entirely flip the timeline. I doubt Clio's parents are even aware of them. We wouldn't be, either, except for the fact that a computer is continually checking for differences between the information in our protected files and those available in the "official" historical records on the public data system. What we've picked up so far are really only ripples. For example, one of the men who will die at Potter's farm tomorrow would have become the grandfather of Isaac Peace Rodman, who was a brigadier general in the Union Army. Rodman was killed as a result of injuries sustained in the Battle of Antietam . . . but so was the person who rose through the ranks in his stead. Different injury, same outcome. His wasn't the only death that caused ripples. The Anomalies Machine in Madi's library listed fifty-eight additional deaths in attacks on members of small fringe religious groups before sanity again took hold in the mid-1790s. And the justification for the purges was always that the group or individual was engaged in some sort of witchcraft.

"Katherine seems to think we won't have to wait much longer," I say, picking up the pace a bit. "Which is a good reason to set the stable points and get back to the library on schedule."

Clio gives me a little eye roll, which is entirely fair. She'd been the one pushing to get a move on while we were at the inn, while I delayed, trying to avoid facing the inevitable.

It still bothers me, though. If Saul and Katherine's jump didn't happen, it stands to reason that my jump to 1936 didn't happen, either. And if it didn't happen, there's no way Lawrence Dennis could have recognized me in 1939. The inconsistency is going to keep gnawing at me until I figure out why that jump is an exception to the rule.

I push those thoughts aside, however, because we're now only a few meters away from the drive leading to Potter's farm. A quick glance at my CHRONOS key shows it's two fifteen, about the same time Katherine's diary had her and Saul arriving. She'd noted there was just one servant in the yard when they approached, a young woman who had been coming back from the well. The girl had pointed them toward the side entrance, where a man named Caesar had greeted them and taken them into the parlor until the Friend could meet with them. Katherine believed Caesar was one of the slaves Potter freed when he joined Wilkinson's group, since the name was listed in the manumission documents she studied while writing her jump plan for that trip with Saul.

Something seems to have changed now, however. There are at least a dozen people outside, mostly women, and about evenly split between black and white. A couple of kids are running around on the lawn, along with a puppy and assorted yard fowl, but the adults are all talking in hushed tones beneath the shade of the front porch. They're gathered around Jemima Wilkinson, who is holding a wicker basket. As in the drawings I've seen, the Publick Universal Friend wears a long skirt, but otherwise is dressed as a male preacher from this era, in a black clerical robe with one of those ruffled white things at the neck. An ascot . . . or maybe it's called a cravat. The key difference is Wilkinson's age. Most of the drawings were made much later, after the group moved to upstate New York. This version of the Friend is at least twenty years younger, maybe more.

"Do you think that's Puffy?" Clio whispers as we walk toward the house. "The one holding the basket?"

"I believe *thou* art correct," I say, emphasizing the word as a gentle reminder that we are about to be judged by our pronouns.

Clio gives a little nod to acknowledge the hint. "Not planning to say anything at all if I can avoid it. I'll wander around staring at my grandmother's locket"—she tugs the medallion out of her cloak—"pretending I'm mortified that you're talking about sex. I'm quite happy to focus on setting the stable points and leave the conversation to you."

I give her a droll smile. "Thou art too kind, wife."

She flashes me a quick grin and a tiny curtsy, then hangs back as I continue on toward the group on the porch, who have taken notice of us. They seem to be watching Clio more than me, though. That's a bit odd, and now I'm wishing she'd stayed with me. Maybe we're violating another norm.

Wilkinson hands the basket to an elderly black man standing nearby, who must be Caesar, and walks directly toward me. "Good day, friend, and welcome. Hast thou come to fetch the child?"

"What?" The question catches me entirely off guard.

"The babe," Wilkinson says, nodding toward the basket Caesar is holding. "Is it thine?"

"No." I glance over at Clio, who is doing exactly what she promised, studiously avoiding looking at us. She has her back to us right now, no doubt setting a stable point. "I'm . . . Thomas Early. My wife and I are here seeking thy counsel, Friend. On the duty of celibacy, in fact, and . . ."

I'm stammering, partly because our cover story seems more problematic now. She could well believe we're contemplating celibacy only because we've found out the hard way what happens when you opt for sex instead. But I've also just noticed her hand. A crude lotus is tattooed on the back. The right side is blue, the usual color for the symbol when worn by men in the religion, but the left side is pink. It's not swollen, but there's a slight scab along one side.

"We have no children," I continue. "My wife would like them, and I suppose I would as well, but with the end coming so soon, I feel we should focus on cleansing our souls. We are here to witness the prophecy unfold and had hoped to speak before . . . When did you find the child?"

Great. Now I've lapsed into non-plain speech. What the hell is a baby doing here, anyway? None of this was mentioned in the diary. Is this another change in the timeline? Or is it something that happened while Katherine and Saul were in the parlor, drinking lemonade or whatever while they waited to speak with Wilkinson?

"Betsy went to fetch water. The basket was not there when she left for the well, but when she returned, perhaps five minutes ago, she found it near the front door. A babe of three months or so. Art thou certain . . . ?" The Friend trails off, looking again toward Clio.

"Yes. Most certain. My wife and I have taken rooms at the inn in Little Rest. We had a late lunch . . . um, dinner . . . and then walked directly here. Many people saw us. The owner saw us leave."

Wilkinson stares at me for a moment and then begins walking toward Clio, whose back is again to us. "What is in thy hand?"

Clio turns around, her head bowed. "My locket, Friend. It was my grandmother's. I hold it when I am troubled, for it remind . . . eth me of her good counsel."

"Did she counsel thee to abandon thy child?"

Clio gives me an incredulous look and then turns back to Wilkinson. "I cannot abandon that which I do not possess. Thomas and I are but recently wed. We have no children, nor is it likely we will, if all thou hast foretold comes to pass."

"I have seen that pendant before. It belongs to John Franklin."

That's the alias Saul used on his jump with Katherine. I scramble for some explanation of why Clio might have the same medallion, but she beats me to it.

"Indeed," she says. "John Franklin and I share a grandmother. My mother inherited this. Her sister was a jealous woman. I had heard she had a copy made, but I have not seen it. Is my cousin here in Little Rest? I've not seen him since he left Richmond several years ago."

I let out the breath I was holding. I'm impressed with Clio's ability to think on her feet. She remembered more from Katherine's diary than I did.

Wilkinson doesn't answer Clio's question, but just eyes both of us for a moment, clearly trying to assess our truthfulness. "I must take my leave. We have a serious illness in the family, and now a foundling to deal with. I've no time to advise thee before the darkness falls upon us. Read the scriptures, pray, and take the Word as thy counsel in The Way. God be with thee."

Given that Clio has set several observation points already, we could simply go. We may need to be able to see closer to the house, however, and we definitely need to set a few points over near the flat rock Wilkinson often uses for preaching. I could pop back in during the night, but they have dogs who would no doubt bark. Better to get everything we need now. So even though Wilkinson is walking away, I follow. "Friend, could we trouble thee for some water? The dust is thick on the road, and it's a long walk back to the inn."

Wilkinson turns back and gives me an apologetic smile. "I beg thy pardon, friend. The strangeness of the past few minutes is no excuse for my forgetting the rules of hospitality. There are benches near our worship area. Please rest a while before returning to the inn. I must get back to Susannah, but I will have someone bring out a jug of switchel."

Most of the others have already gone inside, taking the basket with them. I manage to set one stable point near the front of the house, but a guy in his late teens is seated at the far end of the porch. He's watching us, possibly out of boredom rather than suspicion. I give him a smile and pretend to be interested in the tall flowering bushes running along the side of the house, then I rejoin Clio. An older dog is sprawled at the base of a birch tree. It lifts its head each time one of us activates the key to set a stable point. Not sure what it is about the frequency, but I've never met a dog that wanted to be anywhere near an activated CHRONOS key.

We head out to the clearing, which holds the flat stone known as Inscription Rock, and take a seat on one of the benches. It's where the Publick Universal Friend gives her sermons, but it's currently occupied by a large black rooster keeping watch over several hens pecking near the small rocks around the edge of the clearing. Beyond that, two children are tossing a stick for a puppy. The pup isn't yet trained to bring it back, so there's a lot of laughing as they chase the animal down to retrieve it.

One of the younger servants approaches with a pitcher and two mugs on a tray, telling us to leave it on the bench when we're finished. The drink resembles lemonade, but tastes more like a flat, slightly tart ginger ale.

Clio seems on edge. She keeps glancing back at the farmhouse. After a moment, she turns her back to the house and pulls up one of the stable points she set. Then she motions for my key, so she can transfer the location.

I tap the back of my key to hers, but don't open the stable point. "We can look at these later. Wilkinson is already suspicious, so I'm fairly certain someone has been assigned to watch us."

Clio frowns. "They can't see anything other than the medallion. It's not like I'm blinking out. I just want to check the stable point I gave you. And I need you to check it, too. But sure, we can wait until we're out on the road."

A few minutes later, once we're out of sight of the farmhouse, she stops. "Open the stable point and scroll back to when you were talking with Jemima. Focus on the basket and tell me what you see."

I follow her instructions. At first, I'm not sure what she's talking about, but then I see it. As Wilkinson is handing the basket to Caesar, it tips slightly to the side. I can't see the infant. Only a bundle of cloth. What I *can* see is the faint purple glow inside the blanket. Or at least, it looks purple to me. I'm guessing Clio sees it as teal.

Someone didn't just drop off a baby. They dropped off a baby and a CHRONOS key.

FROM *WITCHERY AROUND THE WORLD* BY JAMES L. COLEMAN (2082)

This tale begins with an ancient tree. Like anything that survives for centuries, a tree accumulates its share of scars. Each of those scars carries a story. With trees, as with humans, it is often the case that the more dramatic the scar, the more riveting the tale. The massive live oak on Hatteras Island is no exception. A jagged scar runs from top to bottom, hollowing out part of the trunk. More remarkable still is a group of four smaller blemishes, each over three inches high, that are burned deep into the tree.

The tree had witnessed hundreds of years of history before our nation was founded. In the early 1700s, Hatteras Island was home to a small band of settlers who made their living from the sea. They were a tight-knit community, and not especially welcoming to strangers. In many cases, that was a wise sentiment. This was an era of pirates, including the notorious William Teach, better known as Blackbeard, who roamed the Carolina coast, plundering merchant ships for gold and valuables. While the villagers on the island were wary of the pirates, they weren't wary of the gold the pirates and their crews spent in the local pub. This was especially true in seasons when food was scarce.

It was during one such season that two notable strangers appeared on the island. The first was a woman who took up residence in an abandoned, ramshackle hut in the middle of the forest. She was alone, except for an infant child, and was known to the locals only as Cora. Some villagers noted the baby was odd. It never smiled, and its eyes would follow a person around, almost as if the child were planning some evil deed. Many felt certain there was some sort of mischief afoot. The most skilled fishermen in the village were bringing in few fish that season, often sending their children to bed with empty stomachs. Cora's catch was always abundant, however. Others who lived near the edge of the woods where her cabin was located noted mysterious afflictions that befell their livestock . . . dead chickens the same day Cora was seen on their property, or crops that shriveled and died after she was spotted peeking out of the forest. One woman claimed the milk from her cow dried up because Cora touched it. A young villager who mocked Cora's baby took ill with a fever the next day and very nearly died.

The second stranger on the island during this time was a captain by the name of Eli Blood, who hailed from Salem, Massachusetts. When his ship crashed against the shoals, villagers helped him salvage whatever cargo they could and he took shelter with them while waiting for his company to send a vessel for him and his crew of former slaves from Barbados. Blood had taken a keen interest in the witch trials in his hometown and fancied himself the sworn enemy of Satan. He listened with interest to stories about Cora and her child—stories that grew wilder by the day—and said she was most likely a witch. The baby, of course, was not a baby at all, but simply a clever disguise for her familiar. Some noted the child did have odd eyes, like those of a cat.

Our story might have ended there, but one morning after a full moon, a body was found on the beach. The numbers 666 were burned into the dead man's forehead, and a set of small, feminine footprints led from the body to the woods beyond the shore where Cora and the child lived. Captain Blood was with the group that found the body. They stormed into the woods and confronted Cora, who denied any knowledge of the crime. Blood decreed Cora be tried not only for the murder, but also for practicing witchcraft.

Cora was bound and tossed into the sea. When she did not sink, Blood declared she was in league with Satan. The captain performed several other tests he claimed had been used by Cotton Mather and others during the Salem trials, and informed the villagers that Cora failed them all.

The men bound Cora, with the baby in her arms, to a nearby tree. Kindling was gathered and Captain Blood approached with a torch, preparing to burn the woman. A few villagers cried out that surely the child should not be harmed, and some stated the law forbade this sort of proceeding.

At this point, the legend takes a turn for the fanciful. Villagers claimed the child in Cora's arms snarled and morphed into a wildcat. Wriggling out of its bonds, it scurried toward the woods. While they were watching the cat, dark clouds rolled in from the sea, obscuring the previously bright blue sky. Before Blood could set fire to the kindling, lightning arced down from clouds straight toward the tree. Splinters of wood and smoking branches flew in all directions. Captain Blood and the villagers were hurled to the ground from the force of the blast. By the time they gathered their senses, it was too late. The rope was still attached to the tree, which was now split down the middle.

But the only thing left of Cora was her name, four letters burned deep into the wood.

If you travel to the Outer Banks, you can still find the Cora Tree. Cora was never seen again, but some people swear her cat lives in the woods of Hatteras Island to this very day.

∞2∞

My garden is missing.

The willow is still in the backyard. So is the patio, the shed, and the large oak. But those are all inside the boundary of the CHRONOS field protecting the house, so they don't really change. The trees and grass seem to fare better in some timelines than others, depending on whether there are high-rise buildings on the other side of our fence, but they've never entirely vanished.

My tiny garden, however, is outside the protective boundary. And it's gone. The seedlings I planted are gone, too, along with the portable greenhouse I placed over them. All that remains is the slightly raised patch of earth about three meters long that suggested someone else had once had a garden here. That's why I chose the spot originally, thinking the ground might be more tillable.

This, of course, begs the question of whether the *other* items planted there are also gone. And since one of those items set in motion the insanity of the past several weeks, I have to know.

In the grand scheme of things, the garden is no great loss. I planted it mostly as a stalling tactic to avoid working on my thesis, but also because the weather was nice, and I'd been thinking about the garden my father and I created on the roof of our townhouse in London when I was seven or eight. In terms of yield, our urban garden was a disappointment—a handful of strawberries, a few anemic-looking aubergines, and enough cucumbers and lettuce for one decent-sized salad. The only things that grew well were tomatoes and sage, neither of which I was particularly fond as a child. But we'd enjoyed planting it together, enjoyed the expectation of our meager crop. I think planting the garden here a few weeks back, smelling the soil and feeling it against my bare hands, was my way of trying to hold on to that place in my soul where my dad was still alive.

Thinking of him was what reminded me that I hadn't checked on the garden since the timeline shifted back. My father was my touchstone, the person I turned to when life didn't make sense. When I made mistakes. When I needed advice. He had an uncanny knack for helping me see the bright side, even when I believed my entire world was shot to hell.

His optimism is something I could use right now. This reality is, admittedly, better than the last, which was brought to us courtesy of tourists from Timeline 27V who were intent on using our timeline as their personal game board. Pearl Harbor never happened, the US never entered World War II, and a slow, creeping fascism spread across the nation. Jack was stuck in the 1960s, and my paternal grandmother, Nora, the only family member who comes even close to understanding me the way Dad did, was erased. Nora exists in this timeline and Jack's home now. Those two factors alone make this reality a vast improvement. And it's better than the reality before that, also the work of the interdimensional gamers, in which the Vietnam War stretched out for six additional months, resulting in numerous changes to our history. In that timeline, my housemate Lorena Jeung and her infant daughter, Yun Hee, would have vanished if they'd stepped outside the boundary.

In fact, there are only minor differences between this timeline and the one I remember as *my* reality—although, if I'm being perfectly honest, my reality hasn't felt as real since my dad died a year and a half ago. Unfortunately, we're fairly certain this relative normalcy isn't going to last. In fact, Katherine seems to think the timeline will flip tonight at ten. We're still not entirely sure what the nature of those changes will be, but she believes it has something to do with witches. Or witch hunts, to be more precise.

We've spent the past several days poring over minor alterations Saul Rand has made to the timeline, small tweaks that haven't quite shoved the time train off its tracks. Katherine and Rich are currently in Austria 1678 setting stable points so we can begin investigating one of those changes. Tyson and Clio are doing the same thing a century later in Rhode Island. I could have tagged along with either group, but neither of them really needed a third wheel. It would also have necessitated scrounging up another costume, so I spent the morning with Jack, Alex, and RJ instead, going through the handful of changes the Anomalies Machine has spat out over the past few days, trying to find patterns amid the chaos.

I've never been good at waiting, and for the past few hours I've felt like there was a giant cartoon anvil hanging over my head with *DOOM* stenciled on the side in big, fat letters. That feeling of dread is what drove me out of the house. It's what had me wanting to talk to my dad. It's why I'm here now, sitting cross-legged in front of where my garden should be, blindly pulling up clumps of turf with my bare hands as tears fill my eyes.

"Maybe this would help?" Jack hands me the spading fork I used to turn the soil when I planted this garden the first time.

I was so lost in my own thoughts I didn't even hear him approach. He sits down facing me and reaches over to brush away a stray tear with the pad of his thumb.

"You okay, Max?"

Jack using my dad's nickname for me very nearly pushes me over into full waterworks, but I sniff the tears back. I'm not the fanciful type who believes in signs and messages from beyond the grave, but it's almost as though Dad is gently reminding me I *do* have someone I can talk to about all of this. I don't have to keep it bottled up.

"I just realized my garden is gone," I tell him. "And I'm fighting off a blue funk and feeling a bit on edge."

"Can't imagine why. Not like you've had anything particularly stressful in your life recently."

He's joking, of course. A month ago, my biggest worries were family finances and the possibility that my great-grandfather, the subject of the master's thesis I've barely started and will likely never finish, was the serial plagiarist my grandmother Nora and most of the literary world believed him to be. Now, I've discovered I have a genetic enhancement that could get me kicked out of university or worse. My great-grandfather—times four, I guess—is a serial murderer intent on changing history with a device I helped create in some alternate timeline. I shot someone in an attic in 1965 and narrowly missed getting blown up by a suitcase bomb in 1940. And we're stuck here *waiting* to see what sort of insane reality Saul is rolling up for his next game. Which Katherine believes has something to do with *witches*.

"Sorry for the hasty exit," I say. "It's just that I was perilously close to shrieking each time the Anomalies Machine coughed up some minor change. On top of that, I was missing my dad. And also kind of wishing I could talk to Nora about everything . . . but that's obviously out of the question."

Nora married my grandfather. They bought the same house in London, the same cottage in Bray, and had a son named Matthew Grace. But this alternate-version of my dad married someone else, because my mother no longer exists. He had a son, rather than a daughter, which for some reason makes me feel better, less like I was replaced. And my dad died one day earlier, presumably from the same undetected heart problem. All of these changes, especially my mother's apparent lack of existence, seem to be due to the decision by my other grandmother, Thea, to toss away the bracelet that kept her under a CHRONOS field. In one sense, it was a selfless gesture, since it prevented us from jumping back and undoing the almost-certainly fatal injury that Saul—or rather, his stupid splinter—gave her right after she shot him. She was willing to sacrifice the remaining years of her life in order to ensure that we didn't take a risk that saved her but allowed Saul to escape. I'm just glad she died before realizing she'd killed a splinter instead of Saul himself.

I strongly suspect Thea came here with the expectation that it could be a suicide mission. But would she have willingly sacrificed my mom for that mission as well? I'd like to *think* she'd have made arrangements to protect her own daughter. Assuming it even occurred to her, which I can't be sure. Thea was a true believer with one goal in life . . . stopping Saul. She convinced my mom to marry my dad in pursuit of that goal. Or at least, I think she did. My parents clearly loved each other. Would Mom have married him if she hadn't? That's one of the many, many things I'll probably never find out, because my mom and Thea lied to me about pretty much everything my entire life. And now, neither of them is around to answer my questions.

Either way, we haven't found any record of Mila Randall Grace, so it seems Thea erased Mom as well when she let that bracelet slip from her fingers. Technically, she erased me, too. There's no birth record for Madison Eleanor Grace, and no student record for anyone with my name in the literary history program at Georgetown. But, unlike my mom, I was under a key, so I'll continue to exist as long as that remains true. Not a huge change for me in practical terms, since I'd already accepted that I'll have to wear one of the damn things for the rest of my days.

We *have* discovered there's another person out there named Madison Grace, however. A distant cousin, with a different middle initial, who is four years younger than I am. All I share with her is a tiny fraction of my genes, two-thirds of my name, and, apparently, an interest in history, since that's her current field of study at Keele.

Is she the original Madison Grace, the one from the pre-CHRONOS timeline who will decide at some point in the future to work with Alex, Lorena, and RJ a few decades from now on a quirky little time-travel project? There's no way to know. I'd be very tempted to drop her a warning to steer clear, except I'm not sure our time-travel band would have any chance of forming in this timeline anyway. Duplicates of RJ, Lorena, and Yun Hee are living in Switzerland, blissfully unaware of time travel, because Alter-Lorena decided to take a different job. Alter-Alex began the temporal physics program at Georgetown but dropped out in his second year. Much to his surprise, he's a holoportrait artist who, based on his posh address in Arlington and the reviews we've found online, makes a very good living creating realistic (or subtly enhanced) avatars for a matchmaking company.

"I wish we'd gotten one of the field-extender bracelets to Nora earlier," Jack says. "You lost one grandmother to the cause. The least we can do is try to save the other one."

"But we'd have had to leave a diary or a key along with the bracelet . . . otherwise, there'd be no field to extend. We can't spare those, and . . . maybe it's for the best, Jack. Pretty sure it's safer for Nora to be kept in the dark, at least for now. She's Katherine's granddaughter. My grandmother. That makes her a perfect target if Saul starts looking for a hostage to give him leverage."

"Good point." Jack winces slightly as he says this, and I'm sure he's thinking about his own family on the West Coast. They still exist and, as best we can tell, he doesn't have a freaky double out there doing something different.

What we can't entirely figure out is *why* that's the case. Jack goes back and forth between thinking there's no way his dad could be under a CHRONOS field and thinking he *must* be. The Long-Range Threat Assessment group, or LORTA, the subsection of the Defense Department where his father used to work, has only one key and as far as we know, it's kept in a vault. They know it's a time-travel device and they know about chronotron particles, or at least they did in the timeline before Team Viper began screwing around with our history. They also know the key can be used to change things, otherwise General John Merrick wouldn't be constantly hounding Jack to help speed up the development of the technology. But we have no clue whether they know about the recent timeline shifts.

Jack doesn't think his father has told anyone at LORTA about this effort to jump-start the time-travel research. All the colleague who loaned him the key knew was that he tested his two kids and neither could use it to jump. Jack's younger sister can't even see the light. Merrick's whole purpose in trying to speed up the technology was to help the US and our allies get a head start on a vaccine for a genetically targeted virus that their simulations say is coming down the pike very soon, which they believe could kill upward of a billion people. According to one of the "alternate" histories published by my grandfather that's currently among the protected volumes in the library upstairs, the death toll won't be quite that high, but 730 million people is still something any sane person would try to avoid if possible. In this timeline, the woman who cooks up that deadly recipe seems to be playing nice with her neighbors, but we have no clue whether that will hold when Saul rolls the dice again.

Apparently, the threat simulations at LORTA agree, because Jack hasn't gotten a single message from his dad this week asking how Project Fast Forward is going. Nothing at all from his family except a text from his stepmother asking about holiday plans. We're crossing our fingers this remains true after the next shift, both because we don't need the extra complication of a looming global catastrophe and because Jack isn't entirely sure he trusts his dad not to have the military swoop in and take over the research . . . along with taking any of us who have a fully expressed version of the CHRONOS gene into custody.

Jack glances down at my grungy hands and then at the small indentation in the dirt. "So . . . are we replanting the garden?"

"No. What's the point if I'd just walk out here tomorrow or the next day and find it bare again? Or find someone has paved over everything that's outside of the protective field?" I stab at the ground with the spading fork. "I'm more curious about whether the CHRONOS key I dug up is still here. Or here *again*, I guess."

"Isn't that the same key you're wearing, though?"

"Yes. Doesn't mean it won't be here, as well. Any time I've spun off a splinter, there have been two copies of me, and therefore two versions of this key."

"Temporarily. Until the splinter . . . goes wherever splinters go."

"I'm just thinking that if I never dug up the key, maybe the events of the past two weeks are simply a bourbon-fueled hallucination. Maybe all it takes to reset this insanity is me digging up this patch of dirt and finding nada."

He chuckles. "You're welcome to keep digging if it makes you feel better, but I don't think that's how it works. And there's a better way to check. If the dog wasn't here to bury the key, then it didn't bury those plastic bones you still have under the table in the living room, either. We'll bring them out here and see if they vanish when they're no longer under a CHRONOS field. That would be a far easier test than digging up the yard, wouldn't it?"

I give him a grudging nod.

"Why don't you put down the pointy thing and come here?"

"Hm. Who put the pointy thing in my hand, Mr. Merrick?" I toss the fork aside anyway, then he pulls me back onto the grass.

For a few minutes, I simply lie there with my head on his shoulder. We watch the clouds drift by, and I feel some of my tension fading away.

"All you can do is your best, babe. At the end, win or lose, no matter what bizarre universe we inhabit, I'm going to be here. And you'll be loved."

I smile. "You could get a job writing for those inspirational posters they put up in classrooms."

"Nice to know I have options. So you're feeling better?"

"Mm-hmm. Apparently, I just needed hugs. And maybe chocolate. I wonder if I could coax a decent pan of fudge out of the food unit."

Jack makes a tsking sound. "You'll ruin your dinner."

"Not if fudge *is* my dinner."

"How about this? I'll wrestle with the food unit while *you* prepare for a quick trip to the beach."

I raise an eyebrow. "As much as I would truly love a beach day, I seem to recall us ruling out any jumps that aren't essential."

"We did. This would be more of a working vacation, and you probably won't have time to do much more than breathe in the ocean air." He gets to his feet and offers me a hand up. "Alex pulled up another anomaly in a small town on one of the barrier islands off the Carolina coast. There's a stable point nearby, but no direct view of the spot we need to see. Some observation points would help us narrow down what's going on. You'd only need to jump back about two hundred years, so RJ seems to think you can come up with something to wear from your closet."

"How does RJ know what's in my closet?"

"Security-camera footage of you in various outfits, courtesy of Jarvis."

That's perfectly logical, and I was already well aware that my virtual assistant has security cameras at locations in and around the house. I still feel a bit like I've been spied upon.

RJ has been helping with the historical-research and jump prep, because it's something he can do and because he's bored. And probably because his wife, Lorena, who is equally bored, is kind of grumpy. Lorena would like nothing more than to be back in her genetics lab, but she doesn't work there now. She's had a difficult time grappling with the fact that there's an alternate version of her family out there. I think the duplicate issue itself bothers her less than knowing this other Lorena has a lab to work in each day, while she had to resort to using the kitchen and the food unit to replicate materials to produce a serum that would get Jack back to this time. Now that the project is finished, she's again spending most of her day with Yun Hee. Lorena referred to it as a *maternal sabbatical*, and she does enjoy taking the baby swimming in the basement pool and playing with her out here in the backyard. But I think she's about maxed out on the pink-rabbit vids that make Yun Hee laugh. Lorena puts on a happy face when she pops into the library or I see her downstairs, but she's not fooling any of us. RJ says if we don't find her another project soon, she's going to crack.

"One of the 1930s dresses should be fine," Jack continues. "You could even get away with the jeans you're wearing, since it's fairly secluded. Might want to change into a T-shirt that doesn't have the date of a twenty-second-century music festival on the back, though, just in case you bump into anyone."

"What do we need to observe?"

"A tree. In the middle of a road. Personally, I'd prefer that you wait until the others get back, but you seem like you need a distraction, and there's a location in the *Log of Stable Points* that's less than a kilometer away. And . . ."

I finish it for him. "Anything we can take care of now is one less thing we'll have to do once the clock starts. *Assuming* the clock starts. I still think it's possible that Saul's changing things for the sheer hell of it. We should just track him down, kill him, and be done with it."

Jack looks a bit nervous at that. Not because he's averse to killing Saul Rand. If he could use the key without the aid of Lorena's serum, he'd be leading the charge.

"No one is listening," I tell him. "We're still outside the barrier. Can't imagine they'd have a listening device in this section of the yard anyway. If they have them in the house at all. And since Thea at least *tried* to kill Saul, I think we can count Sisters, Inc. in the friends column."

"Just because that name was on the deed doesn't mean they're the only ones listening," he says as we head across the lawn toward the house. "And yeah, Thea was on our side. But there are what, fifteen of them? Maybe more. Any group that size is likely to have a few defectors."

I'm tempted to argue that this seems unlikely, since they're clones. But Thea even said there were differences between the Sisters. It was something that puzzled her, given that each group of three was, supposedly, genetically identical, and they were raised in the same setting, taught the same history, and given the same code of ethics. Whether you're a proponent of nature or nurture, or some combination of the two, any differences between three clones raised together would most likely be minor.

"Maybe. But I'm still not sure we made the right decision where they're concerned. It was the only thing Thea asked of me."

"Agreed," he says. "But we were outvoted. And maybe they're right. The risk that someone there is in league with Saul might not be large but it can't be zero . . . and they won't even know you delayed the trip."

Thea's final request was for me and Katherine to tell the Sisters of Prudence what happened last week. And yes, she thought that meant telling them Saul was dead, that she'd finally managed to get revenge for . . . I'm still not completely sure, but I think there were multiple grievances. We can't actually tell them that yet, but it feels wrong not to tell them anything. Not to even let them know what happened to her. The diary she left me has a string of digits under the message, *If I can't share the good news, take Katherine and tell them!* It looked like a stable point, and sure enough, when I entered it into the key it's inside a study or library of some sort at the old Sixteenth Street Temple, on July 12, 2058, at noon. A carbon copy of Thea—or rather, of Thea when she was in her thirties or early forties—was staring back at me when the key registered the stable point, so one of the clones had obviously been told to expect a visit at that time. Thea said the Sisters can't use the key to travel, but they wear a cuff to protect their memories in the event of time shifts. I didn't realize until it was too late that she also wore it as protection because she doesn't exist in this timeline. And that would no doubt be true of the other Sisters of Prudence as well.

I know on a logical level that it makes absolutely no difference *when* we complete that jump to the temple. Regardless of whether we go now or we wait until we can actually deliver the news Thea was so eager to share, the Sister looking back at me from the stable point will wait the same amount of time. We are in her future. She is in our past. It still feels wrong. It still feels like I'm ignoring Thea's last wish.

But everyone else thinks I need to wait. Jack sided with me, but he was the only one. And Jack even said maybe the others were right, so . . . I'll wait. If it hadn't been such a pain to manually enter in that long string of numbers, I'd delete the stable point to avoid temptation.

Jack stays behind to see if he can get the food unit to cough up something palatable and chocolaty, while I head upstairs to the library for a more detailed briefing about the proposed jump. RJ is at one of the desks near the bookshelves that line the walls, reading something on a tablet. Next to him is the newly reassembled SimMaster console that Alex and Katherine have had in pieces scattered about on the desks, trying to figure out how the time tourists on Team Viper were able to use it to communicate across timelines and also to make sure those communications are completely severed. Taking it apart was risky. We have no idea how Saul plans to manage the contest he's setting up, but it seems logical to assume the SimMaster system will be part of it.

Alex is, as usual, in the center of his display cluster. The five screens he has up are currently arranged in a semicircle around his chair. Two of them contain what I think of as his bubble matrix, which is a 3-D visualization of chronotron particles that allows him to track the time and place whenever someone makes a jump with the CHRONOS keys. Another display has the dates of the various anomalies the older computer in the corner has emitted over the past week. The fourth is filled with calculations I doubt I could ever understand, and the fifth is a satellite image.

The one thing that's new is Alex's neural earpiece, which arrived a few days ago. It looks a lot like the sterling silver ear cuff I wore back in high school when they were trendy. This one cost about five hundred times as much, but then mine didn't have a little gadget that extends into the ear canal, enabling Alex to interact with Jarvis and the rest of our computer network. It came with the lenses he's wearing and functions a lot like the clear disk that allows me to interact with the CHRONOS technology . . . just a bit clunkier and without the genetic component. Alex adapted to the device very quickly, in part because he used a less sophisticated version when he entered data as a graduate assistant.

I'll admit the whole thing has me a bit jealous. Jarvis has been my personal assistant for more than a decade. Even though I know Jarvis is an AI and can't actually be my friend, he still *feels* like a friend. If anyone should be neurally linked with him it should be me. But Alex is the one tracking Saul's movements, as well as monitoring possible incursions from the other timelines, and basically doing everything else that isn't historical in nature. He says he can work better and more quickly with this setup, and it barely made a dent in the funds that Sisters, Inc. placed in the household account.

I'm not worried about privacy. I can't fathom Alex having the slightest interest in poking around to see what I've researched or what I have in my private playlists. It probably wouldn't even occur to him. But watching Alex tilt his head and get an answer from Jarvis faster than I could ask the question chafes. Like I told Jack, it's a bit like finding out your dog, the one you've raised since he was a tiny pup, has a stronger bond with someone he just met.

"So you're up for a quick jump?" Alex doesn't wait for a response. He tweaks something on the display with the satellite map and spins it around to face me. "Year 2000. From the protected files for the timeline *before* you found the CHRONOS key."

RJ grimaces. "Also known as reality, before time travel fucked everything up."

I give that sentiment a hearty amen.

The map is now zoomed in on what looks like a live oak parked in the middle of a road on one of several narrow strips of land separated by channels. Waterfront houses, most with docks, line both sides of the road. A red marker directly above the oak reads *The Cora Tree*.

"That's the Brigand Bay area," Alex says. "In later maps, the tree is gone, and the spot is mostly underwater. In this timeline, however, the tree disappears before we even had satellite imagery. When they secured the permits for that housing development in the 1970s, there was no mention of the tree."

Alex taps the display screen and pulls up a different map, on which the houses are the same. The only discernible difference is that the road doesn't split to accommodate a tree. It's just a straight, narrow road like the others on the strips of land between the canals.

I enlarge the map a bit more. "Why do we need to find out what happened to a tree? And, for that matter, why does CHRONOS have a stable point close enough to make a quick jump like this even possible? This area looks pretty isolated."

"We've got a couple of theories on that," RJ says. "One of them, actually, is from a book your grandfather wrote."

"Great-grandfather. And I'm not surprised. You'd have a hard time finding something he didn't write about. Which book?"

"*Witchery around the World*," he says. "It also mentions the Jackl guy Katherine and Saul are investigating now. Anyway, tap one of those images on the right. The tree bark. What do you see?"

"Um. I see tree bark?" When I zoom in as far as possible, something is there, but the image is fuzzy. "It looks like . . . letters. I can make out a *C* and an *R*. And the tree was damaged pretty badly at some point."

"Yeah," RJ says. "Lightning strike. Split right down the middle. The images aren't especially clear, but people who've seen the tree in person said they could make out the letters *CORA*. So, those are the facts. Things get a bit iffy after that point. Local legend has it that a woman named Cora called lightning down from the sky when she and her infant child were about to be burned there."

I read through the article he hands me, which gives a brief overview of the legend. "So . . . this is how they explain a name carved into a tree?"

"Burned into it," RJ says. "The tree was split down the middle, and the letters were burned into the bark. Most people assume the story is only a legend, though."

"Well, sure," I say. "There's no such thing as witches."

"Not just that. They came up with a bunch of other reasons to debunk it. The name of the pirate captain in the legend is the same as a novel written in 1922, *Captain Blood*, and there's no mention of him in records from Salem in the 1700s. Also, one write-up of the legend claims Cora wasn't a popular name until the early twentieth century, but that's false. Jarvis found references to the name going back centuries before that. Some people said the tree couldn't have lived that long, but it's a live oak, and the last time it was measured, a decade or so before it died, scientists estimated it was at least five hundred years old. So that's a point in favor of the legend."

"But you said they didn't tend to burn witches in the US," Alex says. "Which would be a point against."

RJ nods. "Right, although the preference for hanging witches rather than burning them seems to have changed in our new timeline for some reason. Basically, there's evidence both for and against the story."

I'm tempted to note that any evidence *for* the story is clearly wrong, because . . . *witches*, especially since I can see Alex is thinking the same thing. But the only part that couldn't be explained by human ignorance and twisted religious zeal is the lightning strike. That could have happened at any point, though, and some imaginative soul might not have been able to resist incorporating it into the legend.

"This is all very interesting," I say, "but again . . . since when does the Anomalies Machine highlight missing trees?"

"That story was around in the previous reality. I can't find anything about a Cora Tree in this timeline, though . . . and something seems to have triggered a new witch frenzy." RJ gives me a grim look. "We now have nineteen new deaths in and around Hatteras Island as the result of witch hunts in the mid-1700s. It spreads north to Virginia and south all the way to Florida."

"So at around the same time as the incident Tyson and Clio are investigating?"

"Yeah. At least ninety-five people were killed over about four decades, between these in the South and the ones in New England. And it seems like an odd coincidence that the killings in the South would begin in the same general area where a legend about an attempted witch killing happened in the previous timeline."

"Odd that there's a stable point so close by, though, for such a shaky story. Did CHRONOS investigate every spot where there was a legend about a witch?"

RJ shakes his head. "I doubt it. But another explanation for the markings on the tree is that they were a sign left behind by the Lost Colony of Roanoke back in the late 1500s."

"A sign to whom?"

"To anyone who came looking for them. They apparently carved messages into trees to let people know where they were heading, and some say this could mean they were going off to live with the Coree, a tribe native to North Carolina. There were also a lot of shipwrecks along that strip of beach. The area was nicknamed the Graveyard of the Atlantic. One of the passengers on a ship that went down along the Carolina coast in the early 1800s was Aaron Burr's daughter, Theodosia, so historians might have traveled there to find out what happened to her, as well. And back in the 1930s, there was a government camp of some sort . . . ?"

Alex taps his earpiece. "The WPA. Works Progress Administration. One of the so-called Alphabet Agencies put in place to pull the nation out of the First Great Depression." He zooms in on a small cluster of trees at the end of the street farthest from the bay. "Jack says the closest stable point is right there. The whole jump will probably take ten minutes, tops. You could easily be back before the others. At worst, a few minutes after."

Technically, I could be back before the others even left. But we made the decision last week to keep our keys synced to the same time as much as possible. If we spend an hour in the past, we'll jump home an hour later. This is partly to help us keep up with how much time is left on the clock—or rather, at this point, how much time we think we have until the clock begins. Katherine thinks Saul is currently following some variant of the rules from our last game. She says he'll be more likely to stick to the rules if we do. And we definitely need him following those rules. Otherwise, he could do what he did before . . . impregnate a bunch of women in the past and build himself an army of time travelers. As could we, but unlike Saul Rand, we have moral compasses that discourage wholesale mangling of the timeline.

"The question is . . . do I jump in when the houses are there and try to figure out where the tree was, or jump in earlier and find the actual tree? It would be pretty hard to miss."

"Jumper's choice," Alex says.

Once I find the location in the *Log of Stable Points*, I transfer it to my key and scroll back to a random day in 1931, before the WPA project began. A quick pan of the area around the stable point reveals mostly low-lying brush and trees. No houses nearby, although there appears to be a small building of some sort off in the distance.

The ground looks swampy. No way am I wearing a skirt into that.

I go to my room and change into a plain shirt. Then I fetch a pair of mud boots from the garage. They're too big, so I stuff some socks in the toe and head back to the library, which now smells of fudge. I sample a piece from the plate Jack is holding. It's actually one of the better things my food unit has produced, but then it's chocolate, and that's pretty hard to screw up.

"You sure you're okay going on your own?" he asks.

I pat my jeans pocket, where he can see the outline of the laser weapon he gave me before my jumps to Memphis. "I'll be fine. If I can't find the tree within fifteen minutes, I'll come back. Just make sure they don't eat all of my fudge before I get home."

Scrolling through again, I choose a bright, sunny day and blink in. There's a hint of ocean in the morning air, but the water here on the sound side seems a bit more brackish. Once I reach the edge of the tree cover, I give a quick look around, then step out. The ground isn't as mushy as I'd thought initially, but I'm still glad I wore the boots, because I think I'm more likely to encounter a snake than a human. That thought has me a little squeamish, and I'm second-guessing my decision to jump in before the area was developed. But then I spot what I'm almost certain is the Cora Tree near the center of a small clearing.

It takes five more minutes to reach it, but the only creatures I see are a few birds, a dragonfly, and two small deer that startle and scamper off as I enter the clearing. That seems like a good sign. If anyone else were here, the deer would have startled already.

I center the medallion in my palm. When the holographic interface pops up above the key, I set a few observation points about ten meters from the tree. It's easier to see the split now. It hollowed out a section inside the oak's huge trunk. It's a miracle the thing survived.

Then I circle around to see if the word *CORA* is, as RJ's source reported, more legible in person. At first, the sunlight is in my face and I can't really make out anything. I shield my eyes and take a few more steps toward the tree, and now the letters are clearly legible.

If Alex and RJ were searching for information on the Cora Tree in this timeline, it's no wonder they came up empty.

The letters burned into the tree are *KATHY*.

FROM *WITCHERY AROUND THE WORLD* BY JAMES L. COLEMAN (2082)

Long ago, a notorious sorcerer known as the Zaubererjackl (Magician Jackl) lived in the Archbishopric of Salzburg. The Jackl was born Jakob Koller, and as the son of a local knacker, he helped his father render the carcasses they collected from farms and highways. The other job his father performed, when needed, was executioner. Jakob did not help with this task, but the children of Salzburg kept their distance, nonetheless, claiming the boy reeked of death.

When his father abandoned the family, Jakob and his mother were forced into the streets, where they had to beg for their meals. Competition was stiff, as they were far from the only beggars on the streets of Salzburg. Jakob grew into a young man in these back alleys, at the same time the weather grew cold and rations became scarce. Few were inclined to give alms to the poor in such hard times, and fewer still would give a job or a day's wages to an executioner's son.

Legend holds that Jakob grew angry with those who had no compassion. He took the abandoned boys of the town, and a few girls, under his wing, secretly teaching them how to pick pockets and, according to some accounts, how to do magic. If a person was kind to the poor, he or she suffered no harm. But those who did not offer bread or other sustenance to the *zaubererbuben* (magician's boys) soon found themselves wishing they'd been more generous. Their cow's milk would dry up or go sour. A child might sicken or die. And wasn't it odd that since the Zaubererjackl began collecting followers, the weather seemed to get colder each year?

Stories of the Zaubererjackl's wizardry became wilder by the day. He had an ointment that allowed any follower to change into a wolf. Under his spell, wood chips could turn into mice that would decimate stored grain. A single curse from the sorcerer's lips could consign an entire family to die in their sleep, or call down an avalanche to destroy an enemy's house. Some even claimed the Jackl could turn himself invisible. And, of course, he could fly.

But the Zaubererjackl wasn't always the villain of their stories. Often, he was an avenging angel, bringing judgment upon those who failed to act with charity. In some versions, he magicked away the chores of those who shared a meal or lodgings when he appeared to them as a stranger in need.

The prince-archbishop's authorities, however, were convinced the man was in league with the devil. They grew weary of the tales of his exploits and swore to find the cause of the ills befalling their fair city. The more well-to-do in the town supported these efforts. They were tired of beggars who muttered curses at them when they did not offer alms. They complained that there were far too many poor on the streets. Couldn't the leaders do something?

One day, a local shopkeeper lodged an official complaint that Jakob's mother had cursed his oldest son when he refused to give her bread. The mother, Barbara Koller, was brought in to be questioned. Under torture, she admitted to cursing the young man. She not only confessed to witchcraft, but eventually told the inquisitor her own son was the wizard they were looking for, the Zaubererjackl who had been organizing young beggars.

And so the hunt for the Jackl began. Children as young as five were pulled from the streets, along with a handful of adults, for interrogation. Many were handicapped or too frail to work. They were examined for scars that might connect them to witchcraft and tossed into tiny cells in the Hexenturm, or witch tower, to await questioning.

If they didn't answer freely or to the inquisitor's satisfaction, it was determined that the Jackl—or perhaps even the devil himself—had bound their minds and their tongues. Once those bonds were loosened through torture, the children began to spin fantastic tales, implicating not just the Jackl, but others in the town as well. They accused their enemies. They accused their friends, and even their families. All beggars were in league with the Jackl, it seemed. All had signed their souls over to Satan for the promise of a meal.

The cells in the Hexenturm quickly grew crowded. When the authorities could no longer pack any more accused witches into the fourteen cubicles, some were taken to the execution field where they were killed, and their bodies burned.

Each empty spot in the cell was filled by other beggars as the web widened. By the time the authorities were satisfied, 198 people were accused. More than two-thirds were children. The youngest, only eight years of age, was killed along with his twelve-year-old brother. The smallest children were given to foster parents, some died in custody, and 138 were executed.

The Jackl was not among them. Many of the townspeople believed Jakob Koller had been dead for several years before the witch hunt began. There was some evidence to this effect. But how could this be when the inquisitors said so many of the children declared the Jackl was their leader? He was the one who held black mass, who convinced them to sell their souls . . . Why, they'd seen him the very day they were captured!

The more fanciful of the townspeople claimed Jakob had indeed died, and it was his spirit that traveled around the city wreaking vengeance against the selfish. Many say he wanders the land still, punishing those who will not help feed the poor and snatching up small children who refuse to share their toys. But well-behaved children with charitable hearts have nothing to fear from the Zaubererjackl.

∞ 3 ∞

KATHERINE
GNEIS, ARCHBISHOPRIC OF SALZBURG, HOLY ROMAN EMPIRE
SEPTEMBER 22, 1678

As a CHRONOS historian, you make peace with death early on. Not your *own* death. We haven't lost an agent in the field in generations. Many of the events we research, however, took hundreds or even thousands of lives. History and death—including the deaths of innocents—are all too often closely intertwined.

In many cases, CHRONOS could prevent those deaths. In some cases, I could have prevented a number of deaths on my own. But we *don't* prevent them. Our mission is to witness history, not to change it.

Any time my conscience starts nagging at me in this regard, I remember the words one of our trainers told me. *They're already dead,* Rose said as our group watched a line of eager travelers boarding the *Hindenburg* in Frankfurt on May 3, 1937. *They died centuries ago. This is our history. We do not change it.*

In my seven years of field research, I've stood in the drugstore of a hotel in Chicago where hundreds of women were killed and even purchased a packet of headache powder from the man who would eventually be executed for their murders. I even spent several weeks in Nazi Germany with *Werk Glaube und Schönheit*, the young women's division of Hitler Youth, when they volunteered at a kindergarten in Dachau, about a kilometer from the prison where tens of thousands were killed for the glory of the Reich.

Still, knowing the plot of land you've just jumped to has been the site of more than a hundred grisly executions in recent months is one thing. Hearing the sucking sound your shoes make as you step away from the stable point? That's another thing entirely.

Did it rain here recently? Or is the field wet with blood?

Knowing that most of the people executed in this field were children makes the sound all that much worse. A shiver runs through me, and I seek out a patch of ground with less mud and more grass while I wait for Richard.

When he jumps in a few seconds later, he makes a sick face and looks down at his feet, which have just made the same squelching noise. Does Rose's voice echo in his head, too? *This is our history. We do not change it.*

Earlier in the day, Rich and I stood on this exact same spot in the year 2136, outside an office building bearing a historical plaque designating this area as the site of Salzburg's execution yard and the home of the archbishop's executioner, before that building was demolished in the mid-2000s. I can see the house now, about fifty meters to our left. One of the wooden pillars on the attached woodshed is broken, and the entire structure lists slightly to the side. I'm amazed it survived another three decades, let alone more than three centuries.

In a perfect world, we'd have set the observation points on that first jump, strolling around the streets of Salzburg on a crisp autumn day in 2136, when the clothes we're wearing and my more modern take on the German language wouldn't raise suspicion. We were able to set several observation points in the square outside the cathedral and just across the Salzach River, at the site of the Hexenturm, where hundreds of young beggars were imprisoned while awaiting trial for the crime of witchcraft. Our research allowed us to pin down the general location of the execution field, but it did not reveal the precise location of the gallows, and the field has been an office building for over a century. We have a fairly detailed description of events that will take place here tomorrow, courtesy of eyewitness accounts in court testimony, but the stable points need to be close enough for a clear view. I'm almost certain the man who will appear on that stage tomorrow is Saul Rand, but I need to know for sure.

The fact that this field is on the edge of town instead of in the center of the city is a sign that Salzburg is on the cusp of modernity. Until around 1600, executions took place in the city proper, where corpses left on display might serve as a cautionary reminder to those inclined to stray from the straight and narrow. A previous archbishop felt that was a tad barbaric, so this location was constructed to keep the unsightly business of execution more private. The current archbishop is a bit of a medieval throwback, however. The actual executions are still held out here under his rule, but he has no qualms at all about torture taking place mere blocks from his palace. He also has no qualms about allowing inquisitors to parade the condemned, many of them children who've been tortured to the very brink of death, around the square before they're carted off to this killing field.

Moving the executions from the city did little to deter spectators. Townsfolk are willing to hike out here for the show, keeping a careful distance in cases where the execution is apt to be explosive. Archbishop Max Gandolph von Kuenburg's idea of mercy was to occasionally allow the youngest of the accused to wear a sack of gunpowder into the fire so their end came more quickly.

And now it's Saul in my head, not Rose. *Human nature never really changes, Kathy. If you supply even the tiniest spark, you'll always find a mob more than willing to burn everything to ash.*

I startle when Rich taps my shoulder. He gives me an apologetic smile and nods toward the dark shape of the gallows about halfway across the field, faintly silhouetted against the night sky. There's a second platform to the right, which I suspect is where the beheadings take place. Beyond that is a pyre, with a stake rising from the middle, ready and waiting for the next round of justice.

We head across the field to the gallows, our shoes smacking the mud each step of the way. The plan was to separate and circle the platforms when we were within a few meters. I'd go left and set points along the back and Rich would go right. We'd then meet at the far end and blink out. As we're nearing the platform, however, a dog howls from the woods at the edge of the field. A dog, or perhaps a wolf. Perhaps the Zaubererjackl himself is in his wolf form tonight, watching over this field where so many of his followers, his *zaubererbuben*, died.

Instead of turning right, Rich follows me. I open my mouth to protest, to tell him I'm not frightened of a howling beast or whatever ghosts might haunt this field. That would be mostly true, at least in the literal sense. I don't believe in the Zaubererjackl, and despite the gruesome manner in which they died, I don't really think the people killed here, mostly young boys between the ages of ten and twenty, haunt this field. It would also be a lie, though, because I know I'll breathe more easily with Rich next to me than I would if I were standing here alone and he were on the other side of the gallows, where all I could see was the pale orange glow of his CHRONOS key.

And maybe Richard doesn't want to be alone out here, either. Even if he's not worried that ghosts are watching, we both know Saul is. I don't think Saul will jump in, though. He knows we're armed. We have backup, too. Alex is monitoring the location, and if an additional red dot appears on his display at this time and place, Tyson will join us with a gun. If Rich and I still fail to return at our appointed time, Madi will jump back ten minutes to when we were about to embark on this trip and tell us to cancel.

More importantly, however, this is only the opening move in Saul's game, whatever it may be. If he kills us now, his fun would be over too quickly. I think there could come a time very soon when he'll start trying to pick us off one by one. But it's too early. The man loves an audience. And unless he's been extremely busy in the past week, there are only a handful of people in this reality who will know when he makes his move. He'll want as many eyes on him as possible for his opening gambit.

I know Saul well enough to be sure he's watching us right now, if only to revel in the irony of me tracking his movements through this field littered with blood and bone. After all, Saul would never have paid the slightest attention to the Salzburg witch trials if I hadn't mentioned them. He's not a Europeanist. Neither am I. Aside from the one German trip I took in 1943 for comparative purposes and a few day trips, my field research has been confined to North America. I'd probably never have researched the Salzburg trials, either, if my curiosity hadn't been piqued when one of the Hitler Youth girls cautioned a kindergartner that he'd best learn to share with his classmates or the Zaubererjackl would come for him.

Richard and I walk the perimeter of the execution yard together in silence, setting observation points every ten steps or so. The trip is uneventful aside from my foot landing on what is very obviously a finger bone as we pass the halfway point. I fight back a wave of nausea and am relieved to see Rich looking queasy, too. That may sound petty or competitive on my part, but it's really not. I'm just terrified that every odd physical sensation I feel is an indicator that Saul's splinter was correct when he told me, a few minutes before Thea shot him, that the die may have already been cast.

Eventually, I'll take a pregnancy test. It's barely been a week since I was with Saul, though, and the instructions said I should wait a bit longer. And maybe that's for the best. Right now, I need to keep believing he was wrong.

"Ready to go? We don't have much time." Rich's whispered words, almost too low to make out, are the first either of us have spoken since we arrived.

Rich, along with everyone else back in Bethesda, tends to give my guesses about Saul's actions more weight than they merit. True, I lived with the man, but I was apparently less aware than anyone else that he's a freaking sociopath. So in one sense, my judgment is suspect where he's concerned. The one thing I do know, however, is how Saul plays The Game. He's addicted, and I've had a front-row seat to that addiction and his almost superstitious adherence to his routines surrounding it for the past several years.

Today is one week from when we evicted the time tourists. A week was Saul's typical timeframe for research and preparation in his competitions with Morgen Campbell. A new scenario was chosen immediately following the SimMaster's declaration of the previous game's winner, which was usually Saul. Opening night of the next series began one week later with dinner in Redwing Hall. At nine, they went up to Morgen's penthouse for drinks. The Game began promptly at ten, with the previous victor entering his gambit, and went on until four or five in the morning unless Saul had a jump the next day.

Scenarios rarely wrapped up in a single night, and they'd continue the competition during the week until there was a winner. Morgen's schedule was fluid, so it was a matter of how often Saul could play. Sometimes, scenarios stretched on longer than a week. Sometimes they wrapped up earlier. But the opening-night routine was always the same. Seven days after the last series ended, they met for dinner at eight, followed by drinks at nine, and then the victor of the previous game entered his gambit.

My best guess, which could be completely wrong, is that Saul will stick with tradition as much as he can, adjusting for the fact that we're not in the same room huddled around a SimMaster. We're probably not even in the same year or the same time zone. But wherever, whenever Saul is currently, I'm fairly certain he began his dinner—a rare steak and a salad—when the chronometer on his key told him exactly six days and twenty-two hours had elapsed from the end of our last game. An hour later, he poured himself a glass of whiskey, neat. And then, because this version of the game is more complex than simply entering a move into the computer, he headed off to trigger his final change, the one he believes, based on his simulations, will flip the timeline.

"It's only a guess, Rich. I'm probably wrong. If I truly knew the man as well as I thought I did, I'd have reported him to CHRONOS security years ago and we wouldn't be in this mess."

"No, I think you're right. He's still playing the game, only this time, he's not playing against Morgen. He's playing against *you*. The rest of us are peripheral. This is just one more chance for Saul to . . ."

Possibly because he can tell from my expression that he's on thin ice, Rich shrugs and doesn't finish the sentence. *Screw me over? Show he's the boss? Prove he can destroy my life?* Most likely it's all of the above, but none of that is information I shared voluntarily with Rich or anyone else. Madi has read my personal diary, which an older version of me apparently gave to Kate, who saved it for posterity. I must have been in the grip of dementia. No one in her right mind would give her granddaughter a diary detailing each bad decision she made, each private thought she recorded, when she was young and foolish. Everyone else in the house may have read it, too, for all I know. Madi probably passed it around to the others before I took it back. I'm sure they all got a good chuckle out of foolish, lovestruck Katherine.

"Either way," I tell Richard, "it won't be precise. He's not changing the timeline via computer now. Changing real history is messy."

I pull up the stable point for Madi's library. It's nighttime there, as well, but earlier, a little after eight. RJ is doing something with one of Alex's displays. Madi is seated on top of her great-grandfather's desk next to Jack, who's in the chair. For some reason, she's now wearing mud boots, which apparently fulfilled their purpose, since the toes are splattered with mud. Tyson and Clio aren't back yet from their trip to meet with Jemima Wilkinson. We're trying to keep our times synced up as much as possible, so they were scheduled to jump back one minute after our arrival.

Just as I'm locking in the location, Rich puts his hand over mine to stop me. "It's a chance for Saul to prove he's smarter than you. That's what I was going to say. But he's afraid he *isn't* smarter. He's afraid you might be the one person who knows him well enough to predict his moves because you understand what drives him."

"That's ridiculous. If he's so afraid, why bother with this stupid game?"

But I know the answer. He's not merely an addict, he's a narcissist. And no matter how much he changes the timeline, there are only a handful of people on this planet who will be aware of the differences. The one thing a narcissist can't stand is having no one around to appreciate his brilliance.

I lock in the time and location again. As I'm about to blink in, I notice RJ clutching his stomach. The others also look pained. RJ pushes away from the desk and rolls his chair toward the ancient computer we've dubbed the Anomalies Machine. If the CHRONOS keys had been equipped with audio, I'm certain we'd be hearing the odd alarm, a series of bass notes that is apparently the theme from some old movie.

"See?" I give Rich a rueful smile, as he pulls up the stable point on his key. "It's nowhere near 10 p.m. I was wrong. Told you so."

∞

BETHESDA, MARYLAND
NOVEMBER 27, 2136

The nausea I felt a few minutes ago is back and twice as strong the instant I arrive in the library, but now it's combined with a rush of dizziness. It passes quickly, and I step out of the stable point. Rich pops in a second later.

"We should have gone with your first guess," Madi says, giving me a grim look as she glances up from her CHRONOS key. "This is almost seven days to the minute from when Saul gave you the clue about Jemima Wilkinson."

"Which means you were *right*," Rich says. He doesn't add the *told you so*, but just leans toward me and says in a softer voice, "And so was I. Saul's afraid of you."

I'm barely listening to either of them. I quickly pull up the first stable point on my key—the first stable point on any CHRONOS key—expecting to see the same void we've seen in the past two timelines. But it's *there*.

I scroll to November 12, 2304, the day we left. The jump room is dark, but it's a Saturday. No jumps would have been on the schedule because the day is devoted to public tours and education. The only time we work on Saturdays is if we end up with Q&A duty for one of the tours. Otherwise, we steer clear of the bottom five floors of the building between ten and four, because it tends to be swamped with tourists. Even on a Saturday, however, the lights would generally be on. The tour isn't allowed in the jump room, but they do stop at the windows in the hallways on the fifth floor that look down at the twelve jump stations arrayed in a circle like the hours on a clock.

Or at least it used to look like a clock. Now there are only four stations, so it looks more like the points on a compass.

Rich must realize what I'm doing, because he asks, "Is it there?"

"It's there," I say. "But I can't get in."

FROM THE *TD REAL-WORLD*
PLAYER'S GUIDE

Defensive Game (Modified for Real-World Team Play)

1. Once team one (Jackl) has entered its moves, it may not adjust the timeline again until team two (Hyena) has completed its responses.
2. Team members may not actively engage the opposing side during play, nor may deadly force be used against an opposing player to prevent them from making a move. (This is waived if the opposing team has substantially breached the rules.)
3. All participants may be recorded anytime they are within range of an observation point or an official observer from the opposite team.
4. All players and all observers must be within a ten-meter radius of the SimMaster when play begins. Any individual with the CHRONOS gene (permanent, inherited, or temporary) who is within range of the SimMaster

when play begins will be counted as an observer and subject to the rules of play.

5. Initial predictions: Enter the location, the date within one decade, and the precise actions for full points.

6. Final entry: Include the location, date within one decade, and precise actions, along with any style-point considerations. Must be entered within one hour of the move being taken.

7. The system can measure only the moves that are entered based on the information given by each team. Team Jackl is not responsible for unintended alterations to the timeline that occur due to incidental encounters by its team members or observers.

∞4∞

I've never seen *Jaws*. Most of my scheduled jumps were before 1970, so it wasn't a movie I had a chance to watch at the drive-in over in Greenville when Glen and I went on a fairly regular basis while we studied the North Carolina Klan. The theme from *Jaws*, however, was included in my 20th-century US cultural literacy training along with a lot of other seemingly useless trivia. Even though I rarely traveled beyond 1968, I know the lyrics to *The Brady Bunch* theme, can tell R2D2 from C3PO, and recognize a lot of taglines and catchphrases. Radio and TV spread quickly in the 20th century, but there were a limited number of outlets for programming. This meant everyone was steeped in the same culture. For several decades, nothing would mark you as an outsider faster than not knowing certain TV and movie themes or failing to recognize characters everyone else knew. Cultural literacy became a mandatory subliminal add-on for anyone who traveled frequently to the era after an incident in the second cohort. An extraction team had to rescue a CHRONOS agent studying the Manhattan Project after he was mistaken for a Soviet spy. I'm sure there were numerous things that pinged the radar of those who turned him in, but the key issue for most people interviewed was that he kept mixing up Daffy and Donald Duck.

Whoever picked the *Jaws* theme as the alarm for the Anomalies Machine was probably making a joke, but the other day when it went off with one of its minor updates, Rich said it was the perfect musical choice. Katherine disagreed—given the person behind all of this, she said the stabby music in *Psycho* was more accurate.

She has a point, but Richard was right. The *Psycho* music is more of an instant jump scare, whereas *Jaws* evokes a slowly building sense of dread. When the first two notes sounded, it was like a cold hand clenched my gut. The hand squeezes a bit tighter as the music speeds up, and so do the rows of anomalies scrolling upward as the system compares items from our local historical archives, the ones that are protected by a CHRONOS key, to the information available on the public data system. The web, as they called it during the Wild West days of early computer networking before they started curating content a bit more carefully.

The alarm only goes on for about thirty seconds. On the first few occasions I heard it, it ended before one of us could find the control on the ancient computer to turn it off, so we just let it play out now. But even after the music ends, those two notes echo in my head.

RJ glances over my shoulder at the display and sinks down into an empty desk chair. "Well, at least the waiting is over."

"True," Clio says. "But that seems like a whisper-thin silver lining."

Katherine and Rich came in right ahead of us. They're on one of the sofas, both looking at their keys. For a second, I wonder what they're looking for, and then I realize the obvious. They're checking to see if CHRONOS exists in this new timeline.

Rich looks up as I approach. "The jump room looks a little different, but it's there. Stable point doesn't work, though."

"Maybe it's the restriction against jumping to any point later than 2160?" Madi suggests.

I shake my head. "That doesn't apply to the jump room. Otherwise, we'd never be able to get home. But we should try the other stable points we set before we left."

The one Rich set in Sutter's office at the Objectivist Club is completely grayed out. Another one that I set in the courtyard is there, but I can't lock it in, either.

"If you think there's a chance it's the 2160 restriction," Clio says, "there's a really easy way to check. The latest I've been is 2172. I checked, and the store I visited is gone, but if you want to transfer one of the locations to my key, I can test it."

I tap the back of my key to hers. "Why can your key go beyond 2160?"

She shrugs. "Simon gave me this stable point and said if I wanted more of the smokeless smokes I'd have to get them myself. His key was one Saul gave him. Maybe they found a way around that? I don't know if he'd jumped all the way to the 2300s, but he definitely went beyond 2160."

"So did Prudence," Madi says. "She jumped to 2305 on quite a few occasions to visit Tate Poulsen."

"Why on earth would she have been visiting Tate Poulsen?" Katherine asks.

Madi looks a little uncomfortable. "Um, they were sort of . . . in a relationship for a while. I'm thinking Saul ended it. I can give you the diary Thea left behind. It's short, but there's a whole section on Tate and Pru—"

"No, thank you." Katherine shakes her head firmly, clearly not even wanting to think about how and when her daughter from another timeline might have had a relationship with Saul's ex-roommate.

Alex bursts through the doorway and heads straight for his display cave. His hair is wet and his T-shirt is stuck to his body. "I thought I had time for a shower," he says as he drops into his chair. "What's happened? I mean, other than the obvious."

"CHRONOS exists," Jack says. "But they can't lock in the stable point."

"I can't lock it in, either," Clio says. "So it's not just the 2160 restriction."

Alex types something in. "They're probably on a different frequency. Katherine and I were talking about that possibility the other day, when making sure my safety protocols wouldn't block any hope of a CHRONOS extraction team getting through. CHRONOS could exist in this timeline and not be the same organization you knew. Their version of the key could be different. This isn't the same timeline. Whatever Saul did, we're on a different path." He doesn't elaborate, just nods toward the Anomalies Machine.

"Can we be sure it's Saul and not something one of you did in the field, though?" RJ asks. "I mean, probably not Rich and Katherine, since they didn't interact with anyone in the past. And Madi didn't, either. Right?"

Madi shakes her head. "I startled two deer, but there were no humans in that swamp."

Clio and I exchange a confused look. When we left for 1780, Madi hadn't been assigned a jump. She'd decided to wait here for the rest of us to return.

"We can eliminate all three of your jumps as the source of the time shift," Alex says. "The final act that tipped the scale was closer. I've felt several of these now and it seemed stronger than the 1941 shift. Stronger than 1966, too. Which . . ." His eyes widen and I can almost see the light bulb popping up over his head, like in the comics. Then he slides back over to his terminal and begins pulling up data sets. I suspect that's the last thing we'll hear from him until he's chased down the answer to whatever question just occurred to him.

Lorena is at the library door. She gives the Anomalies Machine a loathing look, probably wondering if the thing shows her as erased again, and adjusts a wriggly and very awake Yun Hee, who is perched on her hip and gnawing a teething cookie.

"Can you take her while I get some exercise?" she asks RJ. "I thought she was asleep, but her eyes popped wide open a few minutes ago. I assume that was the actual shift and not more of Saul tinkering around the edges?"

"Yes," Madi says as RJ goes over to retrieve his daughter. "It was definitely the shift. And Alex may be right that it felt stronger, but it was nowhere near as strong as the stomach punch that hit me in Liverpool. I was less than a decade away from the tipping point that time and it drove me to my knees. Same thing happened to me and Jack when we were in the diner in Memphis in 1966, right after Team Viper undid Pearl Harbor. In comparison, this was more like a timid thump, so that may narrow it down a bit."

Lorena looks back at the Anomalies Machine. "Maybe there aren't as many changes with this shift, though. The data is scrolling by at a much slower rate than last time."

As soon as RJ takes the baby, Lorena leaves. She seems to have decided that ignoring the time shift is the best policy. I can't blame her, but it's not exactly a scientific point of view. Things are going to keep happening whether she's around to observe them or not.

RJ asks Jarvis to compare the top five trending stories on the *New York Intrepid* to the ones in the past two timelines, something we did last time as an initial rough cut to determine the long-term impact of the changes Team Viper made.

After a moment, Jarvis says, "Apologies. I am having difficulty locating the *New York Intrepid*."

"Oh, right. It's the *Intrepid-Herald* in one of those timelines," Madi says. "After the 1940s, at any rate."

"I have already located that one, Mistress. But there is no *New York Intrepid* after 1964 in our current timeline. There appears to have been increased media consolidation based on the number of available sources, and I'm unable to access information on whether it continued under another masthead. In fact, I'm having considerable difficulty getting any current information. Would you like me to display the trending stories at this hour for just the two previous timelines from our archived files?"

"No, thanks," she says. "Let me know when you locate a comparable national news source."

"You mentioned something about a swamp a minute ago." Katherine glances down at Madi's feet. "Is that why you're wearing mud boots?"

Madi nods. "Impromptu research trip. I was going to wait until the rest of you got back, but there wasn't much risk in me going solo to an isolated patch of island." She proceeds to tell us about a jump to 1931 where she set observation points near a tree that played a central role in a local witch tale in the previous timeline. "There was no mention of the Cora Tree in current public data when RJ researched it. No information about a presumed witch by that name at all. But an additional wave of witch hunts did start in that exact area in the late 1700s."

"That's around the same time as the witch outbreak in New England that we're researching," Clio says. "Is this Cora Tree what you and Jack were looking at on your keys when we jumped in?"

"Yes," Madi says. "The legend doesn't have a very precise date, though. We still haven't located exactly when lightning hit the tree or when the inscription was burned into it."

"Could it be a carryover from the New England witch hunts?" I ask. "It probably wouldn't have taken much for them to spread farther down the coast."

"No," Jack says. "This is something Saul changed directly."

I'm about to ask *how* he can be so sure it's a direct change, and not something peripheral. One of the main challenges in both of our clashes with Team Viper was the difficulty of pinning down which historical changes are from a specific, intentional move and which are follow-on effects. For example, I had been fairly certain the attempted assassination of Charles Lindbergh was a direct Team Viper move, but it turned out to be an act of revenge for deaths that occurred at a German-American Bund rally the previous year.

RJ, who now has the baby on his shoulders, begins answering the question before I can ask. He spins one of the displays toward us and highlights an image. "This is a still shot from when Madi set the stable point. July 12, 1931. Just a random day when we were fairly sure the tree would still be there. As Madi explained, the tree was called the Cora Tree due to the letters burned into the bark. But that had already changed before the timeline flipped . . ."

He zooms in on the tree. The letters aren't crystal clear by any means. Some of the bark has eroded over time. It doesn't say *Cora*, though. It's five letters now, and I'm almost certain—

"*Kathy*," Rich says. "It says *Kathy*. That absolute fucker."

∞

The final image of the documentary currently playing on the wall screen is a map of the United States. Sort of. There's a square missing at the top left corner and an inverted triangle snipped out near the upper right. Apparently, Washington State and Vermont are now part of Canada. Hawaii and Alaska aren't even on the screen. The remaining territory, shaded in red, white, and blue, is still called the *United States*, although the *United* part seems a bit overstated, in my view.

Music swells as the credits roll over the map background, and the screen goes dark. We sit there for a moment, letting what we've just viewed sink in.

Rich thought a basic video summary would give us some background and context before we start digging into the specifics of what's changed. And it might have done that, but this one seemed heavy on propaganda and light on actual facts. It reminded me of the Universal Newsreels that used to precede movies in the early-to-mid-20th century. We watched a few during classroom training, but the one I remember best was on the drive-in screen in Greensboro during field training with Glen in October 1962. *Red Threat—President Orders Cuban Blockade.* The music was always overly dramatic, and everything was viewed through the ideological lens of the Cold War.

Clio frowns. "Some of that looked different to me, but I'm going to confess to basic ignorance of US history after the mid-1960s. Simon wasn't a fan of the post–Vietnam War era, so we only jumped beyond that to watch Yankees games. And I made a brief solo trip to 1960s San Francisco when I . . . needed to get away for a bit."

"Well," Alex says, "the US was part of the Northern Alliance before, and we're apparently not now. And, the Cyrist Seal of Approval seems to be everywhere in this timeline."

I'm not sure if he means the lotus tattoo or the Cyrist cross. There were frequent glimpses of both in the half-hour video—the former on the hands of people stacking sandbags along the banks of the Mississippi or giving physical exams to children, and plenty of the latter dotting the skyline of the cities and towns. One weird thing was the difference in the arms on the cross. There were two versions. Most have straight arms, closer to the Christian cross. Others have the curved arms with the infinity symbol, the one Katherine told me and Rich she'd sketched out on a cocktail napkin at the OC, back when she thought this was all a gag Saul was cooking up for one of his scenarios with Campbell.

"This felt like a puff piece," Madi says. "Jarvis, who was the intended audience for that documentary?"

"*A Century of Progress* was produced in 2101 by Cengage-Pearson-McGraw on contract to the United States Office of Civic Education. A slightly altered version was shown to those entering management and technical positions. This was shown to approximately eighty-seven percent of citizens as they entered training for service in either the National Guard, the Cyrist Sword and Shield, community police, mission corps, basic infrastructural agencies, or as community monitors."

"You mentioned the National Guard, but what about the rest of the military?" Jack asks.

"The National Guard *is* the military. The various branches were combined under the Government Streamlining and Reorganization Act of 2035. As best I can tell, there are no state guards because there don't appear to be states. Just something they refer to as *constituent communities*. This was also part of the aforementioned Streamlining and Reorganization Act."

Madi asks if he can show us the other version of the documentary he mentioned, but Jarvis tells her that access to management and technical training materials is classified.

"Okay," she says. "Can you give us a side-by-side chart for this timeline and the last, comparing standard environmental and economic indicators, and . . . anything else I should include?"

"Demographic?" I suggest.

Someone else says health. She adds both of those and a satellite map detailing sea-level rise to the list.

"I can post the data only for the previous timeline, based on the information in our archives that was protected by the CHRONOS field," Jarvis replies after a brief search. "Current environmental data is classified on a need-to-know basis, but the sensor outside the house is detecting a temperature increase of four degrees Celsius from the last time shift. If that is part of the general weather pattern, I am able to extrapolate a sea-level rise of around a half meter. Economic data is not available. The query simply informed me that citizens of the United States of America enjoy the highest standard of living in the world."

I'm about to ask him if that's true, but I realize that's a stupid question if he can't access current data on the US. Alex is apparently on the same wavelength, though, because he says, "Jarvis, compare economic data for the Northern Alliance as a whole in the previous timeline to economic data for the current Northern Alliance."

"Unfortunately, I cannot do that, either. That query elicited a warning stating that the US Information Network is restricted to content produced within the United States. For the security of all citizens, contact with persons or organizations outside the US requires permission."

"Permission from whom?" Katherine asks.

After a brief delay, Jarvis says, "That is unclear, and I have been warned that this search is suspect."

The wall screen now shows a large red stop sign. Directly below is a notice that the search we are attempting is a potential violation of US Code Title Six, Chapter Six, Subsection on Efforts to Access Protected Data. It directs us to our community HomeBase, adding that any further attempts to access data outside of our knowledge area will be reported to our community supervisor.

RJ snorts. "Who exactly would that be? Because I have several complaints I'd like to lodge with whoever the hell is in charge. I guess this explains the tepid response from the Anomalies Machine, though. It probably doesn't have a lot of data to compare to what we have archived. Have you checked to see what's on this community knowledge base?"

Several minutes later, it's clear the HomeBase site isn't going to be of much use. It's more of a community rumor mill that doubles as a place to post messages about local events, lost pets, items for sale, arguments between people with too much time on their hands, and jokes with punch lines that don't make much sense to the uninitiated. There is a map of Bethesda, the location of various public services, and so forth. One article has information about shifts for the weekly neighborhood cleanup where you can earn up to two hundred extra game points, but there's nothing to put that into context. There's also an index called Entertainments, but it requires registration.

Church attendance appears to be mandatory, but it's a relief to see that Cyrisism is not the only religion allowed, although the menu is still limited. Two Protestant denominations are listed, as well as Catholic, Jewish, and Buddhist. There's even an option to spend your mandatory weekly worship time in silent meditation, as long as you log in to a special section of HomeBase to meditate with others.

Religious affiliation is, in fact, the one area where Jarvis is able to give us some detailed information. Cyrists make up 94.92 percent of the population in the United States. When we expanded the question to worldwide, however, the answer was simply that Cyrist International is the largest global religion.

Other questions are either not answered or answered vaguely. When asked the racial makeup of the United States in 2136, we were simply told that the US government and all constituent communities do not recognize race as a demographic category.

Our search is punctuated every thirty seconds or so by holographic ads. Some are for local businesses, but most are for various entertainments. One ad is for a movie about a dog. Another is some sort of reality show with a physical-fitness component. The majority, however, are for games, including one that looks similar to a matching game from our own time, although I guess there can't be too much variation in that sort of thing. The logo keeps popping up, with a bunch of fruit avatars that float in front of our faces along with the name of the game, *Forbidden Fruits*. That one catches my eye mostly because the *o* in *Forbidden* is replaced by a stylized lotus flower in pink and blue, which reminds me of the one I saw on the Friend's hand.

The only thing remotely promising as an actual news source is a link to something called the *Cyrist National Examiner*. Unfortunately, it's a subscription site, and Jarvis says he's having trouble getting the banking information to go through.

Madi's eyebrows go up when he mentions banking info. "Jarvis, who currently owns this house?"

"The house is owned by Sisters, Inc."

"Well, that's good news," I say to Madi. "Maybe they can give you some information on our financial situation when you meet with them."

"I guess we could try the public library they have listed," Alex says, "but I'm going to go out on a limb and predict that any society that limits access to government data online isn't going to be especially generous with it in print form. And I don't think any of us should wander around the neighborhood. Or even go outside the house. The entrances are probably being watched."

Madi goes to the window overlooking an apartment building on the left side of the house. She peers out for a moment, then comes back. "Everything looks pretty much the same to me. The building over there seems a bit taller. Maybe a little more run-down. And if you look down the street beyond the apartment complex, the buildings are packed in more densely. Or at least that's how it looks to me. We'll probably be able to tell more in the daytime."

"And we can also go somewhere else to get the international data," Rich says, pulling his key out of his pocket. "A decent research library in Europe might even have information about the US that hasn't been run through the censors. Although the *Log of Stable Points* is probably a better bet than my key. I have some foreign music halls but not many libraries."

Madi fetches the *Log* from the shelf. "I've been to the British Library enough times that I can find my way around fairly quickly." She searches and then transfers a stable point to her key. "There's a location where I can see the piazza and it looks pretty much the same. I think the statue is different, but they must have had the same architect. It's grayed out, though." She starts to make an adjustment, probably to the time, but her gaze quickly snaps back to the center. Another try and then she looks up. "I can't adjust it." She taps her key against mine and says, "You try."

I do, and she's right. It's showing the current time, which is the middle of the night in London. Current time is the default for any stable point in the *Log* that is accessible from your location. If I were in 1965 and opened it to this section, I'd see whatever this place looked like in 1965. The rare exception is if there's a specific historical event the stable point is attached to. Those are often local points that were set by agents. There's this long, convoluted process for getting a location added to the *Log*, a bit like getting a word added to the dictionary—is it widely used, is it something that will be used by future cohorts, etc.

Our stable points inside the US are fine, as long as we're using the slightly narrower definition of the territory. A stable point near the Space Needle in Seattle is grayed out, indicating it can't be accessed. Jarvis notes that the Space Needle no longer exists in this version of 2136, even though RJ says it was renovated a few years back and was doing just fine in the previous timeline.

The others begin pulling up foreign locations on their keys. Most are European, given our fields of study, but Clio has a few in Mexico and Rich has one in Japan. And there are hundreds more in the *Log* that are located around the world. They look normal until we transfer them to the keys, and then they're grayed out.

I try switching from visual navigation to the holographic interface and enter in a coordinate string, but alter the date a century back to 11-27-2036, just as a test. It's still locked. Then I try 1936. Locked. Ditto for 1836, 1736, and back five centuries.

"Hold on," Katherine says. "I've got one that looks live. Rich, try the points you set in Salzburg."

He does and shakes his head. "Not active. Wait. The one I set in front of the gallows is fine. It's just the others."

Katherine sighs. "And the ones I set on the back side are grayed out. Which means the only ones that work are the last few local points we set *after* the time shift."

Alex asks if she can change the date.

"Trying that," she says. "It was an office complex when Rich and I were there in 2136, so I'm really hoping whatever happened over here changed the course of urban development over there."

Richard looks up from his key. "It did. The location grays out even earlier . . . in 2032. Do you think this is something Saul did? I mean, obviously the time shift is, but the lock on international jumps? Maybe the International Council—"

"Of course, it's Saul's fault." Katherine pastes on a patently fake smile. "And if any of his moves are outside the US, aside from pre-2030s Salzburg, we're totally screwed. So . . . where should we start? I doubt we have much time before Saul signals the beginning of the game, and we now know the computers are going to be next to useless for anything other than previous timeline data."

We let that bleak reality digest for a moment, then Jack says, "Your name on the tree makes it pretty clear that Hatteras Island is one of Saul's three moves."

"Agreed," Rich says. "Although it doesn't have to be a three-move scenario. That's what Team Viper was using, but we don't know that Saul will adopt that rule set. I've seen as many as nine moves in a game, although that's definitely not typical."

I glance over at Clio. "Even if it's only three, the attack at Potter's farm has to be one of them."

"So Saul and I *were* there?" Katherine says.

"No. Clio and I waited at the tavern until well past the window you mentioned. Saul has *been* there at some point, though. People were making jokes about Wilkinson and the prophecy, and from what you said, that prediction was the result of Saul's interference. But the two of you never showed up. It's making me more than a little crazy, because of the whole Lawrence Dennis thing. And that's not the weirdest part. Clio can transfer the stable point to you, but it probably won't do any good to isolate a static image for the others to see because—"

A bell interrupts me, and Jarvis informs us that someone is at the front door with a package requiring a thumbprint. As Madi gets up to retrieve it, Jarvis chimes in again to say it requires Katherine's print.

"Show the front porch," Madi says. The wall screen illuminates to reveal a guy about my age holding a rather large and ornately wrapped box. He must be listening to music, because he's humming softly, a bit off-key. The guy himself doesn't set off alarm bells, but the ribbon topped with a massive red bow looks eerily familiar. In fact, it looks almost identical to the ribbon we saw wrapped around two desiccated corpses in a closet at the New York World's Fair.

Katherine huffs and heads toward the door. "He couldn't simply send the damned thing in an envelope or by drone, like a normal person. Of course not. He's Saul Rand."

We'd all wondered exactly how Saul would handle sending us the rules for this new scenario. Katherine was fairly certain he'd at least *try* jumping back in to deliver them in person . . . or sort of in person, since he wouldn't actually take the risk himself but would simply spin off another expendable splinter. Madi said he'd gotten into the house last time through the basement door that maintenance workers used for upkeep of the swimming pool, so we fortified that entrance and set a second alarm down there. And just in case Saul had any ideas about jumping in via CHRONOS key, Alex set up a block for his signal, similar to the one he put in place to keep Morgen's Viper team from crossing back over and screwing with our timeline.

"Hold up, Katherine," I say. She stops at the library door and gives me a questioning look, then I continue, "Jarvis, scan for weapons."

After a very brief pause Jarvis replies, "The gentleman holding the box is not carrying any weapon that I can detect. I *do* detect an odd energy signal coming from the person inside the box, but I do not believe it to be a weapon."

Madi says, "Wait. Did you say the person *inside* the box?"

"He did," Alex says softly. "I'm picking up a CHRONOS field."

At that instant, a thin, reedy wail fills the room. All of us look toward Yun Hee, but she's still smiling as she dribbles bits of cookie into her dad's hair and stares at the colored bubbles on Alex's display.

"Oh my God. Another baby?" Clio is still holding the key in her hand, ready to transfer the stable point to the others, who I'm sure believe she simply means *another baby* in addition to Yun Hee, rather than the one I was on the verge of telling them we spotted in Rhode Island.

The sound is clearly coming from the box, however, because the delivery guy on the wall screen nearly drops it. He recovers, and quickly sets the package on the porch before backing down the steps to the walkway.

When we reach the front door, the crying has stopped, and the delivery guy is on the lawn arguing over his comm-band. He's in the middle of telling someone, presumably his boss, that he's not a fucking stork when he looks up at the porch to find all of us staring back at him.

"Is . . . one of you Katherine Shaw? I need a print."

Katherine identifies herself and he comes forward with the thumb pad, giving the box a wide berth. Apparently, he's decided he's just the middleman and the sooner he's out of here the better.

The instant he has her print, he crawls back into the van and it zips away from the curb.

Clio crouches down next to the package and yanks at the ribbon. Once she has it untied, she pries open the seal, and a pale purple glow escapes the box. Then she reaches inside and pulls out an infant wrapped in a white blanket. "About the same age as the other one," she says. "Assuming Jemima was telling the truth."

"The other one?" Madi asks.

"Yeah. That's what I was about to tell you when Jarvis announced Katherine had a delivery." I look down to see if Clio still has her key out with the stable point ready, but she's focused on the baby. She pulls back the blanket. What looks like a thin purple chain encircles the baby's right ankle. On closer inspection, the color is coming from under the skin . . . about a dozen tiny circles that almost touch. Each circle has a vertical line drawn down the center.

Clio looks up. "Yeah. I thought the light was coming from an anklet, but it's *under* the skin."

I'm about to say it seems like a cruel thing to do to an infant, but she adds, "Too bad they couldn't do that in 1912. It would have made my parents' lives *so* much easier. Mine, too. Maybe we should go inside where it's warmer and you can tell them about the baby in 1780."

RJ pulls a smaller box out of the package as we head inside.

"That was illegal, right?" Katherine asks. "You can't send a baby by delivery service! I mean, I'm *sure* you can't in our time, but there must be child endangerment laws even now." One hand tugs at the silver chain holding her CHRONOS key as she glances out the window at the now-vacant curb. "I shouldn't have given him my thumbprint . . ."

Madi shoots her an incredulous look. "Well, you certainly couldn't have refused delivery. This baby is under a CHRONOS field. It might not belong here, but it definitely doesn't belong with some clueless delivery service."

Both Clio and Madi are looking at Katherine like she's heartless, but I kind of get why she's freaking out. She's the one who pressed her thumb to that pad to accept delivery of a living, breathing human. That alone is probably illegal. What if the delivery guy—or his employer—calls the police? And now they have a thumbprint that, should they choose to check, they won't find connected to anyone living in the country legally.

Clio says, "This blanket is soaked. RJ, do you have any of those . . . diaper things . . . you use on Yun Hee?" She casts a skeptical look at Yun Hee's bottom, making me wonder what sort of diapers they used in the 1930s. Changes in diaper technology isn't something I've ever thought about, but then, aside from this past week, I've never spent much—or really, *any*—time around babies.

RJ says he doesn't think they still have any that small, but he can probably find something that will work. "You might want to take a look at this, though," he adds, handing a small box to Katherine.

Her name is scrawled on the envelope tacked to the front. I don't know Saul's handwriting, but I do know Katherine's expressions well enough to tell it's from him. She slides her index finger beneath the seal and extracts a folded sheet. A message is scrawled across the back.

IBYF. 10 p.m.

Rules on back.

Maximum of FIVE moves, none after 2136.

Katherine hands me the paper. I scan both sides and then pass it around to the others. We all groan at the realization that Saul has stuck us with the stupid name Campbell gave us last time.

The rules printed on the back are cribbed from the legalistic jargon Team Viper used in the previous match, with a few alterations and omissions. One major difference is that the time span for the initial predictions is longer—we have to guess within a decade, instead of within a week. But that's probably not too surprising, since we already have solid indications that whatever moves Saul has taken span several centuries.

"What does he mean by IBYF?" Jack asks.

"I break, you fix." Katherine's nose is wrinkled in distaste. "A Temporal Dilemma variant, although generally not used by serious players."

"What she means is that it's the version you play when you're high," Rich says. "Or when you're nine years old. One guy goes in and fucks things up as much as he can in a set number of moves, then you try to figure out what he did and how to fix it. Or how to screw it up even worse if you're playing for laughs. People even started creating custom mods where you could add zombies or Godzilla or whatever, although the purists would note you weren't really playing TD at that point, since the scenario was ahistorical."

"The purists were right," Katherine says. "IBYF is also a royal pain to solve, because it's harder to determine the direction of the causal arrow." She opens the box and extracts a new game console. It's larger than the one currently in the library, which easily fit inside the front pocket of my jeans when Alisa gave it to me during the last competition. This one is roughly the size and shape of a sandwich, with a button on the front rather than a slot for a fingertip drive.

There's also a small sticker that reads *SimMaster Deluxe*. Unlike the one upstairs, there's no model number after the name.

Alex examines it briefly. "The tech seems more like something from this era than the box Team Viper left."

"Yeah," Katherine says. "I was under the impression that The Game was developed after CHRONOS began. But you're right. This isn't a twenty-fourth-century device. This doesn't even look like something from when my parents were kids." She flips it over. "No serial number. That means it couldn't have been used in any sort of tournament play. Everyone used a player name when they logged on, but even in the earliest iterations, the serial number of your console was your secure ID for major tournament or casual competitions."

Alex heads for the stairs with the device in hand. "This tech is close enough to what we have in the house that I think I'll be able to connect it without your help this time. But I want to check it thoroughly before we integrate. Last thing we need is to have Saul crashing our system. Or breaking into it."

Katherine shakes her head. "He won't do that. What?" she adds, in response to our expressions. "I'm not claiming Saul is too ethical to cheat. He left an infant on our doorstep, so he's waived all pretense of being a moral actor. But he wants a competition, and his ego is too big to believe we can give him one. You should still check it out, though, Alex. If he starts feeling threatened at some point and knows we have security issues, he'll happily go poking around in our files." Then she turns to me. "You're certain there was another baby at Potter's farm?"

"I'm certain there was a device emitting a CHRONOS field inside the basket, along with something that *could* have been a baby. Wilkinson said someone left the basket on the porch with an infant inside. They thought maybe it was us . . . that we'd abandoned it. I'm going to go out on a limb and assume nothing like that happened while you and Saul were waiting in the Friend's study? Do you think maybe they handed the baby off to the servants and just didn't mention it?"

"No. We sat at the table with the family for two meals. We mostly spoke with the children, since the adults were occupied with Susannah's illness. But Potter's youngest son was a chatterbox. If a baby was abandoned on their doorstep, I'm certain he'd have mentioned it." Katherine looks down at Saul's message and then back at the rest of us. Her eyes skip quickly past the spot on the floor near the sofa where Clio is seated next to the baby, who alternates between crying and sucking on one tiny fist. "We have an hour and twenty-five minutes. There's a lot of work to finish before then, so we'd better get up to the library. And, Madi, I'm going to need that stable point on Hatteras Island."

Katherine's hand shakes as she holds her key out toward Madi. Richard watches her for a moment, then walks over to the couch and whispers something to Clio. She shrugs, unfastens the front of the diaper, and takes a peek. "Yep. It's a girl."

Why did he want her to check that?

Judging from the other expressions in the room when she makes the pronouncement, I'm the last one to figure it out. I have an urge to whack myself upside the head for being so dim. In the past week, Katherine has learned she is the mother of twin daughters. Or she *might* be the mother of twin daughters. Or she *was*, in this or some other variant of the timeline. And now, Saul has now inserted not one, but two babies into the game that's about to begin. Apparently, this one is a girl. I don't know the sex of the baby Clio and I saw. At this point, I can't even be positive Wilkinson was telling the truth. But what I do know is that unless that section of the timeline has changed drastically, everyone inside the house at Potter's farm was killed on May 19, 1780.

FROM GESCHICHTE DER SALZBURGER HEXENPEST (2005, AUTO-TRANSLATED)

Fourteen accused witches were executed in Salzburg on 22 September 1678. These entries were made into the official record and submitted to Prince-Archbishop Max Gandolph von Kuenburg on that same day.

- Veitl Fasching (16) Hanged, burned.
- Anton Helmer (11 or 12) Guillotine, burned.
- Barbara Hochleitnerin (34) Hanged, burned.
- Christoph Kienberger (18) Hanged, burned.
- Sebastian Mayr (12) Guillotine, burned.
- Georg Perger (24) Hanged, burned.
- Anna Reinbergerin (30) Hanged, burned.
- Margarethe Reinbergerin (80) Hanged, burned.
- Maria Reinbergerin (40) Hanged, burned.
- Ursula Reinbergerin (32) Hanged, burned.

- Georg Schmalz (15) Hanged, burned.
- Sigma Schwester (16) Hanged, burned.
- Paul Vöstlberger (8) Guillotine, burned.
- Stephan Vöstlberger (12) Guillotine, burned.

It was the last entry submitted by the executioner and the last received by Archbishop Gandolph. Both fell victim to a dreadful wasting plague that swept through Salzburg, killing nearly all of the residents within a matter of days. One of the few people who survived claimed he attended the execution and witnessed the Zaubererjackl—a local magician authorities believed to be the leader of the Salzburg coven—level a curse on the townspeople for their treatment of the poor and disabled.

There is no definitive answer to the mystery of what happened in Salzburg in 1678. Secular experts have posited that some unknown and virulent form of hemorrhagic fever was spread through the Residenzbrunnen well in the city center, or perhaps through the pipes carrying water from the springs at Mount Untersberg. Others maintain the Jackl was an emissary of God, sent to chastise the people of Salzburg for executing children on the pretense of witchcraft. Members of the Cyrist religion maintain this was an act of Brother Cyrus to purge wickedness from the land.

∞ 5 ∞

Madi
Bethesda, Maryland
November 27, 2136

I place the bottom drawer from my dresser at Clio's feet. A soft towel lines the inside, and there's another folded beneath it for padding. "You're sure this will be okay?"

Clio laughs. "Aunt June delivered a lot of babies for women who couldn't afford medical care. Some couldn't afford a crib, either, so they repurposed their dresser drawers. Or potato bins. Little Bit will sleep just fine in her cozy bed."

The baby Clio holds against her shoulder, who seems to have gotten a nickname, has blue eyes. They're blinking now, like she's on the verge of sleep. One tiny fist is wrapped around a lock of Clio's hair.

Prudence has bright blue eyes in the religious iconography I've seen, as did Thea. What about Katherine's other daughter, Deborah? I don't think there are any photographs of her in the house, but Jarvis might be able to pull something up from public records. Driver's licenses, maybe? Even though I'm not sure it matters, it might help us figure out which baby we're dealing with.

"Were you able to get everything else you need for her?" I ask Clio.

"Yeah. RJ brought diapers and another set of clothes, even though they're huge on her. Yun Hee's more than twice her size. Lorena pumped a couple of extra bottles of breast milk, which should hold her until morning."

"So . . . is she sleeping with you tonight?"

Clio nods. "Lorena offered, but she's more relaxed with me. Probably because I was the one to lift her out of that stupid box. And Lorena and RJ will have to keep an eye on her when we jump, so I'll take this first shift. To be honest, Lorena seems stressed enough as it is."

"Yeah. It's been a rough couple of weeks."

We watch as Katherine heads over to the wall screen. She asks Alex to send a file to the main system and then tells Jarvis to display the information. Tyson is still observing something on his key, and he looks as if there are a multitude of things he'd much rather be doing.

"Did you guys elect Katherine as queen while I was in the hall with Little Bit?" Clio asks. "Or did Her Highness simply assume the throne?"

"Definitely the latter." I can't help but laugh at Clio's comment, even though I doubt she's joking.

"Either way, Katherine shouldn't be running things. She's too close to this. Too close to Saul."

"Pretty sure she'd say that's an element in her favor." Clio is probably right, though. Based on what Katherine told us, Saul is picking his targets to taunt her. It's true she knows the man better than the rest of us. She was close to dead-on with her guess about his timetable for starting the game. But she didn't foresee him pulling in her unborn daughters as . . . bait? Hostages? Door prizes?

"I don't trust her judgment right now," Clio says. "Not that I suspect she's in league with Saul or that I think she's incapable of killing him—although I did kind of wonder about both of those things in the past. Now it's more the opposite. I'm fairly certain she'd be capable of killing him with her bare hands, or at the very least, she'd give it the old college try the first chance she gets. And that's just as dangerous."

I'm not sure what a *college try* is, but I nod. I like Katherine, but I don't want her in charge. It is possible, however, that my view could be somewhat prejudiced because I'm annoyed she switched assignments with me. Had I objected to the trade, I'm sure Katherine would have gone all wide-eyed and injured. She's given me the shorter assignment, after all. Sorting out what happened on the island will take much longer than viewing the stable points in Salzburg. We have no idea when lightning will hit the tree, when her name will be carved into the bark, and when (or even if) the villagers actually tried to burn a witch there. Katherine will have to scan through years, maybe even decades, to find the information we need from the stable points I set, which is why she drafted Rich to share the workload. With the Salzburg observation points, on the other hand, I have a single day to watch, so it shouldn't take long at all. While I'm not as well acquainted with Saul Rand as Rich and Katherine are, I'm perfectly capable of making a positive identification if Saul does indeed turn out to be the "sorcerer" who drops in to level a curse on the town. And, to be fair, if someone had burned my name into a tree hundreds of years ago, I'd probably claim dibs on being the one to find out why.

Clio places the baby into the improvised crib, leaving one hand on her tiny chest to calm her.

"I'll talk to the others," I tell her, "and then we can bring the leadership question to a vote."

My reluctance must be clear from either my voice or my expression, because Clio gives me a sympathetic smile. "If you want, I can do it. I mean, she *is* my great-grandmother."

I chuckle softly. "Mine, too, if you add a couple of greats. I don't think she's going to take it well from either of us, but . . . I'm not sure Tyson or Rich will push the issue. She's their friend and . . . maybe they'd feel it was sexist? Assuming that's still a thing in their time."

Clio raises her eyebrows. "I'd imagine that's a thing in *any* time. No matter when Little Bit here was born, as long as there's any sort of difference there will always be some folks who do their damnedest to create a hierarchy." She reaches over and tucks the blanket in around the baby, whose eyes are now closed. "It's human nature. The only question is whether people are taught to respect those who aren't like them or they're taught that it's okay to use them." The baby whimpers softly when Clio pulls her hand away, almost as if she understood this rather bleak assessment of the world she's entered.

"I've got to get busy on my viewing assignment," I say. "Do you think the baby will be able to sleep in here? It could get noisy once we start hashing all of this out."

"Guess we'll see. Can you turn down the lights, though?"

I reduce the lights to 30 percent in their corner, and then head back to the desks in the center of the library, where Jack, RJ, and Alex are combing through the list of anomalies, so we'll have a decent idea for our initial projections. The one good bit of news we've discovered is that it's easier to get historical information than current. A database of old dissertations and other academic work is accessible on the public information system, along with some old books. Information prior to the 1970s is pretty abundant and seems to track fairly closely with what we have in the archives with a few exceptions. But it diverges sharply after that.

As soon as I pull up the observation point Katherine gave me, I see the dark outline of the gallows against the sky. A row of nooses sways gently in the morning breeze and I mentally kick myself.

You really didn't think this one through, did you, Madison?

The full weight of giving in to Katherine's request—oh, let's be honest, Katherine's *decree*—that I let her watch the stable point with the Cora Tree is now sinking in. Although I guess it's the Kathy Tree in this timeline.

I move from the office chair to one of the couches on the far side of the library. Since I have no clue how I'm going to react to watching a bunch of people die, I definitely don't want anyone watching me while I do it.

The historical record is a bit unclear on exactly what time the executions begin, so I start scrolling forward at daybreak. Wood is already stacked into a massive pyre, and a burly man comes out to get the fire going a few hours later. People begin to arrive a little after eleven, so they're probably starting the festivities at noon. I select one of the stable points farthest from the platform. While I may be forced to watch, I'm not volunteering for a front-row seat.

Unfortunately, many of the others don't seem too keen on being at the very front, either. As a result, most of the stable points are completely useless by the time the crowd has fully gathered. Some are *literally* blocked, showing as a pitch-black square disabled by the key, most likely because it's inside someone's body. Other locations merely have a blocked view, including one offering a lovely close-up of the hairy mole on the back of a man's arm.

Great. Guess that means I'm getting the front-row experience after all. I pick an observation point on the right-hand side, a few feet back. But it's soon clear this section isn't going to remain empty, either. A group of younger men and boys is gathering at the edge of the platform. Several carry cloth sacks, and judging from the brown ooze around the bottom of the closest bag, I suspect it contains rotten vegetables. Or worse. Some carry stones, too. An older teen is engaging in target practice while he waits. He's good. Each time one of the marksman's rocks ricochets off the wood, a pack of younger boys scurries away to retrieve his ammo.

These hecklers will not be the direct cause of any deaths today, but they're eager to add a little extra pain and humiliation to the final minutes of those condemned to die. I'm reminded of the young Klansmen at the Beatles' concert who were originally planning to hurl overripe tomatoes and cherry bombs at the band. Team Viper had no trouble persuading most of them to switch to lethal force. I'd love to believe that kind of thing is a relic of our past, but I'm not so sure. Without laws to prevent it, I suspect you can find at least a few people right on this block in 22nd-century Bethesda who would happily shove their neighbors into the mud for ringside seats at this sick exhibition of ignorance.

All I can think is that the wrong group is being executed. If I made the rules, I'd free the ones on the platform and toss the vultures who are here to gawp at them into that fire.

The first act of the day begins just after noon, when the executioner and two assistants haul four boys onto the platform toward a crude guillotine called a *fallbeil*. This sentence is considered an act of mercy on the part of the archbishop, since it's a quicker death than hanging or burning alive.

According to the ecclesiastical court records, the two oldest children are twelve, one is ten, and the youngest, a boy named Paul Vöstlberger, is only eight. He really doesn't look much over six to me, but as a beggar, he's probably malnourished.

And . . . I can't watch this part. Absolutely not. But even though I scroll through as quickly as possible, the stable point goes blood red for a second. The sight startles me so badly that I very nearly blink myself into the location, at which point there would most likely have been one more presumed witch hauled up to the gallows. I put the key down on the couch next to me for a moment, knowing it will be very hard to wipe that red splotch from my memory.

That's good, though. It *should* be hard to forget. If I follow CHRONOS rules, the only bit of history that will change here is that Saul won't pop onto the stage to shout at the townspeople. The spray of blood I saw will still fall to the ground. Thirteen people, four of them children and another three in their teens, will still be killed on September 22, 1678, one of many execution days during this bout of intolerance. I know it happened long ago and I know it's not one of the things Saul altered, but still . . . how do you live with knowing you could change something like that, and you didn't? The words Kate Pierce-Keller sent me in her video message were right. You can't fix all the wrongs of the world, but how do you find peace without fixing the ones you can?

Katherine says something to Richard. She's on the other side of the library, so I can't make out the words, but I imagine they're something like *it's so relaxing watching this tree grow*. Or maybe, *aren't we so very clever for sticking Madi with the shit assignment?*

Okay, I don't really believe they're saying that. They probably aren't even thinking it. But I'd still like to smack both of them.

Jack, who apparently caught my expression, heads my way. When he gets closer, I nod toward the tablet in his hand.

"Please, please tell me you're here to say the timeline shift put everything back in order in Salzburg and we're striking it from the list?"

"Afraid not. In fact, someone else has been added, so it's a total of fourteen now."

"You're kidding me." I take the tablet and am ridiculously relieved to find that the new addition isn't a child. She's not much older, though. *Sigma Schwester (16) Hanged, burned.* "Any idea what was changed that added her to the list?"

"We're not certain. She's not in the interrogation records in the archived materials, so they must have pulled her in recently. It's possible she's connected to one of the other women, since they're both accused of poisoning a well. But it's also possible she might actually be guilty of that . . . because there's a new complication. A big one. Something historians call the *Hexenpest* hits Salzburg the very next day."

"*Hexen* is the German word for *witch*, right?"

He nods. "Yes. And *pest* is pestilence or plague. The so-called witch plague wipes out pretty much everyone in the city. And the description of the bodies sounds a lot like the ones Saul left in the closet at the World's Fair. The ones Kate Pierce-Keller described in her diaries. And that virus was—"

"Waterborne." I take the tablet from him and scan the paragraph. Only a handful of the residents of Salzburg survived. The plague took young, old, rich, and poor. Even Prince-Archbishop Max Gandolph, the man who started the witch hunt, most likely in an effort to clear the city of beggars, was found dead along with everyone else in the palace. Witnesses said the corpses looked dry and shriveled. One of the few survivors claimed to have been at the execution the day before, where the Zaubererjackl appeared and laid a curse upon the town, telling the man that only he would survive to tell the story. The real irony is that they immediately scooped that man up on suspicion of—you guessed it—witchcraft. After all, why would the Jackl have spared the man if he wasn't in league with him?

Sighing, I hand the tablet to Jack and retrieve my key from the sofa cushion. "Guess I'd best get back to the ninth circle of hell."

"That bad, huh?"

I shrug. "Let's just say Katherine *definitely* got the better end of this deal. There's no definitive evidence anything brutal happened at that tree beyond the lightning strike that split the trunk. Those letters could be some lovelorn villager who decided to burn the name of his sweetie into the bark. Either way, they're not likely to have nightmares from staring at a fucking tree."

"My offer still stands, you know."

Jack told me earlier that he'd scan the stable point if I wanted to help RJ and Alex organize the anomalies, but we both know that's not the most logical division of labor. It would take Jack a lot longer to scroll through because he has a harder time locking the locations. And while he'd have less risk of being startled and accidentally jumping in, he has a very protective nature. The one time he was able to use the key without being pumped full of chemicals was to save me from being killed. I doubt he could make a jump all the way to the 17th century, even to save a bunch of kids. But if by some bizarre chance he *did* make it, we'd likely never get him home . . . and I can tell from his expression he knows there's no way I'm willing to risk that.

"You've got plenty on your plate," I say. "Have you found anything on Elizabeth Forson yet?"

"Nope." He gives me a shaky grin. "Which is a mixed bag, in my opinion. On the one hand, not finding a genocidal maniac in the historical record is very good news. The war that breaks out in the mid-twentieth century is regional and not as lethal. On the other hand, we have the lovely moral quandary of knowing that flipping the timeline back reinstates that travesty. And this just came in." He taps his comm-band to show me a message. *CALL ASAP. MERRICK.*

"Your dad actually signs messages to you with your last name?"

"That's his *informal* sign-off. Nonfamily members get the full *General John T. Merrick, Retired.*"

"What do you think it means?" I ask, nodding toward the message. "I mean, if there's no threat from Forson, he can't be calling to get a status update, right?"

"I don't know. I'm still wondering whether he's under a CHRONOS field. I'm apparently on the same path I was before, if there's still no doppelganger out there leading a normal life like the alter-selves of Alex, RJ, and Lorena."

"And me," I add. "Sorta."

He leans forward to kiss me. "That person is not you. Just someone who shares part of your name and a smidgen of your DNA. But, if Alex figured out how to create field extenders, I think we have to assume the folks at LORTA, with the entire range of government resources behind them, could do it, too. And why bother to create field extenders unless they know someone is out here shifting the timeline?"

"What are you going to tell your dad?"

"Nothing for now. I'll message him in the morning and ask what's up. See how much information I can get out of him without reciprocating. Maybe he's just pissed that I didn't give Karis a definitive answer on whether I'm coming out to California for Christmas." He glances down the hallway where Clio is now pacing with the baby, who apparently wasn't quite ready to sleep after all. "Clio might be willing to swap with you."

"Probably not the best idea. I don't seem to have Clio's knack for comforting babies."

"Or . . ." He gives me a conspiratorial look. "You could *say* you finished. It's obviously Saul. I mean, we could be fairly sure of that even before the information I just gave you, but there's really no doubt now. And knowing Saul, he probably left the bodies in the town square, wrapped in red ribbon."

It's tempting. But at some point, we're going to have to stop this stunt of Saul's, and we'll need to know when and where he appears, and for how long. Might as well get it over with.

"I'll be okay. I'm skipping past the worst parts." Jack gives my shoulder a sympathetic squeeze and heads back to anomalies duty.

I set the time for ten minutes after I left off, which would, in retrospect, have been the wiser course of action earlier, rather than scrolling through the scene. The right side of the platform where the *fallbeil* is located is now empty, and the flames on the pyre behind it are arcing a bit higher, so I pan to the left, where the accused are lined up beneath the ropes. Six of the ten are women, which is a bit surprising, since this particular witch frenzy was remarkable in part because the majority of the accused were young men. But four of the women have the same last name. Judging from the ages given, it's probably three sisters along with their grandmother, who was the oldest person executed as a result of the Salzburg trials.

Nope. I can't watch this, either. I look aside, breaking the connection, and then reenter ten minutes later. The stable points are at ground level, which is a mercy. If I don't pan upward, all I can see is feet. A few of those are still moving. I scroll through to speed things up, but that's somehow worse, because it turns their death throes into a gruesome jig.

Just as I'm about to exit and skip forward again, Saul appears out of thin air in front of the gallows, hamming it up in a purple cape with odd symbols painted along the edge. He timed his arrival to the moment the executioner and his two assistants begin climbing the steps of the platform, presumably to tug the bodies of the adult victims down from the ropes and toss them into the flames. There's a look of recognition in the executioner's eyes.

To the people in the audience, with only a 17th-century frame of reference, what happens next would have been a clear act of sorcery. Saul points a tiny wand—which looks quite a bit like the laser weapon I've carried on jumps—and quickly blasts a hole in each of the three men's chests. He shouts something as he fires, then steps to the front of the platform. He's too close to the edge for me to see his face now, and I can't hear what he's saying given the lack of audio. The young men with their sacks of muck and stones draw back from the scaffold. They cringe even farther away when Saul sweeps his weapon across the crowd, aiming at various people until it finally comes to a stop on a middle-aged man who falls to his knees, clearly begging for mercy.

And Saul *does* show mercy. He doesn't fire his wand at the groveling man, who is most likely the lone survivor who was hauled in when officials from neighboring towns came to investigate.

After I watch the crowd, I roll back the time and pan upward. I'm not a skilled lip reader, but I might be able to make out something Saul says. I never make it that far up, however, because something else catches my eye. I freeze the image and zoom in on one of the women on the gallows. Her head lolls to the side and her eyes are closed, but I've seen the face before. And I've definitely seen the long dark curls. In fact, I see very similar curls right now through the door of the library, where Clio is pacing with the infant.

The curls look a lot like my mother's, too. And they look *exactly* like Thea's in the picture I have from when she was younger.

"Jack," I say. "What was the new addition's name again?"

He grabs the tablet from the desk and scans it quickly. "Sigma Schwester, age sixteen."

"Jarvis, is Sigma a Germanic first name?"

"No. Sigma is an uncommon first name of Greek origin. It is also the eighteenth letter of the Greek alphabet."

I feel my stomach sink, as Thea's voice rings in my head. *They're all the way to Rho and Sigma, now.*

"Jarvis, does *Schwester* mean anything, or is it just a last name?"

"*Schwester* is an uncommon last name of German origin. It translates as *sister.*"

I look back down at the key and continue watching. What Saul does a few seconds later removes all doubt as to who the woman is. He steps back, grabs her arm, and yanks up her sleeve to reveal a cuff that looks identical to the one currently on my own wrist, the one that belonged to Thea. It would be an unremarkable plain brass cuff to anyone in the audience, but I can see the glowing orange stone in the center. I probably would have noticed the light from the bracelet earlier, but amber doesn't stand out very starkly in the midday sun, and I was also doing my best not to look at any of the bodies.

As drab as the bracelet might appear to those without the CHRONOS gene, you'd think someone would have pulled it off during her interrogation to check for so-called witch marks. And once they had it off, I doubt they'd have given it back. None of the other accused are wearing any sort of jewelry. This makes me think the girl didn't come in through the regular channels. Is that why the executioner seemed to recognize Saul? How much of a bribe would it have taken to convince the man to add an extra noose to accommodate a troublesome servant, a disobedient daughter, an unfaithful wife?

For a moment, I'm certain Saul is going to yank the cuff. He inspects the bracelet and even tries wedging his fingers between the metal and the girl's wrist. But then it looks like he thinks better of it. Which is a good thing in one sense. If he had erased her, would she even have been on the gallows that day for me to see? Maybe that's what made him think twice. That's one more piece of evidence that Saul is planning his moves not just to win, but to taunt us, especially Katherine, on his way to victory.

What I really want to know is how the woman got to 1678. Thea said none of the Sisters could actually use the keys to travel—whether geographic or temporal. The cuffs with the CHRONOS field were provided to them as an insurance policy and a way to ensure their memories remained intact in case of a time shift.

Was Thea telling the truth? Or maybe this Sister was different? She said something about one who left the fold, but she didn't go into specifics. And I didn't ask, both because it wasn't relevant at the time and because every word that came out of Thea's mouth that day left me more confused than when the conversation began.

The others are looking at me expectantly, clearly waiting for me to tell them why I asked Jarvis those questions. "Yes. The Zaubererjackl is Saul, which all of us knew without putting me through the agony of watching this damned stable point. But," I add reluctantly, "it's a good thing I did watch, because that new woman on the gallows? She's one of the Sisters of Prudence."

∞

I stare down at the stable point Thea left for me in her diary. The Sister is still sitting there atop the massive desk, still staring at the stable point. Her eyes seem more worried now, but it's entirely possible I'm projecting, since *I'm* definitely more worried. My first instinct was to jump in immediately after I realized who Sigma Schwester was, so I could warn this woman that she and the others are in danger. But I can't go in alone. Katherine agreed to come with me once we enter our preliminary moves and have a better idea about exactly what we're facing. And the point Jack made earlier remains true. Waiting a few minutes longer won't make any difference. Yes, the Sister knows the timeline has changed. But she'll have been waiting on me the exact same amount of time, either way.

We're once again gathered around the wall screen, which is now displaying a list. A feeling of déjà vu washes over me. I'm fairly sure I was in the same seat last time, as we all stared at a very similar bulleted list, trying to make our initial, mostly uninformed guesses about which of the changes we'd identified were the three moves that Team Viper used to flip the timeline.

If this insanity is ever behind me and I'm in an everyday office with an everyday job, will I have flashbacks? Will I be sitting in a meeting staring at a coworker's presentation and freak out when a bulleted list appears on the screen, because it brings up memories of corpses, blood, and guillotines? I think it's entirely possible.

The list on the wall currently consists of thirteen bullets and several sub-bullets. Katherine has checkmarks next to the first two, both of which we were already quite certain about an hour and twenty-seven minutes ago when Jarvis interrupted our discussion with news of the delivery.

1. *Book of Cyrus revisions. London 1473?? Others?* ✔
2. *Hexenpest, Salzburg, Archbishopric of Austria—September 22, 1678* ✔

3. Dark Day Massacre, Little Rest, RI—May 19, 1780
4. Cora Tree, Hatteras Island, NC—17??
5. Suffragist and abolitionist Lucy Stone killed along with Stephen Foster and William Wells Brown. Accused of being Prudaeans—August 27, 1848, Harwich, MA.
6. Two youngest Fox Sisters (spiritualists) arrested—1851. Called Daughters of Prudence by a local minister. Scheduled for execution, but they escape before the trial.
7. 1925 John and Lela Scopes are arrested for teaching evolution. Cyrist radio stations and ministers accuse them of being Prudaeans. Crowds from surrounding states descend on the town. Scopes, his sister, and attorney Clarence Darrow hanged.
8. Cyrist Sword raids kill twenty-seven people between 1967–1973 in California. (Prudaean connection in all four.) Cyrist Sword CEO is Larry McDonald (see #11).

• Monterey Pop Festival—hundreds of arrests, multiple injuries, and sixty-five deaths, 1967.
• Five members of the Manson cult killed in L.A., 1969.
• Five killed in a 1970 raid of the Process Church of Divine Revelation.
• Three Process Church leaders executed in 1973.

1. London Massacre—March 6, 1971—13 killed at Women's March (killer is a Cyrist).
2. The Exorcist published in 1971 by William Peter Blatty, not 2067 by JL Coleman. (Blatty was killed in Beirut while serving as a journalist with the US Information Agency in the previous timeline.) Movie debuts December 1973. Set catches fire, rumors of haunting.

3. *Agnew is dropped from the Republican ticket in 1972. Larry McDonald added. Watergate break-in either never happens or is not discovered. Nixon dies during surgery for a blood clot in 1974. McDonald becomes president.*

4. *1977 National Women's Conference is led by Phyllis Schlafly; 2 counter-protesters killed, others arrested as Prudaeans.*

5. *1980 Mazes and Monsters, 1981 Demon Murder Case— first "devil made me do it" acquittal; D&D is banned in 1984. (Character list includes Prudence as a class of demon.)*

There were only twelve entries on the list when I checked a few minutes ago, but Alex, Jack, and RJ, who were tasked with sorting through the anomalies still being generated, just added the last one.

Most of the entries on the screen are gibberish to me. Few of the names are instantly familiar, although I've heard of Nixon, and Scopes rings a bell once I see the word *evolution*. I have no idea what the *D&D* mentioned in number thirteen even is.

The one that does draw my attention, however, is the tenth entry about *The Exorcist*. I've read it. Twice, in fact. Once when I was a teen, just because it was one of the edgier books my great-grandfather wrote. I read it again when I began writing the proposal for my master's research, because while it wasn't one of the books that provoked a lawsuit, it was fairly successful and often cited by his critics as an example of unnatural variance in his writing style. But if a movie was ever made from *The Exorcist*, I haven't seen it.

Jack takes the chair next to me. I lean over to whisper, "I can't decide. There are too many options on this menu. It's an absolute mess, Jack."

"Yeah, well . . . you should see all the stuff we left out. I still think number eight should be three separate entries."

"I thought Alex was going to try to narrow it down by tracking the times and places where Saul has traveled . . . the ones with the red dots?"

He raises an eyebrow. "Have you looked at his bubble matrix lately? A new red dot pops up every few seconds. We were able to weed out several of the anomalies because Saul hadn't traveled to the time and region, but Saul clearly knows Alex can track him that way. He seems to be jumping around like a damn flea to put us off his trail."

"How the hell does Saul expect us to comb through centuries of anomalies and come up with five decent initial predictions in less than two hours?"

"I think the only answer is that he *doesn't* expect they'll be decent. All we could really do for this stage of the game is pick a handful of the changes that seem most likely to be a cause rather than an effect. And also things Saul might have been able to influence directly or through Cyrist International. One positive thing is that he seems to have figured out that he didn't actually need to launch a full-scale Culling if he allowed enough time for his religion to take root. I suspect if we jump ahead a couple of decades, it will still be chugging along, scooping up the cash."

"So . . . we're fairly certain all of the moves happen before 1990?" I ask, nodding toward the list.

"I wish. We just cut the list off after the mid-1980s, figuring those are more likely to be effects rather than causes. Otherwise there would have been an entry for a brief civil war where a few states secede, and a rather sharp shift to the right on social issues. Later on down the pike, you have more deaths in the 2092 terror attacks, and an addition for Elizabeth Forson, who is—"

"High priestess of the Cyrist Church? Or High Templar, or whatever they call them now?"

"Nope. But she *was* something very similar to that in the Church of Prudence." He pauses at my raised eyebrow. "Which I'm pretty sure we're about to discuss with the group as a whole, so I'll hold off for now, except to say Forson and most of her followers were executed as witches in 2119."

"The witch hunts spread beyond the US?"

"Apparently. We have limited data beyond a few entries in world-history textbooks, which are kind of suspect, to be honest. They're all issued by the same publisher, for the US Board of Civic Education, or whatever it was called, just like the documentary we saw."

Richard takes the empty chair near the screen. He's paler than usual and his jaw is tightly clenched. When Katherine looks at him, he says, "Put a check by number four."

"You're sure?" Katherine asks.

"I'll share the stable point later if anyone wants it, but . . ." He shakes his head, although it looks less like an act of negation and more an expression of revulsion. "There's no point in watching it, because it's never going to happen. You're the so-called witch they tied to the tree. You're holding a baby. Babies kind of look the same to me so I can't be sure, but it seemed identical to the one over there. Anyway, both of you are burned. And your name is still smoking on the tree when they take the bodies down."

Now I feel a little guilty. I'm guessing Richard will indeed have nightmares from watching that tree.

"Except now that we know this," he says, "you obviously won't be making that jump to Hatteras Island. I'll handle it . . . or one of the others will."

"Okay." Katherine's fingers tug nervously at the chain holding her key as her eyes dart toward the corner where Clio is sitting on the floor next to the baby's makeshift crib. "We should get started, I suppose. It's nearly nine forty-five, although if we run a few minutes late, Saul really shouldn't hold that against us. Dropping an infant in our laps along with the game files is tantamount to cheating."

I exchange an amused look with Clio. Katherine's split-second glance at the corner just now was the first time she's paid any attention at all to the baby since we entered the library, so I don't think she's slowing her down. Although, I'm not sure how I would react if a baby that was most likely mine was literally deposited on my doorstep. I'd probably freak out at first. Maybe this is Katherine's way of freaking out?

Katherine turns back to the wall screen and taps to highlight numbers *1*, *2*, *3*, *4*, and *9* in yellow. "I think these are the five most obvious choices. Assuming you're certain about that second infant with Wilkinson," she says to Tyson. "Did you scroll back to see who left the basket on the porch?"

"Yeah," he says. "It's the girl who goes to the well . . . the one Jemima says noticed the basket. There's a brief flash of light through the leaves when the girl is in the barn. But that's all I can see. She comes out of the barn with the water buckets, then drops them near the corner of the house and starts searching through the bushes. When she finds the basket, she places it on the front porch. About five minutes later, when she comes back from the well, she pretends to discover it and tells one of the other servants. There's definitely a CHRONOS device of some sort in the basket. Saul was there at some point. Wilkinson's prediction about the Dark Day is more precise now. And I forgot to mention it earlier, but I saw a lotus tattoo on her hand. Pink *and* blue."

"Saul could just be trying to make us *think* there's another baby there," Rich says.

Tyson gives a shrug of admission. "It's possible. Either way, that's a change he made, right?"

Clio waves a hand for us to wait, and then comes over, carrying the baby inside the dresser drawer. "Let me see the stable point on the island."

Richard transfers the location. "There are a few others, but I think that one offers the clearest view."

Clio studies it for a moment and then says, "The babies do seem identical to me. Which is actually a vote *against* them being Katherine's. My mom said her mother and Prudence were fraternal twins. Saul *might* know that, but he might also have simply assumed they were identical and picked the infants accordingly."

"So you're thinking Saul found three similar-looking babies in 2136, in 1780, and . . ." I look at Richard. "Isn't that around the same time as the incident on Hatteras Island?"

"No," he says. "That's what took me so long to find it. The legend was a few centuries off. Early on the morning of October 22nd, 1923, someone pins a flyer to the tree. *Infant found. Inquire at Melcher's.* But why does it matter whether the babies look similar? The fact that they're showing up centuries apart means they're absolutely not Katherine's. I mean, it's not like an infant can lock in a stable point and blink out."

RJ, who has been watching silently until now, says, "No, but you're forgetting that Katherine can use the key. So we can't entirely rule out the possibility that she had one baby in each era."

Katherine snorts. "Oh, sure. I just blinked out between contractions?"

"There are sometimes hours between the birth of one twin and another," he says. "Days, in some cases."

"But that's rare," Katherine says. "Right? It's ridiculous. Saul is just trying to rattle me. These babies can't be mine."

"Can we go back a step?" Clio says. "It might be possible to transport them. Assuming they have the CHRONOS gene. My mom and I have had some interesting and rather intense conversations since my . . . um, encounter with the bomb at the World's Fair. She was never willing to talk about what happened to her when she was pregnant with me. Anything I knew, I'd picked up from my dad. Jack, you remember the dots on the walls at the house in Skaneateles?"

"Sure. Little blips of light up near the ceiling every six feet or so."

"Right," Clio says. "They were cannibalized from a device my mom referred to as the Mirror from Bloody Hell, because it looked a bit like a handheld mirror, only with two handles. It allows two people to view the same location on a CHRONOS key and, more to the point, it's a way to drag a second person along with you, willingly or unwillingly, if they have the gene. That's what Simon used to transport my mom when she was pregnant with me and they drafted her into service as a substitute Sister Prudence. She said the physical effects were really rough if you weren't able or willing to focus on the stable point and blink when ordered to do so. That might explain why Little Bit here was so cranky when she first arrived."

"Sounds like something that would have come in really handy when Jack was stranded in 1967," I say.

"Yeah. Except, like I said, they had to divide it up to protect the house. I'd never heard of the thing, and you told them Lorena was working on a serum, so they probably figured your way would be simpler and quicker. My dad and Aunt June tracked down the mechanic who had lived and worked at the Cyrist Farm when my dad was a kid. The mechanic had no memory of that, of course, since it was his other-timeline-self, but he had the same skill set. He worked with Thomas Edison around the same time Tesla did. This guy had been able to create the device based on Saul's instructions, and after a bit of trial and error, he was able to adapt it to work as a field extender for the house."

"So you think Saul may have stolen the device from your parents' house?" Tyson asks.

"What? No. If Saul Rand showed up in Skaneateles at any point in time, my dad would shoot him on sight. If Mom didn't beat him to it. But Saul had the idea to track down this scientist the first time around. He could easily have done it again. Plus, he wouldn't have been restricted to early twentieth-century technology. I'm sure Alex knows people who could reverse engineer a CHRONOS key given a bit of time. I'm just saying Saul probably has a way to transport the infants, so we shouldn't rule that out as a possibility. And we're going to need to track down that mechanic or see if we can go back and borrow the device before Dad gets the guy to chop it up, because I can't think of any other way to rescue the babies."

"If he was trying to convince me that the babies are mine," Katherine says, "he screwed up by pulling in a third infant, assuming Jemima Wilkinson wasn't lying about there being a baby in the basket. Why would Saul plant *three* babies when I had twins?"

Clio says it could be just one baby that Saul has yanked around to three different locations if he has the extender device. The others join in with theories, but I barely hear what they're saying because all I can think about is the conversation I had with Thea when she explained, in her own rather disjointed fashion, how the clones who call themselves the Sisters of Prudence were organized. She told me there are three in each birth group. *They're all the way to Rho and Sigma now, and I guess there will be a new batch coming soon.*

"No," I say, interrupting the others. "I'm guessing there are indeed three identical babies. And I'm pretty sure all three are Katherine's offspring, in the same way the woman who was executed in Salzburg was her offspring. Jarvis, display the Greek alphabet."

There's a brief delay, probably because he's processing something for Alex, and then the letters appear in a small inset window on the wall screen.

"Zoom in on the letter *phi*."

He does, and we see the symbol Φ.

"That's the symbol on the baby's ankle," Tyson says.

I nod. "Maybe that's so they could tell which baby was which."

"But . . . if that's the case," Katherine says, "they're *clones*. Which means they're not really my children." She stops, her face turning a deep red. "I don't mean that to sound cold, but they're not. Clones aren't legal now any more than they are in my time, and they're certainly not considered legal offspring. There was that civil case, where someone had herself cloned three times to try to get a larger share of inheritance. Do the Cyrists get to break laws with impunity?"

Jack reaches over to squeeze my hand. I'm not sure if the gesture is sympathy or a caution that I might not want to open this can of worms right now. But my mind drifts back to Clio's comment a few minutes ago about hierarchy and differences. That baby didn't choose to be born a clone any more than Thea did. She didn't choose it any more than I chose being born with illegal genetic modifications.

"The Cyrists were no doubt granted a religious exemption," I tell Katherine. "I'm not a fan of that sort of privilege, but I'm glad on a personal level that they made an exception in Thea's case. Otherwise, I wouldn't be here. And even though my grandmother was a bit flaky, I loved her. From what I've read, much of her flakiness was inherent in the original version. Prudence was your *legal offspring* if you really want to make that distinction. But leaving that aside, we have a major problem. Saul seems to be targeting the Sisters. Whatever you may think of the method used to place them on this earth, they aren't expendable."

Tyson says, "Come on, Madi. She didn't say . . ."

I sigh. "Yes. I *know* she didn't say they were expendable. I'm not trying to put words into her mouth. My point is that Thea and the Sisters willingly risked their lives to help us. We wouldn't have a base of operations here if they hadn't. Saul may be targeting Katherine to some extent with these changes, but he was also angry at Thea for shooting him."

"Do you think he knows she fired the shot, though?" Richard asks. "Or that a shot was even fired? I mean, she didn't shoot *him*. Just his splinter."

"Of course he knows," Katherine says. "He would have set stable points in this house. In fact, he's probably watching us now, which is also cheating." She enunciates the last four words carefully, maybe in order to help Saul read her lips.

"But Alex blocked him," Clio says.

"I blocked his ability to jump *in*," Alex says. "But the stable points still exist, so yeah, he could be watching."

Clio shudders and says, "Remind me to shower at my parents' house from now on."

I point toward the wall screen. "If he can see this room, should we really have those options highlighted, then?"

Katherine says it doesn't matter, since Saul will know our initial predictions as soon as we enter them into the system. "And truthfully, it didn't make much difference with Thea, either. Even if Saul figured out what Thea said as she fired her weapon, it didn't make any sense."

She's right about Thea's words not making sense. Thea told us she was acting on behalf of the Sisters and Gizmo. I read through the diary she left me, the one she said would explain everything. It didn't. There was an entire section about Prudence's memories of living in 2305, after the destruction of CHRONOS, with special emphasis on her relationship with Tate Poulsen. I have no idea how much of that was real and how much was romantic fantasy. It could easily have been packaged as one of the lusty-busty romances my great-grandfather published. And we still have no idea who or what Gizmo is.

But she did leave the stable point in the diary. And she did ask not just me, but also Katherine, to contact the other Sisters, whom she definitely referred to as Katherine's *daughters*.

"And now we're off on a tangent," Katherine says, "with only a few minutes left before we have to enter our predictions."

"But it's not a tangent," I counter. "It gets to Saul's motivations. Why is the London march highlighted? Thirteen people killed, and the killer is a Cyrist. So what? Jarvis, are Cyrists more plentiful in 1971 in the current timeline than they were in the last?"

"Approximately fourteen percent of the global population were affiliated with the Cyrist religion in the public historical data for 1971, compared to approximately twelve percent in the most recent capture of historical data for that year. It rises sharply over the next few decades in this timeline. Would you also like the percentage for 1971 in the timeline prior to that?"

"No, thanks." I turn to Katherine. "The fact that the guy was a Cyrist doesn't make it a direct change by Saul. There was roughly a fourteen percent chance he'd be of that religion."

"But the attacker was shouting a verse from the revised version of the *Book of Cyrus* when he opened fire on the group," Katherine says. *"Let women learn at the feet of Cyrus in silence and submission."*

RJ snorts. "There are quite a few verses like that. Lorena offered to read the revised version, since it was something she could help with while watching Yun Hee. She erased it from her reader when she was done and told me not to get any ideas about converting to Cyrisism. Said she liked the Prudence character better."

"So that's where *Prudaeans* comes from?" I ask, nodding toward the list.

"Exactly," Jack says. "Every wicked or evil woman in the Bible and various other scriptures is combined, and wrapped in a nice, neat bow as Prudence. Her followers are called Prudaeans. Hey, Jarvis? Show us a few images of the religious figure Prudence."

The pictures appearing in the corners of the screen are of an attractive young woman. Her eyes are blue or green, or occasionally, a demonic red, and they gleam with either shrewd intelligence or evil intent, depending on the skill and/or religious leanings of the artist. The one feature that remains the same are her long dark curls. They aren't a perfect match for the Sister Prudence images I've seen, but it's far too close for me to view it as a coincidence even if we didn't know they were both cooked up by Saul.

Jack continues, "In the new edition of the *Book of Cyrus*, Prudence is the key antagonist. Or I guess I should say in the new *Books*, because there are three fairly substantial revisions. In all of them, Prudence is depicted as Satan in a skirt. Around 1830, you start seeing a backlash, and the Church of Prudence is formed, aka the Prudaeans. They're either a bunch of pagan nature lovers or a bunch of crazed demon worshippers, depending on who you ask. They've never even come close to one percent of the population, but they're either really active or they get scapegoated a lot, because as you can see, Prudaeans are all over that list. Then in the 1960s, Prudence is incorporated into a New-Age religion called the Process Church of Divine Revelation basically as a stand-in for Lucifer. That's the photo near the bottom . . . the one in the pop art style. A similar group existed in other timelines, called the Process Church of the Final Judgment."

The image he's talking about is an actual photograph, or rather an arrangement of four photographs. Three are of men in long robes and the fourth is of a woman. The photos have an ink wash that shades each quadrant a different color, and the woman could be one of the Prudence clones, but the picture isn't clear enough to be certain.

"It just seems to me that number eight there . . . that looks like a lot going on with these Cyrist Sword raids," Jack says. "I don't know how many died before in these events—"

"None at Monterey Pop," Richard says. "I don't even have to check. That's on my research agenda for next spring. I pitched the proposal three times, and the jump committee finally gave it the thumbs-up as a comparison of accommodations at music festivals, investigating whether there was a correlation between the number of porta-potties and the amount of violence. You've got happy and peaceful Monterey Pop at one end, in 1967—with plenty of bathrooms, by the way, and no violence. The police were super relaxed. No deaths by overdose. Few injuries, and they were well equipped to handle them. Woodstock in the summer of '69 is middle ground, and then it all goes to hell at Altamont in December of that year, with barely any toilets and several deaths. Not saying the lack of toilets caused the deaths. Like I said, it's just what I pitched to get the trips approved. Likewise, I doubt the violence at Monterey actually flipped the timeline, but it's not a minor change."

Clio has been staring at the list for a while, and now turns to Katherine. "None of the five choices we've highlighted has anything to do with these Prudaeans. Why?"

Katherine is silent for a moment, then she says, "Obviously, this is open for debate. If you have another option to propose, I'm all ears. My logic was that if Saul is targeting me, he would hit a location I visited. Or the one we visited together—"

"Except we've established that you and Saul never made the jump to meet with Jemima Wilkinson," Clio says. "Why would the march in London be any different?"

"But I don't have to *be* there physically. Saul would remember me talking about the jump, so . . ." Katherine trails off, looking pained. "And he would know that's what I'd think. You're right. The attack in London *could* have been simply due to his revision of those foul little books of his. All he had to do was toss in a few verses to motivate the faithful. I'm sure there were other attacks on women's groups before and after using that same verse as a trigger. I just assumed . . ." She sighs and takes a seat. It seems more like a sigh of relief to me than one of resignation. "You should take the lead, Tyson. I may be able to predict Saul's moves to some extent, but he can also predict mine. I'll give you whatever advice I can about his motivations. Someone else needs to be making the final calls, though."

"Or you could have us vote," Tyson says. "Like I did."

"That works until we need to make a split-second decision and we don't have a quorum. Besides, you have experience now, and I'm fairly sure the group will be more comfortable with you in the driver's seat." Katherine's eyes flicker toward me and Clio for an instant, and I feel my face growing warm.

There's a general rumble of disagreement from some of the others, but Clio says, "You're right. Tyson is a better choice. You're too close to this to be entirely objective. And the event in London really doesn't seem likely to me. The only question now is which of the others should replace it."

After a brief silence, Alex speaks up from his display cave. "I *think* the decisive change was in the second half of the twentieth century, based on the physical impact this time shift had on us compared to the others we've experienced. But it could be a lot more recent. I'm working on a way to quantify it, to measure the difference in the surge we've noticed in the CHRONOS field each time the timeline flips. But I haven't nailed it down yet, so we're going to have to go with our gut feeling."

RJ groans at the pun, although I really don't think it was intentional. Or maybe he's groaning at the fact that the timeframe Alex suggested doesn't narrow things down much. Nearly half the list took place during that time span.

"*The Exorcist* has a personal connection, too," Richard says. "Less direct, but . . . the original author would be Katherine's great-grandson and Madi's great-grandfather. And Clio's . . . something."

"Yeah," Jack says. "I was looking at that. A fire happened in the previous timeline, too. There was talk about the set being haunted, but the fire itself apparently had something to do with the refrigerator unit they rigged so they could film the actors' breath fogging up."

"And Coleman wasn't the original author of that book," I say. "Or, quite possibly, any book. More likely it was written by Blatty, and he was killed in our timeline before he wrote it. But I'm not sure why that would have changed the timeline. I mean, that's Saul's main objective, right? Taunting us is icing on the cake. I'd think the quickest way to make major changes would be to change the political leader."

"Agreed," Katherine says, glancing over at Clio. "Although I would note that the McDonald guy is a Cyrist, not a Prudaean. What do we know about the men who were appointed as Nixon's VP in each timeline?"

RJ scans the info on his tablet. "Gerald Ford was selected in the other timeline as the safe pick. After Agnew resigned due to corruption—perhaps because Nixon had similar problems of his own—Nixon wanted a straight arrow. Ford had no skeletons in the closet, or at least none that ever came out aside from his wife's addiction, which she turned into a positive by creating a rehab center. When Nixon resigns, Ford is president.

"In the *new* timeline, most of Nixon's pressure is from the political right. Agnew is dropped from the ticket in 1972 because Nixon gets wind of his corruption early. Watergate is a non-event. Either they don't break into the place or they don't get caught. Nixon picks a relative newbie named Larry Patton McDonald from Atlanta. And Nixon doesn't resign. He dies in 1974 after surgery. Had the same surgery in the old timeline, after he resigned, but that time he survived."

The background RJ gives us on this McDonald guy in the two timelines is drastically different. McDonald was a former Navy flight surgeon and a distant cousin of General George Patton and apparently didn't let anyone forget it. He eventually went into politics in the old timeline, but he never made it beyond the US House of Representatives, and he was killed when the Soviet Union mistakenly shot down a Korean passenger jet he was on in the early 1980s.

In this timeline, he started a national group called Cyrist Sword, a security organization focused on reporting suspected communists and extracting people from any religious group McDonald considered a cult—Satanic, Prudaean, whatever. The skullduggery wasn't a complete departure from the earlier timeline, since he helped the Birchers develop an alternative intelligence agency of sorts, but that group, Western Goals, didn't have a strike team component. While McDonald didn't literally kick down the doors himself most of the time, he did just happen to be in California for the raids on the Monterey Festival in 1967 and on the Manson compound in 1969, and used the media coverage for both to springboard his political career. The Manson cult committed some really nasty murders, including a fairly well-known actress who was pregnant at the time, so McDonald got a ton of publicity from that raid. He then ran for Congress in 1970 as a Democrat, won, and ran again in 1972. Right after the second election, he switched political parties.

When Tyson notes that the switch was a little risky in 1970s Georgia, RJ says, "Yeah, but he doesn't end up running again in '74 anyway, because Agnew resigns and Nixon taps him as the new running mate. After Nixon dies, McDonald wins reelection in 1976 and 1980 . . . and thanks to a successful effort to repeal the twenty-second amendment, also in 1984 and 1988. McDonald was *really* far right, a leader in something called the John Birch Society."

"Seriously?" Tyson says. "A Bircher becomes president? Oh, that's fucking fantastic."

"You know these guys?" RJ asks.

"I know *of* them, sure," Tyson says. "They picked up where Coughlin and McCarthy left off. Everyone is a Red. The Birchers are the Bund crowd we just dealt with minus all of the Hitler idolatry. There's still racism, but of the more polite variety . . . Basically the Klan for the country-club set. No sheets or cross-burnings. They even had a member who infiltrated the Mississippi Klan and gave evidence for the FBI. But then they turn around and spread garbage about *civil rights* being a term cooked up by the Communist Party."

Rich nods. "Yeah. They were the focus of several protest songs. Dylan had one called 'John Birch Paranoid Blues.' He walked out on an *Ed Sullivan Show* appearance because Sullivan wouldn't let him sing it. You'd think Saul would mix things up a bit, wouldn't you?"

Katherine shrugs. "Why? He wants to win. Since he's setting up the scenario, he played to his strengths. And extremist religious groups aren't just his *research* specialty. They're also a key ingredient in his ongoing battle with Morgen. Saul maintains religion is the most powerful tool to shape society. Morgen, on the other hand, believes religion only works on weak minds. The strong will never be swayed by it . . . so any leader relying on it will fail in the long run. I'm pretty sure this game we're about to embark on isn't Saul's end goal. He's still trying to prove his point with Morgen."

"Okay," Tyson says, "I say we go with number eleven, then. McDonald is connected to a bunch of the stuff in number eight, but it culminates with his becoming president. Do you think Saul will go for the chronological style points?"

"Ugh," Jack says. "Style points. That's one term I never wanted to hear again. It's not enough to simply screw up the timeline. We have to figure out if the bastard did it backward, sideways, or with one hand tied behind his back."

"The time span is too long," Katherine says. "There's no way he could do it backward. He might get some for the other categories, but with an I-Break-You-Fix scenario like this, it's going to be really hard to figure those out. And . . . we can't worry about any of that. At the end of this, it doesn't matter whether we've fully repaired this reality, or whether the stupid SimMaster says we've won or lost. The only way we win is by making sure Saul can't break the timeline again."

"You're right." Tyson takes a couple of seconds to delete the other options and change the wording around a bit to fit the game format. Then he says, "I guess we're set. Although if past is prologue, the odds of most of these being right are pretty slim anyway."

He taps the list, which now has five options:

1. *Revised Book of Cyrus revisions—London 1473*

2. *Hexenpest, Salzburg—1678*

3. *Dark Day Massacre, Little Rest, RI—1780*

4. *Cora Tree, Hatteras Island, NC—1923*

5. *Larry McDonald becomes President, DC—1974*

"All in favor of the slate on the board?" he asks.

Everyone's hands go up.

"Well, that was easy," Clio says.

And it was. Not because we're enthusiastic about our choices, though. Looking around the circle, it's clear we're simply tired. We're overwhelmed. Everyone in this house, including the babies, has had their world turned upside down multiple times in the past two weeks. There may be five of us and only one of Saul, but he's calling the shots.

We're only at the beginning of Saul's godforsaken game, and we already look like we've lost.

FROM THE PERSONAL DIARY OF KATHERINE SHAW FEBRUARY 27, 2301

I'm *so* tempted to delete my last entry. It just oozes optimism, and my birthday dinner didn't go at all the way I'd planned. If it had, I certainly wouldn't be here in my quarters scribbling in my diary. But I'll leave the entry. It's history now.

The start of the evening was perfect, exactly what I'd hoped for on our first dinner out in public as a couple. No more sneaking in the back of the OC to meet him in a private parlor, but actually sitting together in the Redwing Room like normal people. A nice dinner, maybe some dancing, and then after . . . Okay, after would still need to be in one of the private parlors, because I don't think either of us is ready to simply waltz into the other's quarters, even if our roommates aren't in.

We were discreet tonight, in order to test the waters. If there's any sort of uproar, all Saul has to say is that he took his research partner out to celebrate her eighteenth birthday. He's convinced there will be no complaints, and he's probably right. Angelo has suspected our relationship for some time, based on the oh-so-paternal talk he gave me a few months after Saul and I were teamed up for research. I'm sure Angelo's not the only one—CHRONOS delights in gossip—and if they were going to raise an alarm, you'd think it would have been before I turned eighteen. But we do need to take it slowly. I really don't want Saul getting into trouble about our age gap, especially when he stuck his neck out to protect me after the incident on the Dark Day jump.

The icing on the cake tonight was that Campbell was on vacation, so it could have been a perfect evening. Just me and Saul for once, without having to deal with Morgen-the-Lech's eyes crawling all over me. And it really did start out that way. Dinner was incredible. But as we were finishing up dessert, a chocolate torte with eighteen dark-chocolate candles, Saul said he had access to the private gaming suite attached to Campbell's penthouse, and asked if I was interested in a game. Not a long one, he'd added quickly, especially since I was a beginner. Just a short scenario where he could test a few ideas he had for the longer series he was currently playing with Morgen.

I had to fight back a laugh. For one thing, I can't count the times Saul has complained that Campbell has a major advantage because he owns a top-of-the-line system and has scads of free time as a man of leisure. If Campbell wonders how some idea of his might play out, all he has to do is launch a separate game against the computer or against one of his lackeys, work out the kinks, and then apply the new insights when he and Saul resume their game. Saul is probably right on this point. I've watched them play on several occasions. Campbell hates losing, and I can't imagine he'd be above bending the rules a bit to avoid it. But I'm also pretty sure that Campbell's tendency to cheat in that fashion is the only reason he's any real competition for Saul.

It was also amusing that Saul assumes I'm a beginner. I don't play as much as I did when I lived at home, but it's one pastime my mom and I still share. She'll never admit it, but as much as she loves working in the computing division, a part of her would love to *use* the system she helps maintain. Otherwise, I don't think she'd have been willing to fork over so much money to purchase the CHRONOS gene as my chosen gift. And she'd never get to play Temporal Dilemma if I didn't challenge her to a match when I visit. Dad is truly horrible at strategy games. My parents don't have the latest model and fancy peripherals like Campbell, but Mom is good. She has an uncanny knack for predicting how a small tweak to history in one era can cascade, causing changes for generations to come. And our games are usually close these days, even though I've beaten her only twice.

Saul clearly wanted to sneak in an extra practice, and what harm could come from a little healthy competition? Maybe it was time to let him know I'm not quite the rube he seems to think I am. Dancing wasn't going to happen anyway. I hadn't factored in the fact that it's a weeknight. There's music, and we could dance if we wanted, but we'd have been the only couple on the floor. Not exactly keeping things discreet.

So I agreed to the game and we took the private lift up to Campbell's suite. I fixed us a drink while Saul set the initial parameters. Twentieth century, continental US, three moves "in a basket" as they say, meaning he makes his moves all in one go, and then I have three moves to reverse it. Then he selected the goal—at least 50 percent of the people in the US will believe in demonic possession.

This is definitely not a standard scenario. The usual goal in these games is to prevent (or start) a war, cure a disease, or change the outcome of an election. Macro-level stuff. This seemed really specific. And he had clearly been thinking about his strategy for this simulation, because he completed his three moves quickly. By the time I had our drinks on the side table, the system had processed his moves and was showing exactly 59 percent of the US population stating a belief in demonic possession in the year 1998.

I made my initial guesses as to what variables he had tweaked. Decreased funding for education, a major religious revival, and— mostly because I couldn't really think of anything else—decreased regulations on mass media. All three were misses.

Saul chuckled and settled back on the sofa. For the next hour, he watched as I tried to figure out what moves he'd made so that I could reverse them. His changes were either very small or in areas that seemed unrelated, because I couldn't figure out what he'd done.

As for Saul, he was pretending to read something on his retinal screen, but clearly paying attention, since I caught him smirking on several occasions. He even asked if I wanted a hint, and then laughed when I told him exactly what he could do with his offer.

Finally, I decided to see how much opinions on the issues fluctuated in the decades before and after, and that's when I discovered why my initial projections had failed. Saul hadn't changed anything at all. It hadn't even occurred to me that more than half of the people in a developed nation believed in demonic possession at the end of the 20th century. The system had to do some extrapolation for earlier decades, since it wasn't a standard polling question, and sure enough, it looked at education levels and general religious views to draw those inferences, so despite Saul's little smirks, my initial projections hadn't been off-track. My mistake had been accepting the original premise that achieving his goal would require any sort of change. In retrospect, the fact that the number was exactly 59 percent rather than 59-point-something should probably have been a tip-off.

He clearly wanted me to give up so he could enjoy his little joke. Or maybe this was a test of a similar ploy he planned to try out on Morgen. But even though it was technically within the rules, it felt like a cheat to me. I decided instead to do what I could to lower the number by going ahead with my initial predictions. They weren't wrong. They just weren't the moves Saul had taken.

I flicked a piece of ice from my drink at him. "You lousy cheat."

He frowned, brushing the ice onto the floor. "How did I cheat? I made three moves."

"Not anything relevant! But what the hell? How were people still believing that nonsense? They were three decades past a moon landing—"

"Which a sizable number believe is fake . . ."

"They were on the verge of mapping the human genome! How do they still have fifty-nine percent believing Beelzebub or whoever can float in and take over their bodies? How?"

"It will be a smaller number in a few years. And then it will surge again. Each time you have an era of rapid scientific advancement, you get a backlash."

"I don't believe that's a given."

"So prove it." The tone of his voice clearly indicated I couldn't prove it, but there was a teasing glint in his eye. "Or you could just give up and we could take advantage of our current privacy and this big, comfy sofa."

To be honest, I don't consider that room private. There are almost certainly security cameras in there. But the rooms we normally use downstairs probably aren't any better. Campbell seems the type to have every tryst that takes place anywhere in the OC recorded for his own personal playback.

"Not giving up," I told him. "But this shouldn't take long."

He sighed and stretched out on the couch. "Wake me when you're done."

I debated flicking another chunk of ice at him but decided that would be childish. Instead, I went to work, checking my available resources. I poured 90 percent of my budget into education, boosting science and critical-thinking programs and raising spending as a percentage of GDP to European levels. Five percent was reserved for a public-education campaign on mental illness, and a final 5 percent of the budget was allocated to a skeptics' society to debunk reported cases of demonic possession.

Saul had apparently decided against his nap. He was watching, one eyebrow raised, as I pressed the button to enter my moves about twenty minutes later. When the final screen popped up a few seconds after that, the number of demon-believers had dropped to 49.97 percent . . . which the computer apparently rounded up to 50, because it posted the little victor's medal on Saul's side of the screen.

I groaned, figuring Saul was going to gloat over his win. Because it was a win, even if it was on a technicality. But he didn't seem pleased in the slightest. In fact, his mood was now a bit on the snarly side. He flicked off the SimMaster and said we needed to get back to CHRONOS, since we're on the jump schedule in the morning.

More tomorrow. I have an incoming message from His Grumpiness.

∞6∞

I'm glad Tyson is the one who pushes the button on the SimMaster. Saul immediately pops up in holo-form next to him and Tyson startles, stumbling back into one of the chairs. I'd have startled, too, and Saul would have gotten a good laugh at my expense. Far better for him to see me sitting calmly in my chair.

I'm going for an expression of bored indifference, but once his outfit registers, I can't help but snicker. He looks very much the stereotypical villain in his knee-length purple cape. All he needs is a curly mustache to twirl. It's the same costume he wore to the executions from what Madi said, maybe in an attempt to suggest that Salzburg was the final change he made. He's grown facial hair, something he usually sneers at as an affectation, and his hair is longer than usual. Longer than it should be if only a week has elapsed. He's always worn it short, slicked back or parted near the middle, depending on the styles of the various eras we jumped to. The new look makes him look a bit older than his thirty-one years.

"Wow," Tyson says. "What do you think, Rich? Rand's almost got a Doctor Strange vibe going there."

Rich squints toward the image. "Nah. I'm not seeing it. Closer to a cut-rate Mysterio."

The question of whether Saul is live or previously recorded is answered when he glances at the two of them briefly and disdainfully, and then turns to me.

"I trust you're enjoying your time with our daughter, Kathy? It seemed only fair. That's the beauty of twins, I suppose. One for you, and one for me."

I'm silent for a moment, debating whether to let him know we're on to his game, but Tyson settles the matter.

"And who gets the third?" he asks.

"Ah, that remains to be determined, I guess. The Solomonic judgment is obviously one option. What do you say, Kath? Even split, right down the middle?"

I sigh. "Are you enjoying your little villain's soliloquy? You've even dressed for the part. If you have anything relevant to tell us, please continue. But if this speech is for dramatic effect, let's get on with it."

Saul keeps his face neutral, but his eyes flash the tiniest bit. "As you wish." He reaches forward, finger extended to push a button, and then steps back. The familiar spinning globe of the Temporal Dilemma logo pops up with the words *SimMaster 666*.

Hilarious. I resist the urge to roll my eyes, and I simply ignore his lame joke.

"When I was setting up this scenario," he says, "I couldn't help thinking about our first match. The one we played in Morgen's penthouse, when you were so disappointed to discover how irrational people can be. Do you remember?"

It was our *only* match, but I don't correct him. Given his reaction to me coming even close to beating him, I never volunteered to play him again and he never suggested it. I decided maybe The Game was something that he needed to have as his own. If it bothered him that I'd come close to winning, imagine how annoyed he'd be if the little victor's medal had popped up on my side of the screen. And to be honest, I preferred playing with my mom. She never got all pissy on the rare occasion that I won.

"Of course I remember. If Morgen hadn't had the system set to round the score upward, you'd have lost."

"True. Although, to be fair, you weren't exactly honest about your experience level. I wouldn't have rolled up a child's-level simulation if you'd mentioned that you played regularly with Anya. Your mother was bright, if not particularly imaginative, and your father said she'd finally gotten you to the point where you were a bit of competition."

Your mother was bright.

I bite the side of my cheek to center my focus on the here and now. It would be all too easy to dwell on the fact that my parents probably don't exist in this timeline, or if they do, they're not my parents. I knew that already, but his nonchalant use of the past tense when mentioning her rammed it home again, reminding me that *he* is the reason why we're in this situation. And so I struggle to keep my expression neutral, because I have no desire to let him know how well his blow landed.

Rich is watching me, too. He hesitates a moment, and then says, "Listen, Rand, this little trip down memory lane may be interesting to you, but the rest of us are bored. If we're gonna play, let's play. Tyson is ready with our five initial predictions, so why don't you cut the crap and let us get on with it?"

Saul frowns slightly when Rich mentions Tyson, and I'm again glad I handed over the reins as team lead. He knows he really only beat me on a technicality last time, and I suspect he's been framing this in his head as a rematch. A way to show me he's better, smarter, and superior in every way. A reminder that even with four team members to back me up, I'm no match for him. Will it be as satisfying for him if we aren't facing off head to head? I doubt it.

"Have you been promoted from squire to white knight, Vier? Noble Sir Richard. Ha. I should have known you'd hide behind your menfolk, Kathy. I suppose that's inevitable when it's literally built into your genetic code." When I don't respond to his baiting, he shifts his gaze to Tyson. "Might want to keep those baby-blue lenses in, Chameleon. You're going to be playing a bit out of your league this time. And while I'm sure Delia, Abel, and Glen all did their best with your training, let's face it. You're really only equipped to battle wits with the offspring of slaves and a bunch of inbred semi-literates who want to continue enslaving them. I'd lose the braid, though."

"Thanks," Tyson replies. "But you'll forgive me if I pass on sartorial advice from the guy who's dressed like a comic-book sorcerer."

"Are you so sure that sorcery is merely the stuff of comics these days? The vast majority of people out there would beg to differ." Saul looks back at me. "As I noted in my message, you'll have five moves to reverse my changes. Continental US only."

"What?" Madi says. "That makes no sense. You were in Salzburg. You added an extra person to the gallows. You *started* the *Hexenpest*."

"Correct," he says. "But that was something I did as a test. A proof of concept, if you will. It had absolutely no impact on US history. A *tiny* impact on European history, which is what I was testing, but no lasting changes. The witch hunt was part of their original history and plagues were all too common. As for the woman I added to the gallows, she was completely inconsequential. Let's just say I have a grudge to settle that in no way affects our little game."

Madi's clearly pissed. "Bullshit. You just admitted you altered the playing field before the game even began, and we're supposed to take your word that it changed nothing?"

"Yes," he says. "But feel free to waste your time in Europe if you don't believe me. Now, getting back to the rules. No limit on field observers—"

"Generous of you," Tyson says drolly. He has a point. Saul knows we're limited in terms of people who can jump, so a single observer is pretty much the best we can do. But Saul has the same limitation in that regard.

"As long as they stick to observing," Saul continues, ignoring Tyson's interruption. "Any material participation in the game is expressly forbidden and will result in swift reprisal. That's something your friend over there who decided to stick her pretty neck in during our last match needs to keep in mind. If she can't stick to *observing* this time, I'll make certain there are no pieces around to stitch back together in this or any other reality."

Clio, who is generally unflappable, pales slightly at that comment. I've been so focused on everything else that it never occurred to me she probably has double memories from her attempt to minimize the number of people Saul killed in the bombing at the New York World's Fair. I've dealt with double memories before. They're not fun under the best of circumstances. But a double memory of dying? That's definitely one I'd prefer to avoid.

"As you seem to have figured out," Saul says, "there are some . . . distractions . . . scattered about. Again, I ran multiple checks with the SimMaster. None of the distractions in any way affect the game. Your smartest course of action is to ignore them, but I have no issue with you rescuing them if you really want to waste your time and energy. It might even add a little extra spice to watch you scurrying around to earn karma points for your soul or whatever you think you're doing. I will, however, have a major issue with you preventing them from being taken in the first place. There are explosive devices set to detonate at public events within one hour of the time I picked up each Prudence. If you doubt this, ask Sister . . ." He frowns. "I think it was Rho? Or maybe Tau? They all look alike to me. Whichever one from 2137 was watching over the nursery when I took the infants off her hands. That was a demo. People will die if they try to keep me from collecting them."

Tyson holds up the note that was in the box with the baby. "This explicitly says no moves after 2136."

Saul sighs. "Apparently, I have to say this once for every person in the room. My quarrel with the so-called Sisters of Prudence has *no connection to this game* and in no way influenced the time shift. Getting back to the *relevant* details, the system will read the chronometer on your keys, and it will begin counting down three days from the time it renders judgment on your initial predictions. Your team is not allowed splinters. If you cheat on that count, you forfeit the game. I'm already at a disadvantage playing against four. It would be even more unbalanced if the four of you start multiplying yourselves when I'll be playing with just me, myself, and I."

"The unholy trinity." Rich snorts.

Saul gives him a little nod. "That's actually not bad, Vier. How unfortunate for you that Kathy's never been attracted to sharp-witted geeks. As I was saying, no splinters and no jumps to the year *prior* to the start of play. This SimMaster console is calibrated to detect those."

"Why?" Madi asks.

He looks at her like she's stupid. And it *is* a bit obvious, but probably not to someone who has been contemplating time travel for only a few weeks.

"Because we could give ourselves a lot of extra time to research," I tell her. "Although I'm not at all certain a SimMaster console can measure that."

Saul grins. "You're more than welcome to test it, my love. And with that, I'll leave and allow you to enter your moves."

"Wait," I say. "I have a question. What's the *point*? Why should we bother? There's no prize at the end of this. Even if we figure out what you did and restore the timeline, you're just going to get bored and start screwing with it again. And I think I speak for all of us when I say we have no desire to remain on your little hamster wheel, running around for your amusement, while you play God."

Saul gives one short bark of laughter. "Oh come on, Kathy. Get off your moral high horse. The difference between what I'm doing now and what all of us did collectively at CHRONOS is only a matter of degree. Every single time we went into the field we made changes. People occasionally *died* as a result of our jumps. Others lived who should have died . . . as you know firsthand. The whole purpose of Temporal Monitoring checks after each jump was for them to decide whether the changes we made fell within some allowable range. If it didn't alter our history, if there were no major changes and it all came clean in the wash, no one gave a damn. Water under the bridge, in the grand scheme of things. If I hadn't been the one to exploit the flaws in the system, someone else would have come along to do it eventually."

He steps closer to the camera and locks eyes with me. "I've changed the fate of the entire planet. And I will continue to do so, until I die or until someone stops me. I'm not *playing* God. For all intents and purposes, I *am* God."

"You're *crazy*." Richard's jaw is clenched so tight I'm worried he'll crack a tooth. "I mean, I knew you were unbalanced, Rand . . . but you're actually fucking certifiable."

Saul doesn't look at Rich, but the left side of his face twitches, almost certainly in response to Rich's use of the C-word. It's a tiny movement, but I've seen it several times before, usually right before he hurls something against the wall. He recovers quickly this time, keeping his eyes on me as his grin grows even more smug.

"You *know* how this ends, love. Eventually, I'll get *bored* with all of you, and I'll *erase* all of you. But you're wrong about one thing. There *will* be a prize waiting for you at the end of this game, and that prize is me. Find the move that flipped the timeline, and you'll find me. And I promise it *will* be me, not one of my handsome twins. That means you'll get a second chance to use that little peashooter you had in your pocket at the Fair. And when you fail, I'll have the very personal pleasure of pulling your key."

Saul gives me a slow wink and then he's gone. In his place is a timer set to five minutes. A smaller version of the globe continues to spin as the countdown begins.

As the timer begins to roll backward, the automated female voice asks us to enter our names and positions. Tyson steps toward the box, key in hand, but Clio asks him to hold up. She gives Jack the drawer the baby is sleeping inside, and he carries it out into the hallway. I'm not sure why at first, but then I remember last time when Madi's grandmother was pulled in as an observer. She volunteered, but the rules seemed to suggest she'd have been added to the roster anyway. It would be absurd to include an infant, but as Rich just noted, we're dealing with a crazy man, so I suppose anything is possible. Jack is here this time, too. He definitely has the gene, and he won't be going into the field, so it was smart to get them both out of the room.

Once they're out of range, Tyson taps his key against the black box. "Tyson Reyes, team lead." Rich, Madi, and I register as players, and Clio as our observer.

"You have four players and one observer," the voice states. "Would you like to register additional observers?"

When we say no, the voice says, "The roster for Team Hyena is now full. Your team leader now has three minutes and forty-two seconds to enter five initial predictions."

Tyson gives us a hesitant look. "We need to put something else in instead of Salzburg. And we need a different location for the first prediction."

After several minutes of back and forth, we have our list.

"Prediction One: Harvard University, 1650—first North American edition of the *Book of Cyrus*. Prediction Two: Little Rest, Rhode Island, 1780—Dark Day massacre at Potter's farm. Prediction Three . . ." He hesitates for a moment, looking down at the list in his hand. "Prediction Three: Hatteras Island, North Carolina, 1923—execution of Katherine Shaw for witchcraft. Prediction Four: Dayton, Tennessee, 1925—execution of John Scopes. Prediction Five: Washington, DC, 1974—Larry McDonald becomes president of the United States."

The voice says, "Prediction number one is partially correct. A total of ten bonus points will be added to your score at the conclusion of play."

We all exchange a stunned look. Only *one*? And that one only *partially correct*?

"Woo-hoo," Clio says. "Go team."

The red *START* button appears. Tyson sighs and pushes it.

When the button fades out, the voice continues. "You have three days to complete your moves. All moves must be entered by a registered player or observer. All players and observers must actively participate." The timer dings, resets to *72:00:00*, and the countdown begins.

We all stare at the display for a moment, watching the numbers flip. After the forty-eight hours we were given last time, three days feels almost luxurious . . . until I consider the far longer list of events spread over at least four centuries.

Tyson casts a dubious glance at the SimMaster. "I don't know about the rest of you, but I could use some fresh air. Let's get some food, some wine, and go out on the patio. I'll light the fire pit and we can brainstorm our first moves . . . and also figure out how in hell prediction number two could be wrong."

"And three. And four. And five," Rich says. "Nothing about this makes sense."

"We don't have to go outside, though," Alex says. "Saul can't hear us once the connection is broken. I double checked the simulation box for listening devices before the game started, and it's clean. It's really basic compared to the other one." He tilts his head slightly and his eyes twitch from side to side like he's scrolling. I'm used to seeing people do this all the time with their retinal screens, but it's odd watching Alex search the data system this way. "Jarvis isn't detecting any outgoing audio signal transmissions. Just the signal indicating it's open for communication with the now-nonexistent public data system. And there's a frequency scanner. It *might* be modified to pick up the timestamp from your keys."

"Even if they're not listening," Tyson says, "Saul could still have observation points in here. He could have them outside, too, I guess . . . but he'll have a much harder time reading our lips in the dark."

Alex shrugs. "True. Jarvis, there should be a way to detect stable points and erase them, aside from blocking a specific jumper's signal. An admin feature, since you wouldn't want agents erasing each other's stable points."

Rich is already heading for the door, but he turns back. "They can delete stable points in an area? But . . . how does Jarvis know about admin features on CHRONOS equipment?"

"No," Alex says. "I said there *should* be a way to block them. Jarvis is keeping a list of design flaws. For future reference. It's getting rather long."

Tyson says, "I second this feature request. Is there a wall screen on the patio?"

Madi says there is, and while they work out logistics, I go to my room on the pretext of grabbing a sweater I borrowed from Madi. I've never been one to accumulate possessions, but it's odd having nothing aside from a few changes of clothing, basic toiletry items, and a diary with a few dozen entries from a future that will never happen. It's even odder having to wait several days for clothing to arrive, rather than simply printing something out when I need it.

Ten minutes later, everyone is gathered out back. As I walk through the kitchen to join them, I hear a soft whimper from the far end of the kitchen island that separates the cooking area from the octagonal table and benches built into the wall. The dresser drawer is on the floor between the legs of two barstools. I look down without thinking and see her, wrapped in a pale blanket that glows softly in the stream of moonlight coming in through the patio door. She lies on her side, one little fist pressed against her mouth.

Damn it. I force myself to look away, but my eyes are drawn back. I want to scream because she is tiny and helpless. And I don't know if I can keep her safe.

I apparently failed miserably with the original Prudence. There are several CHRONOS diaries in this house aside from mine, including Kate Pierce-Keller's. A week wasn't enough time to read or watch all of her entries, but she, and pretty much everyone else, read my diary, so I figured turnabout's fair play.

Four days ago, I lay upstairs on my bed after watching those diary entries, in pretty much the same position as the baby, except my fist was clutching my CHRONOS key. For a long time—minutes? Hours? I don't know—I remained curled in a ball, recounting all the ways I'd screwed up. Mistake after mistake, and I had no reason to doubt any of what I'd read. They're all mistakes I can easily see myself making, and I thought how easy it would be just to open my fist and let the key roll away. Then I could walk out back, past the oak tree, and simply blink out, like Thea did . . .

Like *Angelo* did, although it wasn't by choice, in his case.

Did they disappear into nothingness? Into the timeline next door? Would it even matter if I followed them? Would anything change?

Because the one thing that came through crystal clear in that diary was that I sucked as a mom. I pissed one daughter off so thoroughly that she wound up in Saul's hands, and I pushed the other one away in my efforts to get her sister home. While Kate didn't know for certain if either her mother or Prudence truly forgave me for my failings as a parent, she did note we were at least partially reconciled when I died.

I was in such a dark mood the other day, however, that I'm not sure that would have been enough to pull me out. The one baffling thing that gave me hope, that gave me the will to keep my fist curled around the key, was the realization that despite my mistakes, despite the opinions of her mother and aunt, and despite the fact that I placed the weight of a global catastrophe squarely on her young shoulders, my granddaughter clearly loved me. At some point, I must have done something right. I must have learned from my mistakes. Her entry the day after my funeral was the tiny bit of light that convinced me to slip the chain holding my key back over my head.

Not because I think I need to survive so that I can be there for her. We are so far from that timeline I can't imagine how I'd get back there. All I can do is send a bit of love out into the universe to this granddaughter that this version of me will never meet, and hope it finds its way across timelines. That it is the inexplicable thing that gives her comfort in a dark hour.

I kept the key around my neck because her faith allowed me to believe I could avoid those mistakes this time around, if I was indeed carrying some version of her mother and her aunt. That I could protect them. That I had nine months in which to literally make this a better world for them.

Then four short days later, Saul drops a box on the front porch. *Sorry, Kathy. Time's run out. The world is still fucked up, I'm still out here eager to fuck it up some more, but here's a baby for you to protect right this very minute.*

And then another one pops up in the distant past. And a third. A fourth—that one all grown up and on the gallows.

Oops. Failed again, Kathy.

Over the past few hours, I kept finding myself with my hand tugging the chain that holds my key, the chain Angelo gave me on graduation day, although that's not something I've shared with anyone other than my parents. It's the one he used to hold his key when he was a field agent, and he passed it along to me. I could never bring myself to break it. It's sturdy enough I probably *couldn't* break it. But it would only take a second for me to slide it over my head and send the medallion sailing to the other side of the library.

Each time I was tempted, I'd remember Kate's face from the diary entry. Her tears mixed with smiles as she talked about moments we shared . . . moments I'll never know, but which suggest I can learn from the mistakes of that Other-Me.

Each time, I'd feel Rich's eyes on me. Worried. Uncertain.

And each time, I pulled my hand away from the chain.

Rich would stop me before I reached the boundary. But even if he couldn't, even if I somehow slipped past, I watched someone I loved blink out in front of me ten days ago. I can't fathom how Rich can still feel that way about me, knowing everything he now knows, but I'd never put him through that. That would make me not just a failed mother and a failed friend, but a failed human.

The one consolation in all this is that it's highly unlikely I need to bother with a pregnancy test. If I were pregnant, Saul would have found me and brought back *that* baby. Or those babies, if I were carrying twins like before. No, I'm pretty sure this tiny girl is a copy.

A very *human* copy, no matter what the law may say. My face grows warm again, remembering my comments earlier in the library about the legal status of clones. That was more something Saul would say—or worse, Morgen—and I was horrified to hear the words come out of my mouth.

"They're so fragile, aren't they?"

The words jolt me, both because I thought everyone was already outside and because they echo my thoughts so completely. It's Lorena, standing in the doorway.

She comes closer. As she crouches down next to the baby, tucking the blanket around her feet, it occurs to me that she is the one person in this house who might understand my current state of mind.

"They're so small," she says. "So utterly dependent on us to keep them safe. To not screw up. I remember standing in our apartment with RJ the first night we were home with Yun Hee. She was cranky and neither of us knew how to comfort her. All I could think was what in hell have you gotten yourself into, Lorena Jeung? The life of this tiny, frail human being is literally in your hands and you are not fit for this responsibility. RJ later admitted he was thinking the very same. He snapped out of it quickly. It took me longer, but I'd finally gotten past that feeling, for the most part. And then all of this . . ." She glances up at the CHRONOS key on my chest. "All of this proved I was right the first time. I'm not fit for this responsibility. None of us are. And it's not just my Yun Hee we've put at risk, but so many more."

RJ taps on the glass door and motions for us to come outside. Lorena stands up, gives me a tired smile, and goes over to slide the door open. Once the patio door is closed behind us, Lorena tells Jarvis to listen for baby noises in their suite and in the kitchen.

Would I have thought to do that? We'll probably hear the baby in the kitchen if she starts to cry, but still . . .

The others are seated at the far end of the patio in portable chairs and along the low stone wall surrounding a large brick fire pit on two sides. It's one of the old-style pits with actual flames. Gas-powered, I guess. I didn't know those were still legal in the 2130s.

Is this the same fire pit Kate wrote about in her diary? There was a memorial service for a man I apparently loved, a man I'll almost certainly never meet in this reality. Someone else I couldn't keep safe, who had children *he* couldn't keep safe. And the wheel goes 'round and 'round.

I shake my head to release the pressure building up inside. Rich, who is watching me, slides over to make room on one side of the wall, and I paste on a smile. "Sorry. I had to grab a sweater. Have you already called the Temporal Justice League to order?"

Tyson makes a disgusted face. "That's it. You're off the team. Justice League is DC Comics."

"He's right," Rich says. "We're obviously the Temporal Avengers."

Clio nods. "Not a perfect name, but a damn sight better than Team Hyena."

Jack asks how she even knows the difference between Marvel and DC.

"I'll have you know that in 1939, Marvel was called Timely Comics," she says with a sniff. "The Human Torch and Namor the Sub-Mariner. Captain America shows up in 1941. I did some research during my jumps with Simon. Picked up a few comics to take back to my brothers, too. I thought about jumping forward a few years to see if they'd hire a female artist after my engagement ended. And to be honest, I wouldn't have been picky about which one if either offered me a job. But none of them were really hiring women until well after the war ended, and even then it was mostly as inkers, and . . ." She shrugs and holds her glass out for the wine Madi is pouring. "And in this timeline, I'm guessing they're not hiring women for a whole lot longer than that, so it's kind of a moot point."

A platter of cheese and crackers is being passed around, along with apple slices—the one fruit this food processor handles fairly well—and some fudge Jack made earlier in the day. We keep the conversation light for a few minutes as we eat. The only one who doesn't join in is Lorena. She just leans into RJ, observing the banter and occasionally giving a brief smile. I'm guessing she smiled a lot more often before time travel derailed her life.

Another bottle of wine makes the rounds, and then a hush falls over the group. It's almost as if some unseen tenth member cleared their throat and brought the team to order.

Tyson asks Jarvis to put up the list of initial predictions. "Number two doesn't make sense," he says when the list appears. "Even if Wilkinson was lying about the baby—something we're obviously going to have to find out one way or the other—we *know* a CHRONOS key was in that basket. Clio and I both saw it. And Wilkinson's prediction changed. She was even wearing a lotus tattoo, and it looked recent. If the system had said that one was a partial hit, maybe . . . But a complete miss? That's crazy."

"Garbage in, garbage out," says Clio. "It's not like the system knows what moves Saul made. All it has to go on is what he says he did. And before any of you say he takes the game too seriously to cheat, you already said he's basically playing the version of Temporal Dilemma where he burns it all down."

She's right, but something about it feels off to me. "Some of my assumptions may be wrong. He looks older, although maybe it's just that his hair is longer. Either way, his hair has grown too much for it to have only been a week. He gave himself a vacation. Indulged in a little time tourism now that he has an unlocked key. But now that the game has started, I still think he needs to feel like he won fair and square. Not out of any sense of morality, but because he sees this as a rematch." I spend the next few minutes giving them an abbreviated version of my first and only TD game with Saul. At the end, I add, "He knows he won on a technicality. His ego won't be satisfied unless he also wins this rematch. So I don't think he lied about the changes he made. That wouldn't be a clean victory. And he definitely wasn't lying when he said that at some point he'll get bored with this and kill us, assuming we don't beat him to the punch."

"Was he being honest about CHRONOS?" Alex asks. "He said people sometimes lived or died as a result of your jumps, and as long as it didn't change anything major, they considered it no big deal. If a life was historically insignificant, if its presence or absence didn't merit the equivalent of the Anomalies Machine's blue check next to the name, it was just ignored. Is that true?"

"I know it was true in the case of someone living who should have died, because I saw it firsthand with Judge Potter's daughter. She died in childbirth a few years later, along with the infant. Aside from a difference in the dates her death was entered into the record, there was no change to history that we could find, so they let it stand. I've heard a few . . . rumors . . . on the other count, where someone died as a result of a historian's jump, but that was before our time. I know several members of the board who would never have stood for that if they knew. Angelo certainly wouldn't have."

Tyson and Richard back me up on that, noting that there might be a *few* board members who would allow something like that to happen. But enough of them sit in on jump-team meetings for us to know there are others who are absolute sticklers for protocol.

"Okay," Alex says. "The reason I ask is that I think what you said earlier may be right. Saul could have left the babies and maybe even the older Pru Sister, Sigma, simply as a distraction. As a way of upping the stakes, without making a move that in any way alters the timeline. Did one extra woman dying on the gallows that day alter history? And would an extra infant or two dropped off at the last minute to be killed by mob violence change anything at all?"

"No," Madi says. "They'll just add to the body count. But he knows we won't be able to simply stand by and let that happen. He knows we'll divert resources to rescue them, and that will take our focus off the main objective."

There's a general concurrence that this is still cheating, and a far worse form of it than lying to the SimMaster. On the one hand, they're right, but . . .

"It's certainly *immoral* when you're playing with living humans," I say, "but in theory, is it so different from actual, non-temporal chess? You distract your opponent by endangering the queen or a bishop, something you know they're not willing to lose, even though saving that piece may weaken their main defenses."

"Still seems like cheating," RJ says. "In real chess, there's a practical limit to the type of moves you can make. Your opponent can see all of them. This is more like me moving the chess pieces when Lorena gets up to go to the bathroom . . . not that I would ever, ever do that."

"True," Tyson says. "It also screws up any hope of scoring well on initial predictions, because Saul knew we'd assume any event where an infant was added to the mix was a link in the chain that eventually flipped the timeline."

"And we know he was screwing about in Europe," Madi adds. "No matter what Saul says, he can't be certain that didn't have an impact. This isn't a simulation where there are known parameters. What if this *Hexenpest* in Salzburg made it more likely that witch hunts continued in the US?"

"It puzzles me, too," Rich says. "I know you told him about the Zaubererjackl legend, Katherine, but you did at least one training jump to Massachusetts during the witch trials, right? Why wouldn't Saul start there? Was he testing whether an extended witch frenzy would jump the Atlantic?"

I don't answer. I'm pretty sure I know where Tyson and Rich are headed with this and I really wish they wouldn't. Saul could just as easily have been mucking about with the Salzburg trials because he liked the way the word *Zaubererjackl* rolled off his tongue or because the Jackl was a male sorcerer and he wanted to play dress-up.

But I suspect he *was* tweaking things in Europe to see if he could find some other folks willing to play. One of the guarantees CHRONOS made to the International Temporal Oversight Committee, or ITOC, at the UN when they instituted a manned time-travel program was that each of the seven permanent members and a representative of the UN itself would be provided with a device so they would know if the actions of CHRONOS caused any changes to the timeline. CHRONOS complied without hesitation. For a few decades after that, the other member states were a bit haughty about the whole thing. The US was being reckless again, playing around with forces that could harm not just our nation, but the entire globe. They might not be able to prevent us from our foolhardy course of action, but they certainly did not intend to follow us down that path.

"I think he was trying to see if Europe developed their own program," Rich suggests, as I knew he would. "Maybe he changed something over there to see if it would piss them off enough that they'd come out and play? Or, as it turns out, cause them to block our jumps outside of our borders. Which would probably mean blocking their own jumps as well, so I guess that answers our question about whether they have an active program. But at what point would they decide blocking us isn't enough? There have to be spillover effects, and they have to know that, so you'd think they'd offer to try to help us stop him, even if this isn't their mess."

They're not going to drop this, which means I have a rotten choice to make. Like I told Angelo back at CHRONOS, I can *keep* a secret. I promised him and my mom both that I wouldn't tell anyone. And I haven't. Not even Saul. But am I still bound by that promise if CHRONOS doesn't exist, at least not in the form that we knew it? My mom might exist in this reality, but Angelo was a historian before he was a mentor. If the CHRONOS gene isn't on the menu as a chosen gift, he's not really Angelo.

"The real question is *why* they didn't react," Tyson says. "Not just now, but during the last two timeline shifts."

"Unless they were telling the truth and they never developed the technology," Rich says.

"Is this really relevant?" Jack asks, and I send him a silent thank-you for steering us away from rocky shoals. "It seems kind of eso-teric when we can't jump outside of our borders—with the singular exception of six stable points within a twenty-meter diameter in 1678 Salzburg—and they haven't shown any interest in coming to our aid."

Tyson and Rich give a reluctant nod of admission, and Jack con-tinues. "We're assuming Saul went in chronological order, so maybe we should start at the top. The first prediction is the only one we got points on, and it's only partially right. So, what's wrong with it? Unless the current historical record is incorrect, and it may well be, the first printing of his revised *Book of Cyrus* on *this* continent was on the press operated by Harvard University in 1650. Or he's playing word games again and one of the later editions is the one that actually changes something."

"Oh, fuck." Madi's eyes go wide. "Maybe it's not just the *Book of Cyrus*. He almost certainly changed the *Book of Prophecy*, too. That's why it's only a partial hit. The *B of P* is not a public document, so we can't really tell if the publication date changed. In the past, it was a CHRONOS diary. Only Templars who inherited the gene could read it and pass along stock tips and other predictions to the faithful when new information showed up in the book. But that could also be something Saul changed."

She's right. I didn't think of it because the second book wasn't part of Saul's competition with Morgen. A copy of his original *Book of Cyrus* was on our dresser, but I never saw this *Book of Prophecy*.

Tyson walks over to the list. "You've read the new edition of the *Book of Cyrus*, right, Lorena? Which of these could have been accomplished by changes to it alone?"

"Most of them," Lorena says. "Basically, any of those events that mention Prudaeans. From what you said before, Saul invented the Cyrists in a previous timeline and managed to do quite a bit of damage. But he left out one of the easiest tools for motivating people— giving them a nemesis. I don't know what he added to this *Book of Prophecy*, but the vast majority of changes to the *Book of Cyrus* are trash talk about this Prudence character, who looks a lot like she could be Thea's younger, purportedly evil twin."

"One obvious move for us is to change the *Book of Cyrus* back to the original," RJ says. "But that doesn't resolve the issue with the *Prophecy* book. We need a copy of that. You'd think anything that valuable would have been leaked or republished in a digital format by someone looking to get rich quick. Sounds like a project Madi's great-grandpa might have taken on."

"Only if he wanted to end up in jail," Jack says. "Or even more likely, six feet under. From what I've read, the Cyrists are a litigious and vindictive lot in most timelines. In this one, there's a legend that there's a curse on those who share the prophecies, and that legend came about because weird accidents happened to folks who tried it."

"I can see if the Sisters of Prudence have a copy when Katherine and I go there," Madi says.

"And if we're accepting that Saul's only intervention concerning the Dark Day was through revisions to those books, then I think we have to assume Jemima Wilkinson has a copy," Tyson says. "Or at least that she's seen one."

Clio nods. "We can try to find it when we rescue the baby. I'll need to go to my parents' place first and see if my dad can tell me where to find the mechanic who made the field extender. Because that's obviously the only way we're going to be able to transport them."

"You mean you need to come with me when *I* ask your dad where to find the mechanic," Tyson says. "Because you're an *observer*. We can't give Saul an excuse to put a target on your back. You should probably leave your weapon behind so you're not tempted. I'll have my pistol, and Rich can watch the stable points we set at the farm and jump in if we meet armed resistance."

She narrows her eyes. "Fine. While I don't like going back to Potter's farm unarmed, you're right. I doubt Saul has a stable point at my parents' house, though. And speaking of weapons, there's a very real possibility any member of my family may shoot your ass on sight. They're not happy about my involvement in all of this, even though I've told them it's my choice and mine alone. They love me too much to shoot *me* . . . but they're pissed enough that they may be looking for a scapegoat."

"I'll take my chances," Tyson says with a dry chuckle.

Clio shakes her head slowly. "The man thinks I'm joking."

I'm also fairly sure she's joking, but there's an echo of truth beneath the surface. Can't say I entirely blame her parents for wanting to keep her safe. And that, of course, pulls my mind right back around to the baby in the kitchen and the two who will burn to death if we don't save them, thanks to Saul's utter lack of humanity.

No . . . strike that. We're in 2136. Those infants already *have* burned to death. Sigma died at the end of a noose. Even if we rescue them, they'll have double memories, as Clio almost certainly does.

I shiver, and Richard leans forward to turn the knob on the fire pit another notch to the right. The flames inch upward, and I thank him, even though the shiver was due less to the cold and more to horror and revulsion at the thought of someone willingly scarring the mind, not to mention the body, of a child that way.

"So . . . you and Clio retrieve the device from her parents' house and then jump back to Rhode Island to get the baby," RJ says. "What happens if it's just an earlier . . . or later . . . version of the one he dropped off here? I mean, we still don't know for *sure* that the babies are Prudence clones."

"Saul implied they were," Tyson says. "When I asked him about the third child, he wasn't surprised in the slightest. But . . . yeah, he'd probably lie, so I guess that's no guarantee. I've been thinking, though, and I believe our safest bet is to intercept the baby before we—that is, our earlier selves—get to the farm."

Clio groans. I don't blame her.

"You're right," she says. "If we show up afterward, we'll have to say we lied about the baby not being ours, and say we've changed our mind. It makes more sense to retrieve the basket while the girl is at the well. It certainly won't be the worst double memory I've ever juggled. The important thing is to rescue her, then we can figure out a way to stop the massacre itself. If we can manage to stop those foul little books from ever being published, the incident might unravel on its own."

"That option is definitely worth investigating," Rich says. "This is a case of trickle-down effects, so that would solve pretty much everything . . . and it's why I suspect it won't work. We have a printing date and a location, which means we'd have an excellent idea of where and when to look. Saul would have to have been an idiot to publish the revised version there, and he's crazy, but he's not stupid. It was printed somewhere and probably somewhen else, and then simply distributed in the past. So, I think it's going to be a dead end. While the four of you are in the field tomorrow morning, maybe the rest of us should work on a substitute version of the *Book of Cyrus*. We could even come up with some vague, inane substitutions for the prophecies in the other book. Nostradamus-type predictions that could mean anything or nothing at all. That way, if we can figure out where he distributed them, we can sneak in our copy. Or publish a competing version somewhere else."

"I like that idea," Madi says. "You should definitely put Jack on that task. He's got a real knack for that sort of thing." She nudges Jack and they both grin, so this is apparently some sort of joke between the two of them.

"Or we could make sure it never sees the light of day at all. That there is no Cyrist International." They all give me an odd look, which I get, but I continue. "I *know* it feels like we'd be altering our history. And in a sense, we would. But there's every reason to believe Cyrism was entirely Saul's creation, if not in this timeline, then in some other version. Or more likely, versions . . . since it seems to have been built on a lot of small, incremental changes. Maybe we'd be better off erasing the entire religion."

"Maybe," Tyson says. "I just don't know what that history would look like. None of us do. I think we should try to get back to a timeline we recognize. One that has a CHRONOS that can weigh in on this. Then we can raise this issue with Angelo."

Most of them seem to agree that this is a good plan, and we decide to reconvene in the morning. Madi looks a bit disgruntled, but I imagine that's because she assumed my earlier promise meant she and I would be making the jump to speak with the unnamed Sister of Prudence tonight, not tomorrow morning. She doesn't complain, though . . . possibly because it's nearly midnight and we've all had a very long, very stressful day. Lorena in particular looks exhausted. And sad, almost as if she's on the verge of tears.

"Can I add one thing?" I say as the others start getting up to go inside. "This may be stating the obvious, but it can't hurt to reiterate the main goal here. We have to find Saul and we have to kill him. Everything else is peripheral. Because even if we flip the timeline, failing at that main task means Saul will do this again. The timeline won't be safe and we won't be, either. The game is just a way to keep him placated while we *find him* and *kill him.*"

There's a general murmur of agreement, although several of them are giving me slightly confused looks, probably wondering when this bloodthirsty side of me kicked into gear. I just wish it had kicked in earlier when I was standing inches away from him at the Fair with that laser gadget in my pocket. Although that could mean we'd still be stuck with Team Viper as our overlords, so maybe it's best that I'm a slow learner.

Tyson asks Clio if she has any more of the sleeping pills she gave us in New York. She doesn't, but Madi says the food unit can make a natural sleep tonic. I'm guessing it will taste like dried grass, so I opt for a different sort of natural tonic and refill my wine glass.

The others begin clearing things away. Rich and I volunteer to return the portable chairs to the shed near the center of the yard. We stack them in the corner and when we're done, I try to pull the door shut behind us. It's stubborn. Rich lifts up on the handle and we finally get it to close.

"Kate mentioned a shed in her diary," I say as I brush paint chips off my hands. "Do you think this is the same one?"

"It would be about a hundred and forty years old," he says. "Given the condition of this door, it seems possible."

I take a few steps toward the oak tree and rest my hand against the trunk. The bark is cool and rough beneath my palm. It looks so different from the sprawling live oak I saw through the key that it's hard to believe they're part of the same family.

"It's never going to happen," Rich says. "You're not making that jump."

He says the words with complete conviction, but I know him well enough to be certain he's checked the stable point again, just as I did when I went to my room for this sweater. I didn't watch to the end. I'm not a masochist, and I'll be fighting off nightmares tonight as it is, without giving my brain extra fuel. Perhaps things will change once a specific plan has been made for someone else to make that jump, but Richard's conviction alone has not been enough to change the path. It's definitely still me who's strapped to the tree, holding an infant.

But I turn and give him a soft smile. "I know. Thank you."

He shakes his head and looks down. "You don't have to thank me."

"No. Not for that . . . or rather, not *just* for that. We'd make the same decision about any member of the team." I reach out and take his hand, half expecting him to yank away like he did when I was trying to look at his burned palm at the Fair. But he doesn't. He laces his fingers through mine, and I look up at him, trying to find a way to tell him what I need to say without raising his hopes beyond anything I can promise right now. "What I meant was thank you for being there for me today. *Every* day, but I really needed . . ."

I stop and draw in a shaky breath. "Oh God, Rich. I'm so scared. Not of what we saw through the key, but . . . the baby. *Babies.* And I know that before, it went so horribly wrong. I truly sucked as a mom, and how can anyone stupid enough to have ever trusted Saul Rand possibly . . ."

He pulls me into his arms and the dam breaks. I cry into his shoulder, and he holds me and smoothes my hair. "You're not alone, Katherine. Whatever you need, whatever happens, okay? You're *not* alone. We'll stop Saul and then we'll figure out what comes next." He's clearly worried he's overstepping, because he adds, "I mean, not just me, but the others, too. We'll work it all out."

We're both silent for a moment. He starts to move back, but I pull him close again, speaking quickly before I lose my nerve. "When we were in the library and Saul mentioned my parents, I looked away, trying to hold it together. But I could still feel him watching me. I could feel you watching me, too—"

"Oh, God. I'm sorry. I wasn't trying to make you uncomfortable."

"Don't apologize. What I was trying to say is . . . I realized in that moment how very different it felt. Saul was watching me to gauge my reaction to his words. Words he knew would cut me. His eyes were glued to me, trying to see how much power he still had to wound. To measure his control over me." I stop and look up at Rich. "And then, at the other end of the spectrum, there was you. Watching to see if I needed backup. Trying to figure out what you could say or do to help. All I could do was wonder at how unbelievably stupid I've been."

I pull his lips down to mine. If I'd taken time to think about it, I'd have found a million reasons to wait. A million reasons not to take what I know is a huge risk.

Those same thoughts are going through Rich's mind. I can tell from the way he hesitates at first. He's calculating all of the ways this could go so very wrong. Weighing whether it's worth gambling a friendship that has spanned half our lives.

I've shared three first kisses. One was on a dare, when I was four-teen, so it hardly counts. The second was with Saul, and I was terrified because he was experienced, and I was the exact opposite. All I could think was that I'd do something stupid, something that would cause him to write me off as a silly kid. I don't think I ever really stopped worrying about that. And wondering where his mind was when we made love, because I always knew some part of him was missing.

This is different.

Once Rich weighs the risks and makes his decision, his arms tighten around me, and he is *there*, fully present, one hundred percent in the moment.

And because he is all in, I find that I am, too.

FROM THE *BOOK OF PROPHECY*

There are always those who give freely unto Cyrus but lack the resources to make a full investment and join the ranks of the Chosen. The loyalty of all people is important in a vibrant community, and those who cannot fully invest should also know they can expect some reward from the *Book of Prophecy* for their faithful adherence to the Way.

Once each quarter, every local Templar will hold a lottery in which members may purchase tickets at a reasonable rate established by the Templar. A random number will be taken from the *Book of Prophecy*. One half of the proceeds from this lottery will be distributed to the winner, along with the bronze-level prophecy for that quarter.

∞ 7 ∞

TYSON
SKANEATELES, NEW YORK
OCTOBER 6, 1941

I pace along the edge of the lake, waiting for Clio. This is not the stable point she generally uses for family visits, but she didn't think it was a good idea to just pop into the living room with an unexpected visitor in tow. That made sense to me, but she also dismissed three other stable points closer to her house, in favor of this one, near the dock. There's a bank of trees and a wide expanse of lawn between the lake and the house. I can see their porch from here, but just barely.

Maybe she wasn't joking about the guns?

I can also see the small family graveyard, at the top of the hill on the left side of the house. The autumn sun glints off two headstones, one erected in memory of a sister who died as an infant and the other in memory of the woman Clio called Aunt June, although I think the family connection was a bit more complicated than that. In the screwed-up timeline Team Viper and Saul gave us, a third gravestone would have been there on this day, with no inscription and Clio buried beneath it.

It's not hard to understand why her parents want nothing to do with us. Each day, they have a nagging double memory of a reality in which Clio died. She doesn't talk much about that, but she did say her parents considered selling this house, because her mom had a tough time shaking the memory of sitting in the middle of the living room, holding Clio as she bled out from injuries incurred in the bombing. But her mom also has a picture, given to her by Madi, of a much happier timeline where she and Kiernan Dunne grew old in this house, where their grandkids and even great-grandkids swam in this lake. And so, rather than move, Kate decided to repaint the walls the color they were in that Polaroid, as a way of ushering out the old half-memories and welcoming in the new.

We're almost certain this is way before the event that finally tipped the timeline, so they wouldn't have felt any physical effects. They don't have a computer to spit out anomalies, and after the last event, Clio said they'd decided keeping abreast of anything other than local news was probably a bad idea. But her family aren't hermits. I can't see how they could have avoided encountering something that's not quite the way they remember it.

Clio preferred to stay optimistic. She chose a day she knew they would be here. And she cautioned me that I might be hanging out by the lake for a bit while she found a gentle way to break the news.

So, I park myself on the bench at the end of the dock and begin scanning through to make a final decision on which stable point to use for our jump to Potter's farm, still hoping there's enough of a window for me to simply jump in, grab the basket from the bushes where the servant found it, and jump out. Unfortunately, the servant girl is either too nervous or too curious for her own damn good, because she glances back over her shoulder every few seconds on the way to the well and keeps her eyes trained on the spot while she's walking back. I'm tempted to do it anyway, even though she'll almost certainly spot me. It can't have much impact on the timeline. I mean, what's she going to do? Tell Wilkinson or one of the others that she found a baby in the bushes and someone stole it? Unless she was instructed by someone in the household to move the baby, I think there's an excellent chance she'll never say a word to anyone.

Unfortunately, I'm not sure how easy the device will be to use. It could take significantly longer than the usual two or three seconds to pull up a stable point, lock it in, and blink out. What if it doesn't work the first time?

It complicates things, but at least I can spare Clio the worst of it if I can figure out a way to get a message to myself, preferably as late as possible into our previous trip. I run back through the two hours at the tavern and our walk to Potter's farm. We'd set a stable point in the room we rented, so I pull that up and watch as we brush some of the dust off our clothes and splash a bit of water from the basin onto our faces. Any note I leave for myself there would also be seen by Clio.

Then I remember the lens solution I fished out of my leather bag after setting the stable point in the trees just down from Potter's farm. It's been inside the bag for weeks without me ever looking at it. So I jump back to my room at Madi's house earlier this morning, when I was downstairs getting breakfast, and quickly attach a note to the bottle telling myself to abort the trip because there's a basket with a CHRONOS key that may contain a baby, which is pretty much all we knew when we left Rhode Island. I'm about to leave when I remember the multicolored lotus tattoo on Wilkinson's hand, so I add a quick postscript before blinking back to the dock.

A few minutes later, I spot the pale green of Clio's dress coming down the path through the trees. She wanted to avoid letting her clothes announce the fact that she was going to use the key for something more than a cheap and efficient method of travel from Chicago, so the plain clothing she'll change into for our jump to 1780, assuming all goes well, is in my backpack, along with my jacket. The cut of my pants and shirt might be a bit anachronistic for the early 1940s, but not enough to bother with packing a change of clothes.

I can tell from Clio's stride that things didn't go entirely as planned. She's pissed. "You were right. They started noticing changes about a month ago. The blue laws tipped them off."

"Why do you think it kicked in a month ago? And what are blue laws?"

"I don't know why. You'd have to ask Alex. But I know that's about how far back it was because it's baseball season and Dad would have noticed as soon as the first Sunday rolled around. Blue laws are Sabbath restrictions. They're a relic of Puritan days. I have no clue why they're called blue laws. But they ban alcohol sales, for example, in many places. And now, there are no Sunday Yankees games, either, even though in our timeline they got rid of that restriction nearly twenty years ago. I planned the jump for today specifically because it's the final game of the World Series, and Dad would normally be in a good mood. He's *always* in a good mood on days he knows the Yankees are going to win. Not that he'll ever admit he knows, because he doesn't want to spoil the game for Connor and Harry. But we can tell. The only time our predictions on that count were a bit off was during the Yankees' four-year streak because he knew the team was going to win the whole shebang, so he was *always* in a good mood, even on the days they played and lost. Anyway, after my parents realized there were no Sunday games, they started poking around for other differences. I'm guessing if baseball hadn't tipped them off, something else would have eventually. I didn't realize the thing with the Fox sisters was only about an hour away. There's some new local lore about witches, and they searched and found some of the other changes from the 1920s, too."

She nods her head toward the house. "Come on . . . they're expecting you. And no, I didn't ask them specifically about the device, but I may have mentioned that we're going to need a favor and noted that Saul has put *babies* at risk. They're both suckers for babies."

"That's something you seem to have inherited," I say as we begin the hike up the hill. "Did you get any sleep last night? I heard her crying."

"Yeah. Everyone heard her apparently. Katherine came in and offered to take a shift, but she seemed really nervous about it. I get the sense she's never dealt with a baby. Don't folks babysit in your era?"

"Not folks who are training as historians. Those who have child-care as their chosen gift start when they're around ten. Maybe one of the CHRONOS historians in your gene pool had an ancestor who passed it down to you."

She laughs. "It's something I inherited, but I don't think it's a chosen gift. Phoebe—and yes, I've given her a name—stopped crying after I let her sleep next to me . . . or more precisely, next to my hair. It seems to calm her down. Especially if she can wind her fingers through it. Fortunately, she's too small to tug very hard."

It takes a second for me to make the connection. "Oh. Because you have curls like the Prudence clones."

"Yeah. Mine aren't quite as long, but close. So maybe it wasn't the fact that I took her out of the stupid delivery box, but more that I look a bit like someone she thinks of as her mama. Their eyes don't focus very well at that age. And maybe they *are* the moms. Do we actually *know* who carries the next generation of Pru babies? If they're following the whole Madonna Pru thing they did when they were dragging my pregnant mom around, then they'd get extra bang for their buck if one or more of the Sisters was chosen to carry the next batch. Which is . . ."

She doesn't *say* it's weird. Neither do I. But yeah, it kinda is.

We're almost to the porch, so I ask what sort of reception I'm about to receive from her family.

"A civil one," she says. "In retrospect, them knowing something has already changed was a good thing. And not only because my dad wants Sunday baseball back. Mom isn't too keen on the whole witch-burning issue, and . . . I think she kind of sympathizes with the Sisters. I mean, she was forced to live that life for several months."

"From what Thea said, though, I didn't get the sense that anyone forces them."

Clio gives me a sly smile. "I think that should stay on a need-to-know basis, though, don't you? Anyway, they have a brand-new incentive to make sure all of this ends. Connor met a girl, as nineteen-year-old boys often do. Apparently, it's serious, or at least he thinks it is. She's not the girl he married in the other timeline, so he could just be playing the drama queen. It wouldn't be the first time."

I'm about to ask why her brother having a girlfriend is a problem. Neither of her brothers can use the key, so my brain tends to categorize them as normal people with lives a bit less complicated by time travel. But we're now in a timeline where CHRONOS doesn't exist, at least not in the form we knew it. Neither Kate nor Kiernan exist in this timeline, so the odds seem high that their offspring don't exist, either. The field-extender bracelets Alex gave Clio only *extend* the CHRONOS field, which means the wearer needs to be in range of a medallion or a diary, both of which are in fairly limited supply. The current situation would put a serious kink in the possibility of Clio's brothers living any sort of a normal life.

"Why did . . ." I stop, realizing the question I'm about to ask is kind of rude. But then I ask it anyway because it bugs me. "You said you'll never have kids because you don't want to pass along the gene. I know your mom was already pregnant with you, but why risk having more children?"

She shrugs. "They waited five years. CHRONOS existed in the timeline my brothers were born in. Mom and Dad knew Saul was dead. Not just dead but erased. How could they know the whole cycle would start over and come back to bite them on the ass? Unlike yours truly, Connor and Harry had *normal* lives until last year, and we had every expectation they would stay that way. Now everything is screwed up not just for me, but for them, too. To be fair, I can't really blame them for being angry. They have all of the downsides of the connection to CHRONOS without even getting to time travel."

We step into a spacious kitchen that smells faintly of cinnamon and sugar. The walls are painted a pale yellow and decorated every few feet by a purple light about the size of a dime, although I'm sure they'd look like bronze studs to anyone without the gene. It's a very modern kitchen for the era. I've been in kitchens from three decades later that were less well equipped.

Clio catches my expression and laughs. "We had one of the first prototypes of an automatic dishwasher. Mom is chomping at the bit to get a microwave, but those aren't available until after the war and she probably won't make it to microwave popcorn, which is something like 1980. Dad says he's pretty sure something called Orville Redenbacher's is the only reason she wants a microwave in the first place. No matter how much you guys trash Madi's food unit, Mom would think it was amazing." She lowers her voice. "And excuse my brothers. Connor is in a foul mood because he wants to be with this Brenda person, and Harry's almost certainly going to laugh at your braid."

She pushes open the door between the kitchen and the living room, and four sets of eyes land on me. Kiernan and Kate Dunne are on one side of the room. I've met Kiernan, but not Kate, who opted not to come into New York City with her husband during the events in 1940. Two young men who look quite a bit like Clio are seated across the room at a dining table, playing backgammon. The younger of the two, who looks to be around seventeen, doesn't exactly laugh at my outfit, but he most definitely smirks.

Kiernan gives Clio a grudging look and then gets to his feet, hand extended.

"I'm not gonna lie and say it's a pleasure to see you again, because your arrival never seems to herald good news. But I guess that's not entirely fair. You're just the messenger. Saul's the reason the bloody blue laws didn't go away on schedule. That's the one thing that tells me more than anything else that Cliona's right about Simon finally being gone. He'd have killed Saul all over again for screwing with baseball."

I shake his hand and look over at Kate, who is on one end of the sofa with a book.

"Tyson," Clio says, "this is my mother, Kate Dunne. The sulky one is Connor and the other goofus is Harry. This is Tyson Reyes. Who is *not* to blame for the timeline shift and is, like me, trying to fix it. Hopefully, once and for all."

"It's a pleasure to meet you, Mrs. Dunne. I'm sorry for barging in on you like this, and . . . well, for your daughter being in the middle of it."

She sighs, putting the book aside. "Please call me Kate. And I know from experience that my daughter has a mind of her own, so I doubt you're responsible for her being involved. Clio and I have had several chats on this point during her past few visits," she says with a grim smile. "It appears she hasn't been entirely honest about her use of the CHRONOS key over the past few years."

The look she gives Kiernan suggests her daughter isn't the only one in the doghouse. He drops back into his chair with a heavy sigh.

"But," Kate continues, "I don't think she had much choice in the matter. None of us really has free will at the moment. All of our choices are constrained by the reality of that damned key your friends created. Or dug up, I guess . . . although if some version of them hadn't created it in the first place, it wouldn't have been there to unearth. And I know they couldn't have foreseen the exact consequences of their research, but dear God, any fool could have recognized that they were opening Pandora's box. On the other hand, as Clio noted in our last conversation, no one in our family would exist if Saul Rand wasn't a homicidal maniac whose actions stranded his colleagues in the past, so . . . I guess we'll have to carve out the best life we can in whatever reality we find ourselves. That would be a lot easier, though, if we could stop skipping timelines. And that will never happen as long as there's any form of Saul Rand running around."

"Or CHRONOS," Connor mutters.

"You'll get no argument from me or your mum on that point," Kiernan says. "But keep in mind what we've told you about your limitations in that kind of reality. You can kiss the possibility of leavin' Skaneateles goodbye, at least until your mum and I are gone and we can spare a key."

"What do you need from us?" Kate asks. "Clio hedged when I asked her a few minutes ago. Said the request had to come from you, so I'm guessing she has to color between the lines in order to adhere to the rules of one of Saul's stupid games."

"Yes, ma'am. She's technically an observer, not a participant."

"He thinks Saul set a stable point here," Clio says.

All four of the others glance around the room nervously, and I say, "It's not that I think he *did*. More out of an abundance of caution. Clio's safer if she acts only as an observer."

Clio sniffs dismissively. "I was an observer last time, too."

It's a fair point, although it's one I can tell she wishes she'd kept to herself when she sees the pained look on her mother's face.

"Listen," I tell them, "we're on the clock, so I'll cut to the chase. Clio said she told you Saul seems to have transported a couple of infants who have the CHRONOS gene. Who are, in fact, clones of your aunt. Both babies die if we don't get them out, and Clio says you used to have a device that might allow us to rescue them."

"Clones?" Harry says. "What the hell are clones?"

"Genetic copies," I say. "Like identical twins, but . . ."

"It's future science," Kate tells him. "If you really want to know, I can explain the basics later."

Kiernan glances up at the field-extender dots on the wall. "It's sort of in pieces now. But you could go back to when it wasn't, I guess. How long would you need it?"

"For us? A couple of days," I tell him. "From your perspective, though? We could have it back in about thirty seconds."

Kate and Kiernan spend several minutes debating whether and how they'd be able to protect the family without the extender if something happened and we couldn't return it. The consensus seems to be that it would be more difficult, but not impossible. Then they shift to trying to figure out a time before the thing was disassembled that they were all out of the house.

"My birthday," Kate says. "Remember, Kier? The three of us drove into Seneca Falls for ice cream. And then we walked down by the river for a bit, although it would be more accurate to say I waddled like a duck given how pregnant I was."

"More like a penguin than a duck, if I recall correctly," he says with a little grin. "But that sounds like as good a time as any. Come on upstairs and I'll show you where we kept it."

"Clio?" Kate says as we turn to follow him. "No unnecessary risks, okay? And I don't mean risking the device. I'm pretty sure that Swedish guy could make another one of those, but . . ."

She goes over to the couch and gives her mom a hug. "No unnecessary risks. I promise. You won't even have time to know I'm gone."

A cloud passes over Kate's face as she wraps her arms around Clio. It could be normal maternal worry. I've seen a similar look on my own mom's face. That thought gives me a pang of homesickness. I didn't see them often, but if I was back in my time, it would be coming up on the holidays and I'd travel up to Boston for the annual reunion with the rest of my mom's family. We'd eat too much and I'd again realize how little I have in common with any of them these days, even the cousins my own age. Maybe especially the ones my own age. It's hard to keep up with current trends when your head—and often the rest of you—spends most of your time in the past.

Kiernan reverses course halfway up the stairs and pushes past us in the opposite direction, saying he needs to go out to the shed and get a wrench.

We wait in the hallway, which has several framed sketches and one painting of a sunset over a lake. Or maybe it's a sunrise. I'm not sure which side of the water we're on.

"Are these yours?" I ask. When Clio nods, I add, "They're really good. That's the lake outside, right?"

"Mm-hm," she says, looking down. I think it may be the first time I've seen her looking shy. "Hold on and I'll show you."

She opens the second door down to reveal a room with more sketches and paintings, some framed and some not. There's a bed, but I get the sense that the room is used more as a study these days, because a typewriter sits in one corner. Clio pulls back the curtain. Through the window, I see the same scene. Only it's autumn now and the middle of the day, and the leaves are orange, rather than the deep, shadowy green in the painting.

"That's one I created while I was in art school in Chicago," she says. "I wanted to get the water on the lake just right, so . . . Hold out your key."

When I do, she transfers a location. It's the exact view, although when I glance back at the painting, I see that she played up the light on the water so it almost looks like it's moving.

"It's beautiful, but I like your version better."

She smiles and shoos me out so she can change for our jump. By the time she's finished, Kiernan is back with the wrench.

"Why do you need a wrench to show us where you kept the thing?" Clio asks.

"Not for me," he says. "It was bolted inside the closet. Your mum didn't like to look at the bloody thing. It reminded her too much of what she went through. That's one reason I let Herman Scott use it to make the extenders for the rest of the house. He could have built another one, but . . . it was better this way. The coast should be clear from around noon, but if you set a stable point at the back window there, you can watch to be sure the car is gone. I could try describing it, but it might be easier if you just grab it and come back here so I can show you. Leave the wrench there. You'll need it when you put the thing back."

We set a stable point at the window as instructed and scroll through. At a little after 2 p.m. on May 8, 1912, Kate, Kiernan, and a woman who must be June walk out to the barn.

"Oh my God," Clio says. "You're right. She's walking like a penguin."

As soon as the car pulls away, we blink in. The device is in the closet, but it takes a moment to find because a bathrobe is draped over it.

"Well, I see how it got its name," Clio says.

It does look a bit like a two-handled mirror. The markings around the edges are similar to the ones on the CHRONOS key, but more ornate. I loosen the bolts and remove it from the metal brace that holds it to the wall. When I step back into the bedroom, Clio is standing by a wicker crib. She holds up a tiny white gown with yellow embroidery around the sleeves and smiles. "I remember Connor wearing this right after he was born. So cool."

We blink back to 1941 where Kiernan is waiting. "Ugh. I only used the thing once, more than thirty years ago, and it still makes me feel like I'm going to puke my guts up just looking at it." He takes it and taps the empty circle at the top. "Plug in your key and pull up the stable point. To be honest, I don't know how you'll manage it with a baby. And exactly what's the point in this game of Saul's? Is the sick bastard torchin' babies for the pure hell of it?"

"I think it's partly to get back at Katherine," Clio says. "These are clones of their daughter, after all. But it's probably also revenge against Prudence herself."

We fill him in briefly on what Thea said when she killed Saul's splinter.

He laughs softly. "Leave it to Pru to pass a vendetta down through the ages."

"So . . . you knew her pretty well?" Clio asks.

Kiernan colors slightly. "I . . . did. We were on the Cyrist Farm at the same time. I can tell you she hated Saul with the fire of a thousand suns, especially after the son of a bitch killed her dog. Years later all it took was that memory to reduce her to tears."

Clio and I exchange a look, and she says, "Was this dog by any chance named Gizmo?"

∞

LITTLE REST, RHODE ISLAND
MAY 18, 1780

Clio sniffs the air as we step out onto the road. "Now I'm wishing we'd risked jumping in near the farmhouse. How can the air be muggy and dusty at the same time?"

"Yeah. Feels like I'm breathing mud. If there were more than a few seconds where the girl isn't looking, I'd have chanced it. But we don't even know for certain that extender gadget is going to work on an infant, so I'd rather not have an audience while we're trying to figure it out."

"What are we going to do if it *doesn't* work?"

I sigh. "Not a clue. But in that case, she'll be safer back in our room at the inn than she'll be in Judge Potter's house when that mob arrives tomorrow. Let's take it one step at a time."

"Hopefully, we can get back to the stable point before we cross paths with our earlier selves. My dad says it causes a weird feedback loop. You had to do that in training, right?"

"Yeah. Not fun. I take it you've managed to avoid crossing your own path?"

She nods. "I've had double memories, obviously, but I promised my dad I'd avoid incurring them on purpose. And I think maybe I understand why he was nervous about that now, if he was friends with Prudence when they were young. My mom said she was a complete nutcase by the time she was thirty because she'd overwritten so many memories. By the end, she'd actually drop in to have conversations with her earlier selves. So I'd avoid it even if I hadn't promised."

Given the way Kiernan's face flushed when Clio asked, I'm almost certain he and Prudence were more than friends. If I had to guess, I'd say she falls into the category where I'd place Alisa Campbell—not friends, really, just exceptionally well acquainted on a physical basis. But if Clio missed that little cue from her dad, I'm certainly not going to be the one who points it out.

"It shouldn't be a problem," I tell her, explaining about the note I left for myself. "Our memories are going to be a little squishy, though. Hopefully, it won't affect anyone else, since I gave us the basic details from the visit to take back to 2136."

"But what about the stable points I set? We need those . . ."

"They're still on your key. At least, they should be. The key has its own chronometer, so whatever was set in its past should still be on it." Now she has me wondering, though, so I take out the medallion to check. "Still there."

She laughs. "You were worried, too. Admit it."

"Yeah. This was *not* part of our training. We went from the jump room to a specific location and straight back. Occasionally, we might do some part of our research out of order, and some people visited the same event twice, so they had to be careful not to bump into themselves. But if you ever had a situation where an actual retraction was required—where they needed to undo something you did—they sent someone else to tell you."

We turn into the long drive at around five minutes after two. The servant girl is on her knees at the edge of the bushes surrounding the house. She hunts briefly, pulls out the basket, and hurries to place it on the porch as I saw her do while watching through the key. It's not until she turns around that she catches sight of us. She freezes for a moment, glances back at the basket, and then runs to scoop up the water buckets on her way to the well. As before, she looks back over her shoulder several times.

I pick up the pace. The plan is to walk together as far as the barn, then Clio will hang back while I run and grab the basket from the porch. She'd probably have argued the point if not for the fact that she's in a dress she'd have to hike up to her knees in order to keep pace.

If no one raises an alarm, we'll simply get the hell out of here, and as soon as we're back to the tree line, we'll blink out. Clio hanging back also puts her near the stable point where Rich will come in if we run into armed resistance. The most likely hitch in our easy-exit option is the dogs we saw last time. That's why I'm holding the CHRONOS key in my palm to keep it activated. They may bark or howl, but their aversion to the frequency it emits should keep them from getting close enough to bite.

Even if we are spotted, me grabbing the basket and taking off with it makes our story more credible—assuming there's a baby inside. Clio will say she knew I was hoping to join the Friend's church. The baby was evidence of our failure to remain celibate, and I'd told Clio I wanted her to be raised by my brother in Connecticut. Clio didn't want to be that far away from her daughter, and her hope was that if the P.U.F. took the baby in as an orphan, and we joined the congregation, she'd at least be able to see her on occasion. But then I learned

Clio was traveling here and followed, feeling remorse that I'd driven her to such extremes. We'll take our child and go, thank thee kindly, God be with thee, may His blessings be upon thee, buh-bye.

It's a stupid cover story, but not that much stupider than the one we were using earlier, and that one apparently worked well enough to get Saul and Katherine in the door at some point. Any religion that pushes celibacy is, in my personal opinion, not likely to attract the best and brightest minds, so maybe they'll be taken in by it long enough for us to get out of here.

When we're a few paces from the barn, Clio stops as we'd previously agreed and I continue toward the house. As I'm nearing the porch, the puppy the children were playing with on our last visit comes barreling around the house, barking loudly at a small cluster of chickens on the front lawn. The dog screeches to an almost comical stop a few yards away from me, tilting its head to the side.

"Good boy." I reach for the basket. Tiny shards of purple light shine through the weave, and any doubt about whether there's a baby inside is resolved by her feeble cry when I yank the basket toward me.

"Who art thou?" The words are oddly formal coming from the mouth of a boy of no more than six, especially since I'd last heard him laughing and yelling for the pup next to him to bring back a stick.

I nod to him and say, "Thomas Early, young friend. My wife left this basket here."

He frowns and looks in the direction of the well, which is obscured by the barn from this angle. Really wish I'd noticed that in my planning.

"Betsy is not thy wife," the boy says. "And I saw her place the basket on the porch just now."

"Apologies. I meant my wife left it in the bushes." I nod toward Clio, watching anxiously from her spot near the barn. "Betsy must be the person who moved the basket."

The boy cranes his neck upward, trying to see inside the basket, but I'm holding it a bit too high. "But there's a babe inside. Why would she leave a child in the bushes?"

"Dost thou know the Bible?"

He nods, still eyeing me suspiciously. "Mostly we study the *Book of Cyrus*, but the Bible is another testament of God."

"Moses, who parted the Red Sea and freed the slaves from Egypt . . . He was set asail in a basket made of reeds much like this one because his mother feared for his life. My wife was frightened and alone. Knowing of the Friend's kindness, she thought this was a safe place to leave our daughter, but I've arrived now and can care for them both."

His face relaxes slightly and I lower the basket so he can see over the edge.

Betsy rounds the corner of the barn. She stares at Clio and then back at me.

"Please tell the Friend we will be here for the next sermon and—"

"Don't harm the boy!" Betsy yells, dropping the buckets. "Run, John!"

The boy is up the stairs in a flash. I take her words as my exit cue, as well, and motion for Clio to head toward the road.

"Hold up!" someone cries from behind me when I'm halfway to the barn. It sounds like Jemima Wilkinson. I'm not inclined to slow down enough to check, but Clio looks back over her shoulder and stops instantly. One glance at her face and I stop, too.

We have an audience now. Jemima Wilkinson is on the porch steps, in the exact same clothes from before . . . which shouldn't be surprising. Even though it feels like yesterday to me, that's still about ten minutes into the future. Directly behind Wilkinson is the boy named John and the young man who was seated on the porch before, except he's now holding a long rifle instead of a book.

The long rifle isn't a weapon I've ever used personally, but I did learn a couple of things about it and other Revolutionary War weapons in my firearms training. The first is that it's fairly accurate compared to other weapons from the era. Still nothing compared to the rifles I shot on occasion with Glen in the 1960s, but far more likely to hit the intended target than pistols from this time. The second thing I learned is that it takes a while to load them. That means anyone pointing a weapon in your direction probably isn't planning on firing a warning shot. Or even aiming to wing you.

My pistol is in the inner pocket of my coat, but the basket is in my right hand. The odds of me being able to put down the basket, draw the pistol, and fire before the young guy with the rifle gets a shot off seem very slim, so I decide to try talking my way out.

Clio remains by the barn, with her hands clasped in front of her and her head down. I can see the light of her CHRONOS key. What I don't see is Rich, who should have already blinked into the spot closest to the barn.

"My name is Thomas Early," I say. "My wife believed I had abandoned her and the babe, but I was delayed while away seeking work. She had heard from me of the Friend's great charity and hoped thou might house the child. But I found her on her way back to town, and we came together to retrieve our daughter. We do not wish to trouble thee further, Friend."

Betsy has now reached the porch. She gives me a baleful look and grabs the Friend's arm. "I heard a cry from the bushes. When I spied the basket there, I was going to bring the babe to thee straight off, but Penelope said Susannah's fever was dangerous high and I should come quick with the water. So I left the basket on the porch and took up my buckets again. As I was going to the well, I saw these two coming up the lane and thought how much she looks like Prudence. Then while I'm drawing the water, I remembered thy last prophecy.

That basket is woven, so now I think mebbe 'tain't a babe at all, but a witch's familiar in clever disguise."

Wilkinson nods slowly. *"Fear not the fair-haired woman on the eve of the Darkest Day, but beware dark Prudence, who stealeth away with the beast in the woven cage.* Tell thy woman to come closer."

"Friend, my good wife is shy, and truly ashamed that she doubted I would return for her and the child. Please—"

But the Friend is having none of it. "Woman! Come closer that I may see thy face. If thou art innocent, no harm will come to thee."

Clio does as she's told. Her hands remain clasped in front, but the key is tucked back in her bodice. I wish she'd have kept it out so that she could blink away in case the guy with the gun decides to fire. Maybe she's worried Wilkinson will recognize the medallion like when we were here before?

And where the hell is Rich?

Wilkinson's eyes narrow as Clio moves closer. The young man anchors the butt of the rifle against his shoulder and puts his finger to the trigger.

"She is indeed the very spit of the painting of Prudence in thy *Book,*" he says.

"Yes. She is. But hold thy fire, Arnold. That is not The Way. There are tests that must be done and rules on how to proceed." The Friend turns to me and says, "Put down the basket and step aside. John, find Caesar so he and Arnold can hold these two in the cellar while we take the creature in the basket for testing."

The last word sends a chill through me. I'm not an expert on witch trials, but I know enough to be worried about the nature of any witch test. And that goes double coming from someone who would call a child a *creature*. "Wouldst thou kill an infant, Friend? I understood thy message to be one of peace and charity."

The Friend looks pained. "We will not kill a child of God. If this is truly a child, it will survive."

We will not kill . . . It will survive. There's a whole lot of room for doing massive harm to this baby between those two statements. And I'm not about to let that happen.

I nod and crouch down to set the basket on the grass, turning slightly to the side so that my hand moving toward the pistol will be more visible to Rich, assuming he's watching, and less visible to the guy with the long rifle. As my hand closes around the stock of the gun, however, I hear several loud thumps. When I look up at the porch, the Friend and the young gunman have passed out. Betsy is draped over the steps and the boy lies on the grass a few feet away, next to the pup and the chickens.

"Whoa," Clio says, staring down at the Timex gadget Richard usually wears. "It really works. How long do we have?"

"Not long." I scoop up the basket and we take off. The baby begins screaming instantly. Clio grabs her and I toss the basket just as it occurs to me that the CHRONOS field we were seeing might have been inside, rather than attached to the baby. Not that she'd blink out with Clio holding her, but I'm still relieved to see a faint purple glow beneath the thin blanket.

We turn onto the road a few seconds later and immediately see our earlier selves about a hundred yards down, at the tree line. Or rather, we see Earlier-Clio. I'm apparently already in the brush setting the stable point. The current version of Clio stumbles and I reach out to steady her.

"Don't look if you can avoid it," I tell her, just as a hand—*my* hand—reaches out to yank Earlier-Clio into the trees. "Are you okay?"

She nods and we continue at a brisk walk. The two men on horseback I remember seeing as we stepped out of the woods on our earlier trip are approaching off in the distance on the right.

"How long is *not long*?" Clio asks, looking back over our shoulders toward the farm.

"Angelo said it lasts about five minutes, tops. I'm more concerned that the range isn't very broad and there are at least a few others in the house. Why are you carrying Richard's watch?"

"When they looked in to see if I needed help with the baby last night, he said I should bring this, so I'd have some kind of protection in case we got separated. He's at the house today working on the replacement *Book of Cyrus*, and Katherine said they wouldn't be likely to need it. Even if there's some sort of trouble in their meeting, the Pru clone is under a CHRONOS field, so it wouldn't work on her. It's not lethal."

"I think there's a damn good chance Saul will still consider it beyond the role of an observer. But maybe that's why Rich didn't jump in as backup. I was about a second away from shooting Benedict Arnold Potter."

"Is that actually his name?"

"For now . . . or at least it was in the historical info in our archives. In a few months when his namesake defects to the British, he'll decide to drop the Benedict part. Assuming we can prevent him from being killed by a crazed mob tomorrow, that is."

We're close to the tree line, and the woods seem to be empty of our earlier selves. I push away the vague memory that's now coming through—reaching into the pocket of my leather bag, finding the lens solution wrapped inside the note, and then grabbing Clio's arm so we could jump back to the library. In my experience, the more you dwell on a double memory, the more it gnaws at you.

We duck into the woods, but a quick look down the road tells me we're about thirty seconds too late. Wilkinson is headed toward us with Arnold and Caesar.

I reach into my bag and pull out the device. Clio snaps her key into the circle at the top. Kiernan explained how it works for two adults. One grabs one handle, one grabs the other. They both see the same interface and one or both blink on the location. It's a smoother ride if both blink. But I have no idea how to make that work with an infant. She won't understand if we tell her to grab it, and even if she could, the handle is too large for her to wrap her fingers around. Clio will need one hand to pull up the stable point and one to hold her side of the device.

I pry open the baby's fist, hold her palm against the handle, and give Clio a nod, even though I'm wondering if there's a chance my hand will make the trip without me. It doesn't, but then, neither do they. Then we try all three of us blinking out at the same time. Still no luck. Clio starts unbuttoning the bodice of her dress. Not sure what she's up to, but I move a few steps closer to the road and draw my pistol. I don't want to shoot anyone, but as it stands right now, they're all going to die tomorrow night anyway.

"Trying again," Clio whispers as I hear footsteps approaching.

When I look back, Clio and the baby are gone.

I shove the gun into my coat, place the CHRONOS key in my hand, and select the stable point in the library. But I now see five sets of eyes staring at me from the other side of the holographic display. The Friend is there, along with Arnold and Caesar. Just behind them are the two men who passed by on their horses. All five mouths are hanging open like a choir of catfish, so I have absolutely no doubt they saw Clio vanish.

Arnold shakes it off quicker than Wilkinson and Caesar. He shoulders the long rifle and says, "Come out, son of the devil."

I hear the crack of the rifle as I blink.

FROM THE *BOOK OF PROPHECY*

Chicago Head Templar Week of July 11, 1954

Award to top three benefactors for Quarter Two:

- Gold Level: Buy and Hold Kraft
- Silver Level: Buy and Hold Boeing until 7/1997
- Bronze Level: Lassie Stakes at Arlington Park (7/14/54)— Delta, Lea Lane, Alspal

∞ 8 ∞

Madi
Bethesda, Maryland
November 28, 2136

I rinse the last of the shampoo out of my hair. Then I step back, lower the temperature, and hold my face under the frigid spray. It won't entirely compensate for a lousy night's sleep, but combined with a second cup of coffee, it should wake me up enough to get through the day.

My dreams were a bloody mess . . . literally. When I saw Clio in the kitchen earlier, she looked dragged out, too. That's not a surprise to anyone, given that we all heard the baby several times during the night. Around 2 a.m., Jack told Jarvis to pipe white noise throughout the house, noting that it wasn't going to help the situation if all of us were walking around like zombies today. The only two in the house who looked like they slept well were Katherine and Rich, but their rooms are at the far end of the hall, so maybe they were out of range from the beginning.

When I cut the water off, I hear Jack talking to someone. It's on his comm-band, so I can't hear the other voice. I'm guessing it's his dad, but usually Jack sounds a lot more defensive when he's talking to his father, partly because he's having to explain his reported lack of progress in the ongoing effort to form our merry little band of time travelers a few decades early. His dad texted him twice during our meeting on the patio last night. Jack ghosted him both times, putting off the moment when he'd have to once again navigate the inevitable conversational land mines in order to find out how much, if anything, his dad knows in the current timeline.

A few weeks back, Jack showed me a picture of his family taken last Christmas. General Merrick looks almost exactly like I'd have pictured him based on Jack's description. Gray hair, cut super short. In his late forties, not as old as I'd have imagined, but his face is chiseled and lined. Basically an older version of Jack's face, but I hope that when he is his father's age, Jack will have some laugh lines. John Merrick looks like someone deleted his smile setting. Maybe that's a side effect of working at a place that focuses on predicting potential global threats.

Since I didn't think to grab a robe or my clothes before getting into the shower, I stay in the bathroom. It's probably not a video call, but I'd really hate to be clad only in a towel for my first meeting with Jack's father, especially when he's not supposed to know we're anywhere near the cohabitation stage. I dry my hair and use my temporary dye to add in the blue streak Jack likes, since it will be perfectly fine for my trip to 2058.

Jack taps softly on the door and then opens it a crack, giving me an apologetic look. "Yeah," he says, still talking to his dad. "But I visited in September, when there are usually fewer crowds."

So . . . it's not a video call. And apparently not about Jack's mission. I follow him back into the bedroom. He leans against the wall while I look for a top to wear. Nothing I have is really in style for six decades back, but we're not going outside the office at the Sixteenth Street Temple, so it probably doesn't matter. I grab a navy silk blouse Nora bought for me a few birthdays back and begin buttoning it up.

"I stayed in a youth hostel, though. Believe me, you and Karis will be much happier in one of the hotels along the shore. They're fairly reasonable even in the prime season." Jack gives me a grin and runs one finger along my bare thigh. "You should do Montserrat, obviously. Sagrada Família. I'll see if I can find my itinerary and send it to you."

He begins unbuttoning my blouse from the top as he speaks, and I fight back a laugh.

"Listen, Dad, I need to go. Tell Karis I'll let her know shortly about my holiday plans."

There's a long pause. I'm not sure what his father said, but Jack's mood takes a complete one-eighty. The hand that was undoing my buttons just a moment ago falls to his side, and he sits on the edge of the bed.

"Sure. Talk to you soon." When the call ends, Jack heaves a sigh. "He's under a CHRONOS field. Absolutely no doubt."

"But you already suspected that . . . right?"

He nods. "It was weird, though. Dad asked for a status report, and I gave him a bit of techno babble Alex told me. Then he shifted gears and started asking my opinion about vacationing in Barcelona, because I went there during my junior year of college. It was like he wanted an excuse to talk. At first, I thought he was getting sentimental in his dotage."

"Well, you're his son. He loves you."

"Yeah, but that doesn't mean he loves *talking* to me. The length of that conversation just now is close to a record. He usually messages me. Also, I'm certain my stepmom vacationed in Barcelona before she met Dad, because she gave me some travel tips, so why not ask her, you know? And, at the end, I think he lied to me. Which . . . sure I'm lying to him with pretty much every breath, so I can't exactly hold it against him on moral grounds, but I'm trying to figure out *why* he's lying. When I told him I'd let my stepmom know about coming out to California for the holidays, he said I should just plan to stay here. Barring a miracle where timelines are repaired, Saul is erased, and I can take you with me, that was exactly what I intended to do anyway, but . . . his rationale was that Liza Forson wasn't taking Christmas off, and with seven hundred million lives on the line, neither should I."

"But you said Elizabeth Forson and her daughters were killed decades ago in this timeline, during one of the witch purges."

"Exactly. He was giving me info from the previous timeline, which he couldn't know if he wasn't under a field."

"Or . . . maybe it wasn't Forson who was killed? Your dad has access to a lot of intelligence we wouldn't have through the public record. That was true even before we wound up in a timeline where almost anything useful is classified."

"Maybe," he says. "It just seems odd that he'd spout back the exact same number he gave me before. I mean, it's rounded up to the nearest hundred million, so I guess it's possible it didn't change. But we know the First Genetics War went down very differently in this timeline. They didn't even call it the Genetics War. If it hadn't originated in the same geographic area, I'm not sure I'd have connected the two. But yeah, I don't know how much of the admittedly limited information in the public record can be trusted."

"Tyson and Clio have already left. They're scheduled to come back around the same time Katherine and I return from our trip to the temple. Let's discuss it then. I know you're worried about bringing your dad into all of this, but if he's catching on anyway, we may not have a choice."

Jarvis chimes in to let me know Katherine is waiting. I snatch a pair of jeans out of the drawer and pull them on, then we head to the library.

I'm expecting Katherine to be annoyed that I'm running late, but she's in a better mood than usual. She and Rich are on one of the couches near the front windows, each with their keys out. Something seems different, but I can't quite put my finger on it.

"Hey, Madi," Rich says as we enter the library. "Have you scanned forward on the stable point at the temple yet?"

I shake my head. "Just the static image. I panned around the room, though. It's only the Sister and the two dogs."

"Yeah, but we're wondering what it is you see that surprises you," Katherine says. "About two seconds after you jump in, when you step out of the stable point."

"Except Madi knowing she's going to be surprised means that will change now," Alex says from across the room. "You guys know that."

Katherine shrugs. "It doesn't change things *much*, as long as you don't watch for very long. Personally, I like to know what's coming up."

Jack and I sit down on the opposite couch. Alex is right. I really prefer not to watch ahead when I make a jump. Maybe it's easier if you've been doing this for years like Katherine and Rich, but for me, watching for more than a few seconds sets up a feedback loop in my head when I finally arrive at my destination. The trouble is, you're thinking about what you're doing, thinking about what you *saw* yourself doing when you watched through the key, and also thinking about the fact that you're thinking about it.

In addition, the sounds you can't hear through the key are added in, along with other environmental factors, and once you move out of the stable point, things you couldn't see from the earlier position. Part of your brain becomes occupied with thinking about what's different, and that alone can change how you react and interact with the environment, sometimes to the point where the things you watched through the key don't happen exactly the way you saw them unfold. Changes can occur because you're thinking about the fact that things have changed, and the whole thing can snowball. Simply put, it's distracting. Alex tried to explain it once, and said it has something to do with determinism, path dependence, and the forking of a causal chain . . . or something along those lines. That's the point at which he lost me and everyone else in the room, with the possible exception of Richard.

But I pull up the location anyway. Thea's younger carbon copy—quite literally, in this case—is still staring back at me from the large desk at one end of the library, or maybe it's a large office. Bookshelves line three of the walls, including the one behind the desk. The shelves are filled more with trinkets and framed photos than with books, although a copy of the *Book of Cyrus* is on a shelf on the left side of the desk, encased in a clear protective cube. The fourth wall of the office is glass, and it looks out on an enclosed courtyard. A fountain burbles merrily near the center, and beyond that, a pergola stretches along the outside of the opposite wing. The ivy on top provides shade for the bench below, which is white with what appears to be a mosaic of a lotus flower on the seat.

In the center of the glass wall, a stone fireplace rises up from the hearth, where two sleek black dogs are sleeping in front of the unlit logs. As I pan forward, I see them raise their heads when I jump in. One snarls when I step out of the stable point but drops its head back onto its paws when the woman sitting on the desk flicks her hand once in a downward motion.

I then watch myself take several steps toward the glass wall. My head tilts in surprise at something I can't see now due to the angle of the stable point. Later-Me frowns, so I'm tempted to keep watching to figure out why, but I have a better idea.

"Tell me if you see anything dangerous," I say to Jack, who is watching through his own key. He's not making the jump, so there are no problems with causal forks or odd echoes in his head.

After a few seconds, he says, "Nothing unusual, unless you count the fact that Thea's double is a very enthusiastic hugger. But you don't seem too upset about that."

He scans forward a bit more. "She talks, mostly. Shows you something in a book. You and Katherine ask some questions. And then, after about five minutes, the three of you go outside."

"And you're back here at ten thirty," Rich says, squinting at his display.

"Unless you knowing all of that screws something up," Alex mutters just loud enough for us to hear.

Rich and Katherine exchange an amused look.

"So, this is how you did it at CHRONOS?" I ask. "You spent hours before you jumped looking ahead to see what was going to happen?"

Katherine blushes slightly. "Well, no. The keys were kept in the jump room. We didn't use them for research, aside from checking to make sure we wouldn't be spotted by anyone when we arrived. Our stable points were almost always in out-of-the-way places, though, so we couldn't really have seen much if we *had* decided to look ahead. Plus it was . . . contrary to the main goal, which was for us to experience the event so we'd have a fuller understanding of the history and culture. And we had extraction teams to pull us out if things got too dicey."

"Speaking of extraction teams, I need to get back to watching Tyson and Clio," Rich says. "Jack will keep an eye on your trip. If there's any problem, he'll let me know so I can jump in as backup. Or, worst-case scenario, I'll jump back to right now and tell you not to go."

"We'll be back in twenty-three minutes." Katherine gives Rich a smile. And then she squeezes his hand.

Well, that's new. And I'm pretty sure it explains why she wasn't pissed about me being late.

∞

SIXTEENTH STREET TEMPLE
WASHINGTON, DC
JULY 12, 2058

I step aside as I saw myself do through the key and, for the first time, I *hear* the growl rather than merely watch as the dog's lips pull back into a snarl. And as soon as I'm outside the stable point, I see what it was that surprised me. There are actually *two* benches under the pergola in the courtyard. A middle-aged woman is seated at the end of the bench that was previously hidden, next to a large suitcase and several smaller bags. Two leashes are draped over the suitcase. The woman, who is staring at an electronic device—a phone, or maybe a radio?—wears a pink shirt and khaki shorts. Her dark skin stands out in stark contrast to the bright white of the bench. So does the rifle lying next to her. She's also wearing a cuff identical to Thea's, which now encircles my wrist. I need to ask them exactly how you use it as a weapon, since I haven't managed to figure that out yet. The woman glances up, locks eyes with me for a moment, and then turns her attention back to her device.

Katherine has now arrived. I open my mouth to tell her about the woman in the courtyard, but I'm already being pulled into the hug that Jack warned me was coming.

"Madi! Oh my goodness, you're all grown up."

After a brief hesitation, I return the Sister's hug. I think it's her perfume, combined with the blue-and-white caftan, both of which are similar to things Thea wore. Whatever it is, I get a vivid flashback to standing with Thea outside the Palace Theatre on a December afternoon when I was seven or eight.

I haven't thought about that day in years. We'd just attended *The Nutcracker* after a morning spent Christmas shopping. It was one of the fun, whirlwind days that marked Thea's rare visits. I spent summers in Bray with Nora and Pop, and often stayed with them on the weekends when they were in London. They were constants in my life. Thea, on the other hand, breezed in with little or no advance warning. I always hugged her extra tight when she left because I never knew how long it would be before I saw her again.

Thea's younger clone—and I can't help but think of her as younger, even though Thea hasn't been born yet—laughs and apologizes.

"Forgive me, Madi! That was presumptuous, but I watched you grow up, so I feel like I know you. Thea sent back a video every time she visited you. None of us have actual grandchildren, so we had to live vicariously through her. We get to see the younger Sisters, of course, but that's more like looking backward in the mirror. It was nice to see a fresh young face. I'm Beta. Prudence Alpha said I should change the name, because no one should be named after a failed technology, but I like it." She turns to Katherine. "I take it you're Katherine Shaw? I expected someone a bit more . . . imposing, based on Pru's stories."

"Yes." Katherine just stands there looking uncomfortable. I think it's partly because this is, in some sense, her child, but the woman is at least fifteen years older than she is. And it can't help knowing that one of the daughters she *did* give birth to in some timeline has apparently been telling tales behind her back.

Beta clearly picks up on the awkwardness because she smiles and reaches forward to give Katherine's arm a squeeze. "You shouldn't let it worry you. I gave birth to one Prudence and I helped raise several others. There were days when I was ready to run screaming. Every single Pru, including yours truly, was an absolute terror between the ages of twelve and sixteen. And while I loved Prudence Alpha,

I tended to take her pronouncements with a grain of salt. There are many ways in which she never got past adolescence."

Then Beta turns back to me and runs a finger across Thea's cuff, which is now on my left wrist. "I knew Thea didn't make it when there was no message, but it's still so sad."

"Okay, I'm confused. How could Thea send you a message? Or videos of me, for that matter? She hasn't even been born."

Beta walks back to the desk and picks up a CHRONOS diary. "We only have the one book, and it's short a few pages that they took to make our protective devices. But you'd be surprised how much this little book can hold. If we always put the diary back in its secret spot, all of the Sisters can use it." She flips the diary open to a section near the end and taps a link. A video pops up of six-year-old me petting the lion that greets visitors at the London Zoo. "That nearly gave us a heart attack, but Nu, who was in the batch after Thea, told us it's not a real lion at all."

"You're using the diaries a bit like we did in the field," Katherine says. "Only we had to actually send it *back* to HQ the day before we left in order to have our questions answered. I don't see how it could work otherwise . . ."

Katherine reaches for the diary, but Beta shakes her head. "I'm sorry. This is private. But . . . you jumped seventy years back in time using similar technology. Why is it so hard to fathom that someone could send *information* back through time? That's a far simpler task."

It's a valid point. Katherine must agree, because she gives Beta a perfunctory nod and then asks, "Who is the woman in the courtyard?"

"We'll join her shortly. I wanted a private moment first to tell you both that I'm sorry about Thea. We knew based on her last message that there was a chance things could go wrong. We just hoped she'd at least be able to take Saul out with her. That was the fallback plan, but given everything that's happened since then—"

"Thea did kill him," I say. "Sort of."

When I finish telling her about Saul and the splinter, she nods sadly. "Well, that does explain why he's decided to target us. In the last iteration, where we had that weird flag and never fought the Nazis, he mostly left us alone. Now we've not only been disbanded, but he made us out to be some sort of demonic demigod in his new *Book of Cyrus*, and we're down seven more members."

"*Seven?*" Katherine says.

Beta nods. "Maybe even eight. We have the strangest double memory about Eta, from the batch after me. I helped raise her. I even have a scar on my arm from when the little rascal bit me when she was three." She shows us a small scar on the back of her hand. "But my other memory says she died as a tiny infant. As for the others, I don't know for certain they're dead or erased, aside from Thea, of course. And Delta, who was from my batch. She was snatched right after the time shift, during an appearance near Miami in 2049. There wasn't even a trial. The local Templar took one look at her face and declared her a Prudaean. Blamed her for spreading the witch plague and had her burned on the front steps of the temple." Her lip trembles. "They removed her cuff, so she's really gone. Kappa is missing. Sigma and Rho, too. And all three of the babies they were caring for. Poor Tau, she could only watch, because Saul said there was a bomb. And then he set it off anyway. Turns out no one was on the train, but she didn't know that. Prudence Alpha was right. He's an awful, awful man, and you have to stop him. So, yes . . . that makes seven. Eight if what I remember about Eta is accurate. Nine, if you count poor Thea. And I'm not sure how long the rest of us will last with our face plastered in every Cyrist temple as some sort of witch."

I glance around. "But we're at a Cyrist temple right now. Isn't that . . ."

"Risky? Oh, yes, yes. But we worked here in the last timeline, so this is where we kept the diary. It's also the only stable point Thea left, and we obviously needed to talk to you. Fortunately for all of us, the woman in the courtyard is the head of Cyrist security for the DC region. Her office is inside this building, and . . . let's just say they're in the middle of a conveniently timed, unscheduled security drill. The current Templar and his closest allies are in their bunker, where they'll stay until Charlayne gives the all-clear. Which will be about ten minutes *after* she hustles me into the car with Dexys and Midnight, heading back to a more secure location."

Charlayne. It's not a common name and it tickles some corner of my memory. I'm pretty sure I've heard or read it recently, but I can't quite place it.

Beta steps over to the window, but Charlayne is no longer on the bench. She's standing at a narrow gate at the right end of the courtyard, with the rifle over her shoulder and the two leashes dangling from her hand. She says something to a young man on the other side of the gate, who is now carrying the largest suitcase and one of the smaller bags. He nods curtly, then pivots and hurries down the narrow alley between the two buildings toward the parking lot.

Something is wrong. I'm certain of this before I even see her face. She runs toward us, flinging open the door.

"Change of plans." She tosses the leashes to Beta. "We have to go *now*. If you're determined to bring the dogs, get them ready."

Beta doesn't question her, just hurries toward the Dobermans.

"Charlayne Singleton. I'm with the Fifth Column and also a friend of your granddaughter's." She extends her right hand to Katherine. The other hand, which is holding the strap of the rifle over her shoulder, has a lotus tattoo on the back. It's not pink, though. It's amber, and it glows faintly. Not as brightly as the tattoo on the baby's ankle, but it's pretty clear that it generates a low-level CHRONOS field.

She reaches into her pocket, pulls out a small data drive, and slaps it into Katherine's hand, then hurries over to the desk to grab the diary Beta was using earlier. "Get back to your place in Bethesda. You may have to evacuate that location, though. Sisters, Inc. held the title in the previous timeline, and that may still be the case on paper. But . . . we're kinda broke and on the run in this reality, so I'm pretty sure someone else owns that house."

Fuck.

"The drive has coordinates where you can reach us once you locate the missing Sisters." Charlayne stops. "I know you're trying to fix the timeline, but you *are* looking for them, right?"

"Yes," I tell her. "We have one of the babies. We're in the process of rescuing the others."

"Good," she says, flashing us a quick smile. "Thank you. Saul's not going to cut any of them much slack. From what Sister Prudence said, mercy simply isn't within his nature. And he's put a target on every one of their heads with this Prudaean witchcraft bullshit. Beta! Let's go."

"Coming!" Beta clips the second leash into place and the two dogs follow her to the door. The snarly one lifts its lip again when they pass us.

"It was lovely to meet you," Beta says as Charlayne snatches one of the leashes from her hand and pushes her toward the exit.

Just as they reach the door, something explodes in the parking lot. It's a big enough blast that I feel the floor rumble. Smoke now fills the alley between the buildings, and it looks like one of the cars in the lot is in flames.

I expect the two of them to pull back, but Charlayne says, "That's our cue. Go, go, go, go, go!"

She's talking to Beta, but it's clearly our cue as well. I pull up the library stable point near Grandpa James's desk, roll forward to ten-thirty, our agreed-upon arrival time, and blink out.

FROM THE *BOOK OF CYRUS*

(NEV, 12:7)

Cyrus cast her from the Garden, along with the apple of temptation. He watched as she was torn asunder by the beasts of the forests, and knew that it was God's will, for he has said, 'Thou shalt not suffer a witch to live.'

∞9∞

Rich isn't in the library. Neither is Alex.

No one is in the library. And music is playing over the intercom. Very *loud* music. I tap the disk behind my ear and wait for Richard's signal to show on my retinal screen. It's either not active or not in range.

I turn toward the stable point across the room where Madi jumped in. Wincing, she tells Jarvis to cut the music. There's no response. She scans the room just as I had a second before, the music apparently forgotten, and says, "Jarvis, locate Jack."

There's no answer, so she repeats the question, louder. Finally, the AI kicks in.

"Master Jack is not in the house."

"What?" Madi yells. "Cut the goddamn music, Jarvis. Where is he? Where is Alex?"

"I'm afraid they've been taken into custody."

"By whom?" I ask, following Madi to the door.

"I initially believed them to be members of the military, but I may be wrong. Master Alex thinks they are private troops connected to the Cyrists."

"These troops took everyone?"

"Alex, RJ, and Lorena did not resist. Master Jack retreated to the basement to hide the infant, but the troops followed."

Madi's stable point is closer to the door, so she's already halfway down the stairs by the time I reach the hallway. She hangs a right at the bottom and hurries toward the second set of stairs that leads down to the pool in the basement.

"Jarvis, is anyone in the house now?" she asks.

Another delay, and when the voice comes back, it sounds almost hesitant. It's like her assistant is trying to figure out how to deliver difficult news, but that's ridiculous. It's an AI. "I'm now detecting four people in the house. Three just arrived in the library. One is in the basement."

I breathe a sigh of relief. Richard had planned to stay behind and take care of research tasks, but he and Jack were monitoring the stable points for the two jumps in case either group ran into trouble. Since Jack's ability to jump is almost nonexistent, Richard was on point to provide backup. Something must have gone wrong at Potter's farm, and he had to jump in to help Tyson and Clio.

Madi pulls her laser from her pocket. "For God's sake, Jarvis, just tell me who's in the fucking basement!" Her voice is tight, barely above a whisper, although I'm pretty sure the chance to make a subtle entrance ended when we thundered down the stairs leading from the library. She must realize that, too, because she throws the door open. The smell of salt from the pool rises up, along with something else. An acrid scent that takes me back to the locker room at CHRONOS when I played intramural volleyball as a teenager. Sweat. Adrenaline.

There's that weird delay again, and then Jarvis says, "The person in the basement is the infant who was delivered in the box yesterday. She's in the supply closet. I'm so sorry, Katherine."

I stop halfway down the stairs, confused. Why is the baby in the closet? And why is Jarvis saying he's sorry? "Oh my God, is she okay?"

"The baby is fine."

Madi looks back over her shoulder at me and then picks up her pace again. "Jarvis, tell Tyson and Clio to get down here."

When her feet hit the tile floor at the bottom, she tosses the laser aside and begins running. I hear a splash and by the time I spot her, she's already halfway across the pool. Rich is sprawled, face down, at the far end where the light from the CHRONOS field is the brightest. Red tendrils snake out from his chest into the water.

I scream out his name and run toward the pool. Madi knifes smoothly through the water and reaches him before I get to the edge. She flips him over and for a second, I'm completely frozen, staring at the hole in the center of his body. All I can think of is the man in Memphis after I killed him with Sutter's pen gadget . . . the same weapon currently in my pocket.

Saul did this because of *me*. Which means I killed Rich every bit as much as if I'd pointed the damn weapon at him myself.

Madi's voice breaks through and I realize she's yelling for me to get the rescue tube. I'm not even sure what that is, but she nods toward a red strip with a white cross on it. I toss it to her and move toward the pool to help, but Tyson is already there. Clio is heading toward the supply closet. I can see the top of a baby's head peeking over the edge of her bodice. I guess that explains the third person Jarvis reported in the library.

I can't watch them pulling Rich out of the pool. Not without screaming. And I have to hold it together so I can figure out how to fix this. I center the key in my hand and take a few deep breaths until I'm steady enough to set a stable point. Then I scroll backward five minutes, to when Rich's body is still in the pool.

Back five more minutes. The pool is empty now, but someone—Jack, maybe?—is blocking my view. I move three steps to the side and set another stable point.

Tyson grabs my hand. "Katherine. Stop, okay? We need to slow down and think this through carefully."

"Do you think I'm an idiot? Let me go. I'm not planning to blink in on my own." Even as I say the words, I know he's right to be a little worried. I *probably* wouldn't jump in alone. But if I thought I saw a chance to kill Saul and save Rich, can I be sure I wouldn't take it?

"Katherine." Tyson pulls me into a hug. His arms are wet, which reminds me of *why* they're wet, and I again see him reaching down to help Madi lift Rich from the pool. But I don't pull away. He is Richard's roommate, and truthfully, his best friend—a role I more or less abandoned because I was so focused on Saul. Tyson wants to unwind this disaster as much as I do. "We'll fix this, okay? They took his key, but the house is still under a CHRONOS field. Waiting a few minutes to plan things out could make all the difference."

"He's right." Madi brushes away a rivulet of bright blue water running from the streak in her hair down the side of her face as she speaks. "As soon as we find out exactly what happened, we'll make a plan and reverse it."

"I'm afraid you cannot do that." It's Jarvis, which surprises me, since no one paged him. Has he ever chimed in without someone speaking his name first, unless it was an announcement of some sort? I can't remember, but I don't think so. "At least, you cannot do that until the game is over," he continues. "There is a message for you on the SimMaster in the library and . . . I have been instructed to tell you that if you fail to follow the instructions, all of the illegal assistants who were taken into custody will be killed per the stated rules."

"What illegal assistants?" Madi asks.

When the AI doesn't respond, Tyson says, "He must mean Alex, Jack, and the others. Which doesn't make sense. They researched for us last time. In normal play, we'd have access to any publicly available information. Professional players have entire teams of researchers on staff. Why would that sort of help suddenly be against the rules?"

Madi instructs Jarvis to display security footage for this room and all entrances for the past half hour. This time, there's no delay before he speaks.

"I am sorry, Mistress. Security cameras were disabled remotely at 9:32 a.m. I informed Master Jack immediately when it happened, but I am afraid it was too late."

"Damn it," Madi says. "Why the hell do we have to do this without audio?" She pulls out her key and begins setting stable points, leaving wet footprints in her wake as she moves toward the stairs.

Tyson motions for me to follow her, but I shake my head. I know Rich is dead, but I can't leave him here alone in the basement without speaking to him. Without personally telling him we *are* going to fix this, one way or the other.

"Help Clio get the babies upstairs. I'll join you in a minute."

His eyes go to Rich's body and then back to me. "Are you sure? I can stay down here with you."

"No. I need a moment alone with him. I'm okay, Tyson. Because this is temporary."

"I know. That's why I'm asking if you're sure you want to put yourself through this. It *is* temporary. Saul Rand is not taking Rich from us."

"I'm okay," I repeat. "I just need to be with him for a minute."

When I hear their footsteps on the stairs, I cross over to Rich. The tile around his body is soaked. I keep my eyes away from his chest and focus on his face. His glasses are missing, which makes him look different. Younger. Either Madi or Tyson closed his eyes. Would it have been any easier if they were open, unseeing? Probably not, but I still get a totally unreasonable surge of resentment.

I pull off the field extender bracelet I wear as backup on jumps and attach it to his wrist. The field surrounding the house may be active now, but there's no guarantee it will stay that way. Then I lean forward and press my lips against his. He tastes of salt. From the water in the pool, from my tears. Both. "I love you. That's been true for almost as long as I've known you. It hasn't always been the type of love you wanted from me, but I really do think we'll get there, Rich. I'm going to fix this."

As I stand up, I see his glasses, bobbing inside the pool filter. I fish them out and leave them next to his hand. Within easy reach, the way they always were on the occasions I found him napping on a desk in the library at CHRONOS. The way they were on the nightstand in my room last night, when we fell asleep, mostly clothed, thinking we didn't have to rush things. That was a profoundly stupid notion, in retrospect, with the clock literally ticking on the reality around us.

It was stupid to bother with his glasses, too. Stupid that I now ask Jarvis to dim the lights to 50 percent, because one of the fixtures is shining directly into Rich's eyes. Which are closed. Which couldn't see the light anymore, even if they were open.

None of this matters. When we reverse this, Rich will never be shot. We won't find him in the pool. His glasses will never be missing. But somehow doing these tiny, irrelevant things makes it easier for me to leave him. Easier for me to believe that despite the wet tile floor and the gaping wound in the center of his body, Rich is just sleeping, with his glasses in easy reach.

∞

Madi and Tyson are in the kitchen when I get upstairs. One of the babies is on a blanket next to the breakfast nook.

"I thought you'd be in the library," I say. "We need to listen to the message. Check the observation points."

"Yes," Tyson says. "But we have to take care of this first."

There are six bottles lined up on the bar and Madi is programming something into the food unit, probably formula for the babies. *Formula for* your *babies*, says a judgmental little voice in my head, the bitchy one I used to tell myself was Alisa Campbell's, until I heard it coming out of my own mouth about a year ago and finally had to admit the voice was mine.

The baby on the floor doesn't seem especially hungry right now. She's not gnawing on her fist like she was last night. The other baby looked pretty content, too, so it seems like this could wait. But I don't say anything.

"Clio went upstairs to check and see if RJ and Lorena left any baby gear behind," Madi says. "Because there are now four adults to take care of two babies. Three babies, as soon as we can get to Hatteras Island. And the real irony is that there's no *logical* reason for us to prioritize rescuing them. They'll be fine no matter what happens in the interim, as long as we flip the timeline. But Saul knows damn well we won't be able to do the logical thing and ignore them."

"If you think about it in terms of double memories," Tyson says, "there actually *is* a logical reason to get them out first. None of the other people at Potter's farm or on Hatteras Island are under a CHRONOS field. None of them will have double memories of trauma. Maybe the babies won't remember it, either. I'm sure infant minds process memories differently when they're still forming connections. But since we really don't know, we need to get them out of there and get them to safety." He gives me a tired look, and I'm pretty sure he's wondering exactly what place would be safe right now. "I'd love to be able to rescue the girl in Salzburg as well, but since she may have carried out one of Saul's moves, it's going to take a bit of investigation to figure out how we get her out of there without causing additional damage. I mean, it's not one of his *official* moves, but if we can avoid screwing up European history, that would be a good thing, right?"

Madi divides the formula between the bottles. "Either way, the assumption that the bastard won't cheat is bullshit. Yes, his ego is enormous. Unfortunately, his desire to inflict pain is even bigger."

Tyson opens his mouth to speak. I'm sure he's about to take up for me, since the assumption she called bullshit was mine. But if he's going to tell her it's uncalled for, he's wrong. Madi has every right to be angry at this moment. Jack and four other people she cares about are in danger because of Saul. For all we know, they could be dead, too.

"You're right," I tell her. "Although I suspect that when we play Saul's message, he's going to protest that his actions really weren't cheating. He'll have some technical reason, some claim that we broke the agreement first . . ."

"Clio and I ran into trouble at Potter's farm," Tyson says. "So it might not be just a technical claim, although I have some serious questions about the timing. One of the guys at the farm pulled a gun on me. Rich was our backup and that should have been his cue to jump in. When he didn't show, probably because this house was being raided, Clio used the Timex device he loaned her. A half dozen people, two dogs, and a bunch of chickens hit the ground and we took off with the baby. I doubt Saul's going to see that as an appropriate action for an observer. But the other alternative would have been me killing Judge Potter's teenage son, if I was lucky and he didn't kill me first. So as much as I wish we'd had other options, Clio made the right choice. It was damn close getting out of there at all . . . and I think they saw her blink out with the baby."

"They *definitely* saw me." Clio is in the doorway now with a bag over her shoulder and an infant carrier in one hand. The second baby is still asleep on her chest, secured by her dress and apron. I get a flash of déjà vu. For a moment, I'm not sure why, and then I remember seeing myself through the key as the mob is about to tie me to the tree on Hatteras Island. I was shielding the baby with my arms when they wrapped the rope around our bodies to lash us to the trunk, but I was also using a similar apron to secure the baby to my body.

"Another second or two and I'm not sure what would have happened." Clio gives Tyson the bag. "It looks like they may have given Lorena a few minutes to grab some personal items, but most of their belongings are still here. I packed the diapers they had and enough clothes for a few days. Found a couple of pacifiers and two more bottles if you've got extra formula there."

So *that's* why we're in the kitchen. The babies aren't hungry now, but we could find ourselves with unwelcome visitors at any minute. We may need to leave abruptly. And whether we're leaving via the CHRONOS key or we get carted off somewhere by the people who took Jack and the others, it's unlikely they'd have infant formula.

You really do suck at this mom gig, Kathy.

I tell the Saul voice to go to hell and bend down to pick up Baby #1, trying to look like I actually know what I'm doing. I've held a few infants, but never one this tiny.

"It would be a whole lot easier to manage, though, if we stayed here," Clio says to Tyson. "The crib is still in Lorena's room, and they're small enough that they can easily share. Even once we add the third."

Tyson shakes his head as he screws on the last cap and begins stashing the bottles inside the bag. "I don't think we can risk it." He holds up a hand when he sees my expression. "I know, okay? I don't like the idea of leaving Rich's body here, either. I'm just not sure we have a choice. But let's wait until we've listened to Saul's message and figured out exactly what happened here this morning. Then we'll discuss our options."

Clio places the infant carrier on the table and nods toward the baby in my arms. "Phoebe seems pretty relaxed, so she might be okay in this thing." She blushes. "I started calling her that because Phi seems a bit odd for a baby. And she kind of looks like a Phoebe to me."

She clearly thinks it might bother me that she's picked out a name. Like she might have stepped on my toes. And maybe it *should* bother me, but someone already named the child *Phi*, and she's right. It's a stupid name for a baby.

I give Clio a weak smile as I unbuckle the strap on the carrier, and glance at the still-snoozing baby tucked inside her dress. "What are we calling this one?"

"The ring on her ankle is made of tiny linked *Y*s, which I think is the symbol for *upsilon*." She wrinkles her nose. "I can't for the life of me think of a decent short version of that."

The strap on the baby carrier seems to be tangled. "Too bad this dress won't do double duty like yours."

"Good thing mine did," she says. "Otherwise, I'm not sure we'd be here. The guy with the gun decided I look too much like the Prudence character in Saul's little book . . . which must have an illustrated edition in the 1780s. We made it back to the woods, but I couldn't get the extender gadget to work, and the Friend's people were closing in. At the last minute, I remembered that my mom was forced to jump constantly when she was pregnant with me. I couldn't replicate those conditions exactly, but this was apparently a close enough substitute. I'm still not sure if the device worked or if the baby traveled on my signal. Either way, it doesn't seem to have bothered her nearly as much as whatever they did when they transported Phoebe."

When I finally get the strap undone, I place the baby in the basket of the carrier. "I'll take her upstairs," I say, tucking the blanket around her feet. The baby kicks, and one of her feet pops back out again. From what Beta said, and from everything I read in my eventual granddaughter's diary, this is a harbinger of many mother-daughter battles to come. I fight the urge to tuck the wayward foot back inside and instead grab the carrier and head for the stairs, pretty sure that everyone in the kitchen is thinking, just like the Saul voice in my head, that I really do suck at this mom gig.

Five minutes later, when we're all in the library, Tyson pushes the button on the SimMaster and, as expected, Saul appears. I let out the breath I'm holding when we discover it's a recorded message. It will be hard enough to see his face right now, to hear his voice. My eyes are red and puffy from crying, the curse of pale blondes everywhere. If he has a stable point set in this room, he can see me, but at least I don't have to *see* him seeing me.

I still have to see his smirk, though. He doesn't know where I'm seated, so it's not pointed directly at me, but it's there.

"If you're hearing this, then you're already aware that I've leveled the playing field. You registered a *single* observer. Even if you had registered everyone else in the house, you were warned that observers were not allowed to participate. I was already stretching things by agreeing to compete against an entire team. I cautioned you that any attempts to cheat would be met with reprisal. But apparently, the only way to get you to play by the rules is to remove temptation. I've been assured your assistants will not be harmed by their current captors. And as long as you stick to the rules from here on out, I won't harm them, either."

Saul is lying. I'm not sure if the whole thing is a lie, or only part of it, but his face is almost motionless, and his eyes are fixed on a single point. It's not a tiny lie, either. Something has him unnerved and this is a cover story.

There's a long pause, and then he pastes on a look of fake sympathy. "I do apologize about Richard, but I'm afraid that was his fault. He seems to have a pathological need to play the protector. No harm would have come to him or to the infant if he had simply given himself over as ordered. But I suppose he was afraid you'd no longer . . . how shall we say? Bestow your favors upon him?"

This is another lie, but I already knew why he had Rich killed. It doesn't have anything to do with some action Rich took or didn't take in the basement. This is Saul's way of punishing me for daring to care about anyone else. And it probably didn't help that Rich had the audacity to call him crazy.

Tyson spits out a curse and shoves one of the empty office chairs at the hologram. The chair spins slightly as it cuts through the center of the avatar. Even though I know it didn't cause the real Saul any discomfort at all, wherever and whenever he may be, it's still oddly satisfying to see his form break apart, if only for an instant.

"In fact," the newly reassembled Saul continues, "you'd have had one less unnecessary burden to watch over while you're engaged in the game if Rich hadn't acted rashly. Because the babies *are* unnecessary burdens, Kathy. I've arranged it so that you are the only one who can retrieve them, so you can't farm the task out to one of the less skilled members of your team. But they are merely pawns. They have nothing to do with your objective. Each of the Pru clones was inserted into the timeline at a time and place where their death, as tragic as it may be, doesn't change history one iota. Saving them simply means you're condemning them to suffer through another painful death when you inevitably lose. If you defeat me, they will be safe and sound with their mother-sisters without you lifting a finger. If you don't defeat me, I'll just have the pleasure of finding another method of getting rid of them. And it *will* be a pleasure. They planned and very nearly succeeded at patricide. You might be a permissive parent, but I'm not. *For I am a vengeful god, and I will visit my wrath upon those who rise against me, and also upon their progenitors and descendants, even unto the fourth generation.* Something I should add to the next edition of the *Book of Cyrus*, perhaps?"

He indulges in a momentary chuckle, clearly pleased with his cleverness, and then continues. "A few things before I go, Kathy. First, my allies will be watching the basement at all times until the clock on this game winds down to zero. If any of you jump back to reverse Richard's death, it will be very bad news for your temporal physicist and his friends. I would have spared you that temptation by simply erasing him, but the kid who shot him would never have been able to locate the key that generates the field around the house. Second, as much as I'd *love* to see you pack up the remainder of your merry band of travelers and scurry about for a safe house, that will divert your attention from the game and further decrease the chance that you'll provide any real competition. I've therefore instructed my allies to leave your current location alone until the game concludes." He stops for a moment, tilting his head like he's trying to remember something. Then he says, "Oh, I nearly forgot about *Clio*. I've decided to overlook the incident at Potter's farm, even though I'm quite certain those people didn't decide to stretch out and take a nap on the front porch all at once. But please don't assume that because the Hyenas are down one player you can step into Richard's role. Stick to observing. Otherwise, I can't guarantee your safety or anyone else's."

The hologram vanishes in the middle of Clio flipping him off.

"He's right about the last part, though. You should be unarmed from here on out." Tyson winces slightly as he says this, probably expecting Clio to argue with him.

But she doesn't. "Sure. I'll follow his stupid rules. I don't want anyone else to get killed."

That comment, of course, pulls my mind back to Rich and our next task—figuring out exactly what happened in this house while we were gone. If there was security footage, we could watch together on the wall screen, but we settle for the next best option and view the stable points on our separate keys. Madi transfers one of the stable points in the living room that she says will give us a view of the foyer and both of the curved staircases that lead up to the second floor. We agree to begin at 9:07 a.m., which is when Madi and I made our jump to the Cyrist temple. The plan is to scan forward in thirty-second increments. Each time we stop, we'll pan around the area to see if we notice anything. Once we spot a change, we'll continue in real time.

At the first five stops, I don't see anything unusual. On the sixth, however, I spot Lorena halfway down the staircase leading to the foyer. She has Yun Hee strapped into a backpack carrier, and she's pulling a small suitcase behind her.

Lorena is already packed. Which means she knows something is about to happen.

She sold us out.

Madi inhales sharply, so she must realize the same thing.

Lorena grimaces and puts one hand to her ear. Yun Hee, who was happily chewing on the carrier strap, jerks her head up at the same time, and her eyes go wide. Within seconds, Jack, Richard, and RJ come running down the staircase closest to the library. Jack is carrying the dresser drawer with the baby. He gives Lorena a confused look, then turns right toward the hallway leading to the basement stairs. Richard follows him. RJ turns toward Lorena, and if it wasn't clear from his expression that he had no warning about what was going down, he very distinctly mouths *what the fuck?* as he runs toward her. She begins pleading with him, although there's no hope of reading her lips from this angle.

Alex stops on the bottom stair and looks right toward the hallway and then left toward Lorena and RJ. He's clearly trying to decide which way to go, but then a group of heavily armed men in khaki uniforms bursts in through the front door. No one unlocked it for them, so someone, probably Lorena, must have given them the code. All of them wince slightly as they enter. Maybe they set off an alarm of some sort? No . . .

"The music," I say aloud. "That's why they all look like they're in pain. Madi and I heard it when we first jumped in."

Two of the guards take up station near the door. Four others storm up the closest of the two stairways, and we watch as they run along the hallway between the staircases toward the library.

When I pan back to Lorena, an older man, who apparently followed the soldiers in, is now talking to her, also wearing a pained expression. He looks vaguely familiar.

"Damn it, Lor—" Madi stops so abruptly that I look up from the key. "Oh, no, no, no, no."

I catch her eye and she says, "That's Jack's father. General Merrick. Retired general, actually, but he still does contract work for the government. Jack said he was acting weird on the phone earlier. And he was pretty sure his dad was under a key. He probably called to give his son one last chance to tell him the truth."

That's *one* interpretation, and I hope for Madi's sake it's the right one. I don't know Jack well enough to tell whether he's simply in this to get information for his father. Madi knows him better than any of us, but she's not exactly a neutral observer. It's easy to see only what you want to see when you're in love. I'm a bit of an expert on that topic.

We return to watching the stable point. RJ takes the suitcase from Lorena and puts one arm around her, pressing a kiss to the side of her head. As she heads toward the door, I notice something written on the paisley-print backpack in pale-orange glowing letters. She must have swiped some of the material RJ and Alex used to make the field-extender bracelets. The letters, which are crudely fashioned, read: *CRIB PINK*. There's another word below that, but there's a crease in the fabric and I can't make it out. It looks like it begins with *B* or maybe *R*.

"Do you see that?" Tyson says. "It's clearly intended for our eyes only. Anyone without the gene would barely see those letters against the fabric. Not sure what it means, though."

"Maybe she left us a message in Yun Hee's crib," Clio says. "Although I'm not sure what the *Pink* part is for."

I look back at the display. The general turns to Alex and says something. Alex, who is sitting on the bottom step with his head tilted slightly to one side, either doesn't hear the man or chooses to ignore him.

The general speaks again, and this time, Alex looks up. I can't see what he says, but he seems resigned and follows Merrick to the open front door. As Alex goes through, he hesitates, looking down at the guns the guards are holding.

I can see that he stops, but I can't really tell what he's looking at. "Madi, do you have a stable point in the foyer? Closer to the door?"

"Yeah. Hold on a sec."

When she's ready, I tap my key against hers and scroll to the point where Alex is approaching the door. I don't see anything at first, because he's in the way. But once he's on the front porch I realize it's not the guns he was looking at. They're fairly ordinary weapons, at least to my admittedly untrained eye. Alex was looking at their hands. Their *left* hands . . . each of which displays a blue lotus tattoo.

The general motions for one of the two guards to go with Lorena, RJ, and Alex, and one to follow him. I'm almost certain there's a tattoo on his hand as well, but it's hard to tell in the glare of the sunlight coming in through the front door. The younger of the two guards follows the general, who is now talking to the other four guards at the top of the stairs outside the library. Merrick says something and nods toward the hallway on the ground floor that leads toward the basement. One soldier goes back into the library, and the other three soldiers trot obediently down the stairs. The general follows, with the guard who had been at the door taking up the rear.

We're now at the stage where we'll have to move to the basement stable points to see what happened next. I scroll to the first one and take a deep breath, bracing myself. If I could go back right this instant and save Rich, it wouldn't be so hard to watch. But knowing I have to wait, knowing there's a chance I'll *never* be able to fix it . . .

I'm not sure if Tyson sees my expression or if he realizes my hand is shaking, but something tips him off. "We're going about this wrong," he says. "This will move faster if we divide the tasks. Madi and

I will continue watching the stable points. Clio, you and Katherine go to Lorena's suite and see if you can find the message she left."

I open my mouth to protest. But there are tears in Tyson's eyes, and he shakes his head. "Just go, okay? Rich wouldn't want you to watch this. I'll tell you what happens, and if there's anything you absolutely need to see, I'll let you know."

He's right. As much as I want to know what happened, I don't want to watch Rich die.

I pick up the baby carrier and follow Clio down the long hallway to a suite at the opposite end of the house. A crib is wedged next to the bed, and a stroller and other baby gear is stashed in the open closet. Clothing is scattered on the floor, the dressers, and the rails of the crib. The bed, however, is perfectly clear except for a box of teething biscuits. A pink cartoon rabbit in ballet slippers is on the front. *Bellarina Bunny Bites*.

Clio picks up the box. "Ah ha. The message must have said *Pink Rabbit*. Or maybe *Bunny*."

She tips the box over the bed. No teething biscuits, but a folded sheet of paper flutters out. When I open it, I see a printout of a photo. A little girl is wearing a pink snowsuit with bunny ears, not unlike the rabbit on the box. I'm pretty sure the girl is Yun Hee, but she's at least a year older in the photo. RJ is helping her build a tiny snowman from the snow that was shoveled from the walk.

A handwritten message is scrawled on the back of the photo:

Saul has the other us. If it were just me, or even just me and RJ, I'd have told him to go to hell. But he has Yun Hee, too. I know it's not rational. The girl in this picture is not my daughter. But she also IS my daughter. Alex can't guarantee me that these timelines cease to exist after we "fix" them, and I won't be responsible for any version of her dying if I can avoid it. So I agreed to help LORTA. I'm sorry.

"Okay," Clio says. "But who the hell is LORTA? And why are they working with Saul?"

FROM THE *CYRIST NATIONAL EXAMINER*

Lonnie L. Dennis to Lead Cyrist International

(Washington, DC, June 22, 1965) Cyrists around the world, having completed two weeks of mourning for Grand Templar William Dudley Pelley, have now turned to the happier task of welcoming his successor. And unlike the last transfer of power in 1954 following the tragic death of Templar Coughlin, there was no controversy or question about who would take the reins as leader of the fastest-growing religion in the United States. Like Coughlin and the first three Grand Templars for North America, Lonnie Dennis's name is literally written in the *Book of Prophecy*.

Some have argued that Templar Pelley's death could have been predicted, as well, based on the specific passage in the *Book* indicating that Dennis would assume the role in the summer of 1965. Others noted that the prophecy could as easily have been fulfilled by Pelley's retirement. Had Pelley not died on June 5th, plans were already underway for him to officially hand the title to Templar Dennis yesterday, before embarking on his well-earned retirement in the mountains of North Carolina.

Lonnie Lawrence Dennis steps into the role of Grand Templar after a lifetime of public service. He was born in Atlanta, Georgia, in 1893, and from age five, he toured the world as a child preacher, spreading the Christian gospel. The keen intelligence that allowed him to memorize scripture at such an early age served him well at Exeter, and later, at Harvard. He excelled in the fields of diplomacy and finance and published several books on economic and political issues during the 1930s, but success seemed hollow. Dennis felt he wasn't giving back. He missed the ministry, even though he questioned some aspects of his childhood religion.

In the late 1930s Dennis discovered in Cyrisism a religion that balanced his intellectual and spiritual ideals, while providing a sound structure for his wife and two daughters. *Why We Are Here*, Dennis's book about his path to Cyrisism, topped the bestseller lists in the early 1940s. Dennis rose quickly through the ranks, serving first at the state level and leading the East Coast organization for nearly a decade before being tapped as North American Grand Templar and de facto head of Cyrist International.

Dennis relocated to the DC area last month in preparation for his new role. His two older daughters are now married with families of their own, but he will be joined this week by Mrs. Dennis and their adopted daughter, Ada, who will attend Carrington Day School in the fall.

∞10∞

When I look up from watching the events in the basement a second time, Madi is slumped down on the sofa opposite me.

"Come on. Jack's okay. And you can't think he was part of this. He was already upstairs when that guy fired."

"I know *Jack* wasn't part of it. That's not even a question. But his dad?" She shakes her head. "He's responsible. He knew."

"Yes, he knew Rich was shot. But I don't think he ordered it. You saw his expression. He was yelling at the guy."

"Maybe," she admits. "He didn't stop the guy from yanking Rich's key, though. And, what's the saying? The buck stops here. Merrick was the senior officer on location. It was one of his men who fired the shot. He must have gotten tired of waiting for Jack to pump me for information. So he decided to see if his former colleagues could spare a couple of armed goons to just *take* the research by grabbing Alex and Lorena."

I glance around uneasily. "Which means they'll probably be back at any minute for you."

"Why? Jack's dad doesn't know I have the CHRONOS gene, and Jack sure as hell won't tell him. As far as General Merrick knows, I'm the historian, and everyone knows historians are a dime a dozen. He probably figures Jack can take my place now that we've gotten the ball rolling. And he could. I mean, at one point, in some timeline, there was a version of me that wasn't born with the genetic boost. Whatever Lorena did to *that* Madison Grace she can just as easily do to Jack, and he's starting out with a basic ability to use the technology, even if he has trouble with the actual traveling-through-time part. And he's younger, too. That Madison Grace doesn't start working on the project for well over a decade. Lorena probably had to give her constant booster injections."

"You're forgetting that Saul is now part of the equation, though. Merrick may not know you can use the key, but Saul does. If he's looking to level the playing field without admitting he's worried he can't defeat us as a team, passing that information along to Merrick might be his way of picking you off. And we also have no idea how much Lorena told Merrick."

Madi sighs. "Valid point. One more reason we probably need to get the hell out of here, although I don't know how we can research effectively anywhere else."

Katherine and Clio are back. Without the babies, so they must have left them in the crib. Clio hands Madi a sheet of paper. "This was inside an empty box of teething biscuits."

Madi scans it, looking even more miserable now, then leans across the table to hand it to me. "See? Exactly what I thought. General Merrick must be on contract with LORTA again. Or maybe he never retired and is still working for them."

I glance down at the note again. "You'd think Lorena could have given us a bit more detail. How is Saul connected to this? Maybe it was just a way for him to get someone in here to shoot Rich?"

"So, was the soldier stationed at the door the one who shot him?" Clio asks.

I nod and give the two of them a brief overview of what Madi and I saw through the key. "Rich was in the closet where Clio found the baby when we arrived. One of the guards cuffed Jack and took him upstairs. Merrick is halfway up the stairs himself when the last guard in the room moves toward the closet. I don't know . . . maybe he heard something. Rich steps out. I think he was probably trying to distract him, to keep him away from the baby. His key was in his hand, so I'm guessing he was going to try to jump back to warn us after he realized the man was armed. The guy will probably say he fired because he thought the key was some sort of weapon."

Katherine gives me a probing look. "But you don't believe that."

"No. I can't entirely put my finger on *why* I don't believe it, but there was recognition in the man's eyes. I watched from three different angles. Rich was holding the key kind of low, looking down. The guy tilted his head, and it seemed to me that he was looking at Rich's face, like he was trying to make sure he had the right person. He didn't say anything. No warning to drop the weapon, if that's what he thought it was. Just looked at Rich for that extra moment like he was trying to verify his target, and then he fired. Merrick must have either heard the weapon discharge or when Rich fell into the water, because he comes back down the stairs and starts yelling."

"The good news is that it will be easy to undo," Madi says. "I mean, not now, but when we've jumped through Saul's hoops and we know the others are safe. The guy who shot him is at the back of the line, behind Merrick when they go down the stairs to the basement. I'll step out of the laundry room and shoot the bastard."

"Excellent plan," Katherine says. "Now we just have to figure out how to get to that point, which should be fun without Alex, RJ, or Jack's research. Starting from scratch is going to put us at least a day behind. I seriously doubt that anyone who was interested in getting Alex's research would have been stupid enough to leave it on the system. I also doubt they had enough time to go through and pick out which files to wipe. Easier to do a clean sweep."

A query or two with Jarvis, however, reveals that most of what we need is still in the data system. The LORTA guy copied the computers but didn't wipe them. Jack had some information on his tablet, and we don't know the password for that, but Jarvis still has a record of the searches he made, so it shouldn't take too long to reconstruct.

"That's . . . odd," Katherine says. "Why would they leave the data to be used by someone else?"

I shrug. "They may not know anything about the game with Saul. I don't know if they're even aware any of us are in the house . . . although they may now be wondering why Rich was here and why he was wearing a CHRONOS key. And they probably realized Madi couldn't understand Alex's temporal physics research. No offense, Madi."

"Absolutely none taken."

Katherine doesn't seem convinced. "But that wouldn't prevent Madi from selling the data to someone who *would* be able to understand it. That leads me to think maybe Alex was correct that this was Cyrist security. Doesn't seem like the sort of error troops assigned to something called the Defense Research . . . whatever DARPA stands for . . . would make."

"Defense Advanced Research Projects Agency," Jarvis says. "And . . . while I don't know whether the individual who copied the data from the computers was with DARPA, he did *try* to erase the data after copying it. Perhaps . . . he believes he succeeded."

"Alex." I pull up the stable point and view it again. "That's what he was doing on the steps. When Merrick was telling him to join RJ and Lorena. Quick thinking, Alex. And . . . hold on. Did you notice the patch on their shoulders?"

Madi nods. "Crossed swords and a shield."

"Open it again and look at the hilt. At the very top and the um . . . I think it's called the cross guard? The part that protects the hand. One end is looped and the two arms are flared, like the top and the two arms of a Cyrist cross—the new design, at any rate. And if you look closely at that shield . . ."

"There's a lotus along the base," Madi says. "Alex was right. Jack's dad may be head of a DARPA project, but he's using Cyrist troops."

"Or maybe all troops wear those," Clio says.

A quick search shows it's not standard insignia. The brief article notes that there are individual unit insignias, however, so it doesn't really rule anything out.

We begin trying to figure out what to do next, based mostly on notes the others left behind. Deciphering someone else's research is never easy, and most of their work so far was aimed at figuring out which events we should enter as initial predictions. It's a pale imitation of the detailed background packets we assembled prior to a CHRONOS mission. I spent years learning general information about the 20th century, and weeks of prep before starting on a series of jumps. If anything, agents were generally burdened with too much information. When I was embedded with the Klan in Pitt County, the challenge was often pretending to be clueless about people and events when I sometimes had far more background on the situation than the participants.

I pull up our list of initial predictions and am about to launch into a discussion of who's doing which jump and when, but I can't shake the feeling that Saul could have stable points set in here. For that matter, General Merrick and his troops could have left listening devices. Jarvis claimed not to detect any, but I can't say I entirely trust him at this point, since he's part of the computer system they copied. The library feels tainted, and I'm not going to be comfortable making final plans here.

That's even more the case now that Saul flat-out admitted he could get bored of this scenario at any juncture. There's nothing to stop him from deciding fun and games are over, and if he knows exactly where and when we'll be, he'd be able to pick us off like fish in a fucking barrel.

Thinking of Rich's body in the basement makes me want to put my fist through the wall. What are we supposed to do? Leave him down there for three days while we're up here doing research? And yes, I know that at the end of this we'll jump back and prevent him from being shot. He will never have been reduced to a body in the basement, yielding to rigor mortis. But the knowledge that we intend to reverse it doesn't change the fact that we're still going to have to live through it until the game is over.

Even though Saul's knockoff SimMaster seemed to suggest that a Bircher becoming president in 1974 doesn't contribute to the timeline shift, I'm not buying it. Especially when that Bircher is also a Cyrist. That change might not have been a direct cause of the shift, but it's definitely connected. I'm tempted to cut the discussion short and tell everyone to start researching whichever event they intend to tackle once we've rescued the other infant.

I do, however, need to avoid letting Saul know that I suspect his game is rigged. Better to lay down a bit of cover. He assumes we'll prioritize getting the Sisters of Prudence to safety, and I'm not sure any of us would be able to convince him we're going to abandon innocent kids he tossed into the game just for shits and giggles. So I'll leave that bit in, but otherwise I'm going to shake things up. No point giving him a detailed itinerary to follow.

Once the others are gathered around, I say, "I suggest we mark off anything after the 1960s, based on our discussion last night. I also think we should ignore the Dark Day massacre for now. We got the baby Saul dropped off there and a decent idea of how things will unfold the next evening after watching the various stable points, so it's not a location where we need to jump in and do any sort of reconnaissance. And given that our prediction was a miss, the massacre at Potter's farm is apparently not something Saul changed."

"Um . . . unless he's *lying*?" Katherine says, with a confused look. "Yes, I know I've been the loudest proponent of Saul playing by the rules, but we've already established that he's cheating. Depositing the pawns, as he called them, at the various locations may have been an act of revenge for Thea killing his splinter, but he as much as admitted it had the added bonus of throwing a wrench into our machinery, because he *knows* we won't ignore them. If he'll lie about that, I'm less confident we can trust anything he says."

"Including his assurance that this house is safe for the time being?" Madi asks.

"Possibly. But do we have anywhere else to go, especially with two infants to worry about? Three, once we get the other one."

"*Truuue.*" I draw out the word and stare directly at Katherine as I speak, hoping she'll catch on. "But I really do think we should take the jumps in chronological order, starting with the *Book of Cyrus*. We know exactly when and where the book was first printed in the US, and the SimMaster said that event was a partial hit. So *as we said last night*, it's the most logical place to start." I shift my gaze to Clio and Madi as I speak, emphasizing words they should remember are not true in the slightest if they were paying attention last night. It takes a second or two, and I'm kind of wishing I'd stopped to slip them a note telling them what I was planning. But that would have been at least as obvious as this little charade, and we have no idea what vantage points Saul has for viewing this room. "After we locate the book," I continue, "we'll move on to Salzburg and investigate whether we can reasonably extract the sixteen-year-old he inserted into the execution schedule. And once we have all of them—"

"But that's *not* all of them," Madi says. "There are others."

That takes me by surprise. "I thought it was just the one in Salzburg."

"Sorry." Madi gives me an apologetic smile. "Guess I forgot that part when I was telling you what happened at the temple. Beta said another girl who was caring for the three infants is missing. One more, as well, and she mentioned a double memory about a fourth Sister from the group after her, Eta, who seems to have died as an infant . . . only Beta has a scar on her hand from a bite Eta gave her as a toddler. Another one was killed . . . but they took off her cuff, so she's truly gone, just like Thea."

"Do you think Saul could be going after all of the Pru clones?" Clio asks. "He said something about revenge even unto the fourth generation."

"Progenitors and descendants both," Katherine says. "So, yes. I think it's entirely possible."

"What do we know about this—" I stop short of asking about the Fifth Column group Madi mentioned earlier. "Do you think we can trust Beta and her *friend*?"

Everyone is quiet for a bit, all of us trying to figure out what we can safely say.

"I think so," Madi says hesitantly. She's again silent for a moment, but then continues, doing the same thing I did—enunciating a little too carefully with her voice a little too bright. "But we don't need to worry about that yet. If you and Clio are going to do the jump to locate the *Book of Cyrus* publisher, we need to figure out what you'll wear. There are a couple of costume trunks up in the attic. Why don't we go deal with that first? Grab a tablet in case you want to take notes."

I'm not sure what Madi's up to, but we do as we're told. Katherine goes over to print something out from the Anomalies Machine, and then we follow Madi down the hall to the front of the house. She opens a narrow door and tells Jarvis to turn on the lights and ventilation, then we head up to a partially finished attic.

"I thought about the patio," Madi says. "Or out in the yard, although it's kind of drizzly out there right now."

The attic floor is covered with padded exercise mats. One section is clear of junk, but otherwise, the room is pretty much filled with boxes. While there are two decent-sized windows, the day is dreary, and only a few feeble rays of sunlight get through.

"This is better," Katherine says. "I'm not convinced the patio and the yard are secure. Or if they are, I think Saul has a stable point in my bedroom. And he couldn't have known which one was my bedroom, so that would mean *all* of the bedrooms."

I decide it might be best not to ask how she came to that conclusion, mostly because I suspect it has something to do with Rich's cryptic comment as Clio and I were jumping out. Apparently, he owes me a bottle of Jim Beam, and he seemed really happy about it. I don't remember a bet involving bourbon, and I have no idea what the logistics of that wager would be. But the only way he'd be that pleased about *losing* a bet with me is if it somehow involved Katherine.

"I think this used to be a gym of some sort," Madi says as we begin shoving some of the boxes against the wall. "There are some old martial arts punching bags in the closet. Lorena said Thea used the room to meditate when she was here. Grandpa James seems to have been using it mostly to store signed copies of his books, but there are a couple of clothing trunks behind that partition we can look through later. Everything is in those sealed bags they use to store formal dresses. I haven't gone through them, but they look nineteenth century, so I'm guessing they were costumes created for Kate's jumps. No comm system up here, but if we need Jarvis I can use my wristband. There's also no furniture, unfortunately." She taps her commband. "Jarvis, can you please buzz me if the babies wake up."

Once we're settled on the mats, I begin, still keeping my voice low. "So . . . do you think we can trust this Fifth Column?"

Madi shrugs. "I don't know. Kate trusted them, although I think it may have been touch and go at first. And that was decades before the period we're talking about. Organizations can change a lot over time. People can, too. But the group did help defeat Saul during the first go-round. Kate mentioned Charlayne specifically in her diary. I think they were friends in more than one timeline."

"Do you think they might have access to a copy of the *Book of Prophecy*?" I ask. "The new edition. That would be a huge help in checking to see whether Alex's theory is right about Saul being able to engineer a lot of changes just by getting the book into the hands of key Cyrist leaders."

Madi seems skeptical. "Thea said the Sisters weren't given access to it. The Templars doled out occasional bits of prophecy to them the same way they do stock quotes to Cyrists who pay their tithes regularly. But the Fifth Column is apparently a separate entity, so I guess it's possible . . ."

"Can't hurt to ask." Katherine reaches into her pocket and pulls out a sheet of paper and a data drive about half the length of her pinky. "Charlayne gave me this. Said it had coordinates where we could reach her. I was worried we wouldn't have a computer that could read it, but the Anomalies Machine has a USB port. Just a single file on it, so I printed it out. The geographic section of the coordinates seems to put it about forty miles from downtown DC. Roughly fifteen miles north-northwest of Gaithersburg."

The file is another long string of coordinates, with the last section indicating a date and time—10 p.m. on July 12, 2058, about nine hours after Katherine and Madi left the temple. Below that is a single sentence. *Bring the babies once you locate them.*

Madi takes the printout with the coordinates from Katherine. "You've got to admire her confidence. I mean, if Charlayne had any doubts about getting Beta out of the temple and safely to this location, she'd have given us a time *before* that meeting, and she definitely wouldn't be telling us to bring the babies."

"She might just be smart enough not to want to deal with double memories," Katherine says. "Should we wait until we have all three?"

I think about it for a minute. "We'll get the third baby to safety more quickly if we're not having to worry about childcare arrangements. The only question is whether we can trust the Fifth Column. Is it possible we'd be handing the babies back over to Saul? They're Cyrists, right?"

"Yes," Madi says. "Or at least, they're an offshoot. Reformed Rite, or New Cyrists. Kate called them Cyrist Light. But neither Beta nor Charlayne seemed particularly fond of the founder of their religion, based on our conversations today."

"My dad might be able to give us some insight on this group," Clio says. "I don't know that he ever mentioned anyone named Charlayne, but he definitely mentioned the Fifth Column. Do you think Saul would consider it *material interference* if I drop in for a little chat with my family in Skaneateles? He said the Sisters have nothing to do with the game itself, so it doesn't sound like it should be an issue to me. One of you can tag along, if you want, but given the amount of research we need to do . . ."

The general consensus is that it shouldn't be a risk. It bothers me, though. I can't put my finger on why, and I'm definitely not going to push it. I'm the only guy on the team now, and even if they're the ones who wanted me in the leadership role instead of Katherine, I'm pretty sure I'm going to be on thin ice if I start acting like I think the three of them are anything less than capable. And I really *don't* think that, so I just nod and tell Clio to try to keep the visit short.

"Will do. If you start the actual divvying up of assignments while I'm gone, be sure to put me on the concert in California."

I'm a little surprised. If anything, I'd have thought she'd want the ones from the twenties and thirties.

"Why?" I ask.

"Because I spent a couple of weeks in San Francisco in 1967." It's hard to tell in the dim light, but I think she's blushing. "I . . . um . . . let's just say I know one of the bands."

After Clio blinks out, Katherine laughs. "I have a feeling there's an interesting story behind that last statement."

I suspect she's right. I'm not entirely sure I want the details, though. That realization catches me a bit off guard, but I push it aside and open our list on the tablet.

Madi looks at the list and shakes her head. "There's so much on here. I'm torn between thinking we need to use the buddy system and thinking we should split up on these initial intelligence-gathering trips. Some of them are fairly long-distance jumps, at least in chrono-logical terms. The last thing we need is for one of us to get stranded because we've overextended and can't use the key."

"You're probably right. Well, except for Clio. She'll need to be with one of us, since we can't give her a weapon and I don't like the idea of any of us being out there totally unarmed. But I'm hoping we can narrow it down and we won't have to make all of these jumps anyway. Priority one—aside from finding the other baby—is getting our hands on a copy of the *Book of Prophecy*. That may tell us exactly how much of this Saul was able to outsource to his true believers. Jemima Wilkinson might have a copy of the book."

"So your comment that we should mark it off the list was to throw Saul off the scent," Katherine says. "But why do you think they have a copy?"

"Wilkinson's people recognized Clio. They recited something that sounded like scripture, but I checked. It's not in the *Book of Cyrus*, or at least not any version I can find. I can't remember it verbatim, but it was super specific. Referenced the Dark Day and said Prudence would steal a beast in a woven cage. The girl said it was from the Friend's last prophecy."

Madi says, "According to Kate's diaries, only Grand Templars had a copy, and you needed the little disk behind your ear in order to operate it. But . . . that iteration of Cyrist International was mostly using the *Book of Prophecy* to hand out stock tips when Saul had a bunch of offspring who could operate the equipment. He doesn't have that sort of backup now, to the best of our knowledge. And he seems to be using the prophecies to do more than simply enrich the faithful. Maybe his goals are different this time."

"Yeah. So, even though we've rescued the baby, I think I'm going to need to go back in at some point before the jumps Clio and I made. And I should probably go without Clio this time, since she seems to set off Prudaean alarm bells."

"I'll go," Katherine says. "If we hadn't been worried about the slight possibility of me crossing paths with Earlier-Me and Saul, I'd have gone the first time. I've spent several months in the 1700s, so if I encounter anyone, I can blend in. I already know the layout of the house, including where the Friend's study is."

"Okay. That makes sense. You and I will handle this one while Madi and Clio do the meeting with the Fifth Column."

"It really makes more sense for me to go alone. Five-foot me is far less threatening than six-foot you. It's an in-and-out job, and one person can move more stealthily than two."

I look to Madi for support, and I get none. "If you're worried about her using a weapon, she proved herself in Memphis. If Katherine hadn't shot that guy, there's a damn good chance neither of us would be here."

"It's not that I don't think she can handle it." Because Katherine is still glaring at me, I decide to quit beating around the bush and just say it. "You're right, okay? I'm being overprotective. But I know that if I get to the end of this and manage to save Rich, he's not going to view me undoing his murder as a favor if I have to tell him we lost you in the process."

Her anger evaporates, but it seems to take most of her energy along with it. She leans forward, elbows on her knees, and rests her forehead in her hands. "I'll have a weapon, Tyce. If I have to, I'll shoot. But I'm not going to run into anyone. All I need to do is blink in and check the Friend's study when the household is out at Inscription Rock for the Sunday sermon."

"But wouldn't the Friend take the *Book* when preaching?" Madi asks.

Katherine gives us a tiny, slightly smug smile. "Not unless something has changed drastically. The Friend was renowned for a remarkable knowledge of scripture. Even those who detested Wilkinson noted that the sermons were recited entirely from memory. And Saul's books are tiny compared to the Bible. If the Friend has a copy, it will either be in the study or the bedroom."

"Will the costume Clio wore fit you?" Madi asks.

Katherine glances down at her chest. "The bodice might be a little loose. But I've already seen myself in that apron."

I'm about to ask where, but then it occurs to me that she's talking about the jump to Hatteras.

"It didn't really match the dress I was wearing," she continues, "but it made sense after I saw Clio using the apron as a makeshift baby carrier. I'm just baffled at Saul's comment that I'm the only one who can retrieve them, since I didn't have anything to do with rescuing the baby from Potter's farm."

"No, but there was something in the verse Wilkinson recited . . . *Fear not the fair-headed woman*, or something like that. It was the first part of the prophecy about the beast in the basket. Saul probably set up something similar on Hatteras Island. Do either of you remember the name of the place on the flyer Rich mentioned?"

They don't, but it's easy enough to check on the key, since we know the date. Once we find that it's Melcher's, Madi has Jarvis check for any businesses under that name in 1923. There are two stores with that name in the early 1930s, but no information prior to that. One is about a mile away from the stable point, and the other about four miles away. Hopefully, it's the closer one. There's no public transportation, so I'm either going to have to hoof it or go in at a later date when it's possible to hire a taxi, set the stable point, and then jump back to 1923.

We're discussing logistics when Clio blinks in, carrying two shopping bags and a large duffel. She tosses the duffel onto one of the crates along the wall. "Costumes. The sixties and seventies items are based on my mom's memories of old TV shows, but they look pretty close to me. Cash from the mid-1920s, some older bills my dad got from a collector, and some from the 1950s, which is the most recent I had. We're definitely going to need money for some of these jumps. I also have a key to my dad's hunting cabin in Georgia. We vacationed there twice, so he set it up with the field extenders. There's running water and electricity. Way too early for computers, of course. He called the caretakers and told them that his daughter and her friends might be staying there for a few days. We can use it as a rendezvous point."

"But . . . why?" Katherine asks. "We can come up here when we need privacy."

"Saul said the game console would be able to detect if we double back. And we may need to double back if one of us doesn't show up when we're supposed to, so we can tell them not to make that jump." She drops onto the floor next to me with the paper bag. "And this is *food*, because I'll starve if I have to live off the stuff that unit downstairs spits out. Bread, ham, butter, eggs, my dad's macaroni and cheese—which is the best you will ever eat—and some other odds and ends." She grabs five paper-wrapped sandwiches from the top and hands them out, then pushes the bag aside.

"How long did all of this take?" I ask. "I'm guessing your parents don't have costumes from thirty years in the future stashed away in their closets."

"It took me fifteen minutes, which is the exact amount of time I've been gone. Of course, they had everything packaged up and waiting for me," she says around a bite of her sandwich. "I made a jump to the previous month and left a list with my mom, so they'd have time to get everything we need."

I'm really tempted to follow her down this rabbit hole, but I'm pretty sure I'll enjoy lunch a lot more if she doesn't go into specifics, so I unwrap my sandwich and take a bite. It is, in fact, the best thing I've eaten since the pecan pancakes in Memphis, so I wait until I've polished off the last of it to ask her what Kiernan had to say about the Fifth Column.

"Mixed opinion of the group as a whole," she says. "He told me quite a few of the members he knew were bureaucrats who nearly got him killed, but he doesn't think they'd have stopped the Culling without them. As for Charlayne herself . . . he said she's okay. Said she once held him at gunpoint for a couple of hours, and he was pretty sure we could trust her."

"That seems a little . . . contradictory," Katherine says.

Clio shrugs. "She's a Cyrist, but not the crazy kind. At least in that timeline, although if she's wearing a cuff like Madi said, she should remember everything that happened. Dad also said we could leave the babies in Skaneateles if we're uneasy about the Fifth Column, but I don't feel comfortable pulling my family in any further unless it's our only option. And don't look at me like that, Tyson. There's a world of difference between me bringing back some clothes and a bag of food and us dropping off three of Saul's pawns for them to babysit."

She's right, although she conveniently left out the fact that they're also bankrolling our operation if there's cash in that duffel, plus we're already borrowing the field extender. I'm quite certain Saul would see both of those as active participation.

"It's nice of them to offer," Madi says, "but assuming it's safe, we need to get the babies back to the other Sisters as soon as possible. That's their home. Okay, that's not quite right, since we're taking them to 2058, and I'm pretty sure their *actual* date of birth is still a few months from now, based on something Thea said. But the other Sisters are their family."

A slight shadow falls over Katherine's face, but she nods in agreement.

Clio, who has been looking at the list of anomalies, pushes the tablet aside. "Here's what I don't get. Why is there so little alteration of the timeline early on? I mean, we do see changes eventually, but apparently Saul dropped his nasty little books centuries before they kick in. You have scattered witch hunts, but there aren't many significant historical anomalies until the 1970s. You'd think this sort of change to a major religion would shake up the timeline a bit earlier. People were killed in those witch hunts."

"I guess the question is how many of the people killed would be flagged by the Anomalies Machine as significant to the timeline," I say. "Take Salzburg, for example. The witch hunts were used to purge people that the village or town didn't want around anyway, right? You only have a few historical figures who were killed. The rest weren't deaths that would be marked as significant."

"But you have people believing in *witches* the entire time," Madi says. "Actual witch hunts happening centuries after they died out. Surely that kind of change in the culture should have some ripple effects."

"Again," Katherine says, "was it really that big of a change? These seem to have been fairly isolated incidents. And remember what I said about my Temporal Dilemma game with Saul? Even in eras we like to think of as technologically advanced, there is still a whole lot of magical thinking. Moon-landing deniers. Flat-earthers. They don't want to believe in science. They want a simpler explanation. One they can understand. They want magic. Want to believe that a coven of witches hexed their business. That a demon is the reason they can't budget or lose weight."

"But how is a world based on magic or sorcery a simpler world?" Madi asks.

Katherine thinks for a moment and then says, "Your food replicator. Do you know how it works?"

"Aside from not very well? Not really. I know there's a laser, and it separates particles and antiparticles."

"But *how* does it do that? Not to put you on the spot, because I can't give you a full explanation, either. And when you move to something really complex like the CHRONOS technology . . . you need a scientist to explain it, right? Someone like Alex or Lorena. But how adept are either of them at explaining their area of specialty in terms you or I can understand? Now, consider someone with only a very rudimentary grasp of basic science concepts and think how much more difficult it might be for them. Saul's theory was that eras of rapid technological change inevitably create a backlash. People might not exactly think of their televisions or their microwave ovens as magic machines . . . but without a solid grasp of science, they come to accept their function in much the same way they believe in religious miracles or anything else they can't explain. Magical thinking is the human default setting."

"That's a bit like one of Clarke's Three Laws. The third one." Madi gets only blank looks from us, so she adds, "Arthur C. Clarke. Science-fiction author from the mid-twentieth century. And I'm paraphrasing, but the law is something like any very sophisticated technology is indistinguishable from magic."

"Makes sense," I say. "People are surrounded by these marvels that are, simply put, beyond their comprehension . . . at least without putting in a whole lot more effort than the average Joe is willing to expend. Or, really, *able* to expend, when they have jobs and kids and so forth that take up most of their waking hours. In the face of so many things they can't explain, they become more willing to accept *other* things they can't explain. Miracles, magic, wild conspiracies, superstition of every sort. The question, then, is what changed in the 1970s? What pushed these fringe beliefs about the occult into the mainstream? Why do we wind up with a conspiracy nut in the White House whose only claim to fame is that he killed a bunch of cult members?"

"He also seemed . . . lucky," Clio says. "Think about what RJ told us. McDonald gets information about the cult before the police do. And he just happens to switch parties right before Nixon needs a running mate. Nixon finds out about the other guy's corruption earlier this time, too . . . what's his name, the VP . . ."

"Agnew," I say. "You're right. And in my experience, anyone with that kind of advance knowledge usually has access to a CHRONOS key."

"Or access to a *Book of Prophecy*," Katherine says. "Speaking of, we don't need everyone on this discussion. Transfer the stable points you set at Potter's farm to my key, so I can start scanning through to find a good time for me to jump in and see if Wilkinson has a copy."

I transfer the stable points, even though I'm not done arguing about her going in solo. She drags one of the mats off a few feet and pulls up the interface.

Madi has Jarvis send photographs of Larry McDonald to her tablet. The images are small, and I'm debating whether it's worth the risk to go downstairs to view them when Madi flicks her finger upward and a holographic screen appears above the tablet. I didn't realize it could do that, but then my experience with pre-2300s tech falls into two distinct categories—tiny TVs with rabbit ears on top that Glen and I watched during field training and the setup Alex has in the library. This isn't as clear or as large as the wall screen, but it's a lot better than the three of us huddling around the tablet.

She expands the screen a bit and begins scrolling slowly through the pictures. None of them shows anyone with a CHRONOS key. No sign of Saul, either, but I guess that would have been a bit too easy.

The pictures of McDonald as president look a bit like a younger, doughier Ronald Reagan. We isolate the earlier photos, and sure enough, there's one of him outside what looks like the set of a Western movie. He has a rifle strapped over his shoulder as he mugs for the camera. Two men in khaki uniforms carry a stretcher with a body the paper identifies as Charles Manson toward one of the jeeps parked in the background of the photo.

Newspaper photos of the raid on the Process Church of Divine Revelation in 1970 don't show McDonald himself, but there's a grainy image of a woman who looks a bit like one of the Pru clones. We start hunting for more, but then Madi remembers that the group specifically co-opted the Prudence character from the Cyrist mythology. Any woman filling that role would have to resemble Pru to some extent, so we go back to skimming through the pictures of McDonald himself.

Another shows him at the 1968 John Birch Society national convention. He's one of the younger members in the group photo, which is mostly old white men, along with a smattering of old white women. I'm about to move on to one of the others when a face at the end of the table catches my eye, partly because it's a shade darker than the rest of the attendees.

He's older than when I last saw him on the upper level of Madison Square Garden in 1939. He now wears a clerical collar instead of a tie, with the familiar ankh-like shape of the Cyrist cross hanging below it. It's the simplified version with the straight arms. The photo is black and white, so I can't be certain, but the center seems to be glowing.

"That's Lawrence Dennis," I tell the others. "The old guy sitting next to McDonald at the end of the table."

Clio raises an eyebrow. "Are you sure? I thought you said you searched for him?"

"I did."

She reaches forward and expands the screen to the maximum so we can read the text beneath the photo.

"He's going by Lonnie Dennis," I say. "Lonnie is the first name he used as a boy evangelist. Only now it's Grand Templar Lonnie Dennis. And unless that's a weird reflection on the Cyrist symbol he's wearing, I'm pretty sure he's under a CHRONOS field. Although that still doesn't explain how he recognized me in the previous timeline. He definitely wasn't under a key then."

Katherine rejoins the group. "We may have a problem. Whatever you did at Potter's farm changed the timeline. Or changed it back, I guess. That farmhouse is still standing the next day. No fire. No mob. I scanned through the entire day from around noon until daybreak the next day . . . Still pretty dreary, but there's some sunlight coming through the haze."

I pull up one of the stable points. It's not that I don't believe her. But I spent hours yesterday watching that attack. Watching the mob kill literally everyone who lived on that farm.

"The only one who dies is the daughter," Katherine says. "And she was *supposed* to die, so whatever Saul may have done in the past that saved her, he didn't bother this time. Or maybe it really *was* something I did. There are a lot more people at the funeral service than there were when Saul and I attended, but . . . no one is killed. For some reason, they seem to have decided the Friend isn't at fault for the sun disappearing."

Clio barks out a laugh. "We gave them a scapegoat! They saw two so-called witches vanish in the woods after fulfilling the Friend's prophecy. Instead of blaming the Dark Day on the Friend, they could blame it on Prudence and her evil accomplice stealing the basket with the beast, or whatever that prophecy said. The guys on horseback witnessed it, and I'm pretty sure they'd stop in at the Little Rest Inn to share that story. And then the innkeeper tells them the witch was in earlier, eating pandowdy and drinking cider."

"This shouldn't cause any problems with the game, right?" Madi asks. "The Dark Day massacre wasn't one of Saul's moves. We entered it into the system, but it wasn't a hit. So changing it shouldn't count against us."

She's right. It shouldn't count against us. But I have a feeling Saul isn't going to like the fact that the mayhem he took pains to create has sorted itself out.

FROM THE FILES OF THE
FIFTH COLUMN

KEY CHANGES IN CYRISISM

While no known first editions of the European printing of the *Book of Cyrus* exist today, six regional temples for Cyrist International have copies that are centuries old, as do several major library archives. A copy held at the Beinecke Rare Book and Manuscript Library was acquired by Yale University in 1852 with a note that it was printed in the late 1500s, but this date must be false, as a recent chemical analysis revealed it to be printed on acid-free paper. (We have personally conducted an examination of the copy in the library at the Sixteenth Street Temple, and it is also on acid-free paper.) All early editions of the *Book of Cyrus* have long been noted to be in excellent condition for books printed centuries ago, so while the official conclusion is that the Yale copy was stolen and replaced with a forgery, we suspect these books were actually printed in the mid-20th century once acid-free paper was widely available, and then deposited in the past by someone in possession of a CHRONOS key.

Two of the copies held by regional temples are identical to the one at Yale, but the other four (as well as editions in other libraries) contain a variety of textual differences, some significant. In one of these versions, the figure of Prudence is omitted entirely, suggesting some difference of opinion among early Cyrists as to whether these sections are canon or were, as some religious scholars suspect, added in the early days of the religion in an effort to restrain the power of one or more female clerics.

A far simpler explanation is that these copies were kept within range of a CHRONOS field—either a key, a diary, or some form of field extender—when changes were made to the timeline. The fact that there are several variations suggests there have been multiple revisions. A book under a CHRONOS field would be protected and therefore would not reflect any alterations made to the original text.

∞11∞

The room, which appears to be another study, is empty when we arrive. There are two doorways, one fully open and the other slightly ajar. Otherwise, the walls are floor-to-ceiling bookshelves. Most of the shelves have inset lamps that looked almost like candlelight when I viewed the location through the key. The lighting on the holographic interface is usually a bit off compared to the actual location, slightly darker or lighter, possibly because they—or *we*, I guess—needed to optimize the view in order for the link to show up more clearly.

Now that I'm here, however, I'd almost guarantee that the lights are produced by a CHRONOS field, like the shelves in the library back at the house in Bethesda. The sight is comforting, although I don't think it's just because it feels like home. Right now our library doesn't feel especially homey to me given the sense that we're being watched. But I do feel a bit of kinship with whoever owns this house, because they're also making an effort to protect books from alternate timelines.

I move out of the stable point so Clio can jump in, taking a few steps toward the doorway that leads into a large living room. Again, the room reminds me vaguely of my house, which is odd. Our library is on the second floor, so if you catch a glimpse of the living room through the open door, you're looking down.

The baby is crying when Clio blinks in. She has her tucked inside the apron and clutched to her chest. The field extender is flush against the baby's back.

"She was wide awake, unfortunately. I think it's easier on them when they're sleepy," she says.

"Oh, my goodness!" Beta scurries into the room and takes the crying baby from Clio, smiling from ear to ear as she stares down into a tiny face that will, about five decades from now, be identical to her own. She tugs up the blanket to check the anklet tattoo and then calls toward the living room. "They found Phi!"

Her smile fades when she looks back at us. "You weren't able to locate the others?"

"I'm going back for another one." Clio leans forward, placing her hands on her knees as she pulls in deep breaths. She's a bit green around the gills. "Just give me a second to recover."

I offer to take the device and go instead, but Clio shakes her head.

"I'll be fine. It takes a while to get the hang of using this thing. By the time I show you how, I could be there and back."

"Okay. But you look like that ham sandwich is about to make an emergency exit."

Clio gives me a weak grin. "I'm a child of the Great Depression. We don't waste good food." She snaps her key out of the device, centers it in her palm, and blinks out.

"We're still working on getting the third baby," I tell Beta. "But we decided to go ahead and bring these two because I'm not sure our place is safe. When Katherine and I got back earlier today, my roommates had been taken hostage. One of our team members is dead. Well . . . temporarily. We'll go back and change that once this is over. But the new situation means we can't keep the babies there. So we were really glad to get your message."

Beta looks confused. "What message?"

"The one Charlayne Singleton gave to Katherine. It said to bring the babies. Is Charlayne here?"

"Not here in the house. But she's somewhere in the compound," she adds quickly, probably in response to my disappointed expression. "And she'll be here soon. Maybe I can help?"

She looks hopeful, and truthfully, she'll probably know the answer as well as Charlayne would. I just tend to mentally tag her as being Thea, and most of the time, asking Thea a question resulted in a conversational journey that could last hours. You might get an answer eventually, but there would be many circuitous loops and barely relevant anecdotes along the way. Beta seemed a little flustered earlier today, but she apparently knew they were about to evacuate the temple, so maybe I can get a straight answer.

"We're trying to find a copy of the *Book of Prophecy*. The new version, I mean." I glance around at the protected bookshelves. "Do you by any chance have one?"

She begins laughing before I can finish the question. "No. No, no, no," she says as she heads toward the partially shut door. "We were never given a copy of that holy of holies, even in the timelines where Saul had some use for us. They just doled out what information they thought we needed. We didn't even get the quarterly lottery tickets. And now . . ."

"And now he's revamped the entire religion to exclude them."

I turn toward the voice. A woman is in the doorway to the living room, seated on a mobility scooter. My first thought is that it's another one of the Sisters. But she's older than Beta, and there are subtle differences in her face. "Kate?"

She smiles. "I'm afraid you have me at a disadvantage. Although judging from that key in your hand, I'm going to guess that you're Madi and we've met in your past and my future. Or maybe . . ." Now it's her turn to look stunned. I'm not sure why until I glance over my shoulder and see Clio is back, struggling to get the second baby out of the makeshift carrier. She looks even more queasy than she did earlier, which isn't really surprising.

"Madi, can you—" Clio glances up, probably to ask me for help with the straps. When she catches sight of Kate, however, she freezes, with the field extender under one arm and the baby, who is now crying, half in and half out of her apron. "Mom? What the bloody hell . . ."

For a moment, the two of them stare at each other. And then Clio shakes her head. "*Not* Mom. You're Other-Kate." She turns to me. "I thought you said she wasn't around in this timeline."

"No, that was the *last* timeline." I turn back to Kate, who is wheeling her way into the library. Now that she's out of the shadow of the doorway, I see that her right leg is stretched out in front of her in a blue cast reaching to just below the knee. "I've been too busy to scroll through and see if you were ever in the Bethesda house, but Nora exists, so I knew you had to be somewhere. I've seen you in the house in other timelines, though. Even thought about jumping in to ask if you had some advice on how to fix my screwups. That was when you are older than this, but . . ."

"But not in a wheelchair?" Kate gives me a shaky smile. "The chair is a very recent addition. And yes, I lived in that house until a few weeks ago when we became aware of the timeline changes. We held off that first time when the Vietnam War changed. But I told Trey that if things went haywire again, we'd need to clear out and relocate here. My brain isn't quite as nimble at sixty as it was at sixteen. It's harder to snap back from these stupid time shifts. And that's doubly true for those around here who didn't inherit the gene. If not for Trey, I'd have left that damn key in the dresser drawer long ago. But he was kind of partial to the idea of me not blinking out of existence, so . . ."

As she's speaking, I take the second baby from Clio, who is still holding her at an odd angle. It's almost as if she's forgotten about her, which is hard to fathom, since the baby is now wailing at the top of her tiny lungs.

Kate rolls her chair into the room. Her head is cocked slightly to one side as she looks at Clio, who has collapsed into one of the desk chairs. "I'm guessing people have told you your entire life that you are equal parts your mother and father. Are they well in your time? I mean, I know they were in the timeline I remember best. One of your great-great . . . and maybe another great? . . . grandnephews paid us a visit, along with his mother, to hand over the keys and a photograph album. I remember the picture where a sketch of yours won a blue ribbon. That's definitely a talent you inherited from Kiernan. I can barely draw a stick figure. Do you still paint, Cliona?"

"It's Clio." Her voice sounds a little defensive. Is it because Kate used her full name? I've only heard her father call her that. "Haven't had much time for art the past few years. Hopefully, I'll be able to get back to it again once we finish the son of a bitch off. For *good* this time."

There's a hint of judgment in Clio's voice, a not-so-subtle reminder that Kate and company didn't entirely finish him. I want to point out that it's unfair, but I'm also trying to calm a frantic infant.

"I couldn't agree more," Kate says to Clio. "Although I would note that this Saul isn't, strictly speaking, the same Saul we faced. That one was killed and erased. I can't take credit for either of those achievements, but I was there to witness Prudence yank his key. The mistake I made, as a seventeen-year-old, was believing that the cycle wouldn't start again. No, *believing* isn't the right word. Hoping. Even then, deep down, I knew there was a very good chance it would happen again, but I had no idea how we could stop it. All we could do was stay vigilant in case it did and do our part to help fix it. And even if you manage to defeat him, you'll run that risk as well, unless you find a way to prevent CHRONOS from being created."

"That might not even be enough," I say. "Saul is the problem right now, but . . . the last two time shifts were caused by jumpers coming in from other timelines."

She sighs. "Then Dr. Tilson's suspicions were correct. Ben is going to be bummed. Not just that he lost the bet. Tilson isn't around anymore to collect anyway. But also because this complicates the plan we were working on."

I bounce up and down on my toes like I've seen Clio do, hoping the motion will calm the baby. I don't seem to have the knack, though. Kate gives us a sympathetic look.

"Poor little thing," she says. "I never had the misfortune of traveling with that extender, but everyone I know who did said it was horrible. Are you okay, Clio?"

She nods. "Still a little queasy, but it's beginning to fade."

Beta comes in to take the other baby. At least, I think it's Beta, but her dress seems different. She gives me a smile and a nod, then heads back to the side door.

"I'm fairly certain that was Gamma," Kate says. "She's the quiet one. And no, I have no idea if it's a personality thing or if she assumes Beta has already said whatever they needed to convey. We should go into the living room. Charlayne and Ben will be here soon."

"We're *really* short on time," Clio says.

"She's right. We were supposed to drop off the babies, see if you have a copy of the *Book of Prophecy*, and get back. As I was telling Beta, Saul has some of our people hostage, and he's already killed one member of our team."

"I'm sorry to hear that," Kate says. "We've . . . lost some people recently, too, and we're very much looking forward to you flipping this timeline so we can get them back. I promise we'll keep it short. We don't have the book here in our library, but Charlayne and Bensen have some information that may give you an idea of where to find a copy. Charlayne would have been here already, but as I mentioned, we've had some security issues of our own and she needed to check on the guards along the perimeter."

"Along the perimeter of . . . what?" I ask.

"This compound. We have about twenty-five acres. Seven buildings. Kiernan would probably joke that we rebuilt the Cyrist Farm, but none of the people living here were Orthodox Cyrists, even before the last revision of Saul's nasty little book." She looks back at the stable point. "Is Katherine joining us?"

I shake my head. "Sorry. She and Tyson are doing some preliminary research so we can rescue the third baby as soon as we leave here. I can bring her next time, if you'd like."

She laughs nervously. "To be perfectly honest, I don't know if it's a good idea or not. I met the younger version years ago when Clio's dad and I were trying to find our way out of a burning hotel run by a madman. From what I recall, younger Katherine was kind of snippy. And . . . I'm fairly certain she never actually becomes my grandmother if things go the way they have to go in order to end this. It might be better to keep her kinder, gentler version first and foremost in my memory."

Of course, that reminds me I'm in the same boat. Nora never becomes my grandmother in this reality or, most likely, in any other. That thought was hard enough to move past yesterday in my nonexistent garden when my head was on Jack's shoulder and we were staring up at the clouds. Hard enough to deal with when I could hold on to the fact that I still had *him*.

I've pulled up the stable point I set on the first day when I was demonstrating the key to Jack and Alex at least twenty times in the past few hours, wondering if it's worth the risk to jump back and warn him. To leave a note somewhere in the house where I know he'll find it, cautioning him about his dad. Because Saul could easily be bluffing. Katherine even seemed skeptical that the SimMaster could detect whether we loop back on our own timeline.

What stops me is the fear that things could go even worse this time. Jack left the basement in handcuffs, but he was alive. Unharmed. The guy who shot Rich could have a new set of instructions if I break the rules. Next time, there could be two bodies on the floor. Or three, if Jack's dad actually cares enough about his son to try to save him.

"Should we follow or tell her we need to go?" Clio whispers. "The clock's ticking. We could come back later."

I get the sense that this is less about the clock ticking and more about Clio feeling odd around this alternative version of her mother. And I do sympathize. I have a similar reaction to the various versions of Thea running around. "Let's give them five minutes. They may be able to help us find a *Book of Prophecy*, and maybe they can tell us more about this Lawrence Dennis guy."

It's not really the quantity of information about him that we're lacking, but rather the context to place him in. There are multiple books in the public data system written by Lonnie Dennis, Grand Templar of the North American region for Cyrist International. He had a weekly radio show until the early 1950s, and after that, he hosted a ten-minute devotional that played on many TV stations at the end of each broadcast day. His weekly sermons from the Sixteenth Street Temple were televised as well, and there's an entire archive of them online in the HomeBase files that are open access. A younger, more telegenic assistant Templar takes over the routine broadcasts in the mid-1960s, but Dennis retains the title and seems to shift more into political activism. Tyson says it's pretty much the same sorts of causes Dennis worked for as a fascist writer—fighting communism and promoting nationalism and a strong defense. The only real difference is that he's added the religious trappings.

"The Fifth Column," I prompt. "You mentioned the group in your diary, but I thought they disbanded."

"Oh, no." Kate shakes her head. "They were less . . . structured in that first timeline after we stopped the Culling, but they still existed.

I'll admit I had mixed feelings about the whole cloning thing when I realized what they were doing." She glances at the door to the study and lowers her voice a bit. "In my experience, one Prudence at a time was one too many. But my mother convinced me it was one way we could ensure some degree of influence in case there were additional changes to the timeline. My only concern was that they made certain they couldn't actually jump, and they seem to have solved that. The Sisters provide continuity. Having a new crop every generation is sort of a backup in case the Fifth Column doesn't survive. It gives us institutional memory, as the bureaucrats put it."

The front door opens as she's speaking and Charlayne enters, laughing. "We step out for ten minutes and you start bad-mouthing us."

Kate rolls her eyes. "You carry a rifle. You're no bureaucrat. Ben, on the other hand . . ."

Two men follow Charlayne inside. Both are middle-aged. One is slightly pudgy with South Asian features. He's holding the arm of a black man, who carries a cane and seems to be a bit unsteady on his feet. All of them are wearing cuffs like the one on my arm.

Once they're seated, Kate makes introductions. "This is Charlayne's husband, Dr. Bensen Raji," she says, nodding toward the stockier man. He gives me a little wave, and I realize his hand has the same version of the lotus tattoo as Charlayne's—not the typical blue that a Cyrist male would wear, but a slight amber glow.

"Ben is our science guru," Kate adds. "This other gentleman is Stanford Fuller. Stan is a recent addition to our community."

I smile and nod as I try to puzzle out where I've heard that name before.

"And this is Madison Grace, one of the three people who . . ." Kate trails off, and I'm sure she's going to say something rather uncomplimentary but not really unwarranted, given my role in all of this. "Who is technically one of the inventors of this lovely technology," she continues dryly, touching the key around her neck, "although I guess we can't hold this version of her responsible. The other young lady is Clio Dunne. Ben and Charlayne, you haven't met Clio in person, but she *was* in the van with us, sort of, when we rescued Mom and Katherine from the temple."

Charlayne leans in and looks more closely at Clio's face. "Dunne? As in *Kiernan Dunne*? Well, I'll be damned."

"Exactly," Kate says. "These two young ladies are in a bit of a rush, I'm afraid, since this is all connected to one of Saul's games. When you walked in, I was just explaining why the Fifth Column continued after the Culling."

Charlayne sits down on one of the stools at the counter that divides the living room from the kitchen. "It's like Dr. Tilson said at the very first meeting I attended. Pandora's box has been opened. Once the government knew time travel was doable, it was inevitable that we'd eventually get an administration stupid enough to imagine the possibilities without considering the consequences. The government still had several keys in its possession, despite our best efforts to destroy them. Kate knew that, so she kept her key . . . even beyond the point where she or any of our other people had the ability to use it. And further down the pike we knew there was a group of three people out there who were . . . destined? That's not really the right word, but it's all I've got, so yeah, *destined* to create the technology that would eventually lead to CHRONOS. Which might lead to Saul or someone like him, and the cycle would start again."

"At first, the Fifth Column's goal was to stay organized at least through the mid-twenty-second century so we could prevent your group from forming." Ben gives me a grim smile. He doesn't actually say *by any means necessary*, but the words hover in the air, nonetheless. "It seemed a bit too . . . optimistic, though, to think we'd know the right moment or the right way to prevent the project from happening. I mean, if you guys didn't invent it, someone else eventually would. So we shifted gears. We can't reasonably hope to prevent every temporal physicist from developing the technology, so we decided the next best thing would be to control it. Or try to."

"We soon realized that we had an ally in Prudence," Charlayne says, "although not a particularly stable one. Simply put, Saul is a common enemy. And when Cyrist International decided to explore cloning as an alternative to time travel for keeping up the image of a youthful Sister Prudence, the Fifth Column again shifted gears and became the security arm for the Sisters. In addition to our research on the CHRONOS technology, of course."

"So, you're doing temporal physics research here at the compound?" I ask.

Ben snorts. "Not here. We're pretty low-tech, so the work continues at university labs. Most of it would have been funded by the government in previous timelines, but the Fifth Column funneled money through some private donors, trying to keep the research afloat. In the previous timeline, I was employed at the same lab where your friend Alex would eventually have worked. And I can see you're wondering how I know that . . ."

I was wondering precisely that, but then I remember the messages in the diary. "Thea or one of the others told you. That's how you kept track of when Alex was at the point where he might be able to reverse engineer the keys. Or . . . understand them, I guess."

Ben and the other guy exchange a look, and then Ben says, "Yes and no. We've obviously been attempting to speed things up." He looks a little uncomfortable on that front, although I suspect the decision to have Thea's daughter meet and marry my dad was well above his pay grade. And while I probably should resent that intrusion in my genetics to some extent, I'm glad I'm me. Plus, is it really so different from the genetic manipulation that produced Katherine and the others at CHRONOS?

"A few weeks ago," he continues, "right after we felt the most recent shift, I discovered my department at Georgetown had moved to an entirely different building. I'm not even employed there any-more. We do have one Fifth Column member who's still on the inside in a clerical position and a dozen or so members scattered throughout the government, two of them in fairly high-level positions. And one of those put me in touch with Stan, who has been studying multiple timelines his entire life."

The name clicks then. "You're the author of *Many Paths*. Or something like that."

Fuller smiles and says, "*The Physics of Many Paths*, yes. Although I'm not a physicist."

"Alex read your book. And Kate mentioned it in her diary." I turn to look at her.

"But that may not have happened yet."

"Well, it's definitely happened already in this timeline," she says. "The book went on everyone's reading list as soon as Stan contacted us."

"Your description of the paths reminded me of Alex's display," I tell Stan. "Well, one version of it. Did you ever see the display with the different cables that showed the timelines and their various off-shoots?" I ask Clio.

She nods. Her expression is a little confused, however, so I'm not sure she was there when Alex explained it. Although, she may well have been there and simply didn't follow it any better than I did. Plus, Clio may have more experience with the keys, but were physicists even discussing things like the Many-Worlds Interpretation in her time?

Fuller leans forward. "These offshoots you're talking about. Do they sort of unravel off the main timeline? Like the ones you call splinters that eventually fade out?"

"Some of them," I say. "But others are fully formed. Alex col-or-coded the ones that seem to be on similar frequencies. The one conversation I had with him when he was reading your book, he said you spoke of adjacent and intertwined paths."

He nods. "As a theoretical premise, more than anything else, but yes."

"Well, it turns out they're more than theoretical. I actually think your description may be why Alex set up the display the way he did. We were dealing with . . . I guess you could call them time tourists from one of those realities. One of them mentioned that they label our reality 47H. And we later found out they were 27V, which never made sense to me. You'd think they'd number their own reality as 1A. But, anyway, I got the sense those numbers and the frequencies were sort of like a Rosetta stone that helped Alex map things out and eventually allowed him to block travelers from that timeline."

"Time tourists," he says. "Nice to know I'm not losing my mind. I was used to seeing the paths more as layers. One reality on top of the other, and then slowly, one of them comes into focus. That's why I need this cane. When I start seeing the paths, the world around me can seem a little . . . in flux. My balance suffers. I'd gotten used to that, but in the past year, things have become more complicated. More layers, and not exactly parallel. They intersect our paths at odd angles. I'm in a network of people with quirky abilities, and Daniel Quinn, the guy who is our liaison with the government, put me in touch with someone, who put me in touch with someone else, and four or five contacts later, I wind up with Bensen here who was kind enough to provide me with this piece of jewelry." He taps the cuff on his wrist. "It seems to keep me more centered. I still see the paths, even that freaky variety, and I still see when they shift. But at least it's not like everything is flying at my head at once." Stan laughs. "I suspect that makes no sense to anyone other than me, but I'm grateful for the assist."

The cuffs puzzle me. From the sound of it, there are a lot of people walking around wearing them . . . all of the Pru clones, plus the tattoos for people in the Fifth Column. "Have you found a way to replicate the CHRONOS field?" I ask. "Alex devised some field extenders, but you still need to be near an existing field . . . either a key or a diary. And there aren't a lot of those."

"That's true," Ben says. "The bracelets are amplifiers. But one of our technicians figured out that the CHRONOS field is embedded in the material that forms the pages of the diaries. So we cannibalized one. Each cuff has a tiny amount of that material, which is enough to maintain the field around a single person."

"That's what they used to create the tattoos on the babies, as well. And ours," Charlayne adds. "It's a way of identifying us as Fifth Column. The majority of us can't see the light, since we don't have the CHRONOS gene. I like having backup, so even though the Sisters tell me it glows, I always wear a bracelet, too. If you need some for additional protection, I'll look into getting a few more made."

I don't answer immediately, because my mind is trying to make a connection. After a few seconds, I give up and say, "That would be great. My housemates have had to keep within range of a key or a diary, and as I noted, we don't have many of either. Clio's family is in the same situation."

Clio nudges me and glances down at her key. She's right. We only budgeted ten minutes for this entire jump, and I still have several things I need to ask.

Kate must have noticed Clio nudging me, because she says, "They're in a rush, Char."

"Oh. Well, I guess we should cut to the chase, then," Ben says. "Our computers here aren't an exact replica of what Kate calls the Anomalies Machine, but they're close. We've isolated what might be tipping points, although to be honest, there's not a lot of access to public data for us to compare, and things changed at sort of a slow pace. Kate said it seemed more . . ."

"Organic," Kate says. "Less of a sense that the timeline flipped and more that it slowly . . . revolved, maybe? Or evolved. The number of crackdowns on non-Cyrist religions gradually increased. Personal freedoms, particularly for women, gradually *decreased*. Science is still taught in schools, but only at the most basic level unless you're part of a small group of the trusted faithful. And there's very little open information for the general public."

"But the major changes begin around 1970, right?" Clio asks.

Kate gives us a shrug. "That seems right based on what we've been able to piece together. We didn't feel the most recent shift until a few weeks ago, so there hasn't been a lot of time to process all of the changes. I think the cuffs everyone else is wearing are calibrated a little differently, because they didn't register the time shift until the day after my key. Everyone thought I was having a nervous breakdown and I was really hoping that was true, given the alternative. But then I woke up the next morning and found that if I'd lost my mind, everyone else had, too."

"Anyway," Charlayne says, "we've collected what data we could in the short amount of time we've had." She reaches into her basket and pulls out a tablet. "This contains files the Fifth Column has assembled on changes from the previous timelines, especially within Cyrist International. Research is really all we *can* do, given our current cash-flow situation and the fact that none of us can use that key. So, if you need additional background info or simply some place to hide out, let us know."

I take the tablet, even though I'm a bit uneasy about it. "We appreciate the help, but I'm worried about pulling all of you into this any more than you are. As I mentioned to Kate and to Beta, someone broke into the house earlier today and abducted my roommates. They killed one of them, although we *will* be undoing that. So helping us could be risky, and Kate says you've lost people, too, so . . ."

Charlayne glances over at Kate. For an instant, Kate's composure breaks and her eyes are filled with pain. And then the mask is back in place. Maybe there's a reason Grandpa James isn't here. Also, when she mentioned Trey earlier . . . was it in the past tense? I'm wondering what to say, or whether I even should say anything, but Charlayne steps into the breach.

"*Not* helping you would be even riskier," Charlayne says. "And I've got armed guards stationed around the perimeter. If Saul wants to tangle, I say bring it on."

Ben gives her a tiny, indulgent smile, but his eyes are worried. "Our guards aren't going to be much use if he decides to send in a full CS strike team. But Charlayne is right. We're fully committed, so whatever you need, let us know."

"A CS strike team?" Clio says. "As in Cyrist Sword?"

Charlayne nods. "We were Shield and Sword at first. Started back in the late 1950s by the Grand Templar Lonnie Dennis. We provide security for Cyrist Templars and the facilities. This timeline seems to have dropped the Shield part, but it's still on the insignia."

"They're the ones who broke into the house in Bethesda," I say. "Are they connected to the military? Because a general was giving them orders."

"Not in our time," Charlayne says. "But you're nearly eighty years ahead of us. A lot could have changed. Right now, they're just Cyrist security, although the branch I'm with—at least, the branch I was with before this afternoon—occasionally provides extra security for government leaders who are Cyrists. Of course, in *this* timeline, that seems to be most of them."

∞

BETHESDA, MARYLAND
NOVEMBER 28, 2136

I toss the tablet Charlayne gave us onto the bed, intending to stretch out and comb through the files before meeting the others in the attic at three. At a minimum, I need to see if there's anything in here pertaining to the jumps I'll be making. But after a few minutes I realize that if I'm going to accomplish anything, I should probably move to the couch. Or go downstairs. Maybe find a place to practice using Thea's nifty little cuff laser, now that Charlayne explained how. The trick is that you have to pull up on the stone to activate it, then twist to aim and press to fire. Shooting something might release a bit of tension, but I'm not sure where I could practice. Outside seems like a spectacularly bad idea given that the apartment buildings surrounding the yard have a bird's-eye view of everything we do.

Either way, I need to get out of here. There's no way in hell I'll be able to focus on any sort of research in this room.

Because Jack is *everywhere*. Partly because he's every bit as much of a slob as I am. His clothes are intermingled with mine, strewn across the couch and over the iron rail of the bed. I slept in this suite for months before Jack, but I didn't really *live* in here. There were no memories. It was just a place where I came to shower and sleep.

It's odd how this room, this bed, can feel so completely empty now without Jack when two short weeks ago, he'd never even been inside it. I pick up his shirt and hold it to my face, breathing him in, trying to keep my shit together. My lousy night's sleep is catching up with me, so it isn't easy. But I can at least take comfort in the knowledge that Jack was alive when he left this house. Poor Katherine doesn't even have that much to hold on to.

And that reminds me of something I've been meaning to do. "Jarvis, reduce the temperature in the basement as low as possible without freezing the pipes."

There's a long delay. It's not the first time I've noticed Jarvis's responses being slow today, and I'm thinking I should run a diagnostic. General Merrick and his Cyrist Sword squad are probably listening to every damn thing I say. I'm about to repeat my request when Jarvis says he's cut all heat to that floor and will try to maintain a temperature of forty degrees.

"Your stress levels appear to be unusually elevated today, Mistress Max," he adds. "Queuing your normal daily meditation routine."

The wall screen lights up and displays video of a waterfall. Soft music plays over the sound of the water. It would be very relaxing, except for the fact that I don't actually *have* a meditation routine, or any sort of meditation program that involves the wall screen. Jarvis is programmed to adjust the music I swim to, based on my biometric data, but that's the only thing remotely close.

Also, he just called me Mistress *Max*.

I watch the screen as the image changes to a seascape, and then mountains. The mountains seem familiar. I'm almost certain it's the range in Ireland where I used to hike with my dad.

A squirrel is next. Not the gray squirrels that run around in the backyard, but the red variety that live outside Nora's cottage in Bray.

And then I see a picture of Einstein sticking out his tongue at the camera. That's the poster Alex had on his door in the apartment he shared with Jack.

Alex. I pull in a deep breath. That's why Jarvis is responding so slowly. Alex's neural link is still connected to our computers.

The next image isn't exactly peaceful. In fact it's unnerving. A large red-and-black eye stares back at me with a white keyhole in the center of the iris. I'm almost certain it's the cover for a paperback edition of *Nineteen Eighty-Four*.

We're being watched.

Instead of a calm transition to the next screen, the red-and-black eye morphs into a black rectangle and explodes into shards that seem to fly out of the screen. In the void left on the screen, the outline of a lotus flower slowly takes shape. Normally, given the association with the Cyrists, it would ratchet my tension up even more, but this isn't a pink or blue lotus. It's orange. Not quite the shade that I see the CHRONOS light, but it reminds me of the lotuses on Charlayne and Bensen. The connection my mind was trying to make at the Fifth

Column finally clicks into place and I remember where I may have seen that tattoo before.

I'm about to pull the key out to check, but the lotus petals dissolve and the image is replaced by a video of a blue sky with wispy clouds, much like the clouds Jack and I watched in the garden yesterday. A printed message slowly scrolls in over the video backdrop.

You can only do your best. And at the end, win or lose, know I am with you always and that you are loved.

"Thank you, Jarvis. You can stop now. I'm feeling much better."

It's a simple positive affirmation, much like the ones you see on motivational posters in schools and offices everywhere. The words are the same ones Jack said to me yesterday, although he's paraphrased, genericized, and cast them in vaguely religious trappings. He had to do that, for the very same reason I have to sink my face into his shirt again to hide the smile of sheer relief.

The good news, the very, very good news, is that Jack is fine. Alex is fine, as well . . . and hopefully, the same is true for RJ, Lorena, and Yun Hee.

The bad news, of course, is that he can't tell me any of this directly. We can trust no one. Because Big Brother is watching.

My only question is about that lotus flower. I center the key in my palm and pull up the stable point in the foyer when General Merrick and his Cyrist Sword troops were rounding everyone up. When Merrick motions to the soldiers at the top of the stairs, I get a brief glimpse of the tattoo on the back of his hand, but I can't tell for certain.

None of the other locations in the living room are close enough, and the ones in the basement are focused more on Rich and the soldier who shot him. So I head down to the foyer to set a few observation points closer to where Merrick was standing earlier today.

Then I move to the couch and scroll back to 9:10 a.m. The first location is dark, so I'm guessing it's inside Merrick. When I pull up the second one, however, I immediately find what I'm looking for. General Merrick does indeed have a lotus tattoo on his left hand. And it's definitely the same glowing amber shade as the ones on Charlayne, Ben, and the babies. The soldiers with him, however, including the one who shot Rich, all have standard blue tattoos.

I'm about to ask Jarvis to locate the others and ask them to meet me upstairs to go over costumes, but then I remember that this might distract Alex. So I trudge up to their various quarters and deliver the message myself. We have to wait a bit on Katherine, but once we're all in the attic, I tell them about both Jack's message sent via Jarvis and my conclusion about General Merrick.

"The Fifth Column could have changed sides," I say. "But I think that's the sort of thing that might have been transmitted to the Sisters through the diary entries of their later groups. If they passed along the fact that some of the Sisters were kidnapped, I think they would have told them something like that."

Clio shrugs. "Assuming they knew."

"True," Tyson says. "And Merrick could also be a spy in the Fifth Column ranks. But coupled with his reaction when Rich was killed . . . I don't think so. It's also possible that Saul co-opted him. Character Assist is one category of style points, although I think the rules specify major historical characters, and I'm not sure if a military general would count."

"Fuck this." It's Katherine. She rarely curses, and I realize her cheeks are wet with tears. When she joined us up here, she took a seat away from the window, so I think there's a decent chance I interrupted a well-earned cry when I knocked on her door. She wipes her face with the back of her hand and then pushes herself up from the floor. "The game is a distraction. He wants us worrying about style points and a set number of moves because the rules tie our hands. Not his. He proved that this morning. And I am *done* playing his games."

She heads downstairs, with the rest of us in her wake.

"Wait! Katherine!" Tyson catches up to her. "What do you mean you're *done*? I want to go back and save Rich, too. You *know* that. But how is he going to feel if we rush this and he learns a bunch of other people are killed as a result?"

Katherine doesn't respond to his question, but then I didn't really expect her to. She's made up her mind and doesn't want to be talked out of what I'm completely certain is an emotional decision. I'm not even sure she heard what Tyson said. To my surprise, however, she doesn't head down either of the staircases leading to the main floor and the basement below. Instead, she marches the full length of the hallway and into the library.

Tyson gives me and Clio a pleading look, apparently hoping we can tap into some sort of sisterhood vibe and reason with her. I find this highly unlikely, but I give it, as Clio would say, the old college try.

"Whatever you're planning, Katherine, let's sit down and talk it out, okay? Take a vote. I know you're upset, but please . . . don't do anything that could put Jack and the others at risk."

Katherine stops and takes a few deep breaths as she stares at the red numbers hovering above the game console—*55:37:06* and counting. "*This is a distraction.* I don't even think it's a real game console, to be honest. But if it is, who cares? It's like the Prudence decoys he's inserting across the historical landscape. Saul wants us jumping through hoops, worrying whether we're going to be penalized because something was against rules that he set, that he broke, and that he'll damn well break again anytime it suits him. I will wait on saving Richard. As much as I hate thinking of him down there in the basement, Saul found someone willing to kill Rich, and he could almost certainly do the same with Alex and the others . . . although I think Alex and Lorena are safe, given that he needs their skill sets. But this?" She snatches the game console from the table near the wall screen. "This is over."

She holds the console at arm's length and waves it slowly around the library. Tiny spikes of red light from the countdown seep through her fingers. I flash back to Thea smashing the console provided by Team Viper and gleefully crushing the shards under her shoe. Maybe mother and daughter aren't so different after all.

"I hope you're watching, Saul. I hope you're listening, even. Because I have just one thing to say to you. *Game over.*"

Jarvis screams.

It's just the word *NO*, and even though I know it's Alex speaking through Jarvis, and Katherine no doubt knows that, too, the effect is still jarring enough that the hand holding the console pauses a few inches above the table.

Jarvis's voice is always calm and collected. Jarvis does not scream.

"Apologies for the interruption," he continues in more measured tones. "But that would be a *profoundly bad idea.* Like possibly the worst idea ever."

There's a tiny look in Katherine's eye that suggests she's not going to take advice from an AI, and I wonder how closely she was listening to what I said in the attic. I reach out, take the console from her hand, and move a few steps away. At a minimum, she must realize this isn't typical Jarvis behavior, because she doesn't resist.

Jarvis says, "Thank you, Mistress. Perhaps you should place the SimMaster 666 back on the table? Please use caution. *It is very delicate.*"

I do as instructed, relieved to see that Katherine is now looking at the little box as though it might be a snake. Looking down at the console on the table, I remember the transition from the red-and-black eye to the lotus. While it was a bit unusual, I thought Jack had merely inserted it for emphasis. But maybe not. Maybe he was trying to show me that a specific black rectangle could explode.

Large red numbers once again hover above the table—*55:36:12.*

The countdown continues. But I think we may be counting down to more than the end of the game.

Part Two

Kriegspiel

Kriegspiel [from German, "war game"]: a game in which neither player can see the moves of the other side.

FROM *THE PART TAKEN BY WOMEN IN AMERICAN HISTORY* BY MRS. JOHN A. LOGAN (1913)

At an open-air antislavery meeting in a grove on Cape Cod, where there were a number of speakers, the mob gathered with such threatening demonstration that all the speakers slipped away, till no one was left on the platform but Lucy Stone and Stephen Foster. She said to him, "You had better go, Stephen. They are coming."

He answered, "Who will take care of you?" At that moment, the mob made a rush and one of the ringleaders, a big man with a club, sprang up on the platform. Turning to him without a sign of fear she remarked in her sweet voice, "This gentleman will take care of me." And to the utter astonishment of the angry throng he tucked her under one arm and, holding his club with the other, marched her through the crowd. He then mounted her upon a stump and stood by her with his club while she addressed the mob upon the enormity of their attack. They finally became so ashamed that, at her suggestion, they took up a collection of twenty dollars to pay Stephen Foster for his coat, which they had ripped from top to bottom.

∞12∞

"Just put the costumes in the bedroom," Clio says when I arrive at the stable point with the duffel and a backpack. "We'll use it as a communal dressing room."

The main room of Kiernan Dunne's hunting cabin is surprisingly spacious. It's pretty, too, with floors and walls of burnished hardwood. Tiny dots of orange light from the CHRONOS field extenders are spaced a few feet apart near the top of the walls. A braided rug is positioned in front of the fireplace, which Clio is currently stoking. Above us, a loft spans the length of the cabin.

There are only three doors, and one leads outside. The second one is ajar, and I can see the edge of a claw-foot tub, so I pick door number three. I toss the duffel on the bed and hang several of the costumes that are most likely to wrinkle in the closet. The backpack has assorted personal items in case we decide to stay here overnight at some point, and we brought four computer tablets loaded with information the Fifth Column gave Madi and Clio earlier this afternoon. And there are weapons in the bag, of course. Although I can't say I ever thought I'd be in a situation where that would be a given.

Tyson and Madi left about fifteen minutes before we did, jumping first here and then to Hatteras Island, in case Saul now has someone tracking our jumps the way Alex was tracking his. They'll have a mile or more of hiking ahead of them to reach Melcher's store. Saul claimed he'd arranged things so that only I could retrieve the baby, but Madi and I are both blonde and below average height. Unless Saul gave someone a photo of me, they wouldn't know the difference. Of course, that has me worried it will be Madi lashed to the tree, but so far, nothing has changed. Still me. Still holding the baby.

The current plan is for at least one of us to stay here at the cabin and keep watch when the rest of us are in the field. Clio is the designated watcher for this first shift. Our destinations aren't within sight of the stable points, and we can't risk adding a bunch of superfluous jumps to transfer observation points, so she can't do surveillance the way Rich and Jack did when Madi and I jumped to the temple or when Tyson and Clio jumped to Potter's farm earlier in the day. Her job is to keep an eye on the clock. We're all set to return here at 4 p.m., and the one unfailing truth about time travel is that if you're late, it's either on purpose or something bad has happened to you.

Tyson believes we should return to the house in Bethesda briefly at night and hold a few meetings in the library in order to give Saul or whoever is watching false data and a (possibly) false sense of complacency. Madi also hopes Jack will be back in contact and maybe we'll get a few more clues as to where they're being held. I'm not sure it matters, though. Even with our new contacts in the Fifth Column, we're hardly equipped to effect any sort of rescue against an armed force, whether it's attached to the government or to Cyrist International, although I get the sense there may not be much difference between the two in 2136. While they're probably right that we should go back in the evenings, I'm glad we'll be here at the cabin during most of our waking hours. Even though I've only been here a few minutes, I can feel a tiny bit of the stress leaving my body.

What I really need is a good, long, tension-releasing cry, but that was interrupted and there's no time for it now. My secondary plan for letting off steam came damn close to getting us all killed. I feel stupid, even though they all said there was no way I could have known. Madi even said she'd been tempted to smash the thing herself. I'd just found myself doing the same thing Tyson was doing when I huffed out of the attic . . . thinking of everything in terms of the rules Saul set for us. Even though we know he's been cheating every chance he gets.

That tiny plastic box with its infernal countdown is a constant reminder that Saul set the terms. That he is in charge. In control of the game. In control of the timeline. In control of me.

Even if it hadn't been a potentially lethal move, it would still have been best for me to put destroying the box to a vote. I didn't have the right to make that decision for everyone, and I apologized for that before leaving Bethesda. But I stopped short of trying to explain why I did it. It barely makes sense to me, aside from needing to show Saul he does not control my every move. And in the end, the countdown continues. *Tick, tock.* The only question now is whether there's an inevitable *boom* at the end.

The bomb is another diversion, like the damned game. Saul has heard me say many times that he's addicted. He even admitted as much on occasion. I can't shake the feeling he's been banking on the belief that my ego would convince me he'd be so worried about winning—about beating me at a stupid game—that he'd allow rules to constrain his behavior. The simple truth is that he'd never let the rules of any game he was playing against *me* get in the way of his unending competition with Morgen Campbell.

But even though his main goal with the game is to distract and constrain us, my mind keeps going back to his expression in the pre-recorded taunt he posted after Merrick's troops stormed the place. He was lying, which isn't exactly new. But there was something else there. His expression reminded me of the look in his eyes when I took the med kit to him in our quarters, just before the time shift erased CHRONOS. Pain, maybe?

I step into the dress and shoes, happy that I can knock off two jumps with a single costume. One of the beauties of the plain dress adopted by Quakers is that there is almost no variation over centuries. The outfit I wear to search the Publick Universal Friend's library won't be the latest fashion sixty years later, but there are many Quakers in the abolitionist movement, so I won't stand out in the slightest. If I find the *Book of Prophecy*, I'll jump back here to drop it off, but otherwise I'll go straight to Cape Cod.

The 1848 Harwich antislavery meeting was the site of a riot in the past timeline, and even though no one was killed, that was rare enough that two other historians traveled there. Both of those historians were before my time, but there wouldn't be any risk of running into them anyway, since they probably don't exist in this reality. The advantage of those past jumps having taken place, however, is that there's a location in the *Log of Stable Points* that's only a few blocks from the site. I've studied the suffrage and abolitionist movements in Massachusetts in enough detail that I shouldn't have any difficulty blending in.

I pull my hair back into a bun and grab the tablets. Clio is in the kitchen, making coffee. I'm usually more of a tea person, but none of us slept well last night. I could use a jolt of something stronger before I head out. A basket of fruit is on the counter, along with a plate of cookies and a handwritten note, saying the kitchen is stocked, and the car has fuel. There's a number at the bottom, with instructions to call if we need anything else.

"How does the caretaker think we got here?" I ask Clio.

She shrugs. "We took a cab from the airstrip in Athens, I guess. To be honest, it was probably an unnecessary precaution for my dad to let them know we were coming. Bill and Alice live way across the field, so I doubt they'd have noticed we were even here if we completely roughed it. They might have noticed if we light a fire, though, and the pantry wouldn't be stocked. Plus, they handle all of the upkeep on the place out of an account my dad set up, so they'd probably have wondered why there was a spike in the power bill next month."

Clio begins putting away the bag of groceries that traveled with her from 1941 Skaneateles to 2136 Bethesda and now back to 1941 Georgia. She seems a lot more willing to handle logistics and background tasks now than she was during the last time shift or, for that matter, even earlier today. That's good in one sense, because I don't doubt for an instant that Saul will follow through on his threat if he thinks she's strayed out of observer territory. And she's taking a lot of risks for someone who doesn't really have to be in this fight. She could stay here in 1941 and have a fairly normal life. Yes, there are some changes to the timeline this far back, but they're minor. By the time things start going completely off the rails, she'd be in her sixties or seventies.

But Clio was right when she told us we needed her before we began the game against the Vipers. She's actually more skilled at this sort of travel than any of us. Tyson and I are both . . . spoiled, I guess? We've had the luxury of historical archives, costuming teams, era-appropriate cash, and anything else we needed for our trips. Clio is used to scrambling for those things. She's more adept at improvising.

I think the other reason she's not grumbling about holding down the home fort is that she feels responsible for what happened today. Which isn't fair. Saul had clearly arranged that before she strayed outside of his stupid boundaries. If he hadn't, Rich would have been around to provide the backup she and Tyson needed at Potter's farm.

"What happened to Rich wasn't your fault, you know. Saul's playing mind games with all of us."

"That part came through loud and clear," she says. "He likes controlling people."

"True. I guess that's the one part about all of this that doesn't really surprise me. He'd bitch and moan about working with trainees, but thoroughly enjoyed the three months he spent as a field monitor for new CHRONOS agents."

"What does a field monitor do?"

"Every new historian is told that there will be a mid-to-senior-level agent dropping in incognito to observe one of their first solo jumps, making sure they color within the lines. If they do their job correctly and you don't make any major mistakes while they're watching, you don't even know which jump was monitored. I never spotted my monitor and neither had anyone else I knew. Saul signed up for it as a way of getting out of Q and A duty—where we have to answer questions from visitors. I think he may have been a bit too much of a snitch, though, because his request to continue for another three months wasn't approved. That was one of the rare occasions when Saul didn't get his way at CHRONOS. He's good at manipulating people to give him what he wants."

"It's a trait he passed along to his grandson," Clio says. "For nearly five years, Simon popped in whenever he pleased and insisted that I follow him on whatever temporal joyride he'd cooked up. In Simon's case, I think he was also lonely, but he liked knowing he had control over me. There was always the implicit threat that if I didn't trot along after him like a good little puppy, he'd unravel everything my parents did to stop the Culling. Dad is haunted enough by the fact that he couldn't stop the deaths at God's Hollow, and that was only a few dozen people."

"That was near here, wasn't it?"

She nods. "My dad saw a story in the local paper. Otherwise, I'm not sure he'd have realized what was going on. His biggest regret was that they weren't able to just kill Saul then and there, although I think it was some consolation that they did get one shot in."

I shake my head. "They must have missed. Saul never came home with . . ." I stop. "Well, I was about to tell you Saul never came home with a bullet wound, but the story he gave me about an encounter with his Team Viper doppelganger was most likely a lie. Which makes it the *second* lie he told about that injury. When I was bandaging it in our quarters, he said he'd *burned* the arm trying to get a drunken trainee out of a bar on their jump to Atlanta. He's got a scar now, because he was unwilling to risk getting it treated at CHRONOS Med and apparently too lazy to bother getting it done elsewhere."

He came back to our quarters that evening with a fresh bandage on the wound, so at a bare minimum he had Morgen Campbell's replicator cough up something better than the gauze and antiseptic I found in that ancient med kit. If he'd actually gotten someone at the OC to look at it, the wound would have healed cleanly. But there was a thin scar running down his right forearm when we had our unfortunate Valentine's eve tête-à-tête in Miami Beach.

I'd thought his reaction in our quarters that day was because he was in pain and angry at himself for being clumsy enough to burn his arm. But he was covering for the fact that he'd nearly gotten caught while trying out his toxin on that small village in 1911 Georgia. I'm guessing that was also as close as he'd ever come to being killed. And even though Saul tried to play nonchalant as I bandaged the wound, he had to have been afraid his cover was going to be blown. Afraid he wasn't in control.

Something happened between the two messages he sent to us on the game console to make him feel that way again. That was fear I detected, and maybe that's why he sent a recording rather than calling. Unfortunately, I have no idea how much time elapsed for him between the two messages. No idea where he's been or what he's been doing, now that Alex isn't around to track his moves for us.

"I guess the scar is one way we could tell him apart from any Sauls he might pull in from an alternate reality. Assuming he's made progress on that," Clio says.

"And assuming Saul even *wants* to pull them in. He doesn't like to share the stage. I seriously doubt that's different for alternate-reality versions of himself."

"True," she admits. "He did shoot Team Viper's Saul in the leg as a parting gift."

I keep going back and forth on this question. We discussed the possibility that Saul might be attempting to pull in Other-Sauls after Clio and Madi got back from meeting with the Fifth Column. I still think the most likely scenario is that Saul wants the ability to do exactly what Morgen Campbell and Team Viper are doing—jump from timeline to timeline, breaking whatever he likes in these new realities, secure in the knowledge that he can always come home at the end of the day to a world he's recreated in his own likeness. The others don't disagree on that point, but they think he might also pull in other versions of himself to help him get this particular timeline exactly where he wants it. Saul's comment about there being four of us and being forced to compete with *just me, myself, and I* was odd enough that I'm not entirely ruling this out. Actual versions of himself from other stable timelines would be a lot more helpful than splinters, which have a shelf life of ten or fifteen minutes, tops, and then they blink out to wherever splinters go.

They die. Stop using the euphemism, Kathy. Just own it. When you spun off the splinter for your test at CHRONOS, the other you died. Probably not a painful death. But dead, nevertheless.

I squeeze my eyes tight to block out Saul's voice. The last thing I want to think about right now is death. Was Rich's death painful? Is he going to be haunted by that memory? By the memory of being in that basement, in the bone-chilling cold—

STOP.

But I can't, so I do the unconscionable. Or maybe it's not. Maybe Clio wants to talk about it?

"Can I ask you something?"

"Sure." There's no reservation in her voice, and that's probably what gives me the nerve to go on.

"What do you remember about the bombing? About . . . after?"

Her smile fades. "I don't remember being dead if that's what you're wondering. But I *do* remember dying. It's not a fresh, front-of-the-mind memory. Most of it feels distant, as though it's something that happened when I was younger. Vague memories of pain, but the worst thing was my mom's face. I knew I was dying, and I could handle that. It was worth it to save all those people. Even if I knew what the outcome would be, even if I knew the price I paid would be permanent, I'd make that trade again if it was just me."

She tips back her coffee and thinks for a moment. "No. I'd make the trade regardless, but far worse than the physical pain was knowing that me dying that way would destroy my mom. Destroy my dad, too, because I could tell there was no way they'd make it through that together. Even though it was never his fault, she'd blame him for not talking me out of it. And even if she could find a way to forgive him, he'd blame himself. He'd never be able to face that pain in her eyes. There was a tiny hint of that just after, even though I was . . . back. That's when I sat Mom down and we had a long talk about my life being *my* life. My choices being *my* choices. And then we had the good, cleansing cry that we both needed."

"And Kiernan? He's okay, too?"

"He's okay, but I didn't need to have that talk with Dad. He understood. I'm not sure how much you know about everything that happened, but he had to make some god-awful choices, and my mom was spared all of that. Not saying what she went through was easy. It's an entirely different kind of hell having your free will taken away. But it was only about six months for her. Dad spent nearly eight years trying to figure out a way to keep my mom and soon-to-be me safe without trading millions of lives—and his soul—in the process. Maybe that's why he can see shades of gray better than my mother. And I suspect the version of her who is currently holed up with the Fifth Column understands those choices better, too. I'm torn between wanting to sit down and have a chat with her and thinking it would be really weird. And kind of disloyal to my mom . . . because I'm pretty sure she still views her alternate self as the competition for my dad's affection."

I'm about to say that seems like the best competition to have, since it was really still *her*, but . . . it really *wasn't* her. And even if it had been, would that make it better?

Clio smiles and reaches across the counter to squeeze my arm. "Rich isn't going to remember this part, okay? He's not going to remember much about dying, either. And . . . he seemed pretty darn happy when Tyson and I left for Potter's farm yesterday. I think he's going to be so glad to be back that any bad memories will be overwritten in a flash."

∞

HARWICH, MASSACHUSETTS
AUGUST 27, 1848

The jump to Potter's farm was completely uneventful and also a complete bust. As I suspected, the entire household was across the field at Inscription Rock. Even the dogs were with them, so no one was the wiser when I jumped in at the stable point near the porch and slipped into the house. There was no copy of the *Book of Prophecy*, but the *Book of Cyrus* lay open on the Friend's desk along with a partially written letter and several folded, handwritten sheets. The seal was broken, but I could still make out the imprint of a lotus flower in the blob of red wax. Scrawled across the top in a hand markedly different from the letter were the words *Prophesies for the Faithfull Publick Universal Friend.*

Scanning it quickly, I found the prophecy about the beast in the basket in the middle of the first page, near the one giving the date of the Dark Day and one about professing her faith by wearing the lotus. So I snapped a quick photo of the pages, put them back where I found them, and jumped here, between the woodpile and chimney of Snow's Market, a small store a few blocks from the antislavery convention.

I reposition my bonnet on my head as I step out onto Sisson Road, and tie it snugly beneath my chin in case anyone is watching. There's not much wind today, but enough that it might be believable that I'd had to chase the hat down if it blew off my head and behind the woodpile.

There won't be many unaccompanied women at the convention, but I won't be the only one. Quaker women enjoyed a bit more autonomy than most. Granted, it wasn't *much* autonomy. The right to vote was still more than seventy years in the future. Even then, it would take decades longer for women to gain anything approaching true equality.

And, unfortunately, Harwich is a port town, which means there are far more men than women. Plain dress might ward off some unwanted attention, but definitely not all. It's generally safer to travel as a couple, which is why Saul and I made many trips like this together.

Our decision to omit the Harwich Mob from our joint research agenda had been mutual, even though it seemed tailor-made for us on the surface. Saul had heard Stephen Foster—the abolitionist, not the one who wrote songs of the Old South—give speeches similar to the one that incensed members of the audience in Harwich. There was a personal dispute between a local ship's captain and an abolitionist the captain felt had maligned him with a story about his accepting a reward even though he failed to successfully deliver two slaves to a free state, and it led to an exchange of blows. That's more violence than you typically see at antislavery conventions, but it was far from the only event where the speakers were heckled and harassed. And as Saul had noted, no one was killed.

I might have been tempted to add it as a solo jump, given the number of women (and men) in the suffrage movement who attended. But in addition to the awkwardness of traveling solo in this era, my most pressing question had already been answered. Abigail Demmings, a religious historian who retired a bit before I began field training, attended the convention and wrote a full report. Her observations about today's riot confirmed my suspicion that one of the more widely told stories about suffragist Lucy Stone had been seriously embellished in a book by Mrs. John A. Logan, a popular pseudo-historian of the early 1900s. Yes, Stone was a speaker at the event. Yes, she was onstage when the crowd moved beyond unruly and teetered briefly on the edge of murderous. And yes, she had appealed to the chivalry of one of their attackers and he escorted her unharmed through the horde of angry men.

There's no evidence, however, that he placed her upon a stump, then shushed the wild crowd and told them to listen to what she had to say. And also no evidence that she won them over to the point where they coughed up twenty dollars to pay for Stephen Foster's coat, which had been torn to shreds by the angry crowd. It seemed like too good a story to be true.

The size and nature of the crowd is something traditional historians had gotten mostly correct. Abby Demmings's report agreed with estimates given in newspapers of the era that roughly two thousand people are gathered in the large field up ahead, already teeming with people, carriages, and debris. At least three-quarters, maybe more, are men. That's not always true at this sort of event, but again, Harwich is a port town, and a bit wilder than most. There had also been a bit of tension with locals the night before between the participants and the members of the local Baptist congregation. They had heard that some of the speakers were casting aspersions on any Christian denomination or minister that continued to support slavery, but the confrontation ended peacefully. At some point in the night, possibly after ingesting a bit too much alcohol, the "rowdies" from the previous day returned and demolished the crude benches that served as seating for elderly and infirm attendees.

Abby's report stated that one of the men near the front was appalled that Lucy Stone, a white woman, was on the same stage as William Wells Brown, an author and formerly enslaved man recently hired as a speaker on the abolitionist circuit. Most of the men, however, had been angry at what they saw as an attack on their religion, and I suspect her conclusion that they'd been spurred into action during Sunday morning services at local proslavery churches is probably accurate. To be fair, the resolutions presented by the convention seemed designed to rattle the cages not just of politicians, but also of the proslavery clergy. The statement called them monsters for perpetuating and sanctifying the institution. It concluded that there should be no continued union with slaveholding states.

Whatever it was that spurred the crowd to action, her report stated that the men who stormed the stage tossed Wells Brown over the raised back of the platform. Others dragged Foster down the front stairs and into the crowd. At that point Lucy Stone asked one of the rioters to keep her safe and he agreed. The other male speaker, Parker Pillsbury, attempted to help Foster and Brown, as did several members of the audience. Eventually, all four speakers made it to safety, and the only casualty was Foster's coat.

In this new timeline, however, things spiral out of control. That's why I'll be blinking out after Stone's speech, so that I can watch the other events unfold from the safety of the cabin. I've no desire to stick around for the new and deadly finale, but I am curious to discover what she says that tips the crowd from allowing her safe passage to killing her, along with another woman and the three male speakers.

There are no copies of this specific speech by Stone in the previous timeline, but I've read enough of her other speeches that I should be able to spot any substantive changes. Her life and work weren't as thoroughly researched by traditional historians as the lives of Susan B. Anthony and Elizabeth Cady Stanton, in part because Stanton and Anthony literally wrote the history of the movement—a massive, six-volume collection that detailed the contributions of their allies in minute detail but relegated the work of Stone's organization to a single chapter. To understand the actual influence of Stone and her allies in New England, historians had to wade through newspapers and diaries and a slew of other materials, and why go to such a massive effort when Stanton and Anthony had put together such an in-depth study? Many seemed to feel it was easier to ignore the bias and stick with the handy "official" history.

But Lucy Stone is at least as well known as Stanton and Anthony in 1848, and the three women work in tandem for both abolition and women's rights for two decades, when tensions over the Fifteenth Amendment split the suffrage movement into two opposing factions in 1869. All three become angry when the proposed amendment doesn't include voting rights for women. All three will argue that it makes more sense for women to be granted the vote first, given the high rate of illiteracy among the former slaves.

When it becomes clear that women will not be included in the amendment, however, the three will part ways. Stanton and Anthony, based in New York, opt to campaign against ratification of the amendment, both in their public speeches and in their newly formed weekly newspaper, the *Revolution*. Stone and her allies here in New England will take the opposite stance, arguing that the former slaves need the ballot in order to protect themselves and their families. While deeply disappointed at women's exclusion, they will say any step forward is better than none. The differing positions on the amendment cause a schism in the women's movement that lasts into the 1890s.

The day is stiflingly hot, which means I can't rely on my usual subterfuge for setting stable points—hiding the key inside my cloak. As a CHRONOS historian, we rarely set many observation points anyway. The goal was to *experience* the event, which is hard to do if you're wandering around setting locations with your key. Observation points were only to ensure that you could watch from a different spot later, because it was generally a good idea to avoid attending the same event twice, unless you were very careful to keep from crossing your own path.

The platform is at the opposite edge of the field, at the edge of two strips of woods veering off at ninety-degree angles. A few people give me odd looks as I walk about staring down at the key, but for the most part their attention remains fixed on the stage. I set an observation point near the edge of the crowd, one behind and beneath the platform, a few more on either side, and one near the middle. Then I stroll toward the wooded area to get a better view of the terrain. On the left, the woods are fairly dense, but on the right, you can see a road about thirty meters beyond the trees, which could be a possible escape route. Unfortunately, I find no clear path from here to there. Just an overgrown foot trail. Could work, though, if we put in a little manual labor to clear that log and thin out some of the underbrush.

When I return, William Wells Brown is still speaking. He has a pleasant baritone voice, and most of the crowd is listening. As he wraps up his speech and introduces Lucy Stone, there's a distraction on the other side of the crowd. A late-arriving driver is trying to get a parking spot for his carriage as close to the stage as possible. Some human traits seem to be eternal. A man calls the driver a blasted fool, and there's a twitter of nervous laughter at the mild profanity. When it dies down, Brown steps aside to give the podium to Stone, and returns to his seat on the platform.

Stone is my height, or maybe a bit shorter, and at thirty, much slimmer than she'll be in pictures I've seen taken a few decades from now. She's far from an imposing figure, but her voice is clear and commanding as she begins to speak. Her words carry nicely over the ambient noise and casual heckling as I begin slowly backing toward the line of carriages parked near the edge of the crowd, which will provide cover when I need to blink out.

She begins by thanking the committee that arranged the day's events, including two with the quirky names of Elkanah Nickerson and Captain Zebina Small. Then she launches into a speech that she delivered regularly during her time as a speaker with William Lloyd Garrison's American Anti-Slavery Society, stressing the ongoing collusion between government and most churches to prop up the institution of slavery.

"Their support of slaveholding has been so open that none can fail to see it," Stone says. "The church and the government hold hands with one another, and only occasionally does a pulpit remember the slave. Nonetheless, we shall remember him. Let them brand us as infidels if they please. We take no heed."

Her local church does, in fact, brand her as an infidel, due in part to comments such as these. I'm not sure if it happens before or after this speech, though.

"God's balance hangs in the sky," she continues. "On which side will you throw your influence? If the leaders of churches and temples choose the side of commercial interests or preserving the Union over the lives of our enslaved brethren, can we even call them men of God?"

The temple reference is the only bit that's new, and it reminds me that I should have checked to see how prevalent Cyrisism is on Cape Cod in this era. A quick glance at the hands around me reveals only a few tattoos, but the lotus tats apparently weren't required, even for women, until the early 1920s.

One man calls out, "Blasphemy!" This claim is followed by a chorus of agreement.

"Ay, watch where yer goin'," a guy grumbles when I bump his arm. His expression changes to something considerably more lecherous when he takes in the fact that I'm female, young, and apparently unaccompanied.

"My husband will thank you to do the same," I snap, moving closer to an elderly gentleman who is squinting up at the stage. A low hum of excitement spreads through the audience, and when I look up, I see why.

Two other figures are now center stage, just behind the podium where Stone is standing. Judging from the whispers in the audience, I'm pretty sure they appeared out of nowhere. Both faces are all too familiar. Saul is holding a gadget much like the one Clio and Tyson brought back from Skaneateles. One of the Pru Sisters is next to him. She clutches her stomach and drops to her knees.

Saul scans the audience quickly. If he spots me, he doesn't let on. Stone now realizes the audience's reaction wasn't to her speech, but rather to something behind her on the stage. As she turns to see what the audience is staring at, Saul blinks out.

A middle-aged woman a few feet away from me gasps and promptly faints. Her husband, who is staring openmouthed at the stage, doesn't even notice.

The man who had cried *blasphemy* a moment before now cries *witch*, and several people near the front rush the platform. Stone recovers from her shock quickly and tries to help the girl to her feet, but the throng is now on the stage.

I'm still several yards from the carriages and the crowd is moving now, some toward the speakers and others away from them. I could try to get to some sort of cover, but I'm not confident I'd be able to jump unobserved anyway.

So I tug on the chain holding my CHRONOS key, pull up the stable point back in the cabin, and prepare to blink out. The crowd just saw one person vanish and declared it witchcraft. What's one witch more, in the grand scheme of things?

"Uh-uh-uh, Kathy." Saul's hand closes around my wrist, yanking it toward him to break my eye contact with the key. "Were you really about to jump out in plain sight? I can't believe you, of all people, would violate CHRONOS protocol like that."

I bring my elbow back into his stomach, then whirl around to face him. "Don't ever touch me again."

He chuckles, although I'm happy to note that it sounds pained. I'm less happy to see that he's holding one of the planks that used to be a bench. Two fat nails stick out of the end. I reach into my pocket and grab the laser pen. He glances down at it and laughs again.

"What do you want, Saul? Are you so worried you're going to lose that you've decided to just kill me now?"

"Quite an ego you have, love. Not everything is about you. As I told you before, I'm simply teaching our daughter . . . or rather these pale imitations of her . . . a lesson about interfering."

Seeing him face-to-face for the first time since he helped us beat Team Viper confirms my earlier suspicion when I saw his hologram. His hair is considerably longer. The beard doesn't really suit him. And the crease between his eyebrows is several steps closer to the furrow on his father's face. Apparently, he played around in Europe for longer than I thought and was in no rush to start the game after all.

I'm tempted to make a snarky comment about the hint of gray in his beard and ask what he's been up to, but I hold back. He'll think I'm asking because I care what he was doing, and I really don't want to give him that impression.

"What you're doing with the Prudence clones is cheating, Saul, and you know it. First you kill Rich, and now this?"

"I didn't *kill* Rich. If he'd stayed in that utility closet, he'd still be alive. And how can it be cheating when I've already told you these clones are irrelevant to the time shift? You are wasting precious hours tracking them down. I hoped you'd be smart enough to avoid taking the bait, but you've now squandered almost an entire day retrieving illegal copies of a daughter you never even birthed. And, as you've seen, I have more decoys. Are you planning to storm the stage and save this one, too? Along with all the others? If you can't set aside your narrow little code of ethics, you're going to lose far more than your loyal lapdog. The clock is ticking, Kathy, and *you're wasting time.*"

It's there again. That little flicker in his eyes. That hint of desperation.

"You're right, Saul. The clock is ticking. But I think you're running out of time faster than we are, old man. Does that *scare* you? Does it drive you crazy?"

The words are out of my mouth before I consider the board he's holding. But at that moment, a man yells, "There's the devil!" and a beefy hand grabs Saul's collar. Saul holds my gaze, grinning as the man yanks him into the crowd. A punch lands against Saul's jaw, and then Saul lifts the board and spins around toward them. The other man emits a piercing scream and stumbles off, clutching the side of his face.

Saul is up again, swinging his improvised weapon only a few yards away. I stare at his back for a moment, then point the laser and fire. He crumples instantly, and the crowd around him becomes even more panicked. My back is flush against the side of the wagon. Moving right, left, or forward is impossible. Instead, I duck down and roll under the carriage so I can watch.

There is no doubt in my mind that the man I shot is a splinter, so I'm unsurprised when his body vanishes about thirty seconds later. Even so, I'm glad I shot him. Killing Saul's doppelganger won't do a single thing to fix the timeline. And while I could try to convince myself that I shot him to prevent anyone else from being hit by the nail-spiked board he was wielding, that was a minor consideration. The men he was attacking are the very same individuals who will soon burn Lucy Stone and her fellow speakers as witches, so I'm not feeling especially protective toward them. Seeing the massive hole I made in Saul's back with the laser and then seeing his body disappear won't quell rumors of sorcery, either. In fact, it's likely to make them worse.

No. I killed him for Richard. I killed him for the version of me I saw in the video, with the split cheek and the line around her neck from where he tried to choke her.

I killed him because I needed to see if I could do it.

Turns out I can. And it felt good.

FROM THE FILES OF THE FIFTH COLUMN

THE CHURCH OF PRUDENCE

The most notable change in Cyrisism is the shift in the role of Prudence, who moves from a position almost coequal to Cyrus to an adversarial role. She becomes a mash-up of Jezebel, Bathsheba, the Whore of Babylon, and a distaff version of Satan with elements of Kali, the Morrigan, Sekhmet, and various female characters and deities from other world religions.

The most recent version of the *Book of Cyrus* states explicitly that all good in the world is of Cyrus and all evil in the world is of Prudence. Considerable disagreement exists, however, over the definition of good and evil. In the mid-1960s, disaffected female Cyrists, most of them young, split to form the Church of Prudence, noting that the depiction of Prudence in the *B of C* was sexist and designed to justify keeping power and influence out of the hands of women. Rather than remove the pink tattoos that identified them with the religion, converts to the Church of Prudence had the area tattooed again, transforming the tranquil pink lotus to a flame of red and orange.

Despite claims by Cyrist International that the Church of Prudence is a mighty, organized adversary, the group has never numbered more than a few thousand members worldwide. It has, however, spawned a number of offshoots, which often mixed elements of Cyrist, Judeo-Christian, and other world religions. One such hybrid group was the Process Church of Divine Revelation (or Processeans), which flourished briefly in the mid-20th century.

∞13∞

"Too bad they didn't pick a tree on the other side of the island," Madi says as we approach the live oak. "The hike to the store would be a lot more pleasant along the water."

"But there's water on both sides, right? It's an island."

"Water, yes. But no beach. Unless you want to wade through a swamp, we're going to need to head back toward the trail."

The sign is nailed to the live oak just above the split caused by the lightning strike. No name has been burned into the bark yet, however.

"I'm not a tree expert," Madi says, "but it looks to me as though this happened at least a few years back."

"Yeah. Whatever takes place here tonight, the person who turned it into a local legend got a bit creative with the details." I rip the page from the nail, fold it, and am about to stick it into my pocket when I notice a weird smell. When I flip it over, I spot a tiny glob of gel on the back of the paper. At first, I think it's sap from the tree, but the odor seems all wrong.

"What does this smell like to you?" I ask Madi.

She sniffs the paper. "Gasoline. Although . . . it's not liquid. It looks more like this stuff in a tube that my dad used to help start a campfire when we went hiking." She takes a step toward the tree. "And there's more of it. Look."

The gel, which is a pale grayish brown, blends in with the surface of the tree until I'm right next to it. Even then, it's hard to make out the pattern. If you didn't know what you were looking for, it could easily be mistaken for some sort of weird fungus. Up close, however, you can tell someone has pushed the gel into the little grooves between the bark to form the letters *KATHY*.

"An accelerant," I say. "On a tree where they'll burn a presumed witch this evening. Does that seem like a coincidence to you?"

"It does not. And there's no way that the guy who nailed that sign to the tree did it. It must have been here before."

We'd both watched through the key as a tall man with wavy reddish-gold hair walked over to the tree earlier that morning. He held up the paper and nail with one hand and struck the nailhead twice to secure the flyer. Then, he turned back around and left. A few other people wandered into the stable point around midday, stopping to read the message.

"Yeah," I say. "But you'd think the people who walked past would have noticed the smell. Although, thinking back, maybe they did. I remember one of the men wrinkling his nose."

We both take out our keys and begin scrolling through. Madi finds it first. "Last night," she says. "At 9:27. The guy's got some sort of flashlight. Weird looking, and not very powerful."

When I find it, I see that the flashlight is the size and shape of a pocket flask, with a tiny bulb on top. I'm pretty sure it's the type used by troops in World War I. The man appears to be in his mid-thirties, average height and weight. He's in a plaid shirt, but otherwise, it's too dark to tell much else. He shines the light toward the tree with one hand, then uses the other to squeeze a metal tube. His body is partially blocking the view, but I see his hand as he writes the last three letters—*THY*—on the bark. Then he screws the cap back on the tube and shines the light directly on the letters to check out his handiwork before heading off in the direction of the woods on the other side of the tree.

A chill runs up my spine. For the first time since we blinked in, I get the sense we're being watched. It could simply be because using the key reminds me that Saul is probably watching us in the same fashion. But it's also seeing the guy walking into those trees after setting up his fire-starter graffiti. He's clearly working for Saul. He could be watching us from the cover of those trees right this minute. And if he's got a military-issue flashlight, he almost certainly knows how to use a gun. Although, in this era, everyone on the island over the age of seven probably knows how to use a gun.

"Hand me one of those bottles of water," I say.

Madi gives me a confused look but reaches into her bag.

I open the bottle and dribble the contents across the letters. Some of the gel dislodges, but it doesn't seem especially water soluble. Madi crouches down and scoops up a handful of dirt and rubs it into the bark.

When she's done, I check the key for the time the villagers gather for the execution. A quick glance tells me it's still Katherine attached to the tree. But when I scan forward to the next morning, there are no letters burned into the bark. All that remains is a spot that seems a little more singed than the rest.

I breathe a sigh of relief. It wasn't simply that I was worried the letters would reappear. Even though I know it's not reasonable, I half expected the letters to be back, but different. *MADI* or *CLIO*.

That's one reason I initially wanted to do this jump on my own. But Madi pointed out that the tree could just as easily read *TYSON*, if these folks are equal-opportunity witch hunters. Saul also seemed to imply that whoever has the baby was instructed to hand it over only to Katherine. Madi is an inch or so taller, but she's close enough to Katherine's height, weight, and hair color that she can probably pass muster, at least now that she's removed the electric blue streak she wears when we're not on a jump.

At a minimum, we need to get as much information as we can on this trip and set some stable points inside Melcher's store. That way, we can go back to the cabin to observe and find a time when the baby is at the store so we can jump in and grab her. But I'm hoping we get lucky and she's either at the store or nearby so we can check this one off the list.

We walk along silently for a few minutes, and then Madi says, "This situation bothers me more than watching the hangings in Salzburg. Not just because it's Katherine strapped to that tree. I think it's partly that I don't expect that level of wanton violence in 1923, which is stupid because I know there were still plenty of lynchings back then. But I keep thinking about the way the villagers described her child in the story. Cora's child, I mean. Eyes like a cat. Unnatural. Eerie. And, even with that sort of buildup, they still have the child literally *turn into* a cat and flee for the hills rather than admit they killed a kid in the midst of a witch frenzy. It was easier to buy when we thought it happened in the 1700s."

"I saw a lot of similar behavior when Glen and I were embedded with the Klan," I say. "Never was around when anyone was killed or even seriously hurt. That was off-limits, and I am eternally grateful for that rule. But I heard stories. Sometimes when the group acted violently, it was planned—a retribution for a perceived infraction of their damned unwritten rules, like selling fried chicken across the color line or a black man letting his eyes stray toward a woman outside of his assigned territory. But sometimes it was sheer mob mentality. People get liquored up and they get mean. An argument starts over something minor, things get nasty, and you can be damn sure it was never going to be the Klan members who backed down. But still, even those who were proud and open about their membership wanted a cover story for the more heinous offenses. They'd cook something up if they had to, some infraction by the victim that they thought justified whatever they or their buddies did."

Madi huffs. "That suggests they actually had a functioning conscience. It's weird, but that makes it worse."

"True. I suspect it's the same with these witch hunts, though. If your group got into a frenzy and killed not just an accused witch but also her kid, you'd latch on to some sort of rationalization . . . You'd say it wasn't really a kid at all. You'd say it was the witch's familiar. That it had eyes like a cat. In fact, suddenly you're pretty sure it *was* a cat. You even heard a guy say it wriggled out of the witch's grasp and took off for the woods. Probably wouldn't take long to convince themselves of that story. Maybe even the guy who cut the ropes and saw a tiny, charred corpse. Maybe even *especially* that guy."

She takes a deep breath and raises her face to the sun for a moment. "So you think that's what happened in the other timeline? They made up that story about the cat? I mean, obviously they made up the part about a baby turning into a cat, but do you think they did it because they actually killed some woman named Cora and her kid—and then couldn't admit to themselves that they killed an innocent child?"

I don't answer immediately, because I'm pretty sure I know where this is going. And I don't want to start down that path, especially when I've been thinking the same damn thing. But I don't believe Madi is likely to let the subject drop.

"Yeah," I say. "I think that's what happened in the original timeline. And it sucks, because even if it's unpleasant history, it's history. Which means we can't change it."

She mutters something that sounds a lot like *the hell we can't,* but then stops to stare at the sky directly ahead of us.

"That's new." She points toward a tower off in the distance. "When I was here just before the time shift, in 1931, that wasn't there. Is it a communication tower?"

"Yeah. Radio, most likely. You sure it wasn't there?"

"Positive. I blinked in from the stable point in that wooded area, behind that large pine tree. No way I could have missed that tower. I scanned around looking for anything that was human construction before I headed over to the live oak. I saw the roof of a shack over . . ." She pauses and turns to the right. "There. See it? That's the only thing I saw. Definitely no tower, and that was nearly a decade later."

I stop and try to remember exactly when radio became widespread in the US. I know it was pretty much everywhere by the mid-1930s, but 1923 does seem a bit early, especially for an isolated area like this. Maybe that was one of Saul's changes—speeding up the creation of radio and maybe even monopolizing broadcast networks? He would have gotten a pretty good idea of how effective that could be while dealing with Coughlin during our foray with Team Viper.

The map we're using for this jump is hand drawn from the 1930s, and it's several time shifts out of date, so a change as major as a radio tower on the horizon has me a little concerned. It's quite possible that the store we're looking for won't be in the same spot. But it's the only lead we've got, so we begin trudging south on the wide expanse of sand that will eventually be Route 12.

We take a break a few minutes later so Madi can empty out her shoes, which aren't really suited for hiking through the sand, but they were all she had that even remotely worked for this time period. As she's putting her shoes back on, a vehicle approaches from behind. It's dull brown, somewhere between a jeep and a truck, with a cloth-draped back section that reminds me of a covered wagon. A logo on the side shows an orange-and-white life buoy crossed by an oar and a harpoon. Around the edge of the ring are the words US LIFE SAVING SERVICE, and just below it in smaller letters, PEA ISLAND STATION. The driver, a black man who looks to be in his mid-thirties, pulls up next to us and asks if there's a problem.

"Just these stupid shoes," Madi says. "I should probably pull them off and go barefoot."

"Kind of chilly for that," he says. "Where are you headed?"

"Melcher's store," I say.

Either there's only one Melcher's store in this version of 1923 or he logically assumes we're going to the closest one, because he says, "I'm heading up to Creed's Hill Station, so that's right on my way. The back is full of cargo, but I'd be happy to give the two of you a lift if you don't mind squeezing in up here."

"Thanks," I say as we step up on the running board and slide onto the bench seat.

Once we're moving, he introduces himself as Boatswain's Mate Maloyd Scarborough. I give him our names, introducing Madi as my sister-in-law, in keeping with one of the two cover stories we cooked up. Then he asks if we're local, glancing down at Madi's shoes.

"We're down from Manteo, staying at a friend's fishing cabin," I say, really hoping there are at least a few fishing cabins somewhere down the trail we'd just come off of when he picked us up. "My brother was . . . in a mood last night. When we woke up today, he was gone, along with my car and their baby. No note or anything."

"Well, that don't sound good at all," he says with a concerned look. "I sure hope y'all find them and everything is okay."

Madi gives him a nervous smile. "Thank you. He was out of cigarettes, so I'm hoping he went to the store and . . . maybe the car wouldn't start."

"Not having his cigarettes is probably what put him in that bad mood," he says with a chuckle. "I'm a bit of a bear myself when I run outta Luckies."

A cluster of buildings comes into view on the right. Scarborough passes the first few, then turns the truck onto a narrow trail. Up ahead is the store, with a gas pump in front. It's an irregular building that might have been rectangular at some point, but additions now jut out at odd angles. A black diamond-shaped sign reading *Drink Cheerwine for Health and Pleasure* is tacked to the side of the building.

The trail itself leads straight into Pamlico Sound. Several small boats are moored out front, and another is approaching the dock. There are no cars outside, however, which puts a bit of a chink in our cover story.

"Maybe he took the baby down to the shore for a bit," Scarborough says, giving Madi a sympathetic smile. "It's a mighty pretty day."

"Or maybe he went back to Manteo," I say. "I'll call him and . . ." It occurs to me then that this is not only long before the era when people just whipped out their pocket phones and called each other, it's also before answering machines. There might not even be a pay phone here. "I'll call Mama and tell her to go check on him and the baby."

Scarborough says, "Melcher's got a telephone, but he'll make you pay dear to use it. Y'all been there before? To Melcher's, I mean."

I shake my head and he drops his voice a bit, even though there's definitely no one within earshot. "Be careful if you buy anything. He's got a bit of a reputation for leaving his thumb on the scale, if you know what I mean. They're not too keen on strangers in general around these parts, although it could just be colored folk. Pea Island Station is the only all-colored crew in the Life Saving Service. Burk Melcher's willing to take our business when we're down this way, probably 'cause he doesn't want to get on the wrong side of the folks over at Creed's Hill Station who do more of their trading here. But I know several folks, myself included, who been cheated in one way or another, so you might wanna count your change extra careful. If you're lucky, he'll be in the back sleepin' one off and Cora will ring you up."

"Did you say *Cora*?" There's a hitch in Madi's voice, but he doesn't seem to notice.

"Yeah. She's Melcher's hired girl."

We thank him for the ride, and as we're about to get out, he says, "If y'all don't find your husband, ma'am, and you need a ride back to your cottage, I'll be heading back to Pea Island in maybe an hour. I'll keep an eye out when I pass by."

"Thank you, again," Madi says. "Maybe they'll at least be able to tell me if he's been here."

He nods and turns the truck around, giving us a wave before heading back to the road.

There's a bench on the side of the store. Madi and I stop there, and I take out my key, curious to see whether anything has changed in the scene that's supposed to play out at the live oak tonight. Changing future events doesn't seem to be an exact science. At some point it's like the weight of events tips you from one track to the other. But there's no logical reason that Katherine would come to this island. If we don't show up at four o'clock, she or Clio will jump back and stop us from making this trip. One reason we went to the cabin first before jumping here was to keep Saul or whoever's watching the house in Bethesda from knowing if we have to go back and abort a jump.

I pull up the stable point in front of the tree at 10:02 and let out a long breath. No fire. No one lashed to the tree.

"Scan forward to be sure," Madi says when I tell her. "It's possible they're just delayed."

I jump ahead to the next day. There are no singe marks on the tree and no name burned into the bark.

"Nothing." I grin. "We still need to get the baby, but Katherine's safe. And you're not there instead of her, which is the other thing that had me worried."

"And neither is this Cora person," Madi says. "Which is a major bonus. Do you have the cash Clio gave us?"

"In my wallet." The plan is to try to outdo whatever Saul paid. If this Melcher guy knows about the baby, I'll offer him fifty bucks, which is a decent sum in 1923. If he balks, I'll go as high as a hundred.

"Give me half of it," Madi says. "After what Mr. Scarborough told us, I don't trust this guy not to pull a gun on you, ask for the money, and still not give us the baby."

I hand her three twenties. "If he'll steal my wallet, though . . . don't you think he'll do the same for your bag?"

She gives me a point-taken look, and instead of sticking the money into her purse, she tucks it inside her bra. "They won't find it now without a body search. And before anyone gets that close, I'll be blinking out and we'll have to jump back and intercept the baby drop before it happens. Speaking of . . ." She takes out her key and sets a stable point near the bench. "I'll set a few more inside while you talk to him."

As we round the corner, I see that the boat I spotted earlier is now moored. Two men are walking toward the store, fishing poles over their shoulders. One is in his thirties and the other is around sixty. Probably a father and son. I can't decide if having other people around is good or bad. It's possible that Melcher, if he's here, will be less likely to give us trouble if there's an audience. On the other hand, if the two guys approaching are his buddies, they might provide backup if he *does* decide to give us trouble. I'm not too worried about the older guy, but . . .

We're already at the entrance, however, and turning back around to head to the bench would be too obvious. So I push the door open. A little bell goes off as we step inside, followed by the whack of a blade against wood. Someone is talking loudly near the back of the store. A man, but I don't see him.

The guy behind the counter is medium height and stout. Somewhere between forty and fifty. He's holding a butcher's cleaver, which explains the whacking sound. The apron he's wearing was no doubt white at some point in the distant past, but it's now an abstract print dominated by narrow lines of blood and broad strokes of a gray substance. Fish, most likely, given the stack of headless bodies in front of him and the pervasive odor in the store.

The rest of the place is jam-packed with shelves. Even more shelves are behind the counter, filled with bins of dry goods—rice, beans, tobacco, sugar, flour. At the back of the store is a little alcove with windows on two sides, a potbellied stove in the center, and a large cabinet of some sort against the other wall. That's where I hear the man talking. Then I hear the crackle of static. Radio. The speaker sounds familiar, but before I can place the voice, the proprietor of the store calls out.

"What can I do for you folks?" he says without looking up, as his cleaver rises and falls, divorcing another fish from its head.

I'm not wild about starting negotiations of any sort with a man holding a meat cleaver, so I'm relieved when he wipes the blade against his apron and sets it aside. He looks at me and then over at Madi, who is pretending to study the jars of candy on one of the shelves. The man's eyes narrow for an instant, then he pastes on a cheerful look that seems completely foreign on his face. There's no doubt in my mind that this guy knows exactly who we are and what I'm about to ask. And there's also no doubt that he'll do what Madi suggested when we were outside. He'll take the money and we still won't have the baby. We might even find that the night's festivities out at the live oak are back on again.

Acting on instinct, I shift to our alternative cover story. Reaching into my pocket, I take out the FBI badge RJ fabricated for me to use at the World's Fair. It's not the version the Bureau is using currently, and there are, for some unknown reason, subtle changes in the design of FBI badges in this timeline. But in this era before TV, in a part of the country where he'd have to drive more than an hour to reach a movie theater, I doubt this guy is an expert on law enforcement credentials.

"Agent Scully, Federal Bureau of Investigation out of Charlotte. Are you Burk Melcher?"

His eyes narrow again. He glances down at the badge I'm holding, then back up at my face as the door behind us opens and the two men I saw out on the dock step inside.

"Yeah, I'm Melcher. What you want?" He speaks quickly, with an accent that's thicker than any I've encountered even during my time in Pitt County, turning *I'm* into *Oi'm* and the question at the end to a single word—*wachoowan*. It's almost foreign, closer to British, really, than to the accents I've encountered elsewhere in the South.

"Just need to ask you a few questions about a gentleman who was spotted in this area recently with an infant. He's wanted on federal kidnapping charges for illegally transporting a minor across state lines. Among other things. We got a tip that the baby was here."

"Who's she?" he asks, nodding toward Madi.

She steps up next to me. "I'm the child's mother. If you have information on her whereabouts, I'm offering a reward to anyone with information leading to her return. I just want her back safely."

"Stay out of this, okay, ma'am?" I shoot her a stern look, even though she's doing exactly what we agreed. "It's better if I handle the questioning. I'm sure Mr. Melcher here doesn't want any trouble."

The older man who just entered glances at Melcher, then back at Madi. "You talkin' about the baby Cora were watchin'?"

Melcher gives him the side-eye. "Chet, this ain't none of your business."

The younger guy glances around, taking in the situation. "He's right, Daddy. Let's get on back to the boat. We got Co'Colas at the house. You can wait 'til then."

"Hush, Wayne. I'll go when I damn well please. Melcher, I seen Cora walkin' outta here with a baby yesterday. Not her kid, neither. This were a bitty thing. When I asked her about it, she said she were keepin' an eye on it for you."

Wayne exchanges a look with Melcher, then turns back to his dad. "You gonna believe that woman after what happened with my truck? Everything Cora says is a damn lie. Anyway, we both seen these two gettin' outta that Life Saving truck. Pretty sure the driver were from *Pea Island*." He emphasizes the last two words.

His dad ignores him and walks over to a half barrel that might have held ice earlier in the day but is now just bottles submerged in water. He reaches in and pulls out a Coke, snapping the cap off with the opener on the side of the barrel.

"That's a good point," Melcher says. "If you're FBI, how come you ain't got no car?"

"I do have a car," I say. "It's just not equipped for driving in this much sand. My partner and I made it almost to the Pea Island Station when we got stuck. Ms. . . . Mrs. Shaw and I hiked up to the station. I showed them my badge, and they offered to have someone help Agent Mulder adjust the tires on our car and have one of their officers drop us off on his way up to Creed's Hill. We'll be catching a ride with him on his way back, assuming my partner doesn't get here first. And things would go a whole lot easier for everyone if we have this lady's baby with us."

It's a flimsy cover, to say the least, but I'd much prefer to leave a tiny bit of worry in Melcher's mind that backup may be coming. I stick the badge back in my pocket, deliberately gaping my jacket to give him a glimpse of my shoulder holster.

"Someone left an infant here at the store yesterday afternoon," Melcher says. "He's new around here, a dingbatter like you two. Been in a couple times before. Curly hair, that color they call strawberry even though it don't look like no strawberry to me. Told Cora he found the baby down near her cottage at Split Oak Landing."

"Why'd he leave the baby here?" Madi asks.

"Good question. You'd have to ask Cora. She knows the guy better than I do. Maybe he figured it were hungry. Her brat ain't fully off the teat yet, so she's keepin' the other baby fed. I said she'd have to get someone to watch it durin' her shift, but she showed up here this mornin' with both babes in tow. Said she couldn't get no sitter. So I put her on housecleanin' and laundry over at my place. Two brats wailin' all day ain't good for business."

I can't help thinking I'd rather listen to a baby crying than the fire-and-brimstone sermon we're hearing from the radio right now. The voice is familiar, too . . .

Three people come in as Melcher is talking—two men in their twenties and a girl who looks like she's in her teens. One of the guys puts a dime down on the counter.

Melcher pockets the coin. "Y'all need change?"

The one who paid shakes his head. "Nah. She's gettin' a Hershey bar." He steps back and looks over at me, clearly waiting for us to continue our conversation.

"Well, y'all know where the radio is, Dale," Melcher says with a hint of annoyance. "Quit yer gawkin' and get on back there."

When the girl grabs her candy bar, I spot a pink lotus on her hand. I can't see the hands of the guys, although I'm not sure if men even got the tattoos this far back. The three head toward the alcove with the radio, and I'm again struck by the certainty that I know the voice.

"Well, I hope you ain't lettin' Cora cook your supper," Wayne says. "Allie still thinks that bread Cora sold last spring is what killed her aunt."

"I cook my own supper," Melcher says and then turns back to me. "You want the baby, go get her. No skin off my back. Follow the trail through that little patch of woods on the other side of the store. There's two houses back there. Mine's the one with the truck. If you want the basket the kid were in, it's back there behind the stove. And tell Cora to get herself back over here to pack up these fish."

I'm tempted to leave the basket, given that it wasn't much use for carrying the baby when Clio and I were at Potter's farm. But Madi is already headed back, so I follow her.

Dale and the girl are arguing. I'm guessing she's his sister, because she's sitting closer to the other guy. She tells Dale she's not sharing and he should go get his own dang candy bar. He slumps down in the chair and glares at her, looking for all the world like a giant, sulky toddler. The voice on the radio rises again, exhorting listeners to *heed the word*, and Charles Coughlin's face pops into my head. When the girl reaches over to turn the dial, I ask her to wait a moment.

"Who's that speaking?" But before she can answer, I hear the preacher on the radio say something about the message of Cyrus being the hope of all nations, and it clicks.

"That'd be Brother Coughlin. Grand Templar for North America." There's a hint of disbelief in the girl's voice, as if I'd asked an obvious question.

"Thanks." Madi grabs the basket, and we head to the front door. The sound of Coughlin's voice shifts to static as they turn the dial. Then a high-pitched male voice begins singing *Oh, is she dumb! Dumb as they come. She's even so dumb she likes meeeee.* Cyrist or not, they would clearly rather listen to popular music than Coughlin's sermon. And even though the singer's voice is a bit like nails on a chalkboard, I have to agree.

"That went so much better than I thought it would," Madi says once we're outside. "You didn't even have to bribe him."

"Yeah," I say, thinking it was actually a little *too* easy. I take a quick look around the lot. As we turn the corner toward the patch of sparse woods Melcher pointed toward, I feel eyes on me. I look back quickly and see that the girl who was listening to the store radio and her boyfriend are watching us through the windows. The other guy, the one Melcher called Dale, is no longer there, so maybe he decided to buy that second candy bar after all.

As we enter the narrow strip of trees, I spot the two houses at the other end of the footpath. "Melcher knew to be on the lookout for us," I tell Madi. "So his story is bunk."

"So that's why you shifted to the FBI cover."

"Yeah. And it's also why I'm pretty sure we're still going to run into some trouble. I'm just hoping we can get to Melcher's house, get the baby, and blink out before that trouble catches up with us."

Madi nods and we pick up the pace. A few seconds later, she pitches forward, and I reach out for her arm. But I miss, and she hits the ground with a thud. I feel a rush of panic. I didn't hear a gun, but did they have silencers in 1923? Not that Saul couldn't have brought one back in time, but . . .

I crouch down next to Madi, who is already pushing herself up to sitting. So, not a gun.

"Fuck," she says, grabbing her ankle. "I caught my foot on a tree root or . . . something."

I follow her gaze to the overgrown trail behind us.

The something in question is definitely not a root. It's an *arm*.

FROM *WHY WE ARE HERE* BY
BROTHER LONNIE DENNIS (1948)

The simplest answer is that we are here to follow The Way. We are here to fight evil and embrace righteousness. We are here to find our full potential, without limitations, without hesitation. We are destined, and those who refuse to accept the fullness of their inheritance as the Chosen limit the inheritance of us all. We are here to accept our blessings, demand the blessings that are ours as Children of Cyrus.

To follow The Way, it is not enough simply to believe. You must actively claim what is yours. If you can envision it, you can claim it. Those who would limit your rights, your full inheritance, in order to protect those who are not willing to fight for their share are enemies of The Way. Do not listen to those who would have you hesitate, who would have you settle for mediocrity and a smaller slice of the pie in the interest of some purported greater good. Do not listen to those who would have you be content with only some when you can have more.

For the scriptures tell us, in Chapter Six, "Always remember that the strong are the masterwork of all creation. You have no obligation to the weak and the small. Turn your back to those who have chosen the Dark Path, else their weakness poison you."

These are the duties of Cyrists around the world, but we must go beyond the simple answer as it pertains to our individual lives and examine how our faith informs our nation. American values are Cyrist values. Cyrist values are American values. They are synonymous. This does not mean that other religions should be scorned or restricted, but they are not as intrinsically linked to the great American destiny as is our own faith.

As we strive for personal strength and independence, so too must we strive for the strength and independence of our nation. This may require that we cull those who would weigh us down and keep us from achieving our destiny. It may also mean we cut ties with other nations who do not have our singular interests at heart. No man is an island, but a vast, diverse nation such as our own can be. It is far better to go it alone, as island America, reliant only on our own strength and resources, than be shackled with allies who would sap us dry given the chance.

∞14∞

Madi
Hatteras Island, North Carolina
October 22, 1923

Tyson helps me to my feet. "How bad is it?"

His words barely register. My eyes are pinned to the man lying on his back in the tall switchgrass on the edge of the trail. His eyes are open, staring sightlessly at the overcast sky. Someone has carved the numbers 666 on his forehead, and a cloud of gnats swarms above the wound. A thin line of dried blood runs from the last digit into his reddish-blond curls, and I have to fight back a rush of nausea. I take a step away and a bolt of pain shoots through my ankle.

My ankle. Tyson meant how bad is my *ankle*.

"Probably just a sprain," I say. That's true, but I can already feel it starting to swell.

I lean against a nearby pine tree as Tyson gingerly nudges the man's arm off the path with his foot.

"Go ahead and jump back to the cabin," he says. "I'll get the baby. If I'm not back on time send Katherine—"

"I'm not going to tell her to come here."

"Of course not. Send Katherine back to tell us to *cancel* the jump."

Oh. Right. I knew that. I shake my head to clear it. It's like the pain in my ankle is shorting out my brain.

"Let's get beyond that tree," he says, nodding toward a large palm up ahead where the trail curves slightly. "The people renting out Melcher's radio can probably still see us from here."

I nod, and then try to put my weight on the ankle. That's a big mistake, so I lean against Tyson and we begin slowly moving toward the tree.

"Coughlin wasn't on the radio this early in the other timeline, was he?"

"No," Tyson says. "But it's only a few years early. I think he started broadcasting in 1926 or 1927. But that would have been local broadcasts. Radio technology is definitely on the fast track in this timeline. There would have been, at most, a single station broadcasting in all but the largest cities during the 1920s. No way they'd have relay towers out here in the boonies. The radio back at the store was able to pick up at least two different stations. That apparently should have been one of our initial predictions. Not that it matters now."

"But how could we have pinpointed that kind of change to a precise time or place? That stupid game is seriously biased toward whoever goes first."

"True. But so is real chess."

"A bit, I guess. But this is more like you're being forced to play without a queen. I can't blame Katherine for wanting to smash the damn thing."

As soon as Tyson and I reach the palm tree, we spot a new problem. A woman with straight, dark hair and sun-browned skin is watching us from the doorway of one of the two houses. I don't see the truck the store owner mentioned, but the woman is holding a baby on one hip and a toddler is clutching her skirt, so I think it's a safe bet that this is Cora.

I can't blink out with her watching. "Let's just get the baby," I say. "Once we do, we'll go. Even if it means blinking out right in front of her."

What I don't add is that I'll be checking the key once we're back at the Dunnes' cabin. The markings on the dead man's face match the description from the legend, and if they can't pin the blame on one of us, they'll be looking for a scapegoat. There's no doubt in my mind that they'll settle on the woman watching us from that doorway and the little guy standing next to her.

Tyson sighs, obviously unhappy with our limited range of choices. He puts one arm around me, supporting most of my weight, and we proceed toward the house.

"You here for the baby?" the woman asks as we approach. Her accent is thick. *Baby* is very nearly *bibby*. It's closer to Irish or Scottish, and like the people back at Melcher's store, the accent on the vowels reminds me of some of the older people in Bray, where Nora lived.

When I nod, she narrows her eyes slightly and says, "How come you left her out there in the first place?"

"I didn't leave her." I pause, unsure which version of the cover story Tyson wants to go with.

"My brother got angry and took off with their daughter," Tyson says. "Guess he thought he was teaching her a lesson."

Her eyes drift down to Tyson's hand on my waist. I'm pretty sure she now has a working theory about why this husband of mine might have gotten angry enough to leave.

"I *tripped* on the walk over." I extend my ankle, which is already beginning to swell. I don't go into detail, deciding it might be best to leave out exactly what I tripped over. Although now she's probably going to add being drunk to my imagined sins.

Her expression softens, though. "I'd tell you to come in so you can get off that ankle, but this ain't my house. Let me get the baby's blanket. Come on, Joey."

The little boy, who is around two or maybe a little older, steps back when Cora does. "Baby go bye-bye, Mumma? But I *like* baby."

Cora shushes him. As he turns, I see a large port-wine birthmark that covers his right cheek. She closes the door, leaving us waiting on the stoop. After about a minute, Tyson and I exchange a look. I'm about to ask if he thinks she's sneaked out the back when the door opens again and Cora hands a long strip of cloth to Tyson. "Sit down on the step," she tells me. "He needs to wrap yer ankle tight so it don't swell up so much."

I'd really rather take the baby and get the hell out of here, but I obediently park myself on the top step and slip off my shoe. Tyson grabs the cloth strip and begins wrapping.

"While I were in there," Cora says, "I got to thinking. How do I know this baby is yours? You mighta just seen the sign Jimmy told me he were going to put up down at Split Oak."

"The baby has marks on her ankle," I say. "A letter of the Greek alphabet. You can check."

She nods. "I saw it earlier. Why'd you mark a babe like that?"

"It's a religious thing," Tyson tells her.

Cora wrinkles her nose. "Like those Cyrists. Melcher told me I need to get a lotus on my hand if I want to keep working for him, but I don't like some of their teachings."

"You'll get no argument here," I say, as Cora hands the baby to me, wrapped snugly in a white blanket. A tiny, perfect replica of the earlier two. Her eyes blink slowly, like she's on the verge of sleep.

"She's been fed already, and . . ." Cora stops, staring out over our shoulders toward the trail.

We both follow her gaze. Through the trees, we see three men stopped near the spot where we found the body. One of them looks like Melcher. Tyson must be thinking the same thing, because he curses under his breath.

Cora frowns. "Joey, go find Mumma's purse. You can have the rest of your animal crackers, but you gotta stay on the sofa 'til I come back for you, okay?" The boy smiles and she turns to us, but Tyson is already half dragging me and the baby around the side of the house. "Mr. Melcher did say it were okay for you to come get her, right?"

"Of course," Tyson says. "How else would we have known she was here?"

Once we're around the corner, I spot the truck Melcher mentioned. It looks more like an oversized wagon, with a tiny running board on the front. I slide down onto the grass next to the wall and pull the field extender device from my bag. Clio showed me how to use the thing before we left, but I haven't actually tried it with an infant yet. Even if we'd had one of the other two still at the house, I wouldn't have put them through a trip just to test it out, given how cranky they are afterward. I think the odds of success on the first try are slim, but I snap my key into the extender and pull up the stable point for the cabin in Georgia at 4 p.m.

Nothing happens.

Melcher is now yelling something at Cora, but I have a hard time making out what he's saying due to his accent. It's like the man is talking through a mouthful of marbles.

I tell Tyson to go ahead without me. "I'll keep trying. If I'm not at the cabin when you arrive, you'll know you need to abort." When he hesitates, I glare at him. "Just go! I'll tell them you ran out to the highway to flag down your partner. It may buy us some time if they think we have backup coming."

He nods, pulls out his key, and vanishes seconds before Melcher rounds the corner. The younger of the two guys who was on the dock earlier—Wayne, I think—is right behind him.

Melcher looks around. "Where'd he go? And what the hell is that thing you're holdin'?"

"His partner buzzed him," I say. "Agent Scully ran out to the main road so he'll know where to bring the car. I twisted my ankle, so they need to drive back here to pick me up."

"What do you mean his partner *buzzed* him?" Wayne asks.

It occurs to me then that even though this timeline seems to be significantly ahead in radio technology, they might not be to hand-held radios yet. But there's nothing I can do but push forward.

"He called it a walkie-talkie. A radio you keep in your pocket. I'd never seen one before, either."

"*Drime*." The word seems to be a curse of some sort, like Melcher's calling bullshit on what I just said. He pulls a small pistol out of his jacket pocket. Wayne immediately follows suit. "He'd have had to run across my front lawn to get out to the road, and I didn't see him."

"Well, obviously you missed him. I mean, what else could have happened? Do you think he vanished into thin air?"

Cora is watching from the corner of the house. She looks at me quizzically for a moment, and I remember she got cover story A and Melcher got cover story B, which made sense in the moment, but was really shortsighted of us in retrospect. When she opens her mouth, I'm certain she's going to back up Melcher's claim that I'm lying. But she says, "I told the guy to take the shortcut across the ditch. He were runnin' fast, so you mighta missed him. She hurt her ankle pretty bad."

Melcher shoots her an annoyed look and then turns back to me. "You never answered me, girl. What's that thing in your hand?"

It's a fair question. Even though none of them can see the light from the CHRONOS key, it's still an odd-looking gadget.

"I *think* it's the antenna that boosted his radio signal. Agent Scully asked me to hold it. Said he could run faster without it."

There are several major holes in that story, the most glaring one being that the medallion currently snapped into the device is attached to a chain around my neck. But they might not be able to see that due to the baby I'm clutching to my chest.

Melcher says, "That don't look anything like an antenna to me. Looks more like a weapon. And those markings look like witch writin'. Is that what you used to kill the man in the woods?"

"All I know about the man in the woods is that I tripped over his arm."

"Is that why you killed him?" Wayne asks.

"What? No! He was already dead. Why else would he have been lying with his arm stretched across the trail? That's the other reason that Agent Scully was in a hurry to get to his partner, so they could get word to the local police that someone has been murdered."

Having the baby in my lap makes it almost impossible for me to reach the pocket of my sweater where I have the little laser device Jack gave me. Even if I could manage to get to the laser, though, it would be really tough to shoot both of them before one of them shoots me. I can't risk that with a baby in my lap. I also don't know how Cora will react. Katherine has Rich's Timex, which is too bad, because I could reach something on my . . . wrist.

Thea's *cuff* is on my wrist. I never got around to practicing with it, but Charlayne said you pull up on the stone in the center, twist to aim, and then press down to fire.

"Sheriff ain't gonna appreciate bein' pulled into this," Melcher says. "Not with that devil mark carved into the man's head. We ain't had a murder like this around here in ten years, give or take."

Wayne shakes his head. "I don't know as I'd go *that* far, Burk. I don't just mean Allie's aunt dyin' the way she did. What about that Williams girl two years back?"

"I said a murder *like this*, Wayne. Pretty sure none of those people had witch symbols carved into their damn foreheads."

Which means they have had murders like this at some point in the past. That's another one of those things I wish we'd had the time and resources to check. How common are crimes like this in the country—in the world, for that matter—in this timeline?

"You ask me," Melcher continues, "that 666 on his face puts this squarely in preacher territory. Somebody violatin' God's laws takes precedence over violatin' the laws of man. That's why I sent Dale back to drive over to Buxton to fetch Brother Everett. They'll be back long before the sheriff gets here, so we'll have plenty of time to question you."

"Who was the man you found in the woods?" Cora asks.

Melcher says, "You wanna keep out of this, Cora. Get yourself back in the house."

"You sure she weren't in on it?" Wayne asks. "I still ain't forgot what you did to my truck, Cora. It were workin' fine until you and that cursed brat of yours come around tryin' to sell Allie your potions. You ask me, I think there's a damn good chance you helped them kill the guy."

"You may be right. She been flirtin' with him at the store all week." The look Melcher gives Cora as he says this tells me several things. First, his relationship with her goes beyond that of an employer and employee, although I'm not sure that's by choice on her part. Second, Melcher killed the guy in the woods out of jealousy or spite. Probably what happened in the other timeline, too. Third, he framed Cora for the murder last time, and this time he's going to try to frame me. Or maybe both of us.

Melcher looks back at me. "Anyways, it just seems real odd that you and your so-called FBI buddy come pokin' around and suddenly I got a mommucked body on my property, dead as a ferkin' doornail. Now I find you hidin' like a dog, holdin' something that looks like it could well be the weapon the killer used to bash in the guy's head. I don't think that's a coincidence. Drop the thing now. Then get up. And keep your hands to the front where I can see 'em."

I readjust the baby so I can slip my key out of the field extender without being too obvious. Then I put the device on the ground next to me.

"I can't get up while I'm holding the baby. My ankle—"

"Put the damn brat to the ground, then," he says, "and get up like I told you."

I hold the baby out toward Cora, hoping her maternal instincts will kick in. "Would you take her inside until Agent Scully gets back and we can sort all of this out?"

She nods and steps forward to take the baby. Her expression is emphatically neutral, but when her eyes lock on to mine they're practically screaming that I should not trust Melcher. I give her a tight smile and try to telegraph back that I don't trust him in the slightest. I'm just not sure what choice I have right now. And at some point, all of this is going to be undone anyway.

Or will it? When Katherine goes back and tells us to abort, will that spin off a new timeline? Will it make me a splinter, and will the me in this timeline wind up burning to death, strapped to the tree, while the other me dodges that fate?

The truth is, I don't know the answer to that question. Which means I'm going to fight like hell to jump back, to already be in that cabin in Georgia when Tyson pops in at 4 p.m.

Once Cora is around the edge of the house with the baby, I shift to a kneeling position. While on my knees, I twist the stone in the cuff, and sure enough, I feel it pop up beneath my fingers. If I can get my hand to my pocket for the laser, I'll definitely opt for that, because I'd rather go with something I've actually fired. But Melcher is going to be a lot more suspicious about me sticking my hand in a pocket than he will be about me fidgeting with my bracelet. I just need to wait for a moment when one of them is distracted enough for me to use the device on the other guy. I'm hoping the one who gets distracted is Wayne, because he strikes me as being slightly slower on the uptake than Melcher . . . and I want the element of surprise on my side when I go after the smarter one.

We start across the yard toward the trail, but Melcher quickly loses patience with my slow pace, even with him half dragging me. Just before we reach the path, he tells Wayne to carry me. I protest, but there's not much I can do. The guy leans down and flips me over his shoulder, effectively ending any hope I have of reaching the weapon in the pocket of my sweater, which is now pinned beneath me.

For about a minute, he continues down the trail, walking behind Melcher. When we reach the body, Melcher steps off the path to check something. Wayne continues for a few steps, then turns back to watch. I've no clue what Melcher is doing. Maybe he's searching the man's pockets for spare change. But I need to be ready as soon as Wayne turns around. I raise my head to watch Melcher. Charlayne said to twist the stone to aim, but I have no idea exactly how that works until I twist and see a tiny beam of amber light pointing down at the base of a tree about five meters away. I lift my arm, moving the beam upward until it's about at the level Melcher's chest should be.

"You get anything?" Wayne calls out.

"Three bucks in his wallet. Military discharge papers. And an address up in Norfolk. Could be the sumbitch's family."

"Think the FBI guy checked it?"

"Doubt it," Melcher says. "Didn't see no other footprints next to the body. Let's go."

I hear feet scuffling in the leaves as Wayne turns around to head back to the store. Melcher is stepping onto the trail. His gun is back in his jacket pocket. He looks confused when he sees my head arched upward and the bracelet pointed in his direction. I'm not sure if he thinks it could be a weapon or if he's worried about me using it to hex him, but either way, he's reaching for his pistol when I center the beam on his chest and push the stone to fire.

There's no noise, just as there was no noise when Thea fired at Saul. It's not a perfect shot. I was aiming at his chest, and I miss that entirely. I do hit his neck, however. Not the direct center, but apparently close enough, because there's now a chunk the size of my fist missing just below his jawbone. His knees crumple and he falls face down on the trail, much like I did when I tripped over the dead man's arm a few minutes ago. The only difference is that the sand beneath him is turning dark very quickly, even before Wayne realizes Melcher isn't following him.

Now comes the tough decision. I'm currently flung over Wayne's shoulder, and he's a split second away from realizing I shot his buddy. My best guess is that he'll throw me to the ground and pull his gun.

I should be able to beat him to the draw. Assuming, of course, that he doesn't throw me so hard that it knocks the wind out of me.

I think there's a very real chance of him doing precisely that, however, so I pull up on the stone, turn my wrist so I can aim at his thigh, and fire as he calls out Melcher's name. The word morphs into a scream and Wayne drops to his knees. I roll off his shoulder onto the ground. He reaches for his gun, but I manage to get the laser out of my pocket first. It's a textbook point-and-click weapon. I hit him square in the chest. He has time to fire, but the shot goes wild.

I debate shooting again to be certain they're dead, but it's pretty clear they are by sight alone. Still, I give both bodies a wide berth as I head back to Melcher's house, limping badly.

Cora is looking out the window when I reach the edge of the lawn. She opens the door and waits there for a moment, apparently trying to figure out if Melcher is chasing me. About twenty seconds later, she bolts across the yard and begins helping me toward the house.

"They're dead," I tell her.

"Both?" She glances nervously toward the trail. "How? I heard only the one shot."

"My gun is really quiet." I stop, suddenly realizing I have to go back. "Crap. I think Melcher has my extender."

"Your what?"

"The thing I said was an antenna."

Cora shakes her head. "I went back out to grab the baby's basket and it were right there next to it, along with your bag. I took them inside."

"Thank you."

She helps me up the two steps and into the house. Joey is sitting on the couch, dancing a cookie shaped like a giraffe along the edge of the cushion and humming softly. The baby is on the floor next to the basket, still asleep.

"Do you have the keys to Melcher's truck?" I ask. "And can you drive it?"

Cora frowns. "Keys?"

"Yes. To start the truck."

"It has a crank. I never even seen one with a key. But yeah. I can drive it a bit. My husband worked for Melcher, too. We used to take the truck down to pick up supplies when they come in on the boats, before he ran off last winter. I stay here most nights because it's safer than my cottage down at Split Oak. But there's no way I could get this truck off the island. There's only four, maybe five motorcars around here, and the men runnin' the ferries all know Burk Melcher well enough to know he'd not be letting me drive it off the island. Anyway, there's only the one road, and we'd pass right by the preacher Dale is bringing in to examine poor Jimmy."

"Good point. If Jimmy is the guy on the trail, I think there's a very real chance that Melcher's the one who killed him." I reach into my bra and fish out the three twenties Tyson gave me. "You need to get as far away as you can. Otherwise, they're going to pin those deaths on you. They'll claim you're a witch, and neither you nor your little boy will survive."

I expect her to ask me how I can possibly know this, and then I realize she probably thinks I'm stating the obvious, inescapable conclusion to this scenario. Wayne as much as called her a witch a few minutes ago.

She nods slowly as she stares down at the cash in her hand. "This is a lot of money. Are you sure?"

"I'm sure. Just grab your little boy and go, okay?"

"What about you and the baby?"

"We have another way out."

"The same way that guy took? Because I know he didn't run across the lawn. I just told Melcher that because I were hoping maybe he wouldn't hurt you."

"Yes," I say. "It's the same route he took."

I pull out the CHRONOS key and check the time. It's been about forty-five minutes since Scarborough dropped us off at Melcher's store, and he said he'd be passing back through in about an hour.

"Head out to the main road," I tell her. "You know someone named Scarborough from Pea Island Station? His first name was Lloyd, I think."

She nods. "He stops in for a pack of Luckies sometimes, or to use the telephone. Why?"

I tell her to flag down his truck when it passes and to tell Scarborough that Melcher has threatened to kill her. That she needs to get off the island to go stay with her sister or whatever she needs to tell him.

"Do you think he'll help us?"

"I know he doesn't like or trust Melcher," I say. "And he seemed like a good man."

It's true, although if I'm being totally honest, I'm *not* certain he'll stop. It was one thing to offer a ride to me earlier, since Tyson was there, too. But he could be putting himself at a serious risk in 1923 North Carolina by picking up a white woman who's on her own.

"If Scarborough doesn't stop or if he's already passed by, take the truck as far as you can, then walk to the ferry. Does Melcher have a gun other than the one he was carrying?"

Cora nods and heads toward the back of the house. While she's gone, I pull up the stable point for the Fifth Column compound. There's no sense in putting the baby through the agony of jumping with this extender twice.

When Cora returns, she has a small bag of clothes and a rifle slung over her shoulder. Not exactly ideal, but better than her going down the path to pry a gun from either of the men I shot. And it might offer some protection if she encounters that Dale guy and the preacher he went to fetch.

She scoops Joey off the couch, then grabs her purse and stashes the money inside. "You sure you don't need this? And are you sure you and the baby can get out of here?"

I'm not entirely certain we can get out before someone comes banging on that door, but I *am* sure we can get out. Clio has transported the infants using this thing multiple times, and if there's a genetic component to it, I'm a closer match to these babies than she is. Thea was genetically identical to Clio's great-aunt, but she was *my* grandmother.

"We'll be fine. Don't worry."

She stares down at the CHRONOS key in my hand. "So that thing is magic, right? There really are witches."

And . . . we're back to Clarke's Third Law. To Cora, I suspect this device really *is* indistinguishable from magic. It would be much easier to tell her yes. To smile and tell her I'm a good witch. That explanation would probably fit better with everything she's been taught. And even if I could explain the science side of it—which I can't—I'd never be able to explain it in a way she could comprehend.

But magical thinking is a major reason Saul has been able to twist this timeline so easily, and I'm reluctant to do anything that feeds into that.

"No," I say. "It's *not* magic. It's just science we don't understand."

FROM THE *CYRIST NATIONAL EXAMINER*

FIVE DEAD IN RAID ON LOS ANGELES CULT

(Los Angeles, September 4, 1970) Five members of the Process Church of Divine Revelation were killed on Thursday evening when a local unit of Cyrist Sword entered the small café on Fountain Avenue where the Process Church holds its services and runs a financial planning clinic.

Larry McDonald, the founder of Cyrist Sword and a current Democratic candidate for election in Georgia's Seventh District, stated that the group was attempting to rescue two young women, both minors, from the compound when the Processeans began firing on their team. These extractions were requested by the girls' parents, who were concerned about reports of connections between the Processeans and the Manson family. Several members of the Manson group are currently on trial for a string of brutal murders last August, including that of actress Sharon Tate, who was eight months pregnant when she was slain. A Cyrist Sword unit's raid on the Spahn Movie Ranch in September of last year resulted in the death of Manson and four members of that cult, and the arrest of seven others.

Father Malachi, a leader of the Process Church, stated that there is not now and has never been a connection between Manson and the Processeans. He also noted that the church's attorneys would be looking into suing Cyrist Sword for wrongful death of their members and possible libel, if Cyrist Sword leaders continue to make false claims about the group's connection to Manson.

∞15∞

We each set our own stable points in the cabin before leaving so we could avoid a traffic jam when blinking in simultaneously. When Tyson and I arrive at precisely 4 p.m., as scheduled, I'm surprised to see Madi already on the sofa. Her foot is in an ankle brace and propped up on a padded stool, and she seems to be checking a stable point on her key.

She looks up at Tyson. "I came in a couple of minutes early so you wouldn't have to worry."

He glances around the room. "Good call. We can go back for the baby."

"Won't be necessary. We made it out on the first try once I was able to take my time and keep my hands steady. I decided to take her straight to the Fifth Column compound. That's where I got the upgraded ankle wrap. And we definitely wouldn't want to go back to Hatteras Island anyway, because there are now *three* dead bodies in those woods."

"Three?" Tyson asks.

"There wasn't any way around it. Wayne had me literally flung over his shoulder. They were taking me back to Melcher's store to meet up with the local Templar for interrogation."

"But . . . I was going to have Clio or Katherine go back and tell us to abort," he says. "You'd have been fine."

"Would I? Would *this* me have been fine? I thought about that, and I'm not at all convinced. This version of me, the one sitting right here, was being carried off for the Cyrist Inquisition. *I* was the one over Wayne's shoulder. Would I have become a splinter who vanished before their Cyrist priest started poking me with red-hot needles or whatever they do to interrogate people? Would I have wound up being burned at Split Oak Landing instead of Cora or Katherine? Can you tell me for certain that wouldn't have happened?"

She looks at all three of us in turn, and we all shake our heads. I could tell her what we were told in classes . . . splinters simply fade away. But they also said no one could move between timelines, and Team Viper showed us that wasn't true at all. And would Madi have been the splinter or the . . . splintee?

"Exactly," she says. "*We don't know.* And this me wasn't inclined to hang out and risk my life solving that riddle. It was self-defense. Me or them."

"You're right. I wasn't blaming you. I just . . ." Tyson trails off, probably realizing that he sort of *was* blaming her. Although, to be fair, I was, too. Which is way beyond hypocritical given what I still have to tell them.

"Furthermore," Madi continues, "if those two assholes had lived, what would have happened to Cora and her baby? We have a pretty good idea, and I wasn't going to let them die if I could stop it. Which reminds me. We're down sixty bucks. I gave the cash I had to Cora. Told her to take her son and get the hell out of there. I'm certain they'd have pinned all three deaths on her once I blinked out. I don't know if she'll get to safety, and yes, she could still end up on that tree once we flip the timeline. But me simply jumping out and leaving the two of them to that fate wasn't an option. We both know you'd have done the same damn thing, Tyson Reyes, so don't give me any grief about it. And I just checked. No burn marks on the tree. No name seared into the bark, either. Which means we've now gotten all three of Saul's pawns to relative safety, so I'm feeling okay about today's work, even with two extra bodies in the woods behind Melcher's store."

I sink into an armchair. "We've gotten all three *infants*, yes. But I just spotted one of the clones who looks to be in her early twenties at the antislavery convention, so based on what we've been told, I'm guessing her name is Rho. She was dropped there by Saul . . . or rather, one of his splinters. And I encountered a second splinter a few minutes later."

"You're sure they were splinters?" Tyson asks.

"I'm certain about the second one. He disappeared about ten seconds after I shot him."

Everyone is silent for a moment, and then Clio, who had been reading something on one of the tablets, barks out a laugh. "So, Tyson, who did *you* shoot on this killing spree?"

He shakes his head. "My hands are clean this time."

"It may sound bad on the surface," Madi says, "but I would argue that I saved two innocent lives by taking out men who would have killed not only them, but also me. And Katherine merely killed the temporal shadow of a genocidal maniac who was going to blink out ten seconds later anyway. If you look at it in terms of karma, I think we're considerably ahead."

Tyson nods and then turns to me. "Did Saul say anything?"

"Of course. He's Saul. He loves the sound of his voice. The only thing he said that's relevant, however, is that we're wasting time tracking down the Prudence clones. And I'm afraid he's right. Like I said, he abandoned one of them at the convention, and I have no doubt she'll end up dead like Lucy Stone and the other abolitionists who were on the stage that day. We already know he left another clone in Salzburg, and he more or less admitted to me that he's dropping them in as decoys in order to distract us."

"But why *tell* you that?" Tyson asks. "It makes no sense. If I was trying to sabotage someone, I wouldn't point out that I was trying to sabotage them."

"Maybe," Madi says. "But it does make sense if one of his goals is to torment her. It's a classic passive-aggressive move."

"Madi's right," I say. "While Saul is definitely capable of all-out aggression, he's also perfectly willing to employ the passive sort in order to get his way."

"Okay." Tyson paces across to the fireplace. "We've established that Saul wants us jumping around like fleas. He put the decoys out because he knew we would have to defend the helpless. Does he just want to see us in disarray? Or does he have a concrete goal in distracting us?"

"I don't know," Clio says, "but I'm pretty sure he's going to be angry that you killed his splinter. It wasn't really clear to me if they're considered his team members or his observers, but either way, they're probably supposed to be off-limits."

"Doesn't matter," I say. "Gloves off, knives out. Our only objectives at this point are to hunt down a killer and fix this timeline, preferably with as little loss of *innocent* life as possible." I give Madi a nod on the word *innocent*, hoping to make it clear that I don't put the two men she killed in that category. "Simply put, we need to be ready to kill him wherever and whenever we encounter him. Kill him and watch to see if the body disappears. Not only is he trying to distract us with these hostages, he also violated his rule about reentering the playing field after making his moves."

"Are you sure about that last part?" Tyson asks. "I mean, your encounter at the antislavery convention could have been something Saul did *before* his turn ended, right?"

"No. Saul said that he'd already warned me that tracking down the clones was a waste of time, and we didn't speak to him at all about that until yesterday, right before the game started. He said we'd wasted an entire day collecting his decoys. And he also mentioned Rich. It's entirely possible he dropped this Pru Sister onto the stage at an earlier time and then popped back in to taunt me. I actually didn't think he saw me in the crowd when he was on the stage, so I suspect he's set some observation points, just as I was doing, and that's how he spotted me. He looks older now, too, so I think he's stretched this out way beyond the time allotted. But either way, reentering the playing field is a major rule violation. For that matter, so was having his storm troopers kill Rich. And, apparently, setting up explosives in our base of operations."

Clio taps something on the computer tablet. "Moving forward, then. I've been going through the information we brought back from the Fifth Column. Most of it deals with events prior to their time, 2058. But they also provide a few snippets going up to Madi's time, which must have been sent to them by the Sisters using their diary. They have three people within the Cyrist Sword ranks in the 2130s. None of them are mentioned by name, so I don't know how useful the information will be, but next time we're at the house in Bethesda maybe we can figure out a way to convey that to Alex through the Jarvis link."

Madi gives her a skeptical look. "We'd have to be sneaky about it, like Jack was. But yeah . . . if we can come up with a way to get the message across without being too explicit, we should try."

"We can work on that before we head back," Clio says. "Most of what I've been looking at ties in with what Katherine just told us. I've isolated some of the photographs of historical events—most of them catastrophes or massacres—where the Fifth Column's facial-recognition software spotted individuals who have a strong resemblance to Sister Prudence. Several of them sync up with events on our list. I don't know if that means Saul is lying about their presence having nothing to do with the eventual time shift. It's possible he really is simply using them as decoys. Most are scattered about history like the one at the event Katherine witnessed. And it's a little easier to be certain it's them once cameras start recording major events. For example . . ." She opens a file, then frowns and hands the tablet to Madi. "How do you pop up the holographic screen?"

Madi taps a button near the edge and pulls her finger upward, then gives it back to Clio. The screen projected above the tablet now shows four images, one grayscale and the other three in color, although the color on the bottom picture seems a bit off. Clio taps a black-and-white photo of a crowd outside what appears to be a small Cyrist church. Two men are hanging from an oak tree in the field next door, which apparently serves as a parking lot. A small mob is gathering. The image includes several cars pulling into the lot and two other photographers, snapping photos of four men who are about to add a third person to the tree, although the woman they're trying to hang isn't making it easy. Four more men, armed with rifles, guard the group.

"This is the Scopes trial," Clio says. "Commonly known as the 'Monkey Trial.' I remember reading about it as it happened. John Scopes was tried in Dayton, Tennessee. Most of the people in town liked Scopes, especially his students and the guys on the football team he coached. He was found guilty of teaching evolution, in violation of something called the Butler Act, and fined one hundred dollars, although his conviction was later overturned on a technicality. Something about the judge not having the authority to set a fine over a certain amount. He definitely wasn't hanged, and neither was his attorney. That would have been major news, because Clarence Darrow was pretty well known.

"What a lot of people don't know, however, is that Scopes had a sister, Lela, who was also a teacher. She applied for a job teaching math in Paducah, Kentucky, and the school board asked whether she agreed with her brother's views on evolution. When she said she did, they refused to hire her. I have no clue what Lela looked like. After the experience of not getting the job in Paducah and all of the hoopla over the trial, she was a bit publicity shy. There's something in the files about her having a photographer kicked off campus at the University of Kentucky because he took her picture. I don't think she was even in Dayton, Tennessee, when the trial took place in the other timeline. And as they strung him up, John Scopes was yelling to the crowd that the woman they had wasn't his sister, that he didn't know her."

Clio zooms in on the woman's face, and it's now clear she's one of the Sisters. "I'm guessing it's Kappa. The Fifth Column files say she was grabbed at age twenty-seven. She was hanged alongside Scopes. The Cyrists in the crowd believed they were Prudaeans out to cheapen God's handiwork by saying humans are nothing more than animals. There were also rumors that Lela's body vanished from the morgue."

"Why didn't she tell them she wasn't Lela Scopes?" I ask.

Clio shrugs. "She may have tried. But would they have believed her? Look at those faces. They were out for blood."

The next image is of an even bigger crowd, but they're much more relaxed. A band is on the stage, and the area between the photographer and the stage is filled with people, most dressed in bright colors. Two people in the foreground are dancing.

"This," Clio says, "is from Saturday afternoon at the Monterey Pop Festival in 1967. Judging from the band that's playing and the set list, I'd say it's about an hour before the raid happens . . . but the set list is from the last timeline, so there could be some changes. The local police were cool in our reality because the event had gone really well. Yeah, it was pretty obvious that a lot of the attendees were doing drugs. Most of it was LSD, which had only recently been made illegal in California. But there seemed to be a tacit agreement that as long as there was no trouble, there would be no arrests for mere possession. In this timeline, though, the Cyrist Sword crew comes in, apparently with the approval of the federal government, and with a few state officials in tow. It was the first time they'd done any sort of raid on the West Coast. Their troops plowed a jeep into the tepee the organizers had set up as a so-called 'bad trip' tent. Two people inside were killed, along with a guy they grabbed and shot onstage for distributing drugs, or in their words, poisoning people. Everyone began screaming and running out of the place after that. The Fifth Column file says one concertgoer was trampled to death, and two were beaten to death by violent drug users. The rest, according to the official accounts, died of overdose." She stops, looking ill. "I've met the man they shot onstage. He was at a party at the house in Haight-Ashbury where Bobby Weir, the musician I know, lived. He was a guy they called the Bear, who was the soundman—and the supplier—for the band."

Tyson says, "Wait a minute. Haight-Ashbury. Are you talking about the Grateful Dead?"

"Yeah. Are they still popular in 2305?"

"Not exactly, but I share quarters with a twentieth-century music historian. I liked a few of their songs, but Rich is a fan. He once said they were more authentic than a lot of other bands, which I think translates to *rough around the edges.*"

"That was definitely my impression, too, but they put on a good show." Clio zooms in on several kids in the bottom left corner. One girl in a lime-green dress and black tights is standing with her back to the fence, eyes closed, head to one side, clearly into the music. She has shoulder-length dark curls, parted in the middle, that partially obscure her face. A white flower is stuck behind one ear, but that's true of a number of people in the image. "This one seems like a stretch to me, but they've compared it to pictures of the various Prudences between the ages of twelve and thirteen, and they say it's a real possibility. It's a still frame taken from a documentary of the concert. Anyway . . ." She swipes the screen to move on.

The next picture is a group of people, almost all of them women, mostly in their teens or early twenties. One of the girls in the rear of the group, with her back against a tree, could be a Pru Sister. It's hard to tell, though, because her hair is cropped close to her head. She seems a bit younger than the others in the photo, and she stares directly at the camera, eyes wide and slightly panicked, in stark contrast to the others in the picture, who seem relaxed to the point that it's clear they're on some sort of narcotic. The photo is apparently from a newspaper or a book, because there's a smaller image of a man inset in a circle on the bottom right. He's a little older, maybe mid-thirties, with dark, curly hair, an X on his forehead, and a piercing gaze.

"The guy there is Charles Manson," Tyson says. "I'm guessing the others are members of his cult?"

"Some of the members, yes," Clio says. "There were others. Gives me the creeps to even look at Manson. Something about his eyes."

"He was a serial killer, right?" Madi asks.

Clio nods. "Technically, his followers did the vast majority of the killing. Manson was, however, definitely the guy in the driver's seat. The Family, as they were called, brutally murdered a bunch of people in the Hollywood area and were eventually arrested. In the previous timeline, Manson spent the rest of his life in prison. A bunch of his followers got lengthy sentences, too. In this new timeline, a few of them still end up in prison, but Manson and several others are killed during a raid by a Cyrist Sword strike force. One of those killed in the raid was . . ."

I sigh. "The Sister sitting in the back row."

Clio nods. "You got it. This last one should especially interest you, Tyson, since it's connected at least tangentially to Lawrence Dennis. Although, I guess the last two were, as well, since he founded Cyrist Sword, and that was a Cyrist Sword raid at Monterey Pop and on the Manson family. He was Grand Templar during this entire period, and we already have a stable point inside that office from Madi's first meeting with Beta. I think someone is going to need to put in some time scrolling through for additional info."

Madi raises her injured foot slightly. "And I think I know who that someone is going to be."

Clio enlarges the final photo. "This one is from a publication of the Process Church of Divine Revelation, also known as the Processeans. They incorporated Prudence as one of their four . . . deities, I guess? But aside from the long curly hair, the photograph looks more like one of the two Scientology auditors from London who started the group, Mary Ann de Grimston. She and her husband decided there was more profit to be had leading a cult rather than working as middle management. Maybe she just adopted the Prudence persona and hairstyle? What's more interesting, though, is the guy with her. He's not the husband, Robert de Grimston. In fact . . ."

She enlarges a section of the image to center in on a man leaning over to speak to the woman with the long dark curls. The man, who has a neatly trimmed beard and mustache, is in three-quarters profile, and the picture is grainy and slightly out of focus. His hand rests casually on the woman's shoulder. I *know* that expression. I've seen it many times, and I send up a silent prayer that the woman in the picture is really *not* a clone of our daughter, because that would be seriously twisted.

"It's Saul. I'm not sure if that woman is one of the Sisters, but whoever she is, he's screwing her. Probably in more ways than one. Which means that at some point, he's there. Him, not his splinters."

They all give me a confused look.

"Why couldn't it be one of his splinters?" Madi asks.

"The look he's giving her. That's not casual. That's . . . intimate. Possessive, even. A splinter could only be there in ten- or fifteen-minute increments. Saul wouldn't have any knowledge of what was said or done during that time. Nothing for him or the other splinters to build on in the next jump. He can really only use splinters to do discrete tasks."

She nods. "Okay. That makes sense. Kind of."

"You said there was a connection to Lawrence Dennis here, as well?" Tyson asks.

Clio swipes to the next image, which is a newspaper article from November 1972. The headline reads *Grand Templar Dennis Oversees Inquest of Process Leaders.*

"It's long, and I merely skimmed it," Clio says. "But the gist was that the Grand Templar, who is also spiritual counsel to President McDonald, determined that an example must be made. There's a lot of talk about the tendency to make evil and deviancy *cool*, and he says in no uncertain terms that this evil must be . . ." She enlarges a section of the article and reads aloud. "'This evil must be combated with all of the resources of Church and State, united in the effort to protect our citizens from the Forces of Darkness.' The rest of the materials in the file say she was publicly executed along with three other leaders of their religion. We still don't get a clear look at her face in either the photos or the handful of film clips, partly because her hair is down, and they're hooded for the execution. But I don't think she's one of the Sisters. I think it's de Grimston. She was just convinced to change the deity she represented from Jehovah to Prudence."

I reach over to enlarge the other image Clio pulls up, of Mary Ann de Grimston. It's hard to tell for certain, but I think it's fairly likely she was the woman kneeling before the Grand Templar in the photograph as she awaited sentencing.

"At first," Clio says, "I thought switching from Jehovah to Prudence was a pretty major change of character for the religion. This new *Book of Cyrus* has Prudence cast basically as a female version of Satan. But the files from the Fifth Column note that there are also elements of Kali and other female gods of vengeance, and the Jehovah from the Old Testament wasn't exactly sunshine and puppies. There was a whole lot of smiting. So it kind of makes sense. The Processeans assign someone else in the role of Jehovah. They have a guy playing the role of Christ and another playing Satan. All four were burned on Cyrist crosses on the National Mall, in a televised ceremony broadcast nationwide. As you can see, Lawrence Dennis is looking pretty frail by that point. He dies the next year."

Madi makes a sick face. "They *broadcast* the executions?"

"Oh, yeah," Clio says. "Broadcast, recorded, and even made kids watch it in school. These are the consequences of playing with the occult, kiddies, so toss out those Ouija boards. Cities held burnings of *The Wizard of Oz*, and some game called *Dungeons & Dragons* was banned, along with a bunch of other things they decided were demonic. Some of it was challenged in the courts and initially overturned, but by the early 1990s, even the courts were supporting the restrictions on the pretext of public safety. The Fifth Column files say there was something people referred to as the Satanic Panic during the original timeline, but this raised things to an entirely new order of magnitude. It waxes and wanes, with a revival in the mid-twenty-first century."

I lean back into the couch and rub my eyes, trying to put myself in Saul's head and figure out what the hell the man intends to accomplish with this timeline. Given the theme of this disaster, I still think it's connected to his ongoing competition with Morgen Campbell, and I really wish I'd bothered to listen more closely on the rare occasions I tagged along with him to the Objectivist Club. The conversation I remember best is, probably not coincidentally, the one Saul was in the middle of the first time he noticed me. Or at least, the first time I was *aware* of him noticing me. It was during my last month of field training, and our cohort had finally been sent invitations to one of the OC's gatherings for CHRONOS agents. When I arrived at the OC with Rich and two other guys from our class, Morgen had been on his throne in the Redwing Room engaged in a verbal jousting match with Saul.

Morgen had been goading him on some religious topic, although I can't remember the specifics. At some point, however, he'd asked Saul if he believed in sin. Saul more or less dodged the question, using Cyrus, Morgen's ancient Doberman, as an example. He said old Cyrus probably thought it was a sin that society allowed him to be owned by Morgen, when the dog was smarter and better groomed. One of the guys near me chuckled, and that's apparently what drew Saul's attention to our corner of the room. He then said the young man in the corner probably thought it was a sin that I wasn't as in love with him as he was with me.

To be honest, I think Saul was spitballing. Find any group of four teens, and the odds are decent that at least one will have a crush on someone else in the group. But I blushed, of course. I suspect Rich may have, as well, given Saul's knowing smile as he stalked off to the bar where Morgen hides the better brands of booze.

Saul left shortly after, never bothering to fully answer Morgen's question. But I know the answer. It's in one of the verses he included in his stupid little book of scripture. *Those who settle for mediocrity when they are capable of greatness have sinned in the eyes of Cyrus.* Saul occasionally has his moments of self-doubt, but he generally believes himself to be the smartest person in any room.

Saul also made it very clear to me that he believed history would be better off under *his* guidance when we were outside the police station at the New York World's Fair. *People make shit decisions as a group unless they are led by a strong hand. And we could do that through the Cyrists.* Saul had used the word *we* on the pretext of including me in the plan, but I suspect it was more a case of the royal *we*. He'd also prefaced the statement by adding in a lot of noble causes and historical wrongs that could be righted, but they were mostly filler. Much of what the man believes lies in that one sentence—*people make shit decisions as a group unless they are led by a strong hand.*

And who better to lead than the self-presumed smartest man in the room?

He's enough of an egotist that I'm sure he gets off on seeing his face plastered on temple windows and knowing his half-assed aphorisms are hailed as holy writ. But surely he can't look at the current timeline and actually believe it's an improvement? Surely he's not so naive as to think that a society based primarily on superstition could be superior to one based largely on science? Or that such a society could be competitive on a global scale?

The limited information we've gotten from the Fifth Column suggests the nation really isn't competitive at all. Our country is large enough, with a diverse enough economic base by 1970, that isolationist policies wouldn't necessarily have resulted in massive starvation or anything like that. But I can't think of any nation in history where turning inward resulted in the country becoming stronger over time.

Saul knows that, too.

And why would he be playing what is, essentially, a kid's variant of The Game? Why would a man who prides himself on his command of Temporal Dilemma opt for the version people play when they're stoned out of their gourds? This seems especially pertinent after his snarky comment that he wouldn't have rolled up a child's level simulation for our first match-up if he'd realized I had any skill at TD.

Something about this doesn't fit.

"Whoa," I say. "I think Saul screwed up. I don't know what his *original* goal was, but things didn't go the way he planned, and he's not entirely happy with the paradise he created in his own image. That's why we're playing an I-Break-You-Fix scenario."

"But if he screwed something up," Madi says, "why doesn't he go back and undo what he did?"

"What if he doesn't *know* what he screwed up? Maybe it's something that got out of his control. Changing real history isn't as clean as a simulation game, and he's farmed a lot of this out. The only thing we know with some certainty is that he deposited revised editions of his two books. Maybe some of the people took those in directions he didn't intend. And maybe he tried to fix it. Could be that's why we have all the different versions of the *Book of Cyrus*."

Tyson shakes his head. "What would he be unhappy about in the current timeline? He apparently has financial control over Cyrist International, which gives him massive wealth at his disposal. The citizens aren't giving his selected government much grief, from the sound of it, at least by this point in time. Sure, the society is a bit restrictive, but you can always give money or play a game of *Forbidden Fruits*. And they've been brainwashed into thinking they're better off than the countries outside their bubble. Which brings me back to what's been bugging the hell out of me periodically since this whole thing started. Rich and I were talking the other day, and it doesn't make sense that we haven't had some sort of pushback from ITOC. I mean, aside from blocking the stable points."

"What is ITOC?" Clio asks.

"The International Temporal Oversight Committee," Tyson explains. "It's part of the United Nations. ITOC was formed a decade or so before CHRONOS was created. Everyone was fairly certain when the committee was formed that at least two of the other member states had already done several time jumps, although there was nothing to indicate they were pursuing a full-fledged program like the US. Alex said he hadn't detected any chronotrons originating from either location, but I have a hard time believing that Europe or China would simply ignore the massive changes we've seen in these past few shifts. We're not an island. And we already know from the only stable point we have that works in Europe that there are ripples.

Rich said that building on the execution grounds pops up decades earlier."

I take a deep breath, then just spit it out. "They're not ignoring the changes. They don't know. Or at least, they wouldn't have known in our timeline. If I had to guess, they're a bit more hesitant about trusting the US around the time CHRONOS is developed. Maybe because we have well over a century of antidemocratic government in our fairly recent past."

Tyson frowns. "Okay. There's a lot to unpack in that. But the seven permanent members were given CHRONOS keys when the agency was created, before the first cohort went out into the field. Unless all of the member states stashed their keys away in a sock drawer, how could they not know about the changes?"

"They were given keys, yes. And temporal physicists in each country were able to verify that the keys emit a chronotron field. But the keys they were given were purposefully set to a different frequency. It was apparently a national security decision. If the US ended up at war or in any other situation where they needed to use the technology, they didn't want to have any constraints. So whoever is wearing those keys is as clueless as everyone else about the time shifts."

There's a long silence in which Tyson simply stares at me. Then he says, "How do you know that?"

I debate giving a partial answer, but it's sort of tied together and I've already spilled the explosive part. And so I send a silent apology into the universe in case my mom and Angelo are out there somewhere, and barrel ahead.

"My parents and Angelo had a relationship for a while. He dated my mom briefly before she met Dad, when she first started working at CHRONOS. My folks have always gone through polyamorous phases. I didn't really understand the details back then because I was maybe four or five when things cooled off. He was just around a lot and always game for piggyback rides or sneaking me ice cream between meals. The one time I asked my mom about it she said Angelo started dating someone who preferred monogamy. But they remained close. If something was troubling Angelo, he used my parents as a sounding board. And . . . I've never told anyone this next part. Not Rich, not Saul.

"I overheard something I shouldn't have when I was on break after my third year of classroom training. My parents had rented a place down near Virginia Beach, and Angelo joined us a few days later. He'd taken over the additional role of liaison between CHRONOS and the government a few months prior, and he'd come across some encrypted files. He needed Mom's help unlocking them, and he was *livid* when he found out about the government deceiving ITOC. As a result, he had way too much to drink that night. Ranted about exposing the whole thing, but my dad talked him down. Pointed out that other countries probably wouldn't take that sort of deception very well. That we could end up in a war if they thought the US had been tampering with the timeline in order to advance our national interests. I wouldn't have heard any of that discussion if not for the fact that I was reading on the upper deck when my dad was trying to reason with Angelo. When they realized I was up there, Angelo swore me to absolute secrecy. Said he could lose his job. For that matter, so could my mom. This is the very first time I've spoken about it since. And if we're ever back in a reality where this is relevant, you're all sworn to secrecy, too."

Tyson shakes his head. "No worries there. That kind of secret could get you killed if people in power find out you know."

"Exactly. I'm a little worried that Saul may have pieced some of it together, though. I think the whole *Hexenpest* thing in Salzburg was his way of testing the waters, either to see how far he could go without getting pushback or maybe just to see if there was anyone over there willing to come out and play time games with him. Or willing to stop him. And they sort of did, by locking down foreign access. I just don't know whether that was because someone spotted changes or because of generally greater suspicion of US actions."

"So . . . when was this?" Madi asks. "I mean, when did the US government give these other member states the keys that are under a different frequency?"

Tyson says it must have been around 2247. "That's when the Chrono-Historical Research Organization merged with the Natural Observation Society to form CHRONOS."

"That's what, nearly sixty years before your time?"

Tyson nods, clearly wondering where Madi's going with this.

"Don't you think at least one of them would have reverse engineered the technology?" she continues. "That they would have created keys using that frequency, which is a different one than our keys use? I would assume someone at CHRONOS would have been under a field of that frequency, just in case. But none of *us* are . . ."

Clio's mouth falls open. "They could be changing things, too. And we'd *never* know. How's that for a kick in the pants?"

I'm not entirely sure how to feel about that. On the one hand, the notion that someone, or even multiple someones, could be altering our reality is definitely unnerving. If one of those keys was lying around this cabin, I'd most certainly slip it into my pocket to be on the safe side. But the fact that we don't have access to those keys is also oddly comforting. If it's impossible for us to know, we can't be expected to try to fix it. And we've got enough on our plate at the moment dealing with our homegrown temporal terrorist.

We're all silent for a few minutes. It feels like I just sat through a particularly painful Temporal Conundrums class. I suspect they're all thinking the same thing and feeling that annoying ache at the front of their heads. Madi is at any rate, because she rubs her temples and then says, "Like Jack said the other night, this is esoteric. We can't know, and therefore we need to set it aside and focus on what we can, hopefully, fix."

"Exactly." Clio tosses the tablet onto the couch. "San Francisco seems like a logical next stop, since the Fifth Column info says some of the Process Church members and the Manson crew lived there within a few blocks of each other in Haight-Ashbury in 1967. In this timeline, the Process Church sets up camp a bit earlier in the year. Their chapel was also a coffee shop. I don't have an address for it. It's not the same location as the previous timeline, but I'd almost guarantee that's where the photo with Saul is taken, probably in the spring or very early summer of 1967."

"Why do you think that?" Tyson asks.

Clio enlarges the image and points to a bulletin board in the background. Saul's head is blocking part of it, and the blue font at the bottom is really hard to read even after she enlarges the photo. I can see the face and torso of a semi-clad woman against a green background that reminds me of peacock feathers. The only word I can make out is *JUNE* at the top, in fat red letters.

"Because," Clio says, "that poster was plastered everywhere when I was in 1967 San Francisco. It's for the Monterey Pop Festival."

FROM THE *MONTEREY PENINSULA HERALD*

QUESTIONS MOUNT OVER CYRIST PRIVATE SECURITY RAID ON FESTIVAL

(June 21, 1967) Despite more than fifty deaths and at least twice that number injured, last weekend's Monterey International Pop Festival started off on a peaceful, happy note. During the preparations and the first day's activities, local police and music lovers joked outside the arena, accepted flowers from the participants, and in one notable case, an officer even stuck a flower through the brim of his helmet. Friday evening's concert went flawlessly, and the second day of the festival seemed to be off to a good start.

About two hours into the afternoon's performances, however, the medical tent set up by the event's organizers began to see an unusual number of visitors. The facility, which was dubbed the "bad-trip tent" because it was a relatively quiet place that any attendees who might be using narcotics could retire to if they had a bad reaction, also dispensed first aid, and had tended to only a handful of guests the previous night. One of the hired medics who was on staff Saturday was among the two people killed when an officer with Cyrist Sword and Shield (CSS), a private security firm on contract to the State of California, lost control of his vehicle and crashed into the tent. Moments later, a man identified as Owsley Stanley, a suspected drug dealer, was shot onstage by a CSS officer, as the band Country Joe and the Fish was still onstage. According to multiple witnesses, however, Stanley was not running from the officer as stated in the official CSS report but was, in fact, shoved onto the stage before being shot. Several eyewitnesses also claim that CSS fired additional shots into the audience, with three of them stating that the woman who was reportedly trampled fell only after being shot in the head by the officers onstage. We have spoken with hundreds of attendees and can find no one to corroborate CSS reports that fights broke out and people were killed and injured prior to their arrival. The vast majority of casualties were reportedly the result of drug overdose.

Larry McDonald, the national leader of CSS, said the group was hired by the State of California to act as backup should the Monterey police find themselves overwhelmed. They received an anonymous tip that narcotic use was rampant, that several individuals had died due to overdose on a new variant of LSD known as Monterey Purple, and that dozens more were seriously ill. According to CSS Chief McDonald, his men arrived to find that two people had been killed in violent clashes in the audience, and located the suspected dealer, Owsley Stanley, hiding backstage. McDonald said he then contacted Lieutenant Governor John Schmitz, a personal friend, and requested helicopters from Fort Ord to transport victims to the hospital. More than three hundred individuals were treated at Fort Ord and Cyrist Mercy in Salinas, which have reported a combined total of fifty-nine drug-related deaths as of this time, with several still in serious condition.

McDonald told reporters outside the fairgrounds where the event was held that while they were surprised at the number of deaths, they were prepared for casualties. "These drugs are merely a symptom of the evil that has permeated American society. The young people who take these substances claim they want to open their minds, and the drugs do precisely that— they open the mind to demonic forces."

Most of the event's coordinators could not be reached for comment, but one who agreed to speak on condition of anonymity said, "The whole thing stinks. Yeah, there was some acid use . . . but LSD doesn't do that, man. I took multiple hits from that batch and know hundreds of people who did . . . we had no issues. The police weren't overwhelmed at all until people started getting sick. Why were victims taken to Cyrist Mercy and Fort Ord? Monterey Community Hospital is closer and larger. And they flat-out lied about Owsley resisting. He's not stupid and he can afford lawyers. We'd have proof of that, too, since we were filming for a TV special . . . but the [officers] smashed our cameras and took the [expletive] film."

An assistant medic, who refused to give his name, was outside the tent when the raid happened and agrees that the symptoms seemed inconsistent with LSD, noting that there were well over a dozen children among the victims. "Most people I know don't give their kids acid. One or two you might write off as an accident, but . . . not this many."

Local leaders have questions, as well, and are calling on the state to begin an official investigation. Governor Reagan's office declined to comment, but the anonymous event coordinator for Monterey Pop has little hope that any investigation by his administration would be open and honest. She noted Reagan's staunch antipathy toward the counterculture, his claim that support of free speech was simply a license for "filthy speech," and his comment on the campaign trail that a hippie was someone who "looks like Tarzan, walks like Jane, and smells like Cheetah."

∞16∞

TYSON
SAN FRANCISCO, CALIFORNIA
MAY 28, 1967

The sky has an odd, shimmering quality, despite the fact that the day is a bit overcast. Much like the last jump Clio and I made together, the air is heavy and smells of smoke. It's stronger this time, though. Not the faint whiff of a massive forest fire in the distance, but multiple sources. Most of it is auto exhaust, which I'm used to. Any city street in the 1960s reeks of car fumes. Cigarette smoke, too. Here, however, those familiar scents bring with them a trace of incense from the store we just passed. Patchouli, sandalwood. And there's definitely marijuana in the mix.

Music is in the air, as well. We're still a few blocks away, though, and it's hard to make much out over the sound of people talking, cars passing, and the occasional blast of a horn to shoo the pedestrians out of the street.

Looking around, the thing that strikes me hardest is the fact that this is not even one year after the Beatles concert in Memphis, but judging from the hairstyles and clothing alone, you'd think at least a decade had passed. Admittedly, the South tends to lag a bit behind national fashion trends, and the average age of the young people at

Mid-South Coliseum was at least two years below the people here, but the differences are still stark.

The clothes Clio's mom sent are fine, but to be honest, I think we could have worn almost anything. We've been walking for nearly a mile, and I've seen a fairly wide array. Mostly jeans, some with wide legs, some not. A man in a top hat with flowers laced through his beard was selling newspapers on the sidewalk near the exit of the alley where we jumped in. A black guy around my age with his head shaved and another whose hair is wider than his shoulders. Girls in skirts that skim the ground, girls in skirts that barely cover their bottoms. Clio's pink-and-green flowered jumper hits mid-thigh. She wears it very well and I remind myself to focus on my surroundings, not my jump partner.

One welcome difference from last year's concert in Memphis is the racial mix. There were some black and brown faces in that crowd, notably Toni Robinson and her friends, because the Beatles refused to play to segregated audiences. But they were scattered around in clusters, not intermingling. As in Memphis, most of the faces here are white, but there are several mixed-race groups chatting on the sidewalk.

It's nice to be somewhere I don't need the damn colored contacts. But I have to admit I'd be happier if it were less crowded.

"I thought you said this was before Haight-Ashbury gets overwhelmed."

Clio makes a face. "It's worse now than when I was here two weeks back. It will be worse yet in a month. Give it two, and they'll be packed in like sardines. By the end of the summer, a lot of the people who came here seeking human connection will head home to where they have room to breathe. The hotels and boarding houses are booked solid, even now. People are sleeping in the parks and crashing at some houses a local commune bought. From everything I've read, the movement had some wonderful moments, and even some long-lasting impacts, but it ended on a sour note because there were too many people here, many without money, and a whole lot of them extraordinarily high."

"So . . . knowing all of that, what made you decide to come here during the Summer of Love?"

"Well, technically, I came during the *spring* before the Summer of Love. And . . ." She hesitates, and then asks, "Have you ever gone through a major breakup?"

"Not really. I've had a few relationships that lasted a month or so, but they weren't serious. Too busy with CHRONOS. There's a reason they encourage you to hold off on relationships until you're done with your field training, and preferably until field work is over entirely. It can be awkward managing relationships with people who aren't agents. Plenty of time for settling down after your ability with the key begins to fade and you're stuck in a desk job."

"What age is that?"

"It varies. Usually in your early-to-midthirties."

"I guess it takes a little longer to fade for second-gen CHRONOS. My mom could still use the key in her late thirties. June could use it almost all the way through her forties, but she gave herself some sort of booster when she was at the Cyrist Farm. But anyway, what I was getting at was that after Matt broke off our engagement, I needed to get away for a bit. I wanted something completely different. Some place where there was no risk of Simon. And no stuffy white-picket-fence guys like Matt. Which isn't exactly fair because he's not really all that stuffy, but . . ."

"But it was right after your breakup and you were thinking only bad things."

She looks at me out of the corner of her eye and laughs. "You really *haven't* had a major breakup, have you? Yes, you think about the bad things. And then ten minutes later you're thinking of the *good* things and crying into your beer because he was perfect or at least damn close, and you're certain you'll never love anyone ever again. Rinse and repeat."

We wait for a break in the traffic and cross Oak Street, heading for the strip of green that Clio says is called the Panhandle because it looks a bit like the slightly off-center handle to the much longer, much wider Golden Gate Park to the west of us.

"But sure," she continues, "I could have gone to Vegas or pretty much anywhere, I guess. You're probably going to laugh, but I decided on San Francisco because of a song. Simon insisted on going to the Yankees game where Mickey Mantle hit his five hundredth home run, in mid-May of 1967. This was maybe a week after Matt broke things off. We're walking out of the stadium and Simon says *Sweet Charity* is at the Palace, and we should go. Normally, I would have said nope, time to go home, you've stolen enough of my day, but it occurred to me I really didn't have anything better to do. So I agreed, and while we're in the cab, Simon lights one of his god-awful cigars and I'm feeling kind of despondent and also kind of nauseous. Thinking I desperately need to get away. To go somewhere, anywhere, any*when*, without Simon. Then, as I'm debating whether I want to throw him out of the cab or throw myself out, this *San Francisco* song comes on the radio. Talking about gentle people and flowers in your hair, and . . . that's sort of the direct opposite of Simon. I had to get a few costumes ready, but three days later, I'm on Baker Beach, soaking up sunshine and making sketches of the Golden Gate Bridge."

"So if the song had been 'Last Train to Clarksville' you'd have headed to . . ." I trail off, not entirely sure what state Clarksville is in.

"Maybe. But I also knew this was one place I could escape without being worried I might stumble across Simon, as long as I timed it right. He'd mentioned Haight-Ashbury once when he was drunk. Said he dropped in during early August of 1967, and it was a shithole. That's why he decided to avoid any trips after 1965 that weren't strictly baseball or Broadway related."

"Guess he didn't like crowds."

She shrugs. "He absolutely loved New York, so it's not like he was a stranger to packed streets. To be honest, I think he tried some acid while he was here. Had a bad trip or maybe he just didn't like the person he found when he went in search of himself."

The music is louder now, and I spot the bandstand through a gap in the crowd. I don't recognize the song the band is playing, but it's heavy on guitar. Some of the chords feel a little shaky to me, and I immediately hear Rich's voice in my head. *The LA sound of the late 1960s was packaged, processed, cookie-cutter. San Francisco, though . . . that was authentic.*

Rich should *be* here. I know he's got a Woodstock jump coming up. I'm almost certain the Monterey concert is on his long-term research agenda. Is that another reason Saul decided to remove him from the game? Rich would likely have recognized that poster on sight, something that Saul would have known. It was sheer luck that Clio had seen it before.

The cover story we worked up has me as her cousin. Just graduated from LSU, about to ship out for Vietnam, and I'm looking for a girl I know. She followed the Processeans here from New Orleans, which is where they set up one of their first locations.

Our original plan had been to find their headquarters, which functioned as a coffee shop when the building wasn't being used for services. We'd had absolutely no luck in that regard, however. There was no record of an address for the Process ministry in this timeline, and when we checked the address they used in the previous timeline, we found that it's now a private residence. So we're resorting to Plan B, in which Clio will try to get the information from her friends in the band.

Something pops into my head then that probably should have occurred to me earlier. "What if you didn't make the trip in this timeline?"

"I made it," she says. "This jump wasn't connected to Simon, and nothing I've ever done was directly connected to CHRONOS, so there's no reason it wouldn't have happened. But I checked the stable points for that date to be sure and saw myself pop in right on schedule."

Younger kids are seated near the front, cross-legged on the grass. A small section of lawn seems to have been set aside for dancing, or maybe people just cleared out to avoid the flailing limbs of this one very tall, lanky white guy who is in his own universe right now.

There's a short break in the music as we approach the edge of the bandstand. When the band picks back up, it's a song I do know, mostly because it's a cover. "Dancing in the Street." Martha and the Vandellas. 1963 or maybe the year after. The guy singing lead seems younger than the others. He's exceptionally good-looking, with long, straight, light brown hair, topped off by a white derby. Clio catches his eye during the first few notes of the song. His brows go up in surprise and he grins at her. And when he reaches the part about people dancing in Chicago, he sings it directly to her.

I find that I do *not* like this. In fact, I don't like it one bit. I'm not the only one, apparently. Several girls near the front are shooting dagger stares in Clio's direction. She's not paying any attention to them. Instead, she's digging around in the woven bag she's carrying. After a moment, she pulls out a pad and pencil, and begins sketching the band.

The next song is a much longer bluesy number. Clio continues to sketch. She includes all of the band members and one of the girls dancing on the edge of the stage. But they are clearly the background. Even though the dark-haired guy sings lead on the next song, the focus of Clio's sketch is definitely the heartthrob at the front. The only other person whose face is drawn in detail is the short guy near the edge of the stage. He looks familiar. It takes a moment, but I realize he's the guy Clio mentioned. Owsley somebody, the sound engineer and creative chemist Cyrist Sword makes an example of at Monterey. Unless we manage to fix this, he has about three weeks to live.

When she finishes the sketch, she stashes the pencil back into her bag.

"It's good," I say.

"Thanks. But the question is whether it will have Bobby curious enough that he doesn't get distracted by his harem," she says with a tiny smile. "It's the reason I got his attention last time."

Judging from the look he gave her a moment ago, I suspect it's not the only reason she got his attention. The song is either the end of the concert or the end of the set, because the long-haired guy, who is apparently Bob Weir, rests his guitar against the amp and hops off the bandstand. He scoops Clio up into a hug, followed by a long, enthusiastic kiss.

"You said you were going back to Chicago!"

"Change of plans," Clio says. "This is my cousin, Tyson."

"Bobby," he says, extending his hand. "Good to meet you."

We shake, then he nudges her sketch pad with his knee. She hands it to him, and he holds it out slightly to get a better look.

"Your cuz is good," he says. "I told her she ought to set up a shop here. Who needs art school when you can do this? Or is that why you decided to come back?"

She gives him a sad face. "No. My parents will kill me if I don't finish school. But Tyson is shipping out in a few weeks and wants to find this girl he knows from LSU who took the semester off to head out here. And since you guys seem to know pretty much everybody in the Haight . . ."

He glances around at the crowd and shakes his head. "We *used* to know most everyone. Not quite as many familiar faces these days." He turns to me. "Do you have a picture?"

I shake my head. "But the girl I'm looking for is part of an odd church with a branch here. They're called the Process?"

"Oh, sure. They've been around a couple of months. Apparently put on a good show with their services, but members keep to themselves, aside from selling that paper of theirs. They bought out the building where the Diggers were running the Free Store. The Diggers had to move again, and they aren't happy about that." He points to the other side of the park. "Over on Frederick, just across Stanyan. I haven't been there, but I heard they started a coffee shop called Satan's Cavern. Bought out the Jeff Haight and ousted a bunch of folks who were crashing there, too, which really wasn't cool. Jerry says the Process Church are scam artists. And kids need families, you know? He's debating whether we should even do the Monterey gig, since he learned they're pumping a lot of money into it. But we're already on the poster, and the organizers are running ads, so we'd feel kind of bad about pulling out."

There's a lot there that I don't understand at all. For one thing, we've seen the poster for Monterey Pop, and I don't remember any band names. I also have no clue what the Jeff Haight is. I do have a vague memory of the Diggers from the background data on the Summer of Love that I glanced through before we left. The group was staunchly anti-capitalist and tried to live their beliefs. They operated not just the Free Store, but also a free clinic and a free soup kitchen, with the costs borne by several wealthy donors. Unfortunately, the Summer of Love would essentially bankrupt them, as thousands of young people poured into the neighborhood and overtaxed their resources. They viewed the influx as a horde of locusts—young people who weren't interested in giving back to contribute to the community, but simply hanging out in California for a few months of readily available drugs, partying, and free food before returning to their hometowns or colleges in the fall. The Diggers were so disillusioned by the experience that they held a symbolic funeral for the hippie lifestyle at the end of the summer and gave up on the idea of an urban collective, leaving Haight-Ashbury behind to form a rural commune.

What I can't remember is whether that was the group's history in *this* timeline or the last, since the Fifth Column provided info on both. Everything is beginning to run together. And maybe that's Saul's grand design—get us so confused we can't tell what's new and what's old.

Clio's eyes travel over to where the Owsley guy is loading something onto a flatbed truck. "Yeah. I guess you don't want to disappoint people . . ." She looks like she wants to say something else, but she just tears off the drawing and hands it to Bobby. Then she tiptoes up and gives him a quick kiss. "Thank you for the info on the Process crowd! We're going to check it out."

"Yeah. You're coming by the house later, though, right?" he says, looking a little concerned. "You, too, man. And bring your girl if you find her. We're having a party!"

"Wouldn't miss it!" Clio blows him a kiss over her shoulder as we begin working our way through the crowd toward Oak Street.

"We're not actually going, are we?" I ask once we're out of earshot.

"No," she says, with a look that suggests it was a stupid question. "They're *always* having a party. Bobby is a sweet kid, but he's still very much a kid. While I don't exactly put the week I spent here in the category of *mistake*, it's not an experience I'm particularly keen to repeat."

I'm ridiculously relieved to hear her say this, and thoroughly annoyed at myself for feeling that way. *Get a frickin' grip, Reyes.*

"And every damn thing in that house seems to be laced with acid," she adds. "I'd swear it's in the water supply. Have you tried it?"

"Acid? No. Although I did have a concoction at the OC—that's the club Morgen Campbell owns—that contained a proprietary blend of so-called *mood meds.* I remember everything being floaty and surreal for a few hours. Alisa said I actually giggled, but she's been known to lie."

Clio grins. "Now I'm wishing we had time to go to the party. I'm guessing the stuff Owsley makes is way stronger than your OC's mood meds. It might be fun to see you giggle."

"If we flip the timeline and find a way to stop Saul for good, I'll consider obliging you. What's the Jeff Haight?"

"An abandoned hotel where kids crash, especially when the weather's bad. It's on the way."

We cross the road again and head down Cole. At the intersection with Haight Street, she nods to one of the row houses on the other side, just to the left. "That was the Jeffrey Haight. Except there were no bars on the windows before. I never slept there, but one of the girls I met said she sometimes did on cold nights. Said they'd all curl up in there with their sleeping bags like a giant litter of puppies. Wonder where she's sleeping now . . ."

We cross the street and take a slight right to continue on Cole. When we walked past number 636 on our way to the concert on the Panhandle, there had been no signs of life outside the house where Charles Manson is currently living with the first members of his cult. The fact that there was no one around gave us a chance to set a couple of stable points outside the building so we can observe them later.

Now, however, two young women are sitting on the front steps. Each has one half of a grape popsicle. When they catch my eye, the blonde slides the ice pop in and out of her mouth slowly, then gives me a grin. The other girl, who can't be more than sixteen, follows suit. I don't know who they are. It's possible the younger girl isn't even part of the group that follows Manson to LA, but I'm pretty sure the older one was in the photograph the Fifth Column gave us.

Clio flips them off. They laugh and go right back to their popsicle fellatio. Once we turn the corner onto Waller, she shudders. "The older girl is Susan Atkins. One of the crew that committed the Tate murders."

We continue in silence, then she says, "Do you think there's any chance the Sister he drops off with Manson is in that house right now?"

"No way to know until we watch the stable points. But probably not. The file said the group was pretty small until they got to LA, which is where that photo was taken. And the girl looked frightened in that picture. Like she was looking for an escape route. If she'd been there a year or more . . ."

Clio nods. "She'd either have escaped or been more resigned. Thinking there was no way out."

We bump into a member of the Process Church before we reach the church headquarters, a few blocks from the Manson house. The young man wears a hooded black robe. Next to him, sitting patiently at attention, is a black-and-tan German shepherd. The dude in the robe is clearly going for ominous and foreboding, with a broody scowl above his goatee, but the effect is ruined by the fact that he's hawking a religious newspaper on the street corner and his dog's tongue is lolling comically out of the side of its mouth. I fork over two quarters and take a copy.

Clio glances down at the paper. "Oh, wow. Are you with the Process Church?" She slurs her voice and gives him a wide, slightly dazed smile. "What a groovy coincidence. We're looking for your café. Someone at the concert said the Oracle is there today. I want to ask her a question."

The man's scowl deepens. "Satan's Cavern is up ahead on Frederick. It's not far. But if Prudence is there, she's not going to answer your question. The Oracle doesn't even answer questions for acolytes. Only full members. And only then if you've proven yourself worthy."

"Oh, well. We can try. Ask the Oracle and the wisdom of the universe will be opened before you."

Tall, Dark, and Goth literally looks down his nose at her. "Here's another one, Gidget. Bother the Oracle with trifles and the woes of the universe will befall you. And if you really piss her off"—he leans in even further—"she might tell you the exact day you'll die, like she did this guy in New Orleans. And then she'll laugh and laugh when she's right." He then turns his gaze on a group approaching from Stanyan Street.

"Well, isn't he just a bucket of sunshine," Clio mumbles as we cross the street. "How much of that do you think is true and how much is mumbo jumbo?"

"I'd guess mostly the latter."

She shrugs. "If Saul is there with her, it wouldn't be hard for him to give her some accurate predictions along those lines."

We stop at a bench outside Kezar Pavilion to scan the paper, which upon closer examination is really more of a magazine than a newspaper. *Process* is printed in bold black caps across the top. The cover of the edition, which is entitled "Freedom," features a stark aqua-and-black image of a young woman standing next to a spiky metal fence. At the bottom is the Process Church logo. Four black lines are inside a circle, pointing north, east, south, and west, with the interior edges forming a square in the middle. The idea was apparently to depict four letter *P*s that overlap at different angles. Madi said it looked a little like one of those martial-arts throwing stars, but the main thing it evokes in my mind is a swastika. The group switches to a version with flared rather than straight lines in a year or so, and in this timeline, a lotus flower now obscures the white square in the middle. And it *still* looks like a swastika. Which was probably the intent, given that Mary Ann de Grimston fell into the *Hitler-had-some-good-ideas* camp in the previous timeline and told several members of the Process inner circle that she was the reincarnation of Joseph Goebbels.

It's not the edition that had the picture of Saul. There are also no photographs of three of the four Process leaders, who don't claim to actually be the various gods or demigods, but simply their representatives or spokespersons here on earth. Before the time shift, the only one whose photos were spotlighted in the magazine was Mary Ann's husband, Robert de Grimston, the so-called Christ of Carnaby Street. The two split up in the mid-1970s. Mary Ann got custody of the cult in the divorce and Robert was kicked unceremoniously to the curb.

In this reality, however, Mary Ann seems to be a little less camera shy. The second article, "Financial Freedom," includes an image of a woman with long curls. Her face and body are dimly lit, almost to the point of being silhouetted against the blue wall. Only her hands, spread above a vivid crystal ball, are fully illuminated. The gist of the piece is that one of the benefits of becoming a Processean is freedom from financial worry.

That part isn't new. The group was known for giving its devotees room and board, taking pretty much everything they owned in exchange.

What's new is that the Oracle now claims to guarantee those who join the Processean family a substantial return on their investment. "Give us all your loaves and your fishes for a year. They will feed multitudes, and yet come back to you fourfold. You are free to go at any time after that, or you can stay and reinvest in the collective." There's also a Friend of the Process option. It's less lucrative—they only guarantee to *increase* your loaves and fishes. It's pitched as the perfect choice for those who are curious about the Processean Way but not ready to fully commit to collective living.

Turning over your loaves and fishes apparently means turning over responsibility, too. Children are raised in a collective fashion, benefiting from the wisdom of the community. Each child's nature is determined, and he or she is paired with a spiritual guide. One of the articles has a rather chilling depiction of the horrors of childbirth, and another dispenses little nuggets about parenthood that seem to boil down to the idea that sacrificing to make a better life for your kids is a bad thing. It just pisses you off and instills a sense of guilt in their young minds. And children are manipulative little tyrants, anyway.

I hand Clio the magazine, open to the image of the Oracle. "Looks like the Process adopted more than just the lotus flower and the Prudence personae from the Cyrists. They seem to be managing finances this time, not simply handing out stock tips to the faithful in exchange for a tithe."

"So . . . what the hell are they doing in the Haight? There doesn't seem to be a surplus of cash around here. It's mostly teens, and a good many of them are sleeping in the park."

"Maybe it fulfills the part about feeding the multitudes? A little side of feel-good to convince you that your money is in safe, altruistic hands? I mean, a lot of religions add in a missionary component. And the group hasn't been around long."

She shrugs. "Sounds more like the Diggers to me. I didn't get the impression from Bobby that the Processeans are letting people crash at the Jeff Haight. And why would Saul bother with an upstart group like the Processeans when he's got Cyrist International?"

It's a good question. I don't have a good answer, however, and any speculation is halted when she flips the paper open to a two-page spread near the back. The stylized Monterey Pop poster is on one side. Opposite that is a more legible poster with ticket prices and a list of the bands. The Grateful Dead are, indeed, prominently featured in the center column, just below the Jimi Hendrix Experience and the Who. I feel a wrench of pain as I look at it. I know many of these names—Simon and Garfunkel, Otis Redding, Jefferson Airplane, and the Byrds, among others. I can pull up a song for the performers in most cases, thanks to cultural-literacy training, and can even hum a few bars. But the fact that I know deeper cuts on the albums, and the background to the artists and the songs . . . that's all Rich.

"We should get going," I say. "We don't have long before we need to be back."

Clio nods. "A two-page spread in their magazine," she says as we turn onto Frederick. "Bobby's right, they're definitely promoting the concert. Wonder how that ties in with the Oracle and Saul?"

"No clue. No clue about anything. Not even sure there's logic to what Saul does. I mean, I-Break-You-Fix. That's a fucking madman's game."

She must pick up on the fact that my mood has taken a turn for the bleak, because we walk along in silence until we're approaching our destination. The storefront across the street appears newly painted in deep red. A black sign above the door has the words *Satan's Cavern* in the center, flanked by Process Church logos with the white lotus in the middle. They're the later variant, with the flared edges to each tail of the *P*.

The top half of the bulletin board with the Monterey Pop poster is visible through the window as we approach the café, which is crowded, with all of the tables occupied and several people leaning against the bookshelves lining that side of the store. They're painted black, but have panels decorated with a floral motif with droopy purple flowers. At the back is an altar, covered in black, of course. The Christian cross is on the left side of the wall above it, the simplified Cyrist cross on the right, and in the middle is the goat's head emblem sometimes used in satanic worship.

I start to open the door, but Clio grabs my arm.

"We just need to set the stable points, right?"

"Right . . ."

"Then let's go. We can just as easily do that a few months back, when it was still the Free Store run by the Diggers. This place gives me the creeps. And don't look now, but we're being watched."

Her warning comes a little late, as I was already looking up before she reached the last sentence. We are indeed being watched by a woman with long dark hair, held back by a red band. She's sitting one table over from the poster.

It's almost certainly Mary Ann de Grimston, and the fact that I looked up really doesn't make much difference. Her eyes are on Clio.

FROM *PROCESS*: "FREEDOM" (1967)

Freedom to Grow

The Process Church of Divine Revelation has its roots in London, where the Oracle first began counseling people in 1964. In the span of three short years, the church has grown into an international phenomenon, with locations in seven US cities—New Orleans, New York, DC, Chicago, Miami, Los Angeles, and San Francisco—as well as nine foreign missions.

We continue to grow because we help others grow. Our spiritual and financial counseling form the mainstay of each local assembly, but we offer many other services to meet the needs of the community. Most assemblies have a local spiritual bookstore. Many offer holistic medicine and a range of natural therapies to help relieve the stress of busy lives. Our Los Angeles assembly will soon be branching out to form a media company, so we can explore new ways to spread joy and the divine prophecies of the Oracle.

Interested in starting an assembly in your city? Come grow with us!

∞17∞

The Templar's office at the Sixteenth Street Temple in the early 1970s looks remarkably like the Templar's office where Katherine and I first met Beta and Charlayne nearly a century later, in 2058. As best I've been able to tell over the past half hour or so of chronospying, the only structural change is that somewhere along the line, the wall between the office and courtyard was knocked out and replaced by glass.

There were also a lot more books on the shelves in the 1970s. The *Book of Cyrus* still holds the spot of honor to the left of the Templar's desk, although there are three noticeable differences. First, the book has the straight-armed version of the Cyrist cross embossed on the front rather than the infinity-sign version. Second, it's on a simple wrought-iron bookstand, not inside a protective glass cube. Third, and most important, that bookstand is designed to hold two books. On the right is a second slim volume, the *Book of Prophecy*.

Bingo.

The man behind the desk is different, too, of course. I didn't meet the Grand Templar for North America in 2058, and I'm not curious enough to scroll forward to see what he or she is like. But I'm going to assume they're a major improvement over Templar Dennis.

This isn't really a rash judgment. Tyson and I listened to the man speak at a German-American Bund rally in 1939, where a giant portrait of George Washington was surrounded by swastikas and racist slogans. I know Dennis was a Hitler apologist, heralding the German dictator as the greatest political genius since Napoleon, because Hitler understood that the masses must be led and united by their emotions, not by an appeal to reason. Dennis was billed as the thinking man's fascist, as if supporting vile views with academic footnotes somehow makes you better than a garden-variety, working-class Nazi.

I don't know much about the man in this timeline, aside from the fact that he oversaw witch trials and public executions. Given that I'm currently sidelined by an injury incurred when I tripped over the handiwork of someone who would have hauled me in front of a similar tribunal, however, that's all I need to know. And I'm almost certain that Lawrence Dennis is fully aware that witchcraft is bunk. Like Saul, his only quest is power.

My general dislike for him is amplified by my recent discovery that at least once a week for the three-year period I've just scanned on the CHRONOS key, a young woman arrives at the side door of his office—the door that will eventually be a glass wall opening into the courtyard. It's not the same young woman each time, although there were a few repeat performances. All the girls wear the same plain black shift with a discreet red logo above the pocket. None are much older than twenty and, in some cases, I suspect they're younger. Sometimes, the girl brings a small package, which she places on the desk. It appears to be marijuana, or at least something he puts in a pipe and smokes after she's gone. But whether or not there's a package, the girl always gives Dennis's neck and shoulders a perfunctory massage, removes all of her clothing from the waist up, and drops to her knees behind the desk where the good Templar is seated. Several minutes later, she gets up, puts her dress back on, and departs. On most of these occasions, the Templar retires to the couch for a long nap. Sometimes he snoozes in his chair. Not too surprising that he'd need a nap, given that he's in his late seventies and doesn't appear to be in good health.

The girls aren't his only visitors, of course. My tablet is currently displaying pictures of several key historical figures who apparently play a role in this insanity. Dennis isn't in the office much, so I suspect he pushes a lot of the day-to-day work of running Cyrist International on to others. I start just before the execution of the Process Church members in 1974 and move backward, pausing when I see someone new take the seat to the right of the massive desk so I can check their face against the virtual mug shots. None of the leaders of the church are ever in the Templar's office as best I can tell.

Larry McDonald is the first familiar face that I spot. Well, familiar in that he's currently looking back at me from the display hovering above my tablet. I'd never heard of him before all of this began. I'd definitely never heard of Robert Welch, the founder of the John Birch Society, who's about the same age as Lawrence Dennis. Welch accompanies McDonald on a few occasions, but McDonald is one of the more frequent visitors, popping in about once a month. McDonald always brings cigars, and Dennis usually pulls a flask of something out of his desk. While I can't hear what they're discussing in these meetings, I get the sense in most of them that McDonald is giving him a report, because he does most of the talking, with Dennis nodding until the last few minutes of the meeting, at which point McDonald usually grabs a pencil and starts taking notes.

The other face I recognize from the Fifth Column mug shots is Spiro Agnew, Nixon's vice president. He's listed as being a Cyrist, and the meeting was on a Sunday in April 1972, after weekly services, so maybe he was a member of the Temple. The mood seems friendly for a few minutes, then Agnew's face goes pale. He starts to protest, but whatever Lawrence Dennis says next stops him midsentence. Agnew doesn't resign from the vice presidency in this timeline, so this would be a few months before he was dropped from the ticket in preparation for the Republican Convention. RJ told us there was some flak within the party about the choice of McDonald as his replacement because the guy is in his first term in the House of Representatives and was, until early 1971, a Democrat. Others weren't too keen on McDonald's connections to the Birchers. But it was Nixon's choice, and his mind was apparently made up.

Otherwise, visitors to the office are a steady stream of church and civic leaders, none of whom I recognize from the photos, and, of course, Dennis's "massage therapists" a few times each week. I was watching June 1969 and was about to the point of moving on to something else, thinking we were probably at the edge of the window where I'd see anything pertinent, other than the *Book of Prophecy* behind his desk. I'd also gotten so accustomed to zipping past as soon as I saw any young female in the doorway that I very nearly missed one of the main things I've been watching for.

I can barely see her face in the shadow of the doorway. My first thought is that it's one of Dennis's regularly scheduled massage therapists. But she's much too short. This one isn't even close to legal age. As soon as she steps into the light, the resemblance becomes clear. Then Saul follows her inside, erasing any doubt. Two armed guards enter behind him and close the door.

The girl is around eleven or twelve, and she looks similar to the girl we saw in the image taken at Monterey Pop. Saul could have grabbed any of the Sisters at this age if he timed it right, and we can't rule out the possibility that he's still snatching them. But this is probably Eta, the one taken as an infant, triggering Beta's double memory. Her hair is shoulder length and she's dressed in a plain gray tunic with buttons up the front, pants the exact same shade of dull gray, and black shoes. I guess it could be a school uniform, but I don't think I've ever seen one so devoid of style. She's holding a blond wig.

Templar Dennis seems surprised to see them, but he gives the girl a warm smile and a hug when she approaches. She takes a piece of candy from a jar on his desk, then whispers something to him. As she cups her hand around her mouth, I spot the field extender bracelet. Not a cuff like the one the other Sisters wear, but a narrow band on her left wrist. Dennis nods, and she heads for the door on the other side of his desk. Saul must say something, because she turns back and gives him a withering look along with a quick one-finger salute before disappearing inside. A bit cheeky for a kid that age, but neither of the men seem shocked. Dennis appears not to notice at all, but when I scroll back to watch again, I see one side of his mouth twitch upward.

Based on Kate Pierce-Keller's description of the events that prevented the Culling, I'm almost certain there's a coat closet and a bathroom behind that door, and that she had a stable point set there. No clue whether she still has it on her key, but I could blink in at some point when the office is empty and set my own. That way, all we'd have to do is wait for the Sister to step out of the bathroom and get her to leave with me. Then I could scroll through for an opportune time to jump in and grab the *Book of Prophecy*.

Of course, that assumes she wouldn't scream when she saw me. Even though she clearly doesn't like Saul, she knows and seems fond of Dennis. Both relationships seem to be the sort that would take time to develop, especially the latter. I can see how Saul might be a person to whom many people could take an instant dislike, but Dennis doesn't strike me as the sort of person a young girl would warm toward easily. Everything I've read and seen, and everything Tyson has told me, suggests he's a bit prickly.

And even if the girl didn't scream, even if I could convince her to leave with me, Saul and Dennis would quickly realize what I'd done, since they're under CHRONOS fields. If Saul is still even pretending to play by the rules he set, he *shouldn't* jump back to stop me. But *shouldn't* and *wouldn't* are light-years apart with that man. And who knows whether this is before or after he realizes we aren't exactly playing by the rules and that Katherine made a valiant, if foolhardy, attempt to destroy the judge, jury, and quite possibly executioner that he set up in the library?

Saul plops down in one of the chairs facing the desk. Whatever he says must not be especially congenial, based on Dennis's expression. After a couple of acerbic exchanges between the two, Saul gets up from his chair, takes two menacing steps forward, and bangs his fist against the desk. Dennis simply watches, unimpressed by the display of temper, probably because there are two armed guards in the room. He listens again as Saul continues to rail, then gives a noncommittal shrug and says the only words I'm able to decipher at all from the entire meeting—*and then you'll have nothing.* At least, that's what it looks like he says.

The girl steps back into the room at that point, but a movement outside the window of the cabin catches my attention and jolts me back to the here and now in 1941 Georgia. A woman is peering through the gap in the curtains covering the little window on the door. I reach over and flip the cover of the tablet closed and slide it under one of Clio's drawing pads. Then, I slip my key back into my sweater and hobble over to answer the door.

The woman is in her mid-to-late thirties, slightly plump with cheeks pink from the wind outside. She's holding a paper bag and smiling, but her expression looks a little strained.

"Hello," she says. "I'm . . . Alice Owens, the wife of the caretaker Mr. Dunne hired to watch over the place. I was just stopping by to see if y'all needed anything. You're not Clio, are you?"

"No, ma'am. Just a friend of hers."

"I didn't think so. It's been a while, but I remember her having the cutest dark curls when they visited. Is she here?" Mrs. Owens cranes her neck to look beyond me into the cabin. Her eyes rest for a moment too long on the coffee table where my tablet is. It looks like a thin notebook now, so I'm guessing she saw ghostly holographic faces hovering above the table when she looked in the window. And she's probably racking her brain trying to come up with a logical explanation for what she saw. A trick of the light? A reflection?

"Clio's not here," I say, and then I remember that the vehicle they provided is currently parked outside. "Everyone else went out for a hike. I sprained my ankle earlier, so I'm stuck on the sofa."

"Oh, goodness gracious, sweetie. Don't mind me, then. I'll just set these jars of jam in here on the counter." She steps inside and heads toward the kitchen. When she comes back into the living room, she again glances at the coffee table.

I thank her for the jam, and she leaves, but I can't quite muster up the nerve to use the tablet again, even without the extended screen. We're supposed to meet back in the library at eight Bethesda time, just over half an hour from now. But I need to soak my foot. Better yet, my whole body. I hit the ground pretty hard when I tripped and again when Wayne dumped me off his back. While I could use the tub here, I want to go *home* to my room. I want to stretch out on my bed, if only for a few minutes, and hug Jack's pillow. I'm past the point of caring that the place is being watched. If some creep actually wants to stare at my banged-up body sliding into a bubble bath, they can have at it.

Most importantly, Jack may need to reach me, and he can't do it here. So I grab my computer tablet, step into the bedroom where we've stored our various costumes, and blink back to my room at 7:23 p.m.

∞

BETHESDA, MARYLAND
NOVEMBER 28, 2136

Even though the lights are off, no room is ever entirely dark when you're holding an active CHRONOS key. It feels strange, though, since Jarvis usually turns the lamp on when I enter. Must be the lag from his connection with Alex. I'm used to being here in the dark when I sleep, but it feels oddly disorienting right now. I take a step toward the lamp on my bedside table to turn it on manually, but someone grabs my hand from behind.

I pull in a breath to scream. Before I can get it out, however, familiar fingers lace through my own and I hear a gentle shushing noise in my ear.

Jack. Turning toward him, I bury my face into his shoulder, and he wraps his arms around me. We stay that way for a long moment, then he nudges me toward the bathroom. Once we're inside, he turns on the light, then cranks up the fan and turns the water on full blast.

"I'm *pretty* sure there are no cameras in here, but there are both cameras and listening devices in the bedroom. Tell Jarvis to play something," he whispers. "Your loud swim mix. And switch the lights to the lowest setting."

Not exactly the musical choice I'd have made for a relaxing soak. In fact, just thinking of swimming in the basement pool tenses me up, and also causes this weird, scratchy sort of headache at the front of my brain. But my loud swim mix is definitely the sort of music you'd want to mask a conversation, so I follow his directions. Once the music begins and the only illumination is the tiny tea-light candles surrounding the tub, I put the stopper in and adjust the temp. If it's listening devices he's worried about, that's probably something his dad's crew put in place. But wouldn't they know he's here? Even if they didn't realize he's missing from wherever they're being held, surely they're watching the entrances to the house?

Not if he used the key, genius.

"Why are you limping?" he asks, still keeping his voice low.

"Tripped over a dead man's arm on the jump to Hatteras. I came back early so I could soak my ankle."

"Ice would probably help more." His voice is tight, and he seems kind of . . . twitchy, I guess?

"Already did that. My whole body hurts. I'm going to have a nasty bruise on my shoulder and my knee, and no way am I getting into a tub of ice. Are you okay?"

"Yeah," he says. "Side effects."

"So . . . Lorena gave you another booster shot? I take it your dad doesn't know you used it to come here?"

"He does *not*. And more to the point, his CO doesn't know, and Saul doesn't know."

"Are the others safe?"

Jack nods. "Try not to be too mad at Lorena, okay? She—"

"I know. She left us a note. And it's not like we can really say much when we've been off rescuing Thea's sisters."

"Where did you all go? I've been watching the library stable point, this one, and the ones downstairs. I was getting worried."

"We're supposed to meet back in the library at eight. Tyson and Clio are in San Francisco. We've located a picture that places Saul there with that Process cult, probably in the spring or early summer of 1967. The ankle injury meant I had to settle for watching stable points from the cabin—"

"What cabin?"

"One that Clio's family owns. In 1940s Georgia. After you said we were being watched, we decided it might be wise to use some other place as a base of operations, to the extent we can. We were in the attic for a while. Jarvis doesn't extend up there, so we weren't as worried about them using him to spy. And then I guess you heard about Katherine's um . . . I guess it was a panic attack."

"With the game console? Yeah. Alex screamed and the guy monitoring him got suspicious. He told him there was a spider under his desk. Alex is almost certain that Cyrist Sword has this place wired in more ways than one. Dad thinks he could be right. He's got two of his trusted people looking into it. Hopefully, they can get someone in there to disarm it, but this house is pretty much surrounded. And, of course, they have Jarvis set up to spy on you, but Alex is being selective with what he allows through."

"Which is why we're whispering in the bathroom?"

"Exactly. I don't want to overtax him. He's swamped. He was already on the verge of exhaustion, and Saul has this manager overseeing his work who has just enough knowledge of the field that he may be able to spot if Alex is dragging things out. The guy has had him working every waking hour for the past three months. Lorena, too, and—"

"Past three *months*?"

He nods. "Yeah. Dad wanted me to wait until everything was a bit further along, but—" He stops when he sees I'm about to interrupt with another question. "Let me back up, okay? Dad's not happy that I was keeping secrets, but he is on our side. Or, at least, he isn't on the other side. There's a large group within Cyrus Sword that would be delighted to see this house blasted to kingdom come in order to cleanse it of evil spirits."

"I take it your dad is Fifth Column?"

He frowns, then shakes his head and laughs. "Okay. That saves some time. How do you know about the Fifth Column?"

"Kate's diaries," I say. "That's also where we took the babies. They're apparently behind the whole Sisters, Inc. thing, and they have a compound about fifteen miles north of—"

"Gaithersburg," he says. "Yes. That's where Lorena, RJ, and the baby are now. They were in one of the cramped on-call rooms at DARPA for the first week and they were miserable."

A tiny voice in my head says it serves Lorena right. Which is totally unfair. I wasn't lying when I told Jack I don't blame her for this, and I definitely don't want any of them to be miserable. I'm almost certain things would have happened in a similar fashion even if she hadn't decided she had to save their alter-selves. And I get it. As much as I'd like to think I'd have made a different choice in order to save some version of me and Jack, what if we had a child who was also at risk? I don't know what I'd have done. But I still wish she'd told us. That she'd given us some sort of advance warning. Maybe Rich would be here and we'd . . .

That weird sensation in my mind is back. I shake my head again, trying to dislodge the cobwebs so I can focus. "So you and Alex are staying at DARPA?"

"Yeah. Alex needs to be close to his research and . . . I need someplace quiet to focus on writing my magnum opus."

"Your what?"

He grins. "How soon they forget. You're the one who suggested me for the job. And when I pitched it to my dad and the other two people he's working with, they said it was something we should have in reserve, in case the opportunity presents itself."

"Oh. You mean a revised *Book of Cyrus*. But your dad and the guys who were with him . . . they were all wearing lotus tattoos. How do they feel about you overhauling their scripture?"

"Most of them don't know, to be honest. Will never know. And my dad's not Cyrist. He just works with them. One of his coworkers at LORTA is Fifth Column, going back four or five generations. He came to my dad after we fixed the Team Viper timeline and hooked him and several others up with the Fifth Column tattoos before this latest shift. In this reality, a lot of the projects DARPA was working on have been outside of the government, since they did this whole military restructuring thing in the late 2040s. That included temporal physics, but then someone came through with a massive private grant, and . . ." Jack glances at the tub, which is almost full, and then down at his key. "Do you have a stable point for the attic? I'll meet you up there after your soak so we can finish this conversation. The others should be here by then. I'll give you a couple of minutes to bring them up to speed, so . . . five minutes after eight?"

"Okay. Or you could join me in the tub?" I'm only half-serious. There's really not enough room for two, especially if one of them is dinged up.

He gives me a rueful smile and pulls me close. "Don't tempt me. It's been three long months, and I have missed you more than you know."

I make a sad face and tap my key against his to transfer the location.

"And I'm only *mostly* sure there are no cameras in here," he adds. "If they're watching, I'm already going to have to admit to my father that I've been lying about only being able to jump a few minutes back. I'd rather not add the awkwardness of him first meeting his hopefully future daughter-in-law while we're making love in the tub. And yes, I think there was an implied proposal of marriage somewhere in the middle of that, but feel free to ignore it until we have time to do things right."

It's not the first implied proposal on either side. In fact, it's becoming a bit of a running not-exactly-a-joke. "Duly noted, Mr. Merrick. I'll have Jarvis remind us the next time we have a boring afternoon. Are you sure you can jump again?"

He rolls up his sleeve and shows me a small patch on the inside of his arm. "I'm going twenty minutes forward to a different location in this house, so I'll be fine. I'll also be fine to get back to my room at DARPA, but I wouldn't push it much beyond that. And Lorena is pretty sure this stuff will require increasingly large doses to be effective, so don't get your heart set on honeymooning in Victorian England."

"I'll settle for right here in this house and this year, as long as all of our friends are alive, and Saul Rand can't screw with the timeline."

"Works for me. We'll kick everyone out, put island scenery on the wall screen in the basement, and pretend it's a clothing-optional beach once this is all over."

I shudder at that, thinking both of Rich's body in the pool and the current frigid temperature down there. Yes, it's been three months for Jack, and yes, he knows we're going to undo Rich's death, but the comment still seems uncharacteristically flip for him. "I think it's going to be a little while before I'll feel comfortable swimming in the basement."

He frowns. "True, but it could have gone *so* much worse." He presses a quick kiss to my lips and blinks out.

I slip into the warm tub and feel the tension slowly melt. That's when it occurs to me that Jack might not know Rich was killed. Maybe his dad didn't tell him?

But as I sink below the surface of the water, the odd sensation in my head is back, full force. And along with it comes the double memory.

I sit bolt upright in the tub and reach for a towel.

FROM THE *CYRIST NATIONAL EXAMINER*

Templar Dennis to Give Guidance on Demonic Possession Film

(Washington, DC, September 13, 1973) Never one to hide his faith under a bushel, Vice President Larry McDonald has made civic virtue a key talking point in his campaigns and public appearances. Indeed, pundits have noted McDonald may have been chosen as a replacement for Agnew to bolster Nixon's reputation among those on the right who disapprove of his willingness to tolerate the growing laxity in public morals. The president's appearance in 1968 on the short-lived television series *Rowan & Martin's Laugh-In* was a prime example. While a self-deprecating sense of humor is certainly not a bad thing in a leader, the appearance lent the imprimatur of the White House to a program that championed crude humor, inappropriate music, implied drug use, and sexual immorality.

Cyrists have long recognized, however, the value of the media in shaping minds and hearts, and steering Americans away from casual flirtation with the dark side of religious faith. There is always a place within the Cyrist fold for art that honestly reflects the price that people pay when they, wittingly or unwittingly, embrace evil. Such works come along rarely, and when they do, it's worth reaching a hand across the aisle to our Christian brethren to applaud it and help it reach a wider audience.

William Peter Blatty's *The Exorcist* is precisely this sort of work. While sections are undeniably crude and may offend those with gentler sensibilities, evil is not polite. Demonic possession should not be treated lightly. Witches should not be depicted as suburban housewives or peppy teenagers, for that only tempts the young to assume that Ouija boards and tarot decks are merely harmless fun, and there is no such thing as true evil.

Those who read *The Exorcist* do not come away doubting evil. Despite the unfortunate decision of the author to focus strictly on his own faith, Cyrist International recognized the potential of investing in a film adaptation that could spread the message of this book to a wider audience.

Grand Templar Lonnie Dennis, who is also spiritual counselor to the vice president, has thrown the full weight of his office behind the project, which will debut in December. Dennis served as script consultant.

He also played a major role in convincing British composer Mike Oldfield, a recent convert to Cyrisism, to allow a track from his album *Tubular Bells* to be used in the film, despite Oldfield's concerns over the movie's graphic nature.

∞18∞

KATHERINE
BETHESDA, MARYLAND
NOVEMBER 28, 2136

A pale green light pops up on my retinal screen when I arrive in the library at 7:40. Another morbid reminder that Rich's body is in the basement. There's another light, too. Tyson must be back, although his light's color looks wrong to me. More pink than purple.

I wish we'd stayed at the cabin. This place feels off. Something has changed. Not like a time shift. Or at least not *exactly* like a time shift. More like my mind is trying to work through a conundrum. It scratches at the front of my brain.

Probably because I'm exhausted. It's been a long, emotionally and physically draining day. In the past twenty-four hours, I've jumped from 2136 Bethesda to 1678 Salzburg. Back to 2136 Bethesda, then to 2058 DC and back. Then 1941 Georgia, 1848 Cape Cod, then back to 1941 Georgia, then back here. That's more travel than I'd normally see in two months at CHRONOS, even if you ignore the emotional turmoil. My retinal screen is keyed to my vital signs. Maybe the sensor being on the fritz is the first cue that I'm on the fritz, too. I need a shower. A drink. And, after reporting out to the others, I need a good night's sleep.

Assuming, of course, that I *can* sleep. At a minimum, I can get the drink and the shower before the others return. I open the bar on the far side of the library and find that my great-grandson was an adventurous drinker. There's a wide array of brandies, liqueurs, whiskies, and vodkas. I finally spot what I'm looking for hiding behind a bottle of ouzo. It's Tanqueray, not the brand my dad preferred, but as soon as I open it, the scent takes me back. Most of the year, my father made do with the replicated version our food unit created, but each Christmas, Angelo gave him a bottle of Hendrick's. I pour a tiny bit of the gin into a glass, find it to be palatable, and toss back a full shot.

I'm debating whether to pour a second when I hear familiar laughter. "Is that wise, love? You're on the clock, after all."

I slide my hand into my pocket.

"Oh, come on. A laser's not going to have the slightest effect unless you're aiming to burn a hole in the wall."

When I turn around, I can see that's true. Saul is seated in a leather armchair in front of a fireplace. The projected room behind him reminds me a bit of Redwing Hall at the OC, with dim lighting and dark wood panels. The effect is odd, because even though Saul is relatively solid, the background shimmers a bit around the edges, and through it I can see vague outlines of the whiteboard and sofa here in the library. Saul's beard seems darker, but I think it's been dyed to hide the flecks of gray I saw earlier, because the crease between his brows looks even deeper.

He's holding a glass, most likely of scotch, which he raises. "Nice work on my splinter back on Cape Cod. I wasn't sure you had it in you. Do you feel better now?"

"Much. What do you want?"

"To talk to you alone, obviously. I know you're still angry. You have every right to be. I overreacted when it came to Richard, and as much as it chafes, I have to acknowledge that you were due a little fling. Turnabout being fair play and all that. I was angry and . . . jealous."

"I thought his death wasn't intentional. Isn't that what you told me earlier?"

He shrugs. "You know what I'm like when I'm angry. But I know he's your friend, and it's not like it's permanent. In fact, you can reverse it when we're done here if—"

"Then we're done here." I turn on my heel and head toward the door.

"*If* you agree to the offer I'm about to make. You need to hear me out first. And if you really want to do the poor gox a favor, you won't simply go back to save him. You'll go back and tell yourself not to play games with his heart. It's going to kill him all over again when you grow tired of him. And we both know you will. If not now, eventually. You're too bright and too beautiful to be satisfied with Vier."

Ah, he's doling out compliments. He wants something.

"What sort of agreement, Saul? I'm tired. I need food and sleep if I'm going to keep playing your damn game."

"To be honest, I'm finding the game to be a drag. Playing in the real world is more complex than a simulation. This timeline went a bit off the rails, love. When I break something, I don't take half measures. I don't think you can fix it. I'm not even sure I could . . . I seem to have created Frankenstein's monster."

"Frankenstein's monster turned on its creator. Have the Cyrists turned on you?"

He laughs. "Not literally. But really, can you imagine me creating any system where people trade good behavior for porn access? Because that's mostly what that *Forbidden Fruits* thing seems to be. Fortunately, however, our friend Alex is on the brink of unlocking the same access Campbell's team had. I can start fresh somewhere else. Pick and choose my timeline."

"So what's stopping you?"

"I don't want to go alone. Traveling isn't the same without you. Simply put, I miss you. I still love you. And I'm willing to forgive if you are."

It's a struggle, but I manage to keep my face neutral. I really want to hurl the nearest heavy object at him and scream that I'm not asking for his forgiveness and that he'll never have mine. That doesn't seem likely to play to our advantage, however, so I just say, "What about Rich and Tyson? Madi and her friends? I can't simply leave them stuck in this timeline that even you admit is screwed up."

"You talk about *my* ego. Do you really think you're so invaluable they can't muddle through without your help? They're welcome to continue trying to fix it. Without you. And without a countdown to limit them. They can tweak away to their hearts' content. Yes, Vier will miss you. But that's going to happen anyway. A clean break is kinder."

What I'd really like to break is Saul's neck. I don't for one minute believe this has anything to do with him missing me. He *needs* something from me. And I need time to figure out what it is and how I can use this knowledge to our advantage.

"This is a lot to spring on me, Saul. One minute, you're threatening to kill me and the next you want me back. I need some time. Like I said, I'm exhausted."

His lips tighten, but he shrugs. "Push the button on the console when you've reached a decision. But please be aware there's an expiration date on this offer. In the interim, the game and the countdown go on. Sleep well. Oh . . . and Kathy? Rich stays where he is, obviously. And if you're even thinking of double-crossing me, remember that I have hostages."

And then he's gone. Apparently, he thinks professions of love and pleas for forgiveness go hand in hand with threats.

I indulge in that second shot of gin and then head to my suite. It's at the far end of the hall, just beyond the door leading up to the attic, where we had our meeting earlier in the day. That door is now open about two inches, and I don't remember us leaving it ajar. In fact, I'm quite certain we closed it. If General Merrick's Cyrist troops drop in again, we don't really want to draw attention to the one spot in the house where Jarvis isn't currently active. Maybe one of the others got back early, too?

As my hand slides again to Sutter's pen laser in my pocket, someone pulls the attic door shut. I debate calling out, or asking Jarvis who else is in the house, but on the off chance it's not someone on our side, do I really want to let them know I'm suspicious and give up the element of surprise?

I pull the laser out and take two steps toward the door. As I'm about to open it, the pale green dot appears again on my retinal screen and a message pops up next to it. *Please don't shoot. Those things sting like hell.*

"Rich?" The word comes out as barely a whisper, but it must be loud enough for him to hear. The door opens and he pulls me inside. Above and off to the right, I see the faint glow of a CHRONOS field.

For a long moment, I stare at him, unable to form words or even a coherent thought. It's partly because I'm so relieved to have him here, but also because I now realize what was nibbling at my brain in the library. The double memory hits me full force. One version where Tyson and Madi dragged Rich's body out of the pool, and one in which he was simply gone, along with Jack and the others.

"Oh, God. You have no idea how glad I am to have you back, but we were holding off on undoing that because Saul's people grabbed all of Madi's housemates. He said he'd kill them if we saved you, so we had to wait. What made Tyson change his mind?"

Rich is silent for a moment, then says, "That explains a lot . . . but could complicate things. It wasn't Tyson." He gives me a confused look. "And why would you think it was Saul? But come on up and I'll let them tell it."

I expect to see Madi and Clio sitting on the exercise mats, but it's Evelyn and Timothy Winslow. My grin grows so wide it almost hurts and I blink back tears of joy and relief. "An extraction team? Yes! We can go home, Rich! We can go home!"

Evelyn smiles sympathetically. "It's not going to be quite that easy, I'm afraid, but we *are* here to help. Maybe you should sit down."

"When will Tyson and the others be back?" Rich asks.

"At eight."

"Then we should jump forward," he says. "Otherwise, they're going to need to go over everything twice."

Timothy and Evelyn exchange a look, then Timothy says, "About that . . . We're still not sure Angelo would want us to share this information with anyone aside from the two of you. He specifically said this shouldn't go outside CHRONOS."

I'm happy to hear them speaking of Angelo in the present tense, but . . . "Tyson *is* CHRONOS," I say. "He was in the training group right after mine and Richard's."

"Not in this reality," Evelyn says. "Only twelve active agents, with a maximum of four allowed in the field at any time. They started phasing us out a few decades back. Your cohort was the last group of trainees."

"Tyson *is* CHRONOS," I repeat. "And Madi and Clio are part of this team, too. Madi helped invent the technology. Madison Grace? They're both descendants of CHRONOS historians. Descendants of mine. And . . . descendants of yours, as well."

Their eyebrows go up, and I realize Rich must have omitted that fact. I probably should have done the same. But I know Timothy. He loves kids, to the point that he actually looks forward to Q&A sessions with school groups. He wants a family. Evelyn does, too. They're among the very few people I know at CHRONOS who don't seem to dread the idea of retirement from field work, most likely because they're looking forward to the next stage of their lives.

Having dropped the family-connection bombshell, I sit on the mat opposite them, pulling Rich down next to me. It occurs to me then that Rich shouldn't have even known about the attic. "How did you know to come up here?"

"When I was finally cleared to leave the basement, I asked Jarvis where all of you were. He said your last location was in the hallway near the attic."

I shake my head, unable to say it. "I watched them pull you out of that pool in the basement."

He laces his fingers through mine and presses his lips to the back of my hand. "I don't remember that bit, fortunately. I do have a memory of stepping out of the utility room and the guy shooting me. The last thing I remember is falling into the pool and thinking that the water was warm. That we should make time to come down for a swim. But I have a *much* clearer memory of Timothy's message popping up on my retinal screen just after I stepped into the utility closet to hide the baby, telling me to leave her at the front and wait at the very back of the closet until they gave me further instructions. And then when I got up here, I found them, but not any of you."

Evelyn says, "When we arrived and discovered Richard in that basement, we scrolled back to see how we could prevent it from happening."

"How did you get in? I thought Alex was blocking . . ." I stop. "Oh. Not from CHRONOS. We hadn't entirely given up hope for an extraction team."

"It still wasn't easy," Timothy says. "Angelo had to extrapolate from the signals TMU received, and then we had to find a time when the house was empty to set observation points. I wasn't too keen on just the two of us coming in, given that there were so many different signals coming out of this location. Rich was the first familiar face we saw, and he couldn't really tell us much if he was dead. Then we scrolled back further and saw Katherine, and knew we'd need to minimize overlapping memories. Sending Richard a message to stay hidden seemed like the best option. What he's omitting is that we had to send four or five additional messages to get him to *stay* back there once he realized what was happening in the basement."

"Yeah," Rich says with a hint of annoyance. "I was worried about the infant I was hiding. I was worried about our friends. Friends that Katherine has just told me Saul is holding captive and has threatened to kill if they jumped back to save me. So that wasn't me being irrational or impulsive. You acted without complete information."

"Okay," Evelyn says. "Point taken. Our goal here is to preserve history, not make things worse, so obviously we want to avoid anyone dying who's not supposed to."

It's not until this instant that I fully comprehend that this isn't really the Evelyn Perry Winslow I've known for the past twelve years. Not the same Timothy, either. They seem physically identical in every way—she has the same coppery hair and light dusting of freckles, he has the same green eyes and cheery smile. They might even have had almost the same life experiences. In fact, I can envision Evelyn, or anyone at CHRONOS for that matter, making the same comment under the circumstances we're currently in. But the two people sitting here in front of us are native to *this* timeline that Saul has utterly fucked up. From their point of view, everything we're trying to undo is history they're sworn to preserve.

"Of course," Rich says as he squeezes my hand. I don't know if the same realization that hit me has only just now occurred to him, or if it's something he's been thinking about for the past few hours while hiding out in the pool utility closet. But we're clearly on the same wavelength. We're going to have to navigate this very carefully.

All four of us jump forward to right before eight o'clock, and I head downstairs alone to the library, since it seems unwise for Rich to be flaunting the fact that he's once again among the living. Madi steps out of her bedroom into the hallway as I pass her door. Her hair is wet. She must have gotten the shower that I didn't.

"I was just coming to tell you I found another trunk with costumes," I say. "As soon as Tyson and Clio are back we should go take a look."

She nods and gives me a strained smile as she adjusts her backpack on her shoulder. "Good idea. You smell like gin. Does that mean we're celebrating?"

"More like I needed something to take the edge off a horrible day. Hope you don't mind that I raided your bar."

"The gin is all yours," she says with a shudder as she limps along beside me. "That's some nasty, nasty stuff. But cheer up. I think things are going to get better soon."

I'm not sure what has brought on this wave of optimism. Maybe she's already worked through the double memory? Either way, it's something best discussed when we're away from any snoops. Tyson and Clio blink in as we step into the library. When I suggest going to the attic, Tyson says we should debrief first. By which he means we should sit on the sofas and regurgitate the cover stories we decided on back at the cabin, in hopes of misleading whoever may be watching about what we've been up to for the past few hours.

"Later," I say firmly. "I want to show you this *now*."

"Katherine is right," Madi says. "If these costumes won't work, then we'll have to come up with something else entirely, so we really *do* need to check them out now."

Tyson is barely listening, though. He frowns, rubbing his forehead, and looks over at Clio, then back at me. "Something's . . . different." And then in a louder voice. "Yeah. Let's go check out those costumes. But I need to make a pit stop first."

"Me, too," Clio says. "We'll meet you up there."

I don't argue. I'm pretty sure they're not going to their rooms but rather down to the pool in the basement in order to confirm the double memory that just hit them. Sure enough, they take a right and head down to the main floor as soon as we exit the library.

Madi follows me. I was a little surprised that she backed me up. Maybe she's already confirmed that Rich's body isn't in the basement? But then I open the door to the attic and see Jack standing at the top.

Rich is in the middle of making introductions. Timothy and Evelyn were hesitant enough about talking in front of Tyson, Clio, and Madi. And now we have Jack up here, too. Great.

"You're *the* Jack Merrick?" Timothy says. "The first person to time travel?"

Jack looks baffled. "Definitely not the first. I can barely use the thing. I think that honor belongs to Madi. Madison Grace? One third of AJG Research? I'm not even in *A Brief History of Time Travel.*"

"You're in *our* version," Evelyn says. "Along with Ian Alexander and Lorena Jeung. You developed the technology while working with a military research unit. You get stran . . . ded . . ." She sighs. "And I shouldn't have said that. It's only for a few months on a jump to the future, though. You make it back safely."

I'm not entirely sure she's telling the truth about the last part. Judging from Jack's expression, neither is he.

"It's a moot point, anyway," Madi says as she joins him at the top of the stairs. "They'll have to change that bit of history because Jack won't be getting stranded anywhere. Who are you guys?" She leans closer to look at Timothy. "Never mind. Same eyes as Kate and Clio. You're the Winslows."

Rich, who is now seated on the costume trunk he pulled up, chuckles. "Your genetic-design team clearly decided to make those green eyes a dominant trait."

Tyson is pounding up the stairs now. The attic is small and there's a traffic jam at the top as we squeeze into the tiny space. But Tyson pushes past all of us and practically tackles Rich.

"You have no idea how glad I am to see you, man. We wanted to go back and undo it, I swear, but Saul's people—"

"I know," Rich says. "It's okay. I'd have done the same thing."

Then Tyson turns to Timothy. "And you guys, too. Damn. We'd given up hope at this point . . ." He trails off, probably in response to Timothy's strained expression. "What?"

"There's no you at their version of CHRONOS," Rich says. "Apparently, there are quite a few differences. We don't have full details yet, but they can fill us in now that the gang's all here . . ."

But then I realize the gang *isn't* all here. There's not enough room for everyone in this section of the attic, so Madi and Jack were sitting on a box on the other side of the staircase. Now it's just Madi. And then, a split second later, Jack is right there next to her again. Only, I'm almost certain he's in a different shirt. I don't think anyone else even noticed. I give Madi a questioning look, and she mimes the word *hush*.

Evelyn is staring at Clio, who has taken a seat on the floor next to Tyson. After a moment, she shakes her head and says, "Just tell them, Timo. If Angelo gets pissed, so be it. We didn't create this mess. Start with Abby."

"Shouldn't I tell them about what TMU saw first?"

"No. I mean start with Abby five years ago. Then TMU. And then the *new* stuff with Abby. That's the only way it makes sense if they're used to a CHRONOS with field agents."

Having listened to many of Timothy Winslow's tales over post-scrum lunches at the OC, I suspect this would go a lot faster if Evelyn told the story. Timothy tends to wander a bit. But as he proceeds, with her filling in bits and pieces, I realize she had him take the lead so she'd be able to focus on watching us and gauging our reactions.

"Okay, I don't know if you remember this or if it even happened in your reality. It was about four-and-a-half or maybe five years ago. You might have still been in classroom training. Anyway, Abby

Demmings was called in because there was a TMU error . . ." Timothy glances over at Clio and adds, "That's the Temporal Monitoring Unit. When we came back from a trip, they checked to see if there were any changes."

"We've had a crash course in CHRONOS operations over the past few weeks," Clio says. "You can skip detailed explanations. So there was a TMU failure when Abby Demmings came back from a trip?"

"No," Timothy says. "See, that's the odd thing. Abby wasn't in the field when it happened. One thing that seems pretty different between our CHRONOS and yours, from what Rich has told us, is that most of our research is done remotely. I've been in the field three times in just over ten years as an agent. That's been true since the second cohort. It's only for things where you absolutely can't get the information you need through observation points. If you can see or hear it through a key—"

"Hear it?" Madi says. When Timothy nods, she turns to Jack and gives him a high five. "Kudos to your future development team."

Jack chuckles. "Glad to hear the feature request went through. And I'll pass the kudos along."

"We have to follow CHRONOS rules, of course," Evelyn says. "No stable points in private quarters, obviously. Public settings only. Can't use it in times and places where there are laws against recordings. No government or corporate settings, of course, unless the information is public domain. And so on."

Madi looks a bit less excited about the audio feature now.

"Anyway," Timothy says, "Abby had pretty much closed out her research agenda. She was working in Archives for a couple of months to wrap things up before heading out to teach somewhere in Vermont. So, she wasn't in the field, but when the two historians who *were* on schedule to go into the field that day come back, it turns out Abby had been erased. One step outside a CHRONOS field, and she'd no longer exist."

He continues, noting that the situation completely baffled TMU. No changes to any of the time periods they could spot, but Abby's great-great grandparents decided to wait and start their family a few years later. As a result, Abby was never born. But that was the *only* impact on the timeline as best they could tell, and they were worried they could screw things up more trying to fix the situation. The jump committee determined that Abby should continue to work at HQ rather than taking the teaching job, so she'd be under a CHRONOS field.

They failed to consult Abby on that decision, however. When she learned she'd essentially be on house arrest for the rest of her life, she had a nervous breakdown. Angelo took pity on her. Pleaded with the board to give her a portable device—not a key, but a field generator like the diaries—so she could work outside CHRONOS. But they said no. She eventually got her act together, however, and continued working in Archives.

"So . . . did any of that happen in your reality?" Evelyn asks.

Tyson and Rich shake their heads, but I say, "I knew she had a breakdown and Angelo tried to help her. We were already doing field work when that happened. First year. I didn't know the details, but . . . Abby wasn't *at* our version of CHRONOS HQ, so I'm thinking maybe the board said yes in our timeline and she took the teaching job in Vermont."

"In this reality," Timothy says, "Abby's erasure was the end of field research. Which was a bitch, because Ev and I had finally gotten approval for a jump to Dallas 1963. But there had been rumblings about minor changes to the timeline since we started, and a few members of the jump committee were increasingly nervous that over time, even those very tiny changes could add up."

"Over time, and over time*lines*," Rich says. "That's how we got the damn Cyrists."

They give him a look like he's crazy and are about to go on, but I jump in. "He's right." I pause for a moment, debating whether to mention my recent conversation with Saul in the library. My gut says to wait, because I haven't really had time to process it yet, and I'm not sure how much information we should share with Timothy, Evelyn, and this strange new iteration of CHRONOS. I'm not even sure how much of that conversation I want to share within our team. If all else fails, I would go with Saul to save the others. I'd kill him first chance I got and try to make my way back, but I'd go. I'm sure the others, especially Rich, would be vehemently opposed to that, and I'm not even sure it would keep them safe. I certainly can't take Saul's word on that count.

With all that whirling through my head, I decide to stick with the basics for now. "Saul created the Cyrists. I don't know how many steps we are away from the timeline where he first had the idea, and he may have built on a group that actually existed before he started tweaking. He wrote the *Book of Cyrus* that is currently in our protected archive, as well as the revised version. The symbol, I'm afraid, was my design. It was for a scenario Saul was playing with Morgen. I don't know about your reality, but in mine, Saul was constantly competing with the old gox." They're giving me odd looks, so I add, "They played Temporal Dilemma. It still exists, right?"

"Yes," Timothy says. "And Saul still plays at the OC. But if you're talking about Morgen Campbell, he died five years ago. Rumor has it he overdosed on mood meds, but he'd been in bad health for a while."

I'm not sure I can describe the emotion that hits me with this news. It's not glee, although I'm not sorry Campbell is gone. He was toxic in the two timelines where I've known him, and I suspect that would be true in *any* timeline. His clone was toxic, too. But it feels odd to think that he's dead. So much of the past few years of my life has in some way revolved around Morgen Campbell. Yes, he was Saul's competitor, but in some sense, he was mine, too. I always felt like we were engaged in a battle for Saul's time, Saul's attention, maybe even Saul's identity. Is the Katherine that Evelyn and Timothy know happier since Campbell died? And did her Saul bother with creating the Cyrists without Campbell around to spur him on?

"Who runs the OC now?" Tyson asks.

"Campbell's daughter, Alisa." Evelyn's eyes are now on my hand, which is resting on Rich's knee. "You do know that you and Saul . . . I mean the version of you back at CHRONOS. You know you're together, right?"

"Yeah. We were together in this timeline, too. But I finally wised up."

"Good for you." Ev gives Timothy a playful nudge with her elbow and whispers, "I was right, and you were wrong."

It's clearly an in-joke, and even though it kind of feels like it's at the expense of some version of me, I don't press the point.

Timothy doesn't seem eager to follow that conversational path, either. "So anyway, they grounded all of us. Remote viewing only after that. Temporal Monitoring is basically abandoned now with no one in the field, but I guess they still had one or two people keeping an eye on things because all of a sudden, we're on lockdown. We were in the cafeteria at lunch when Sutter comes in. He grabs you two and Saul, and we haven't seen you since. Angelo says you—or *they*, I guess—are confined to quarters. TMU apparently picked up signals suggesting you were making jumps, even though that's not possible. None of us have access to keys. But it looked like your signals . . . Did you know their monitors track us by the color we see the key?"

We all nod, and he looks a little disappointed that his big reveal fell flat. "Trouble is, the jumps keep happening while you're in lock-down, even though security cams show you haven't left HQ and your signals are still locked. The theory then shifts to the possibil-ity that someone was mimicking your signals, which Angelo said actually made more sense because they weren't identical. A lot of the activity they were spotting originated from this location and time, so they're also wondering if it's some glitch dealing with the creation of the technology, since CHRONOS records show most of the research happens near here around this time. Anyway, Angelo said they've locked things down extra tight, and Sutter started the process of getting a legal waiver for a team to jump back and investigate. That was what . . . about a week back?"

"Not quite," Evelyn says. "Five days ago. We didn't know it at the time, but more than just you three were popping up on the charts. TMU was showing seven distinct signals . . ." She does a quick head count. "Which now makes sense, I guess. Angelo said some of the jumps appeared to be attempts to breach security at headquarters."

"That would have been us," I say. "We tried to jump in when we realized CHRONOS was back."

She nods. "Anyway, we were under strict scrutiny after that. No one was allowed to leave CHRONOS for the first couple of days, but I think Alisa complained that it was cutting into her revenue, because we were eventually cleared to go to the OC and a few other places near campus. That's where we were yesterday at lunch. As we were leaving, Abby intercepted us, saying she needed to talk to Angelo, but she didn't have a pass to enter HQ. She was wild-eyed. Her clothes were filthy, and the poor thing looked like she hadn't slept in days."

Timothy picks up the story at this point. "Only, I'd just seen Abby in Archives earlier—like, two hours earlier, tops—and she seemed fine. Wearing scrubs like everyone else, joking with the guy at the desk next to her about some historical detail the holodesign team screwed up on the series she's working on. Now she's telling Ev she lives in Vermont, but one morning her house isn't her house anymore. Her fiancé and her cat disappear. And then she finds out CHRONOS doesn't exist. And then it *does* exist, but it's only CHRO, because the two groups never merged. And now it's back as CHRONOS, but she still has no house, no fiancé, no cat, no bank account."

"Oh, God," I say. "She must have been under a field when Team Viper erased CHRONOS. Can you imagine going through all those time shifts alone?"

"The only thing she had was the *Log of Stable Points*," Evelyn says. "And the field extender she said they gave her when she relocated to Vermont. It had the local points she'd set during her research, and she'd been poring over everything, trying to see if she could figure out why things kept changing."

"She kept clutching Ev's arm," Timothy says, "terrified that we were gonna disappear. Luckily, Angelo was in his office. After she told him what she'd seen, he got her set up with a hotel room and some clothes. Given the fact that Sutter was on the rampage, I thought he'd send her straight to security. There was already some chatter that maybe these signals were evidence that people could cross over from other timelines."

"Well, that's true," Jack says. "That's what erased CHRONOS a few time shifts back."

Timothy shrugs hesitantly. "I don't know about that part, but it's obviously true. I mean . . . *you're* here in our timeline."

"That's different, though," I say. "We're here because we were under a CHRONOS field when Saul made the changes that created this timeline. Jack was talking about time tourists who were using our timeline as a real-life version of Temporal Dilemma."

Timothy nods, but it's like he's humoring me.

And . . . to be fair, I can see why the two things might seem much the same from their point of view. So I give a verbal nudge to get Timothy back to the topic. "Why *didn't* Angelo take Abby to security? Other-Abby, I mean. The one from our timeline. I know Sutter's a jerk, but he's still got the eye thing, right? Sutter would know she was telling the truth."

"Well, yeah. And Sutter would also find out that you shot Saul on a jump to some antislavery thing in 1848. If Abby . . . Other-Abby . . .

had seen anyone aside from you through the key, Angelo might still have turned her in. But . . . we get it." He glances over at Clio. "And the versions of me and Ev from whatever timeline *she's* from probably get it on an even more personal level. I think it comes with the job . . . You go to whatever extremes are necessary to protect your kids."

PRESIDENT LAWRENCE PATTON MCDONALD—SECOND ADDRESS TO THE AMERICAN PEOPLE (OCTOBER 24, 1974)

Fellow Americans, we have, as a nation, been in mourning for the past month. President Nixon was a good man. No one will question that, and it is not my goal today to speak ill of him so soon after his passing. He led this nation through a period of turmoil, and his death was a tragic blow.

But as I assume the vast responsibility of leadership, I must acknowledge that Nixon was not always honest with the people of this great land. Perhaps it was out of a sense of paternalism. Perhaps his motives were pure. But a great nation such as ours cannot be preserved by coddling its people. That only serves to make them weak and corrupt. So I will be honest with you. I will share the truth as I know it. The things my administration will reveal in the coming weeks may confirm many of your suspicions. Others will, no doubt, shock and deeply trouble you.

The goal of our enemy is to combine super-capitalism and com-munism under the same tent, all under their control . . . Do I mean conspiracy? Yes, I do. I believe there is a plot, international in scope, generations old in planning, and incredibly evil in intent. If we are to defeat this foe, all people of good character, good conscience, and noble ideas must take up arms against it. For it is not an enemy we can defeat with tanks and missiles, not a problem we can send troops to solve.

We are the army. We are the defense. And the enemy could be right next door.

∞19∞

"Oh, wow," Clio whispers. "I don't think Katherine knew that. Do you think she knew that?"

I shake my head. Given what she told us earlier about her parents' connection with Angelo, I'm guessing she might have wondered. But one look at her face makes it clear that she didn't know for certain.

Evelyn must notice Katherine's surprise, because she quickly adds, "We don't really know if that's true in *every* timeline. I mean, sure . . . you look like the Katherine we know, but that's due more to your genetic design team than to your base DNA. You could have had an entirely different set of parents, theoretically, and still look the same."

"It's okay," Katherine says. "I'm just a little surprised it's open knowledge. I thought there were rules against historians' kids getting the CHRONOS gene."

"There may have been at one time," Timothy says. "But it's been encouraged for the past few decades. Offspring inherit some ability with the equipment, so keeping it within families decreases the pool of people who've had the more intensive genetic alteration."

"Angelo realizes you're not the exact same Katherine as the one we know," Evelyn says. "I mean, some of your experiences are obviously different. And, well, she's at CHRONOS with Saul, and you're . . . here. But he asked us to find out what's going on rather than sending an extraction team to bring you in . . . especially considering what you did in 1848. I'm not even sure how something like this would be handled in the legal system. Is it still killing someone if another version of them exists in this timeline? And I guess there are mitigating factors if you can actually prove he was behind that guy shooting Richard, and that Saul was trying to screw up the timeline."

"There's also the mitigating factor that she didn't kill *Saul*," I say. "That was a splinter. And are you really saying the only reason you're here is to consider . . . I don't even know what to call it . . . extradition? Are you here to extradite Katherine back to our time for something she did in 1848?"

"Sounds to me like that's way beyond the statute of limitations," Clio says.

Evelyn pulls a water bottle from her bag, then looks up. "There's no statute of limitations for murder. Although it would probably be manslaughter. And we're not—"

"*Manslaughter*?" Rich says. "Saul Rand is a genocidal maniac, so I think a decent case could be made that killing any version of him is a service to humanity. In one timeline, he strangled Angelo, stuffed him in a closet, and blew up headquarters, killing everyone there and stranding me and Katherine and the two of you in the past, along with twenty other agents who were in the field that day. At a bare minimum, Katherine killing him was proactive self-defense, because he was dead set on killing her along with the rest of us. And we've got video evidence to prove that."

Timothy raises both hands. "Let's calm down, okay? To get back to Tyson's question, no . . . we're not simply here to extradite Katherine. And we know Saul's an asshole. I wouldn't have guessed genocidal maniac, but I'm definitely not ruling it out. Our main goal is to simply make sure there are no changes to the timeline."

"And at a minimum," Evelyn says, "Katherine shooting him in public like that, with an anachronistic weapon . . . well, there's no evidence that it *did* affect the timeline, but surely you see how it *could*? And we can't let anything like that happen."

Well, I guess that answers my question.

We'd already accepted that the odds of getting back to our original timeline weren't great, although Alex seems hopeful that he'll eventually figure that out. Obviously, we have to stop Saul. Surely, they'll agree on that point. But they're going to resist if we go beyond that. And is this current timeline one we can live with? It doesn't exactly sound like there's a place for us in this 2304. I'm not at CHRONOS, and Rich and Katherine probably won't be too happy hanging out around carbon copies of themselves. Katherine, Rich, and I at least have other options as long as CHRONOS doesn't try to prevent us from finding a time and place to relocate. Same goes for Madi and Jack. Clio and her family would be okay for a few decades. But Alex, RJ, and Lorena are stuck both in this time and, given the current political isolationism, this place. I'm not cool with abandoning them to that fate.

"Unfortunately, you're protecting a timeline that's *fucked*!" I say. "We've got some sort of information lockdown, superstition is running rampant, and you expect us to just trot back to CHRONOS?"

Jack nods. "Tyson is right. I've spent the past two weeks in the top scientific lab in our nation. It's a lab that I've been in during previous timelines, when it was part of the Defense Department. I know people there who are exceptionally familiar with technology, including one who is under a CHRONOS field. He says science in the US, in general, is a good three to four decades behind where it was in *our* 2136, before the time tourists and then Saul started screwing around with things. Alex says that's absolutely the case for temporal physics, although the information he's been allowed to see from international sources is a few years out of date, so he's not sure if the lag is global or due to the US closing ourselves to international initiatives. Lorena says her field is way behind, too, judging from the information my dad's office has given her."

Tim runs a hand through his hair. "This isn't the *best* era in American history, obviously. The country is in a rut. We go through sort of a scientific drought during the isolation years. But we do come out of that period. Things start to improve pretty quickly in the next few decades. They're already starting to look up, in fact. You're a historian, right, Jack?"

"Not a historian of this screwed-up timeline," Jack says. "But generally speaking, yes."

"Then you know these things are cyclical. History isn't a steady march of progress. And you're not *really* trying to lay all of this at Saul Rand's feet, are you? That's an awful lot of credit or blame for one man."

"Oh come on!" I say. "You know better than that, Timothy. A single person can start a movement. Generate an idea that inspires people for good or for ill, and other people carry those ideas forward, creating a much greater impact than one person could alone. Christ, Gandhi, Martin Luther King, to name only a few. And, unlike Saul, none of them had the advantage of a crystal ball that could literally make their followers wealthy in exchange for their loyalty."

"You actually think Saul invented Cyrisism?" Evelyn says.

"I *know* he did," Katherine replies. "Not just in this reality, but in bits and pieces over several timelines. While there may have been other people who carried the movement forward, the seeds were entirely planted by Saul Rand, violating the rules and regulations you hold so dear. He *broke* this timeline. Hell, the man even stated that this was an I-Break-You-Fix scenario. Leaving aside the people who died or had their lives radically altered because they live in a very different reality, he's killing people directly. The people who saw me shoot Saul's splinter in 1848 watched Saul and one of his hostages magically appear on the stage as Lucy Stone was speaking. Saul's sole purpose for doing that was to add the girl on the stage to the death toll for that day. In the timeline we know, *no one* died at that event. Saul was spinning around like a madman in the crowd, swinging a plank with nails in it, when I fired. Shooting him almost certainly saved lives."

"But what if those people were supposed to die?" Evelyn says. "Your history may claim no one died in Harwich that day, but ours says the crowd turned on the antislavery speakers and on each other. If the people who died were supposed to die, if their deaths were history, then you know we can't interfere."

The comment is so damn predictable I nearly laugh. It's the same thing Rose said to me. The same thing she said to Richard. The same thing she said to Evelyn, Katherine, and Timothy, assuming they didn't land the other trainer who takes students out on that grizzly field trip. *They're already dead. We don't change that.*

"Bullshit," Clio says. "Your history was created by a madman. Do you expect us to just let that stand? I have family in this timeline who can't skip forward to whenever it is that things get better. How many people have died because of the changes Saul made? How many more have lived their entire lives under a theocracy that kept most of the population ignorant and impoverished?"

"Even if everything you're saying is true," Timothy says, "do you have any idea what fixing this timeline would mean? What kind of anomalies that would cause? Because I don't even know how you'd calculate something that massive. All we can do at this point is take the evidence to the board at CHRONOS and let them decide. Although, I'm pretty sure this will have to go to the High Court. And there are international ramifications to consider, as well. It's a lot more complicated than you think."

"No." Jack's voice is calm, in stark contrast to the rest of ours. "It's actually very simple. Here's the only thing you or anyone at CHRONOS needs to understand. Right now, we've got a madman out there screwing around with history. If his recent actions are any indication, he's going to make the current situation even worse if we don't find a way to track him down and stop him. That's going to seriously alter your history. I think you know that. I think part of why you're here is because small changes are continuing to happen. And that's being picked up at CHRONOS, isn't it?"

There's a slightly rehearsed quality to this speech. While everything he's saying about Saul is completely true, I've got a strong sense that at least some of the rest is bluster. I really hope Jack knows what he's doing.

He continues. "Katherine mentioned that Saul set this up as I-Break-You-Fix, but it goes beyond that. He's aiming to break it so badly that it *can't* be fixed, or at least not easily. He really doesn't care what kind of mess he makes, because he's not planning to stay. And he's definitely not going to leave any loose ends, such as a time-travel organization that might decide to track him down. Do you understand what that means for CHRONOS?"

Timothy and Evelyn don't answer, but their faces make a verbal response a bit redundant. They completely get what he's saying, and this isn't a wrinkle they'd considered until he mentioned it.

"I think you do understand," Jack continues. "The rest of the people in this timeline won't know anything has changed, but those of you living at CHRONOS would find yourself in a seriously altered reality. And that's assuming you even exist. So, here's the deal. We intend to stop him. And while we could use your help, we do have other allies and will handle it alone if need be. Cyrist Sword, the military wing of the organization Saul *thinks* he has under his thumb, has a pretty strong underground that's been organizing to combat him since around 2030, which is why I think he's cowering in the last half of the twentieth century. They're also the group with control of the time-travel research that could, but not necessarily *will*, become CHRONOS. Still . . . they're Cyrists for the most part, and they have two preconditions for helping any of us. First, we make a good-faith effort to rescue the Sisters of Prudence. All of them. Second, we reinstate this."

Jack hands Evelyn a thin volume with the Cyrist cross—the variant with looped arms—embossed on the front in gold leaf. The cover looks old, but I'm guessing it's either been roughed up or repurposed from another book.

"This is *their* version of the *Book of Cyrus*," he says. "They're okay with abandoning the *Book of Prophecy*, because they understand that the stock tips, blackmail fodder, and political dirt contained in that volume were a perversion of history. It's done far more harm than good. They just want to keep the scripture."

Rich gives a silent chuckle. I glance around at the others. They're all keeping their faces carefully composed, but I'm sure they're thinking the same thing. I don't know how much time has passed for Jack since this morning, but he seems to have kept himself busy with the task Rich and Madi were advocating last night on the patio.

"But you said the religion was created by Saul," Evelyn says.

Jack shrugs. "It was. And if you've studied world religions at all, you know there are dozens of versions of the book, which is why you have so many offshoots of Cyrisism. This is the least problematic version, in the view of the Cyrists who could pull the plug on time travel and CHRONOS, so even though I'd personally prefer to toss this religion into the trash and be done with it, I think a compromise may be in order."

"Seems like a bad design on Saul's part," Timothy says. "If he wanted to shape society, wouldn't one definitive volume make more sense?"

It's a valid point. "Could be part of the whole burn-it-all-down scenario," I say.

Madi doesn't look convinced. "Maybe. But . . . it may also have been unintentional. Regional temples were under a CHRONOS field, at least in some timelines. When Saul made his changes, any copies of the *Book of Cyrus* in those temples would have been preserved. On the other hand, the copy I saw displayed in the office at the Sixteenth Street Temple had a Cyrist cross with *straight* arms, instead of that infinity symbol in the middle, so they've clearly been willing to make some substitutions, at least for the cover. I don't know about the contents of the book, obviously, since I was viewing the office through the key. But Lawrence Dennis was the head of the denomination that approved the public execution of so-called Prudaeans, so I'm going to go out on a limb and guess it's the version that says all things evil are of Prudence."

I make a mental note to find out what else Madi learned while watching that stable point. Tim and Evelyn thumb through the book for a moment and then exchange one of those *couple's looks*, as Madi once called them. No words are spoken, but an entire conversation seems to have taken place in the space of maybe two seconds, because Timothy says, "Can you make a list of exactly what it is you intend to do and what help you're requesting? You might want to keep that request small, because . . . this will never be green-lit by the board. Angelo took a risk just sending us here. There's no way he'd be able to authorize a full contingent of agents on his own."

"So much for *Temporal Avengers, assemble*," Rich says in a side whisper.

Timothy asks if they can take the copy of the *Book of Cyrus* with them. Jack agrees, saying there are plenty of copies where that came from. I'm sure that's true, since it was almost certainly printed very recently at DARPA. Unfortunately, that's probably something the lab at CHRONOS can figure out, as well, if they do even a basic chemical analysis, but there's no way to warn Jack about that now.

Evelyn adds, "I also think it may help to have one of you—Katherine, perhaps—record a message for Angelo describing the previous timeline and the events you've told us about, including your reasoning for using the weapon at the antislavery convention. You might also want to mention your current relationship, or rather the lack thereof, with Saul."

That's when I realize the two of them are tentatively on our side, or at least willing to honestly plead our case. Otherwise, Evelyn wouldn't be suggesting things she believes might sway Angelo. He didn't like Katherine being involved with Saul in our timeline. I think the odds are exceptionally good that he'll latch on to any information that would convince his version of her to dump him.

"I can do that," Katherine says. "It's going to take a little while for us to get all of this together, though. We've all been on separate recon jumps and haven't even had a chance to debrief. And . . . this has been one hellaciously long day for all of us. I don't know about the others, but I need sleep or I'm not going to be clearheaded enough to do anything."

There's a general murmur of consensus. Timothy and Evelyn agree to jump forward to this location at 11 a.m. tomorrow, pick up whatever we have, and take it to Angelo at HQ.

Before they blink out, Evelyn adds, "Just to be clear, you can request additional personnel as backup, but I don't know anyone else Angelo could ask, among those who can still use the key, who would risk being booted from CHRONOS for this. It's not a huge sacrifice for us. We're headed out the door in six months, and we already have teaching positions lined up . . . although . . ." She gives Timothy a slightly sick smile. I'm pretty sure it's because she's realized those teaching positions could evaporate if the right people at HQ pulled their recommendation, which totally misses the point that there probably won't even be an HQ if this fails.

When the two of them blink out, a collective sigh of relief spreads through the room. I start to speak, but Madi clears her throat and cups a hand to her ear. It takes a second before the rest of us catch on to what she's not saying . . . *our* stable points may only be visual, but Evelyn just told us *their* version has audio. And we watched them set a stable point so they could jump back in.

Clio suggests we go to the cabin, and it does seem like the best option given that this place is now under three different sorts of surveillance.

Jack says, "I'm not sure I can make that long of a jump."

Madi reaches into her bag and pulls out the field-extender gadget. "Mr. Merrick, let me introduce you to my little friend, the Nauseator."

∞

Bogart, Georgia
November 5, 1941

"I don't know, Tyce." Clio pulls the edges of her sleeping bag around her shoulders and then looks back down at the stable point on her key. "That looks like bait to me. Which I'm okay with, as long as it's an actual worm on the hook. But I'm a little worried that it's only a lure. How easy would it be to pop a fake up on that shelf? They have to know we have a stable point there. Maybe they're just trying to get us to bite."

She's definitely right. The wrought-iron book stand is directly behind the desk. Both books have the more recent version of the Cyrist cross, with the flat, slightly flared arms embossed in gold. On the left section of the stand, we have the *Book of Cyrus*. On the right, the *Book of Prophecy,* with the same white cover as the other volume. A matched set, except for the fact that the book on the right is about half as thick as the other one . . . the same thickness as a standard CHRONOS diary.

I hear a rustle from the open loft where Madi and Jack are sleeping. It's probably Madi. She's the most coffee-addicted of the bunch, and I'm sure the aroma has drifted upward, like most of the heat in this place and, possibly, our whispered voices.

We were all too tired to think by the time we got to the cabin last night, so we delayed the debrief until morning. When we finished eating our hastily assembled sandwiches, Clio ticked off the potential sleeping options: one double in the bedroom, another double up in the loft, and the couch or sleeping bags here. Clio and I wound up here in the main room, which was plenty warm until around a half hour ago when we both woke up with teeth chattering. After several wickedly cold minutes getting the fire started and coffee brewed, we're now back inside our sleeping bags, sitting on the couch, warming our hands against the mugs, waiting for the fire to work its magic as the sky gradually shifts from navy blue to a deep purple.

Luckily, we remembered to exchange stable points from the various spots we each visited so any early risers could get started. As tired as I was, I still lay awake, staring up at the rafters, for a good half hour, wondering how much of what Jack told Tim and Ev was made up on the fly. It was the first thing that popped into my head when I woke up, as well, but the fact that I had Madi's stable point at the Sixteenth Street Temple to observe was a decent distraction. The mystery of how Lawrence Dennis fits into all of this was gnawing at me even before this latest time shift.

"You could be right," I say to Clio. "Why would Dennis risk leaving an actual *Book of Prophecy* out in the open? Although, to play devil's advocate . . . it's risky, but it's also a show of power."

Clio thinks for a moment. "But is it *really* all that risky? It's not like your average person who tried to snatch the book could read it. They'd need to have the gene and the ear disk, depending on whether

Saul wrote the predictions out or recorded them. And anyone else who picked it up would think the book was a fake, because they would see the pages as blank. Or not blank, but just not dynamic."

"Right. They wouldn't be able to scroll through to see anything other than what appears on the page. It would look like a bunch of static, handwritten pages in an old diary. Or typed, even. We generally opt for handwritten while in the field because it looks less suspicious in most eras, but that's tough on the eyes. There's a setting to convert it to type. Translate it, too."

Clio looks annoyed. "*Really*? Wonder if my dad knows that. He made me learn Gaelic so I could read his grandfather's diary. But think about it. Saul has a few entries he'd need to sneak in there to set the game up . . . and a few for red herrings like Jemima Wilkinson and the Dark Day. The prophecy predicting Prudence and the beast in the basket, for example, but that would only be a few lines. A few more to point them toward suspected witches, but . . . all of that would only take up a few pages. That would leave dozens of pages that any of the Templars could read. And it would already be translated, apparently, given this magical setting I never discovered. Plenty of room to include prophecies for a few years. Or even decades, especially when there are fewer sheep following The Way."

"But we're talking more like seven centuries. And there are supposedly some pretty specific tips in that book."

She grins. "'And lo, Brother Cyrus came down from the heavens to deliver knowledge unto his children who follow The Way. Under his blessed hand, as the Chosen watched in amazement, new words appeared upon every page.' I don't know if that's actually *in* either of the books Saul wrote, but it could be. Drop in, work your so-called magic to reveal the new set of prophecies, and jump to the next location on your list. It would take an hour or so to visit all six regional temples and update their crystal ball. Rinse and repeat two or three times a year, or whatever it takes. The only real question is whether he'd have had that many diaries with him."

"Maybe," I say. "I usually only carry two on a jump, a personal journal and the official research diary for that project. But I haven't been in the field very long. Unless it's a day trip, historians will generally pack a diary or two from earlier research. They're not something that's closely regulated, in part because anyone looking at the things without the CHRONOS gene sees a standard diary. The paper may be a little thicker than usual, but it's nothing that would set off alarm bells for most people. Delia Morrell, one of our trainers, traveled with a binder that held at least six."

As I suspected, the smell of coffee has drawn Madi down from the loft. One foot is bare and the other is clad only in the ankle wrap, and she winces when they hit the cold floor. Although that could be from her injury. She's still limping pretty badly, too, which is going to limit how much she can do in the field. Once she has her coffee, she heads for one of the armchairs, draping her legs over the side closest to the fire to warm her toes.

"I think Clio is right that the *Book of Prophecy* on the shelf is probably bait," Madi says. "He wouldn't leave the real thing sitting out like that, even if people could only read parts of it. The real thing is probably inside a safe somewhere. And there's not much logic in taking risks specifically to get it. The countdown may still be ticking away in the library back home, but we're not in this to win Saul's game. If we want help from your friends at CHRONOS, we're not allowed to fix this timeline anyway. And even if we *could* 'fix it'"—she makes air quotes around the last two words—"what does that really mean? This screwed-up timeline goes on. Those of us under a key just won't be in it."

She's right, but it's a little depressing having it all spelled out.

Clio must agree, because she says, "On that cheerful note, I'm going to go scramble some eggs. If one of you will slice bread for toast, we can get this show on the road a bit faster."

Madi stifles a yawn. "That reminds me, there are some jars of jam on the counter that your caretaker's wife delivered. And . . . she may have caught a brief glimpse of the holoscreen on this." She holds up her tablet. "Sorry. She said she'd be stopping by again today to check on us."

Clio rolls her eyes as we head for the kitchen. "That was my one hesitation about Dad telling them we were going to be here . . . although that fire would have been a dead giveaway, and we definitely needed it. It's usually not this cold in early November. Alice Owens is a sweet lady, but dear God is she nosy. Did she ask about the tablet?"

Madi shakes her head. "I stuck it under your drawing pad on the coffee table, but she kept eyeing the spot as she backed out the door, so I think she saw something. Getting back to the girl in Dennis's office, though . . . something just occurred to me. Did he have a much younger adopted daughter in the last timeline?"

"No," I say. "Two daughters, around the same age. His marriage broke up in that timeline, mostly for financial reasons."

"It breaks up in this one, as well. This is wife number two. And take a look at this." Madi pulls something up on her tablet and hands it to me. "I found this in the files Charlayne gave us. Note the name of the daughter."

I scroll down to the last paragraph and read it. At the very end, it says his wife and their adopted daughter, Ada, will be joining him in DC. I give her a confused look.

"Now say the name aloud. Beta, Zeta, Theta . . . ?"

"Eta. Ah, got it. It's pronounced the same."

Madi nods. "Eta is from the second batch. The one who bit Beta's hand when she was little . . . or who died as an infant, depending on which branch of the double memory you follow. So it seems like Saul delivered someone to Lawrence Dennis who could read the full *Book of Prophecy*. Why would he give up that much power?"

We toss around a few ideas while getting breakfast on the table, but none of them feels right to me. Those who were not roused by the scent of coffee gradually come to life when the smell of bacon fills the cabin. Or maybe it was the rooster crowing. Either way, by the time the sun is above the horizon, we're all awake and reasonably alert.

Everyone else is as curious as I am about the story Jack told Tim and Ev, so he gives us an overview while we eat. More of it is based in fact than I would have assumed. His dad is a fairly recent addition to the Fifth Column ranks and was under a CHRONOS field when the last time shift happened. Several of General Merrick's colleagues, including the one who convinced him to get the special version of the lotus tattoo that shielded him, have Fifth Column roots going back a couple of generations—not for religious reasons, but because it was one of the few places consistent about funding and encouraging scientific research. LORTA's funding was in constant flux, with the government tending to keep alive only the programs with immediate, direct military uses or ones that might have major economic applications. Many of the scientists who were let go, especially those working on genetics or temporal physics, found a home with the Fifth Column. The group also helped other scientists to get out of the country, asking only that they do what they could to keep their colleagues here in the United States updated on advances in their field that were happening in other countries.

"So, why would Saul gut scientific research if his goal is to be able to skip to other timelines like Team Viper was doing?" I ask. "Or were we wrong on that assumption?"

"You weren't wrong," Jack says. "That's definitely what he wants. But, yeah . . . it doesn't make sense to gut scientific research if that's your goal. Based on the information I've seen, the whole science-versus-superstition thing started veering out of control in the late twentieth century. It cycles back around for a bit, and then everything goes completely off the rails sometime around 2050. Full isolationism, religious control over education, and—as usual in that scenario—science gets the ax. The field of history isn't faring too well, either, with anything inconvenient being either written out or profusely edited to fit the desired narrative."

He stops and finishes off the last of his coffee. "This next part is speculation, but Alex and I both think it's really the only thing that fits. Once Saul was satisfied with the job he'd done screwing up the timeline, he jumps ahead, probably to the late 2150s if his key has the same restrictions against jumps after 2160. He arrives in our future ready to throw a little money and influence around, hoping to build on the research Alex was doing, trying to figure out how Team Viper moved between timelines. Only, when he gets there, he discovers science is literally decades behind. Alex, all alone in our library, was doing more cutting-edge temporal physics than the university labs he finds. And Alex appears to be his best, maybe even his only, hope for replicating that research."

"So who exactly stormed into the house to grab them . . . and to shoot me?" Rich asks.

"A Cyrist Sword team, led by my dad. Ordered, indirectly, by Saul. Rumor has it he's been paying massive bribes along the chain of command. The bulk of the paramilitary group is still under the joint control of Cyrist International, and has strong ties to the National Guard. DARPA is a major exception. And LORTA, their Long-Range Threat Assessment group, is almost entirely Fifth Column. Saul apparently doesn't know the extent of it, but he must at least suspect there could be traitors in the mix. Otherwise, he'd have just sent down instructions to kill Rich, rather than tasking a specific individual with the attack."

"Was Lorena one of those scientists they got out of the country?" Madi asks. "I mean, the Lorena from this timeline who was in Switzerland. Not the one we know."

Jack shakes his head. "That was a nasty bit of subterfuge on Saul's part. There is no Lorena Jeung in this timeline. There's no RJ and no Alex, either, so it's a damn good thing they were wearing field extenders. The photos—along with the video she received—were faked. She's having a really tough time dealing with that. It was hard enough when she felt like she sold us out to protect this other version of Yun Hee. To find out she did it for a computer-generated fantasy was gut-wrenching. I'm just glad she didn't know the full extent of what happened in the basement." His jaw tightens as he looks at Rich. "I didn't know, either, until Madi told me in the attic last night. Although, I think my dad knew it was reversed, because there was this big drama about your key vanishing. They think it was stolen."

"Why go to all that trouble with Lorena, though?" Madi asks. "Last night, you said they'd been pushing her really hard, too. They have plenty of ways to get samples of the CHRONOS gene. Saul, for one, but also the Sisters of Prudence he's been kidnapping. Surely they have geneticists who can reverse engineer that? I mean, they already did it with the cloned versions of Prudence and were even able to isolate and edit out the ability to actually time travel."

"Yeah," Jack says. "But I don't think Saul really wants to create more time travelers. I was being honest when I told Tim and Ev that he'd prefer a timeline without CHRONOS. The fact that they still exist is one hundred percent Fifth Column. Saul just wants a stronger, longer-lasting version of the booster serum Lorena makes for me that he can carry with him when he blows this joint. That's why we've been trying to drag this out as long as possible. She's been giving him really low-level patches and telling him that she's trying to increase the strength, but she's worried doing so too fast could be lethal." He glances over at Katherine. "How old was Saul when Team Viper erased CHRONOS?"

"Thirty-one," she says, her eyes widening slightly. "But I noticed he looked older in one of the recordings. And again when I saw him in the . . . I mean, when I saw his splinter at the antislavery convention. Are you saying he's aging out?"

"That's the hope, although it's something we might want to play close to the vest around your friends at the new and not-so-improved CHRONOS, since it could reduce his threat in their eyes. But yeah, we haven't had a visit from one of his splinters in over two weeks. And the last one disappeared before he could blink out. He only lasted six minutes."

Rich shakes his head. "I'm not sure that means anything, though. Saul could have simply moved on to bugging Alex and Lorena six months in the future."

"Alex thought about that. There's a wall screen with a monthly projects calendar at LORTA. The bottom section is for regular office maintenance items. *Replaced PIK Filter* is a nonsense task we had one of the Fifth Column people add. I set a stable point in front of the wall screen, and the folks in the organization put a green check in that box on the calendar on any day when they get intel that one of Saul's splinters has dropped in at the Cyrist Sword offices to ask the commander about progress. I scroll through to check every day. I haven't found anything new at any point in time for the past sixteen days. There were fourteen visits overall. Alex was able to track Saul's general destination. After most of them, he goes back to 1969 California. Los Angeles, mostly, although there were a few to San Francisco a couple of years before that."

"You're saying Saul keeps checking back year after year, to see if Alex and Lorena have made progress?" Katherine says. "That's way more patience than I'd expect from him, especially if he's worried that his time is running out. And I'm a little surprised he'd trust any serum Lorena makes."

"He trusts her because he has hostages. And a guinea pig." Jack pulls up his sleeve to show a little gray med patch. "What she hasn't told him is that my serum isn't a permanent fix, and not even a good temporary fix, for his problem. I'm young enough that my body hasn't started the long, slow process of decline. Lorena says once that happens, usually in your thirties, the body starts making imperfect copies of the genes in the CHRONOS alteration. My body still makes decent copies. I just lack one element allowing me to use the key without the boost. But you're right about his patience level. It doesn't last. They're supposed to put a green check on the calendar anytime Saul shows up . . . and a red check if anyone on the project is killed."

We all brace because we know where this is going.

"A few days ago, I found two red checks had popped up on the calendar in September of next year," Jack says. "I have a stable point at Alex and Lorena's workstations. He continues to show up for work, although he looks pretty rough. She doesn't show for a few days, and then she's back, too, looking even rougher than Alex. One red check was either RJ or Yun Hee. And I don't see my dad anywhere around."

I stop him because I'm confused. "You said Saul hadn't made any jumps for more than two weeks, but you spotted new red checks on the calendar a few days ago?"

"Yeah. If I had to guess, there's some version of a dead man's switch. If he doesn't show up, Alex and Lorena's supervisor metes out a punishment. There's a third red check the following January, and . . ." He shakes his head. "I thought about changing the plan, having them put letters instead of the checkmarks. Initials so that I'd know who they killed. But screw that. It was making me crazy. And we're not going to let it happen."

He gets no argument from any of us on that point, although I have to admit the information he just gave us about Saul raised almost as many questions for me as it answered. First and foremost, why would Saul jump back to the 1960s once he realized that he was losing his ability with the key? Why not camp out at the local Cyrist temple in 2140 or whenever, and put his money and influence toward the development of the serum and the advancement of interdimensional travel?

I think it raised similar questions for Katherine. After breakfast, she comes over to ask if Clio and I noticed anything in the stable points from Satan's Cavern in Haight-Ashbury that we set after we jumped back to earlier in the year when the building was still the Diggers' Free Store. That was a good call by Clio, in retrospect, although I can't say I caught as much of a bad vibe from the Process Church. They really do strike me as nothing more than a bunch of people playacting at being occultists. But the Free Store had piles of clothing and small household items on a maze of tables. Dozens of people, many in states of altered consciousness, were poking around in those piles, hunting for donated treasure, and no one paid any attention to us as we wandered around setting observation points. Didn't even need to be stealthy about it. There were plenty of folks doing far weirder stuff than staring at the space above a strange medallion during the Summer of Love in San Francisco.

"We haven't had time to look through them yet," I tell her. "We were trying to figure out whether the *Book of Prophecy* on Lawrence Dennis's shelf is real, and why Saul would have him adopt a kid who can read the full book, not just static pages."

"And Jack's information solved that bit of the puzzle," Clio says. "Saul's supply of jump juice started running dry before he'd accomplished everything he wanted to. If he wanted this timeline to stay screwed up, he needed someone to continue what he'd started, so he had to trust someone else to dish out the updated prophecies."

Katherine nods, but she seems distracted. "Is there any chance you could take a few minutes and scroll through the stable points at the Process Church's café to let me know when Saul appears? I still think that's our best bet to find actual Saul, rather than a splinter. I'll see if Richard can help. I need to make the recording for Angelo and edit some things out of the diary I'm sending back with Timothy and

Ev. Oh, and Clio, you said there was some information here about the killing at God's Hollow. I'd like to send a copy back to Angelo. Because if the Saul in this timeline was up to the same tricks, then that's something that should have already happened."

"Sure," Clio says. "It's in the storage space under the bed up in the loft. But I don't know if that even happened in this timeline. We haven't had any way to check the local papers. Mr. and Mrs. Owens might know, but . . . it would be kind of an odd question to ask."

"It's okay," she says. "If it happened, Angelo might be able to find something about it in the CHRONOS archives. Or at any rate, he'll know whether there was a time that Saul blew off his TMU check."

After Clio tracks down the clipping and gives it to Katherine, we split up the observation points and begin scrolling through. It's a little harder to spot Saul than I'd have thought, because he's grown out his hair and beard more than they were in the video at the start of the game. He actually looks a bit like one of the other guys who seemed to be in charge for the first week or so when the various members of the Process Church were putting in some sweat equity by scrubbing the place, painting the walls scarlet and black, and laying floor tile. Even the kids get in on the action. There are about twenty of them, ranging in age from around six to twelve, all dressed in black or gray, with identical haircuts cropped at the jawline. They're brought in for a few hours a day, always in a group, so maybe this is part of their schooling?

"Do we have anything on children in the Process Church?" I ask Clio.

"Nothing beyond a few articles from people who left. Those who were on the periphery lived normal family lives, but the ones with parents who went full Process were raised communally."

I share the location and current time I'm viewing with Richard, who has joined us. "They've really nailed the stereotypical cult-kid look, haven't they? What's the name of that movie? *Children of the*

Corn? Or maybe it was *Children of the Damned*? Maybe both, come to think of it. Kind of an Aryan vibe, too. Just two little dark-haired sheep in a sea of blond."

When I mention the bearded guy to Clio and Rich, and give them the coordinates to check, Clio takes a quick look and grabs one of the computer tablets. After a brief search through the files, she shows me a picture from one of the earlier publications. "I think that's Robert de Grimston, Mary Ann's husband."

"Yeah," I say. "I saw his picture in the magazine we got from the goth guy on the street corner. Just didn't recognize him in the different lighting. They've almost got a halo effect going on in the magazine. You're right. There's a resemblance."

Rich shakes his head. "I wouldn't say it's very strong. Saul is thinner. His hair is straighter, and a little darker."

"Oh, I'm not saying they're trying to *fool* anyone," Clio says. "Just that I think she may have traded de Grimston for someone who could offer her more. They're not supposed to split up until the early 1970s. Mary Ann claimed to be an oracle, though. Robert was simply a pretty, Christlike face she could put out front. But she could be a damn good oracle with Saul as part of the team."

This seems more and more likely as we continue scrolling through. Robert de Grimston isn't around, but we find two other times when Saul is in the café in 1967, including the one when the photograph with Mary Ann was taken. Charles Manson is in the café, as well, on a few occasions, along with Susan Atkins, one of the two women Clio and I saw eating popsicles on the stoop outside the house. She eventually begins working a daily shift waiting tables.

"Crazy conspiracy theories aside, isn't that a closer connection than Manson is supposed to have had to the Process Church in the previous timeline?" Clio asks.

I nod and keep scrolling. Then Clio finds Atkins at the stable point we set in what is now the kitchen, talking to Saul. I'm jotting that one down when she says, "Oh my God, look at this."

She taps the stable point to the back of my key and then Richard's. It's the first time I've seen Saul in the all-black outfit the rest of the Process Church wears. He and Mary Ann are near the altar that's the center point of the café, about six feet away from the table near the bulletin board with the Monterey Pop poster. She nudges Saul, and he walks over to a man of around thirty in a brown suede hat with a floppy brim that shadows his face. The guy has just stood up and his wallet is in his hand. He pulls out a couple of bills as Saul approaches, and slaps them on the black tablecloth, next to a plate with a steak bone in the center, swimming in a pool of leftover juices. An untouched plate of toast and a glass that once contained milk are on the other side.

The guy looks kind of familiar. He's not as short as Manson, but still well below average height. Saul towers over him, and like a lot of tall men, seems to be trying to use his height to his advantage, getting into the shorter guy's personal space. If he was trying to intimidate the man it doesn't work, however. He gives Saul a look of disgust and turns toward the door.

Something Saul says must catch the man's attention, because he turns around and walks back. He still looks annoyed, but also mildly intrigued. And then I can't see his face at all because it's blocked by Saul's shoulder. His hand is visible, however. They exchange cash and also a tiny square of gray paper.

Saul says something else as the guy walks toward the door. He turns back and points toward the poster. I can see his face, and after watching it twice, I'm almost certain what the other man says ends with the words *busy with that*, which would make sense given what Clio said about him supplying most of the concertgoers with

Monterey Purple. And the last sentence he says is crystal clear. *See me after.*

I look back at Clio. "Okay, was that—?"

"Yes!" Clio says. "It's Bear. His last name is Owsley. No, that's his first name, I think. The guy the Cyrist Sword goons make an example of at Monterey. You saw him at the concert."

I'd actually been going to ask her if that was a drug buy, but I guess her answer confirms it indirectly. And that's why he looked familiar. This was the guy in the background of the sketch Clio made.

Rich's eyebrows go up. "You mean Owsley Stanley? Sound technician for the Grateful Dead, and LSD supplier to . . . well, pretty much every musician in the world in those days. Rumor has it that John Lennon flew people from Britain to try and sneak the stuff back in film canisters. The chem lab Owsley set up produced such pure product that his name *literally* wound up in the dictionary as a synonym for primo acid. You know him?"

"Not really," she says. "But he's a friend of a guy I do know."

"She means Bob Weir," I tell him, fully anticipating his jaw drop. "And while I'm sure that's a story you will want to hear every single word of eventually, take a look at the stable point. Seems Saul is *also* a customer of this Owsley guy."

Rich stares at his key for a moment, then shakes his head. "Look again. Saul gives him money, but he also hands him something else. That little square of gray. Owsley doesn't give Saul anything in return. I mean, *maybe* he slipped him some tabs of acid with his hand that's off camera, but . . . Whoa." He glances up to the loft where Madi and Jack are working. "Hey, Jack. Can you come down here for a minute?"

When Jack joins us, Rich asks him to roll up his sleeve. Jack does, revealing the booster patch he showed us earlier.

A tiny square of gray paper.

PART THREE

ZUGZWANG

Zugzwang [from German, "compulsion to move"]: when a player is at a disadvantage by virtue of having to move; where any legal move weakens the position.

∞20∞

After a little over four hours of discussion and scanning through our various stable points, we jump back to the attic in Bethesda at five minutes before eleven. Once Jack has a couple of minutes to recuperate from the Nauseator, he heads to LORTA to explain our current plan to his dad and his Fifth Column contacts and get their input.

This was the cause of some disagreement, to put it mildly, and was eventually subjected to a vote. I'll admit I was hesitant at first. I have never met General John Merrick, and I do not trust him. He apparently didn't think it was important to inform Jack that Rich was dead, and Jack has said the man is the type who accepts collateral damage as part of his job. I suspect all of us, maybe even Jack, could wander into the collateral damage category if the circumstances seem dire to General Merrick. But I trust Jack completely. He swears his dad is the only reason any of us inside this house are currently safe. And so, I voted with Jack. I can't blame the others, however, for wondering if he's really the best judge of his own father's conduct and motivations.

The final vote was four to two. Tyson and Katherine were both on the *hell-no* side of the equation, with Tyson adding that he was concerned there might be a Fifth Column *inside* the Fifth Column. Double agents aren't unheard of, especially when dealing with someone like Saul, who has plenty of money for bribes and a moral compass flawed enough to use babies as temporal pawns. Clio seemed torn, but in the end, she decided the Fifth Column might have information we need to pull all of this off. Ironically, it was Rich who decided the matter. I think it helps that he doesn't remember lying dead on my basement floor. It's a pretty vivid memory for me, though, and I suspect it's even stronger for Tyson and Katherine. Rich argued that we're taking at least as big a risk working with this version of CHRONOS, and with things this screwed up, we need all the help we can get.

I just hope Jack is right about his dad. I also hope he's able to make it back, because it took him two tries to leave the attic. The good news is that he can rest up for a bit if he needs to, and Lorena can give him another patch, but it's clear he was right when he said it would be risky to assign him any long-distance jumps.

The other question we debated long and hard is whether Saul actually set a bomb in each time and place where he grabbed the various Sisters. It would be so much simpler if we could jump in and keep him from ever abducting them. We're still not entirely sure when and how Eta was taken, but in the other cases where he snatched clones, it's possible we could prevent the abductions without risking any lives at all. It would be very much in character for Saul to have set off that one bomb simply to make his point. He might even have chosen to abduct the babies and their caretakers on a day when a totally unrelated explosion occurred in order to minimize his effort.

In the end, though, we can't risk it, especially since Jack says Alex is certain there's a bomb here, as well. That's why Tyson is staying back at the cabin in Georgia. It's why all of us will, from here on out, never be in this house at the same time. We're going to need to be here occasionally, but if Saul or his Cyrist Sword crew decides to blow the place before the countdown ends, we need someone on the outside who can jump back and warn us not to make that trip.

The first items on the agenda we'll be sending back to CHRONOS are rescuing the remaining Pru Sisters from the locations where Saul dropped them. While Charlayne didn't make rescuing them an explicit precondition for helping us, the Fifth Column members working with Jack's father did. I don't think any of us would have been cool with abandoning them to their fate, anyway, when we have no idea how all of this will end. Sigma's rescue should be simple. Given that Saul appears out of nowhere as the Zaubererjackl, it's unlikely to make the situation worse if another wizard appears out of nowhere to shoot him and save Sigma from the gallows. The hardest part will be dealing with the fact that we're leaving children to die up there. Yes, their deaths are history, but that history is seriously fucked up, and I'm not ruling out fixing it.

Saving the Sister at the antislavery convention is also fairly direct. Someone only has to jump in immediately after Saul's splinter disappears, grab the girl, and go. There's the issue of people who aren't supposed to die in our timeline, and I can tell this one bothers Katherine a lot. But at least none of them are eight years old.

We didn't have a chance to do a reconnaissance jump to the Scopes trial, but that event was a big historical deal in previous timelines. The *Log of Stable Points* has two locations in the area, including one beneath a platform on one side of the courthouse. Tyson and Clio are planning to use the Timex thingy. And yes, I've been informed it's called a neural disruptor, but I like our name better.

The jumps to the late 1960s and early 1970s are the iffiest. I need to check with the Fifth Column to be certain there have been no more abductions. If there haven't been, then the good news is that this is Eta at different ages, and we have multiple chances to rescue her. From what I've read about how Manson treated the women and girls in his "Family," we need to get her before she ends up with that group. We can't wait until just before the place is raided, which is the one time we know exactly where she'll be. Spending that long with a group of serial killers would have to leave a scar on her psyche. The easiest opportunity would probably be at Monterey Pop, since she is with a group of other kids. Locating her as a small child would obviously be best for her emotional health. As an infant would be better still, but none of the other Sisters know when she was taken, so someone within Cyrist International must have been involved in getting her to Saul, who eventually handed her over to Lawrence Dennis. Even if Dennis was kind to her, and I get the sense he was, she seems to be a pawn in some ongoing game between the two of them. And she's obviously not very happy even being in the same room as Saul Rand.

I'm lost in my thoughts about all of this when Jack arrives, as planned, a few minutes before Timothy and Evelyn. I'm not sure how long he's been away, but he's in fresh clothes and there's at least a day's worth of scruff on his face.

He turns his hand toward us to reveal a lotus tattoo. It glows a faint amber, at least for me, in the dim light of the attic.

I wrinkle my nose in disgust. "You've got to be kidding. How will this help us in any way? You said your dad was worried—and rightfully so—about you attempting long-range jumps."

"That still holds," he says. "I'll only be going in if we need to liaise with the Fifth Column."

"I don't get why they even have the special tattoos if they don't have the CHRONOS gene. They can't see it." I don't add that I very much *can* see it, and it's not exactly something I *want* to see resting on his pillow at night if we come out of this okay.

"There's a two-step verification process. They see the plain blue tattoo, with a slight tilt to one of the petals. And there's also a password. Once you reach the point in history where they have the Pru clones, you're presented to one of them, who *can* see the special tattoo and can confirm you're in their book."

"The *Book of Prophecy*?"

"No. They have one of the diaries, and they keep a running list of Fifth Column members. Sorry about the ugly tat, though. Maybe I can get it removed after?"

I tell him it's not a big deal. And really, it's not. Maybe he can have someone tattoo over it and turn it into flames or something like the Church of Prudence members did. It still leaves me a little unsettled, though.

Timothy and Evelyn appear in the very same spot at 11 a.m. Evelyn is still holding the bottle of water she took out of her bag, with the single sip taken from it, so either they really did jump straight here rather than reporting back to CHRONOS or she's an absolute master at attention to detail.

Katherine and Rich take point, since the rest of us seem to unnerve the Winslows a bit. I simply open the document we came up with during our final hour back at the cabin and display it on the holoscreen above my tablet. It includes details of each planned jump, along with our reasoning behind them, and a short wish list of things we could use from CHRONOS. The same information is on the first page of the diary Katherine will be sending back to HQ, along with her message to Angelo and details about the massacre at God's Hollow. And we have another, slightly more detailed list back at the cabin of things we intend to change as soon as possible, although they may have to wait until we stop Saul. It seems like a bit of a risk to share all of that with CHRONOS at this point, however.

Timothy and Evelyn don't bother with pleasantries, but immediately begin reading the list. And immediately start shaking their heads.

"Item number one isn't going to happen," Evelyn says.

When we were coming up with the wish list, Rich and Tyson were both adamant that we should ask for them to send Delia Morrell and Abel Waters. Tyson said that he trained with them, that you couldn't ask for two people with clearer heads in the field, and that they work together seamlessly. Rich agreed, saying Abel would also be a good man to have on your side in a physical confrontation. Katherine was a bit more hesitant, noting that it would be awkward for Abel in pretty much any period before the mid-1960s, especially in the South, because his skin is dark enough that he can't simply insert blue contacts and divert attention from his race like Tyson can. But most of the earlier missions are simply a matter of popping in and popping back out with whichever Sister of Prudence it was that Saul dragged along for the ride. It might also include killing a Saul splinter, but they all agreed that, never having been a member of the Saul Rand Fan Club, Abel probably wouldn't balk at this.

I was less certain, of course, partly because I don't know them, but also because there are a few things in Kate's diaries that suggest to me that even though Delia and Abel may be incredible with trainees, they might be less perfect in the field than Tyson and Rich think. Clio chimed in, noting that her dad said Abel could be unreasonable and Delia was a basket case one time when Abel was in danger. But since neither of us know much about the alternatives, we didn't argue the case very strenuously.

"Why *not* Delia and Abel?" Rich begins to tick off the merits of pulling the two of them in, noting first that we really need some extra muscle to rescue the various Sisters.

Evelyn raises a hand to stop him. "They retired this past spring. Delia's about five months pregnant. No way Angelo would send either of them."

Rich sighs. "You said there are only twelve active agents. Why don't you tell us which twelve, so we don't go poking around in the dark again?"

Timothy says, "Aside from the alternate versions of the two of you, there are the two of us, Saul, Adrienne, Esther, Shaila, Mariah, Rob . . . oh, and Wallace."

Katherine makes a face, clearly unhappy with our menu of choices. "Esther's not an option. She's fierce—she has to be to study the ancient Akan—but she and Saul are thick as thieves in most time-lines. I don't think we can trust her."

"This Esther doesn't study the Akan," Evelyn says. "We stick exclusively to history within our borders. Other countries prefer to research their own history, and I mean, who can blame them? Regional biases are hard to overcome."

Rich asks them to repeat the roster of agents and counts off on his fingers. When they finish, he says, "That's only eleven. You missed one."

Timothy shakes his head. "Tate Poulsen is on a one-year suspension. Still has another few months to go. Which is kind of moot now that no one is jumping, but . . ."

My head jerks up. "Is he on suspension for fathering a child in a Viking village?" Everyone gives me a questioning look. "Just something Thea noted in the diary she left me. It was in her long list of their grievances against Saul, but I wasn't entirely sure why."

Evelyn frowns and gives me a shrug. "Maybe? All we know is that he's been suspended. We didn't ask what he did. Personnel records are private. The only other thing we know is . . ." She glances over at Katherine. "It would have only been a six-month suspension, but he attacked Saul right after the hearing with the jump committee. Just stormed into the cafeteria and literally threw him into a wall. The med unit had to reset Saul's nose, but to be honest he's lucky he got away with only that much damage. I seriously thought Tate was going to kill him."

Timothy gives a dark chuckle. "A few of us were kind of okay with that possibility. Then some damn fool went and called security."

Evelyn colors slightly, digging an elbow into his ribs. "Hush, Timo. *Of course* I called security. But they were on their way already, so . . ."

"Wait," Katherine says. "Tate studied Vikings. But you said you can't jump outside the US."

Timothy looks confused. "Territories aren't off limits. Tate studied the Vikings in Greenland. And . . . I'm guessing that's *not* a territory in your timeline."

"Right," I say. "That's who we want, though. Tate. If this Abel guy isn't an option, we want Tate. Does he still look like Thor?"

Evelyn looks a little dumbfounded, but she nods.

Katherine stares at me for a moment, and then seconds it. "Tell Angelo that Saul set Tate up. He did the same to me. One of Saul's roommates' birth-control methods failing might be accidental, even if they're statistically foolproof implants. Two roommates having those failures, however, suggests he was dosing us with something that counteracts the medication. And he is probably *still* dosing your version of Katherine."

"Okay," Timothy says. "I'm not sure we're even close to following that logic train, but Tate might be the best option anyway, especially if what you really need is someone willing to throw Saul Rand against a wall. If Angelo can track Tate down, that is. And if he's even willing to pull in anyone aside from us. As for the other items on your wish list here . . ." He reads for a moment, then tugs up his sleeve to show the watch on his wrist. "The neural disruptors are probably doable. They're standard issue for security. I've never personally seen one of these field-extender things you mention, but . . . extraction teams must have something of that nature. Otherwise, how would they retrieve a wounded or unconscious agent?"

"That last one, though . . ." Evelyn says. "I'm pretty sure we can get something to neutralize any listening devices in the house. You could probably order that now if you had the time. But we don't have anything that wipes out the stable points at a destination. You can erase the location from your key, but the end point still exists."

"Can you do us a favor and just . . . um . . . *ask* about that?" Jack says. "I reminded Alex that we really need that admin feature about five minutes ago. Five minutes ago for me, but it's about three-and-a-half months in our future. Theoretically, that gives Alex, his team, and whoever comes after over a century of R&D time before you'd be inquiring about it."

"Sure," Timothy says. "Can't hurt to ask. The research requests and resources on the list shouldn't be a problem, assuming of course that Angelo doesn't simply decide the safest course is to ignore all of this."

Jack says, "I probably don't need to say this, given that the others seem to trust you and this Angelo guy. But, to be clear, if he should decide that the best bet is not simply to ignore it, but to send one of your extraction teams or whatever you call them to take all of us out and preserve this timeline entirely as it is, it won't work. The Fifth Column is organized in cells. If I don't show up on schedule, the leader of my cell will contact someone, who will contact someone else . . . and they *do* have backup plans. None of them will result in the creation of CHRONOS."

"Understood." Evelyn nods down at my ankle, which is still in the wrap. "What's going on with that?"

"Tripped," I say, deciding she doesn't need the full story. "The brace helps, but it's still swollen and I'm not moving at anything close to normal speed. Looks like I'm going to be stuck on couch patrol."

"What size shoe do you wear?"

I tell her, even though it seems like a bit of a non sequitur. She nods, puts the cap on her bottle of water, and sticks it inside her bag.

Katherine takes a deep breath and hands Evelyn her diary. "This includes everything you asked for, along with a few extra items Angelo may want to consider. Even if they haven't or won't occur in this timeline, it may help him to understand why it's absolutely imperative not just for us, but for you, that our version of Saul is stopped. And that your version is watched very, very closely."

"Okay." Evelyn sticks the diary in her bag. "We won't keep you waiting."

True to their word, they're back in thirty seconds, this time in different clothes. Each is carrying a large suitcase. Evelyn has a pair of shoes with chunky heels in her other hand.

Timothy steps aside and someone else arrives in the stable point he set. The guy is also holding a suitcase. He's hunched over slightly in deference to the low, sloped ceiling in the attic. For the first time, I wonder whether we're exceeding the maximum occupancy limit for this floor.

Timothy grins. "Glad you listened to me now when I said to duck, aren't you? For those of you who don't know, this is Tate Poulsen. We've brought him up to speed. Turns out even after a few months to cool off, he's still quite eager for an assignment that could involve killing or maiming multiple versions of Saul Rand. You know Katherine and Richard . . . Well, actually I guess you don't know *this* version of them, but you can put a name with a face. That's Clio, *the* Jack Merrick, and . . ."

"Madi," I say. "You'll be meeting Tyson later."

Tate nods at us but remains silent. He sits on the floor, keeping his eye on Katherine and Rich. Maybe he's trying to see if they look different from the versions at CHRONOS?

Evelyn hands me the shoes she's carrying, along with a pair of tights.

"These should fit. They're the lowest heels I could print that have a stabilization field. The tights have one, too. I still wouldn't advise trying to run. The ankle might twinge if you do, and it could slow down the healing. But you should be able to walk on it for a bit if you don't overdo things."

"Thanks."

Timothy returns Katherine's diary. "Angelo was initially pissed and convinced that you guys were trying to manipulate us. But whatever you said in this turned the tide."

She pales slightly. "Most likely the video. He needed to see exactly what Saul is capable of when he's angry." Rich puts an arm around her, and she leans into him. I hadn't really thought about what she was sending back, but I have a pretty good idea now which video she's talking about.

Timothy says, "He was even more on board after I mentioned the possibility that Saul gave you—and Tate—something that interfered with your birth control. That's a felony. And administrators' keys now have the feature you mentioned. Angelo acted like it was something we should have learned in training, and I actually kind of remembered that once he told us. So did Ev. Does that mean there was a time shift?"

"No," Rich says. "Little changes like that won't create a shift. It takes something big, or many things that add up over time. What hit you was more of a garden-variety double memory, like when you did the interview with your splinter. If there's a time shift and you're under a key, you'll feel it here." He taps his stomach.

"Yeah, well, we're already feeling it *here.*" Timothy taps his forehead. "And I know what a splinter is. But why in hell would you ever interview a splinter? For that matter, why would you even create one if you could avoid it?"

"Guess you didn't have to go through that during your training," Katherine says. "Consider yourself lucky."

"What about the *Book of Cyrus* I gave you?" Jack asks.

"Oh, right," Timothy pulls it out of his bag. "Angelo's friend in TMU is working on that now. And Angelo is talking to Abby about possible points where that version could be inserted with the least damage to the overall timeline. The usual person to ask about religious history would be Saul, but he obviously can't do that."

"Wait," I say. "Demmings is a religious historian? Did she train Saul?"

Katherine gets my point before I even finish the sentence. "Yes. She did. That's another thing you might want to mention to Angelo. Seems a bit too much of a coincidence for one of Saul's trainers to have been the only one in—how long? Ever?—to have been erased like that, given everything else we know."

"I think that's already occurred to Angelo," Timothy says. "To a lot of us, actually."

Evelyn leans forward and says, "You've given us your terms and we've shown you what we can offer. We *want* to help. But I need to let you know that we have conditions, too. After each jump made by anyone on this team, we'll be going back to HQ. Angelo has someone in TMU that he trusts. She's taking a risk, but she's agreed to check whether actions on each move make a substantial difference to our timeline. That goes for the jumps you'll be making, too. Angelo hasn't given us the specific parameters, but if they determine the move was too risky—say, if it causes a war that kills a lot of people—then we'd have no choice but to jump back and tell whoever made that move that they should not do it. I'm not saying we could or would stop you from taking it, but we have limits to how much we're willing to damage our own history." She shakes her head in disbelief. "I can't believe I'm even saying that much. We're CHRONOS, damn it. We do not *change* history."

∞

BOGART, GEORGIA
NOVEMBER 5, 1941

Jack jabs the log in the fireplace one last time, then puts the poker back in the tool stand. "I think that will do it. But if we're going to survive here in the wild, we need to bring some fuel to start the fires."

"You think *this* is the wild? We should go camping for our honeymoon." I'm joking, because I can't actually imagine Jack in a tent.

But he says, "Sure. I'd like to visit that Glendalough place when this is over. It looked . . . peaceful. I'm looking forward to peaceful."

"Me, too." When Jack requested the stable-point eraser, I thought it was for the house. I really wanted to go through each room and exorcise every single stable point Saul Rand placed there, so the house would feel safe again. But Jack pointed out that would make it obvious that we know we're being watched. The main reason for that feature is that we can selectively wipe other stable points when we jump in at a location. That way, we don't have to worry about another one of Saul's splinters popping in after we do and shooting us in the back. Apparently, we have his dad to thank for that idea. I guess having a military mind helping out with tactics isn't a bad thing.

So we all came straight here from the attic, along with costumes and some tools we needed. Alex is patching in old security footage of the various rooms via Jarvis to Cyrist Sword. Hopefully they don't catch on to the fact that Jarvis isn't as reliable of a spy as they believe him to be. While Jack's dad and his Fifth Column friends seem to be on our side, the same can't be said for the DARPA supervisor who is apparently in Saul's pocket, and we can't afford to do anything that would put Alex, Lorena, and the others at risk just because we're tired of being under constant surveillance. The only snoop we have to worry about here at the cabin is Alice Owens, and if she comes back around, she'll find the filmy door curtain she peeked through yesterday has been replaced by an extra thick towel.

The cabin is small, but it has more arrivals and departures than a Dryft terminal at rush hour. Tyson went to 1848 with Katherine and Rich to help get things set up for the rescue at the antislavery convention, and then dropped back in to say they also needed Tate. From there, Tyson jumped directly to join Clio at the Scopes trial, and Tate jumped to Salzburg to join Evelyn and Timothy at the stable points in front of the gallows. They were kind of psyched for the assignment, in fact, given that they've never been able to jump outside of the US, although I think they're going to find it's really not a vacation spot. The plan is to use the neural disruptors to knock out the executioner and his assistants as they bring out the prisoners. Then they'll grab Sigma and blink back here, so I can take her to the Fifth Column. Katherine will take the other Sister, who we're pretty sure is Rho, directly to their compound, and I thought about giving Evelyn that stable point. I hate to make Sigma take multiple trips, even though Jack says the mini-Nauseator isn't quite as bad. But I'd prefer to keep the Fifth Column's exposure to a minimum.

Barring an emergency, Jack and I will be holding down the home front, although that may change once we get all of the Sisters to the Fifth Column. I'm wearing the tights Evelyn gave me, and the shoes with the stabilization field definitely help, but my ankle is still puffy, so I'm keeping it elevated as much as possible. Another advantage to us being here in 1941 rather than in 2136 is that Jack is closer to any emergency if he does have to go in. He has a half dozen of the booster patches and we have the extender, but I don't want to push it. For one thing, I don't like how jumpy the booster makes him. His leg has been twitching away, even though he's normally not a fidgeter.

And, of course, we're safer here in the cabin than we would be literally sitting over the powder keg at home.

"How did Alex figure out that there was a bomb?" I ask.

"RJ actually helped piece it together. Remember that night, before we went out to the patio? Alex said it wasn't a listening device, that it was much more basic than the other console. I wasn't there when the game started last time, but RJ and Lorena both remembered that the system repeated back your names and your roles . . . team lead, players, observer. It didn't do that this time. In fact, it didn't do anything that couldn't be programmed into a networked holoprojector."

I stop and think back, trying to remember. He's right. It didn't repeat our names or our predictions.

"The only thing it did was patch in the call from Saul and pronounce Team Hyena as having four players and one observer—something Saul already knew. Oh, and it awarded ten points for your first prediction, which it also didn't repeat. Either Saul made an educated guess as to what it would be, or he simply didn't give a fuck and set it to award a partial credit for whatever the first guess was. After Lorena passed along the message from RJ, Alex used the Jarvis connection to reexamine the file directory he saw when he was connecting it to the system. The reason his security program hadn't detected any problems is that there was literally nothing there. It's a shell. From what you told me, Saul called in with a second message after Cyrist Sword stormed the place, but aside from that countdown, it's just a holophone . . . and a fairly basic one at that. The only unusual things are the frequency scanner and the countdown, both of which are linked to that lone signal going out to keep the channel to a nonexistent data system open. Alex is convinced it's a kill switch. When the countdown ends, or that signal is otherwise broken—say, by someone smashing the case—the house blows up."

"Could Saul send a signal back to the console and blow the house up before then?"

"In theory, yes. But he waited."

It takes a second for the full impact of the past tense to hit. I knew Jack jumped back from three months in the future, and yes, logically, that would mean any explosive set to go off a little over a day from now would have already gone off.

"Are you saying our house *actually* blew up?"

I feel very stupid for not realizing this earlier, and I also want to cry. It's ridiculous. It's just a house. A house I'd never even been inside two months ago. But the house held a lot of love and history. A lot of chaos and pain, too . . . but that's not the house's fault.

He puts an arm around me. "Yes. It blew up. I know you love the place. I do, too. And I knew you'd look exactly this miserable, so I kind of danced around it. No one was inside, but the house itself was gutted. And this kind of twists my brain, because I don't know if you weren't there because I told you this, or you weren't going to be there anyway. I'm glad we have this place as a backup base of operations. It's obviously not ideal in terms of tech, but no one knows about it, and thanks to the old security footage, Alex was able to keep Saul's lackeys at Cyrist Sword from catching on for the full seventy-two hours."

I shake my head to clear it, feeling dense again. "He only had to do it for seventy-two hours? Thank God. I'd been thinking of poor Alex having to run interference with Cyrist Sword for the three entire months you've been gone, which in retrospect doesn't make any sense at all. At least he got one thing taken off his plate."

"He does miss the Jarvis link, though," Jack says.

And that brings the tears. I obviously have a backup for Jarvis, but not in this timeline or any other I'm likely to get back to. "Sorry," I say. "I know it's stupid. He's a virtual assistant. I can create another. But he has most of my photos of my parents. Vids of me with Nora and Pop. With Thea."

"Hey, hey," Jack says. "Come on. This isn't a done deal. It's not. Your house blew up, but that doesn't mean we're going to let it *stay* blown up. And Jarvis is still there for now. We have time to rescue the photos."

"That would be a big red flag that we know about the bomb, though. Otherwise, why would I be getting all nostalgic in the middle of Saul's idiotic game?"

I glance at the time and try to stop the tears. If it were Katherine, Rich, or Tyson, I wouldn't really care. But the first group arriving, in less than a minute, will be the Winslows and Tate with Sigma. And after that, I need to get her to the Fifth Column.

So I wipe my face on my sleeve and watch the stable point, praying they show. I saw all that I ever want to see of 1678 Salzburg through the key, and if they don't arrive, I will—at a minimum—have to watch the events through the key again to see what went wrong.

Twenty-seven seconds later, Timothy and Evelyn blink in. Tate arrives shortly after that, with one arm around Sigma. Both of them are clutching one of the handles on the field extender. All four of them look drained.

"Did it go okay?" I ask.

"I think so," Timothy says. "Some of the crowd could probably see the jailers and the other prisoners pass out when we hit the neural disruptor. But we ducked around the side of the building. They didn't see us jump out. And . . . she already knew we were coming."

Sigma nods. "We got a message in the diary. If we resisted, Saul would kill innocent people. And so we had to watch as his splinters showed up and took our babies, one by one. Then he came for me. I don't know what happened to Rho and Tau." She looks up at Tate, then over at Timothy and Evelyn. "So when are we going back? We have to get there earlier. They took those kids out *before* you saved me."

When they don't answer, she turns to me and Jack. "Someone has to go back! There were *children* in there with me. One little boy who barely came up to my waist. He was hungry. And there were marks on his fingers. They tortured him and then they fucking killed him! I heard the crowd. The man . . . When he came back there was blood . . . *Please*. We have to go *back*!"

Evelyn sinks into one of the chairs. "We can't." Her voice is tiny, almost inaudible. "That already happened. It is our history. We do not change it. Right, Timo?"

Timothy squeezes her shoulder, but he doesn't respond. I'm not even sure he *can* respond.

Sigma grabs Tate's arm. "If they won't rescue them, Tate, then take me back with you. I'll help. We'll save them together. What if that boy was your son? Wouldn't you want someone to save him?" When he doesn't respond, she pulls back her foot and kicks him in the shin. "What good is your strength if you won't use it to protect the helpless?"

Tate makes a sound that can only be characterized as a growl and storms out of the cabin.

Sigma glares at all of us, tossing her dark curls back over her shoulder in an angry gesture I remember all too well from a few arguments with Thea and many more arguments with my mom. She takes a deep breath, clearly trying to regain her composure. "Thank you for rescuing me. But I'm not going home until I know that those children—that all of those people who were in that little cell with me—are safe as well. They're *not* witches. There's no such thing as witches, damn it! And none of them deserve to die."

Then she turns on her heel and follows Tate outside.

FROM *THE BOOK OF CYRUS*
(NKJV, 5:9–15)

May Cyrus, the beacon of Hope, fill thee with joy and peace at each step along The Way. Knowest thou always that hope is stronger than fear. Hope helpeth thee to be at peace with change, for it is in the waves of change that one findeth true direction. If thou wilt but take life day by day, understanding that small pleasures are the greatest riches, thou wilt find peace, joy, and a blessed stillness in thy soul.

Verily, despite the sham, drudgery, and broken dreams, it is still a beautiful world. Be cheerful. Strive to be happy.

∞21∞

I shiver as soon as I blink in. Even at 2 a.m., you wouldn't think it would be this damn cold in August. Rich is already climbing the steps onto the platform. A second shiver that has nothing to do with the cold hits me as he walks right through the stable point where Saul will appear this afternoon. I doubt he's watching at this hour, but still . . .

"Right there, Rich." My voice, which is barely above a whisper, seems dangerously loud above the soft hum of insects. He stops on the stage, sets a stable point, and then walks a few paces away and sets another.

Off to the right, I see the faint glow of a CHRONOS key in the narrower of the two strips of woods. A moment later, another hum hits my ears, as Tyson starts Madi's GardenGenieXL to carve an escape route big enough for a wagon. The tool is a bit louder than the insects, but since the nearest house is about a quarter of a mile away, I think we're fine. Madi said the only thing that looks too big for the GardenGenie is the log lying across the path, so Rich and I are heading over to help.

Before we get there, however, the light from Tyson's key blinks out. Then it's back, along with a second key.

"What the hell?" Rich says, pulling out his pen laser as we keep moving toward the woods.

We watch as the slightly higher of the two lights bops around for about thirty seconds, then we hear a large crash. A moment later, the second light vanishes again as the GardenGenie hums on. There's a soft rustle as it scythes down the underbrush, along with the occasional crack as it cuts through something a little larger.

Tyson meets us at the edge of the woods. "There was no way the three of us could have moved that damn thing. So I blinked back and told Tate I needed his help. Which . . . basically meant I got out of the way and Tate moved the tree."

"Are you sure that was a good idea?" Rich asks. "I'm not sure Evelyn is going to see this as being within the scope of our agreement."

Tyson shrugs. "I don't really see us as having an agreement. Seems more like Jack gave them an ultimatum. If you want CHRONOS to exist in any form, help us defeat Saul. And . . . Tate didn't ask why, anyway. Just blinked in, moved the tree, and said he needed to get ready for the goddamn jump to Austria. His words. Either this version is grumpier, or he's pissed about something. Listen, I need to get moving, too." He nods toward the black drone a little larger than my hand that's merrily lasering a pathway through the brush. "Can you go forward and grab that thing when it's done?"

∞

Rich and I arrive at the stable point behind the woodpile at Snow's Market around noon, about a half hour before my earlier self is set to appear. We tossed around the idea of me doing the Salzburg jump instead, because of the risk of crossing my own path. But I've studied both this event and Lucy Stone's personality in considerable detail.

She's a bit on the stubborn side. Most suffragists were. A young woman who was easily diverted from her goals wouldn't be part of a movement pushing against social, religious, and political norms in order to effect change.

If we're going to achieve both of our objectives for this jump, however, either Stone or Foster needs to listen and follow my directions. And if we succeed, I'm likely to have a double memory of the event anyway. I'd prefer to minimize that as much as possible, however, so we definitely need to avoid me spotting Rich. Would I have been able to muster up the anger to shoot Saul if I thought Rich was alive? I *think* so, but I'll admit I'm not sure. So Rich and I will be parting ways before we get to the field where they're holding the antislavery convention. He'll be behind the stage and behind the wheel—or rather, the reins—of our getaway vehicle.

Which we still need to rent.

Snow's Market is closed, given that it's Sunday. I'm a bit concerned we're going to have to just walk around Harwich Center and find the livery stable on our own, since most of the town is probably in church. Luckily, however, we happen upon a heathen who apparently celebrates the Lord's day on his porch with a pipe and a book. Rich asks him for directions. We follow his instructions, passing the turnoff for the field where the convention is being held, and two blocks down, we find Rogers Livery Stable.

There's a very real chance that the place will also be closed on Sunday. But having a large antislavery convention in town requires lodging for out-of-town horses. There's no one out front, so we go around to the side of the barn and find a middle-aged man barking orders to a boy of around fourteen, who is busy attending to their four-legged guests.

If there are any rules against doing commerce on the Sabbath in 1848 Massachusetts, the man happily ignores them. The only thing he has available, though, is a two-horse carriage with high wooden sides. I give Rich a skeptical look. It's a bit wider than we'd planned, but . . . maybe?

"Five dollars for the day," the man says, wiping the dust from his hands on a grungy towel flung over one of the stable dividers. "Plus the full hunnerd-and-forty deposit. Unless you got someone local you can bring in to vouch for you?"

That's nearly twice what Rich has in his pocket. The stable owner sees the hesitation in his face and says, "Stranger come into town and took off with my best carriage last year, so I'm not as trustin' as mebbe I once was. Or ya can take Willie here as driver, in which case there's no deposit, but I'll be raisin' the fee to ten dollars for the day."

A five-dollar wage for a driver is tantamount to highway robbery. That's closer to a month's pay, and we really don't want the kid tagging along anyway. There's not much choice, however, unless we want Evelyn and Timothy to go back to CHRONOS with a second request for era-appropriate cash, and we can't really afford that sort of delay.

Rich pays him the ten dollars and we wait while they harness the horses.

"Maybe it's for the best," I whisper. "How long has it been since you drove a carriage?"

He gives me a mock offended look. "My last year of field research with Scott. We did a two-day stint as drivers for Barnum's Jenny Lind tour. It's not, as they say, rocket science. But we can't take him with us. I'll get him to pull over when we're out of sight of his boss."

We climb onto the rear of the wagon, and as we round the corner, the kid asks where we're going. Rich slides down the bench and begins negotiating with him. He turns out not to be a hired hand, but the owner's son.

"No, sir. You have any idea the whoopin' I'll get if I come back without this wagon?"

"Do you know Captain Zebina Small?" I ask.

"Yes'm."

"This carriage and the horses will be at his home at 4 p.m. We'll give you an additional ten dollars for the trouble of walking there to retrieve it. You're free to report the extra wage to your father or not, as you wish."

He thinks for a moment. "Make it twenny. I don't know you, and if this carriage ain't at Captain Small's house, ten dollars won't be enough for me to get outta Harwich. And I'll most surely *need* to get outta Harwich if you don't return this horse and buggy."

Rich peels two tens off the dwindling roll of bills and hands them to the boy, who flicks the reins to direct the horses to the side of the road. After turning the carriage over to Rich, he gives us a grin and a little salute before disappearing into the woods on the opposite side of the street.

"Two month's wages for four hours of hanging out in the woods," he says. "Not a bad deal. How did you know this captain's name?"

"Someone Lucy Stone mentioned in her speech," I say. "Odd name, so it stuck in my memory."

It takes far less time for us to get to the field than it does to gradually maneuver the carriage through the crowd toward the stage. There are a number of wagons near the platform, although I'm guessing they all arrived earlier in the day. We get a few rude comments, including a man who yells out *ya blasted fool, leave yer wagon at the back.*

I curse softly as I hear the crowd laughing, trying to remember if I looked over to see the driver when I heard the man say that. I'm almost certain I only saw the side of the wagon, and since I'm not hit with a double memory, I must be correct.

Once Rich has the wagon in place, pointing toward the very recently cleared path through the woods to what we now know is

Bank Street, I squeeze his hand, then hop down and pull out my key. "Back in a second." Ducking down, I slip into the shadows beneath the platform and blink back to 11:26, thirty seconds before Lucy Stone will walk around the corner. It's the one time she is alone before the convention begins, and I suspect she's heading toward the patch of woods that serves as a latrine for gatherings like this. I'm not sure whether the fact that she's in a bit of a rush will be a good thing or bad, but hopefully one of the two interventions I'm about to make will get the speakers off the stage and into the wagon that will be parked in this spot while I rescue the Sister of Prudence that Saul will abandon in the middle of the stage.

Lucy Stone's eyes are locked on the woods ahead. She doesn't see me at first and startles when I speak.

"Miss Stone? May I have a moment of your time? The matter is most urgent."

She turns back and gives me a polite but somewhat confused smile. "I'm sorry. Have we met?"

"No. My name is Katherine Shaw, and . . ." I look nervously over my shoulder. "My mother says I should stay out of the matter, that it's none of our concern. But I overheard my brother and his friends last evening. They're angry at some of the things that were said during your last session and they're planning trouble."

"I'm afraid you're late, Miss Shaw. The rowdies were rather busy last night, breaking up the benches built for our audience."

"That was only the beginning, I'm afraid. There are plans to storm the stage. They said you were a Jezebel . . ." I pause, realizing that's what they called her in the previous timeline. "A Jezebel and a daughter of Prudence. They plan to take you and your friends to the nearest tree and hang you for maligning their faith. When one of them shouts the word *blasphemy*, that's their cue to storm the stage. And I'm convinced they mean to do it."

Her face grows somber. "I am sure you mean well, Miss Shaw, but threats will not keep us from speaking the truth. We are all willing to give our lives to the cause of freeing our enslaved brethren if that is the price that must be paid."

"No doubt *you* are willing to pay that price. But you have no children to consider, Miss Stone. I understand Mr. Foster has a small child. Mr. Brown has children as well. I would not ask anyone to stay silent on such an important matter, but I want to do my part to ensure that you can continue your work. My intended will be behind this stage with a wagon. If you hear a man yell out the word *blasphemy*, I beg you . . . tell your friends to come to the back of the platform, and we'll get you and the others to safety."

Stone considers this for a moment and then nods. "Thank you so much for your concern, Miss Shaw. I'm sure everything will go smoothly. The young men of this town vented quite a bit of anger on our benches. Let's hope that is all they have in them and they'll be peaceful on the Lord's day." She gives me another smile and squeezes my arm, then continues toward the woods.

There was absolutely no guarantee in her words, but I didn't really expect her to believe there's a serious threat. I duck beneath the stage again and blink forward thirty minutes to when Stephen Foster makes a similar pilgrimage to the woods. I repeat my story, adding that the men made some truly horrible statements about Miss Stone. At this point I stare down at my shoes and think of every embarrassing moment in my life, willing the blush to my cheeks, and then look back up at him. "If you hear a man yell *blasphemy*, that means they're about to storm the stage. There will be a wagon behind the platform. If you, Miss Stone, and the others can get to the wagon, take it through the path to Bank Street and on to Zebina Small's house. Someone will pick it up there at 4 p.m."

Foster gives the newly widened path a quizzical look, and then assures me that if there is trouble, he'll do as I've asked. He keeps glancing back toward me as he walks away, so I have to wait before ducking under the platform. I definitely need to get out of here, because William Wells Brown is beginning his speech, which means my earlier self is approaching from the main road.

When the coast is clear, I duck beneath the platform again and scroll forward to thirty seconds after I left. The wagon wheels stare back at me, and I blink in to the sound of Lucy Stone thanking Elkanah Nickerson and Captain Zebina Small. Less than five minutes from now, Saul will appear with Rho on the stage behind her.

Rich is standing next to the wagon now.

"We have about four minutes until Saul appears onstage." My voice shakes, and Rich reaches forward to pull me into a hug. "I'm too nervous to wait."

Rich pulls the mini-Nauseator out of his breast pocket. I clip the handle to my key, give him a quick kiss, and pull up the stable point. Saul and Rho jump in, which should be just after the man yells *blasphemy*. There's about three seconds as Saul glances around the audience, and then he's gone.

"Go," Rich says. "Then I'll clear the stable points."

Before my eyes open, I hear the woman from the audience scream.

I expect the reaction of the four abolitionists to be different now, and it is. Last time, Lucy Stone rushed toward Rho, who had dropped to the stage clutching her stomach. This time, Stone doesn't even have a chance to look at Rho. Two of the men are already lowering her over the raised back of the platform. Also, Rho isn't clutching her stomach.

People begin pushing toward the stage.

The man screams, "Witch!"

I'm about to tell Rho that I'm here to help, but I don't have to. She grabs onto the tiny handle and says, "Just tell me when to blink."

I pull up the location for the Fifth Column, just as I see a man with a club climbing onto the platform. Someone grabs his leg and he falls back. I lock in the stable point and say, "Blink now!"

∞

BOGART, GEORGIA
NOVEMBER 5, 1941

I'm delighted to see that Rich is already in the bedroom of the cabin when I arrive, standing next to the GardenGenieXL, which is right where we left it before jumping back to Harwich. He's staring at a stable point above his key. At first, I assume he's checking to see if Stone and the others got away, but then he says, "I like this better. It's bad enough seeing the Anomalies Machine on and scrolling. At least we don't have to listen to the ominous soundtrack. Still that annoying countdown flashing, though. I don't blame you for wanting to smash it. Did you take Rho straight to the Fifth Column?"

"Yes. She already knew what was going on. Beta or one of the other Sisters from 2058 sent a message in their diary. They told her not to resist Saul or people will die . . . but also not to worry, because help was on its way."

I pull up the stable point in front of the path through the woods in Harwich at about a minute after I blinked out. My view is briefly obscured by the wagon, which then disappears down the path. It's wide enough, but I realize we should have had the GardenGenie make another pass at a higher level. The men duck down, but not before one of the branches snags the hat off Parker Pillsbury's head.

Again the stable point is blocked, this time by several men chasing after the wagon. They stop about halfway down the path, as they see it turning onto the road and realize they won't be able to catch them.

I then pull up the library in Bethesda that Rich is still observing. The Anomalies Machine continues to scroll, but I think it will stop soon. As best I can tell, Stephen Foster's daughter will never marry and will have no children, although she will touch many lives teaching five decades of girls in Boston. Alice Stone Blackwell, the daughter Lucy Stone will give birth to nearly a decade after the convention, also had no children. Only William Wells Brown had additional kids—two sons and a daughter—after 1848. I can't zoom in close enough to see the Additions column, but along with whatever progeny those three children produce, it will include numerous books—six by Alice Stone Blackwell and nine written by Brown. One of his works, *Clotel*, was the first novel published by an African American and told the story of Thomas Jefferson's daughter by a slave. I'm sure there are people and accomplishments under the Erasures, too, due to those who would have been born in this timeline, but weren't, because their parents never met.

As we watch, the list stops scrolling.

"See," I say. "Barely a ripple."

"That only tells us about changes up to 2136," he says, "and we don't have access to a lot of public data in that timeline thanks to the government censors. There will probably be a lot more anomalies when they run a CHRONOS TMU check, if only because they'll have had a century and a half longer to accumulate."

"Could be. But really, all we did was give the abolitionists a heads up."

Rich snorts. "And provide a wagon. And clear out a path through the woods so the wagon could get through. Am I the only one hearing Rose's voice right now?"

He's mostly joking, but I suspect there's a bit of truth in the comment. We were raised CHRONOS. Those warnings are seared into our consciousness.

"I heard her," I admit. "But I told her to shut up, because she's wrong this time. Those people did *not* die in our timeline. We are under no obligation to preserve this screwed-up history Saul created. Even if there are red lights flashing away at TMU, there's a huge difference between what we're doing and what Saul broke, and I'm increasingly suspicious that it wasn't entirely by design. We're obligated to *fix* it, because we know it can be better."

As I say those words, it's not Rose's voice echoing in my head. It's Saul's, as we stood outside the World's Fair Police Station and I tried to work up the courage to kill him. And failed.

Do you really think we couldn't do better?

It's not the same, though. We've *seen* better. It wasn't perfect. It had flaws. But from everything I've seen, it was objectively better, and not because those of us working toward it had access to massive wealth and power.

It was *better*. And we can get the people we know who are stuck in this timeline back to better.

"THE JOHN T. SCOPES TRIAL" (1925)

Then to Dayton came a man with his new ideas
    so grand;
And he said we came from monkeys long ago;
But in teaching his beliefs Mr. Scopes found
    only grief;
For they would not let their old religion go.
You may find a new belief; it will only bring you
    grief;
For a house that's built on sand is sure to fall;
And wherever you may turn there's a lesson you
    will learn;
That the old religion's better after all.

FROM THE *BOOK OF CYRUS*

(NEV, 9:3–5)

Do not compare man to the beast of the field and the jungle. Each is a separate work of God. If you lower yourself to the status of an animal, you should not be surprised that true men treat you as a lesser being.

∞22∞

The instant I arrive, I get a flashback to standing near the fryer in Ida's kitchen in Spartanburg 1963. Even here in the shade, not just of the trees around the courthouse, but also of the platform built for the day's events, the heat is staggering. That flashback could also be, in part, because I smell food. The court has recessed for lunch, and families are seated on the lawn surrounding the courthouse with their picnics and paper bags.

The heat shouldn't have taken me by surprise. The judge is less than an hour away from deciding to move the trial outside rather than deal with a packed upstairs courtroom with no air conditioning and nowhere near enough fans or windows to make a day this hot even remotely tolerable. That's partly because the plaster on the lower level was cracking from the weight of all the spectators standing on the upper floor, but I suspect it was also planned.

If the trial follows the same basic trajectory as the one in our history, Clarence Darrow, the defense attorney for John Scopes, will call his opposing counsel, William Jennings Bryan, to the stand. What follows is just each side trying to get their debate points out to people who don't read that often. Darrow tried to put scientists on the stand, but the judge ruled their testimony to be irrelevant. His only recourse now is to poke holes in the biblical account of creation. And Bryan has said repeatedly that he'll answer any and all questions in defense of his religion.

The questions aren't really new to Bryan. In fact, Darrow had already asked Bryan many of them and had some of them answered in a magazine interview. The two men may have stark differences of opinion on religion and evolution, but they both like publicity. This section of the trial is being broadcast live. Newsreel cameras will even capture a few minutes of footage, and that would have been harder to do in the cramped courtroom. Also, the benches and platform here on the lawn didn't sprout up like mushrooms. One story holds that the only reason town leaders pushed the issue with Scopes was to drum up a bit of tourism for Dayton. And, at least in the previous timeline, it backfired for the most part. Aside from the media, the vast majority of people who attended the trial were locals. Other folks mostly stayed home and listened on the radio.

Clio and I thought we would have to either jump in the night before and set stable points or else use the location about a quarter mile away and walk over, but we found two moments, about a half hour apart, when the crowd's attention is locked on the front of the courthouse. Clio took the first, saying she'd walk down and set a stable point closer to the hanging tree, and then once I arrived, we'd get into place for the rescue.

I take a few steps out onto the lawn. While I don't see Clio, I do find out what's holding everyone's attention. They aren't looking at the front lawn, as we thought, but rather at the other end of the platform I ducked out from under. A man, whom I realize is William Jennings Bryan when he turns his head, is seated at a table on the far side, talking to a group on the bleachers. The wax paper and empty Coke bottle in front of Bryan suggests he's just finished his lunch. Two banners are draped along the wall on either side of the platform. One says *READ YOUR BIBLE*. The other says *OUR GOD MADE US MEN!* That one is flanked by Cyrist crosses.

"As I have said before," Bryan says, "this contest is a duel to the death between evolution and Christianity—and I include our Cyrist brethren in this term, as we all follow Christ. In the past, this struggle happened in the darkness. In classrooms, often without knowledge of parents. My hope is that from this day forward it will be a death grapple in the light. If evolution wins here in Dayton, Christianity will die a slow and gradual death because the two cannot stand together. They are as antagonistic as light and darkness, as good and evil."

One of the men looking up at the platform says, "'What do strength and weakness have in common? What fellowship can light have with darkness?' That's the *Book of Cyrus*, Chapter Six, Verse Seven."

"Why, certainly that is a true statement," Bryan says. "I think you'll find a very similar quote in the Good Book, um . . . I mean *our* Good Book, of course. That's the case for a lot of your Cyrist verses, in fact. The Cyrist apple didn't fall very far from the tree, even if it was Prudence who fed it to Cyrus, rather than Eve feeding it to Adam."

This is met with a polite chuckle from some in the audience, and hostile glares from the dozen or so people seated near the man who was spouting Cyrist scripture. They clearly don't find Bryan's quip amusing.

"Except *Cyrus* didn't eat that apple now, did he?" The man's face, which was already a bit on the ruddy side, is reddening fast. "Cyrus threw the apple out of the Garden, along with the witch who tried to feed it to him. Because he understood that light cannot even *coexist* with darkness. He resisted the evil Adam was too weak to push aside. Maybe the sons of Adam evolved from lesser beings. But those who follow Cyrus did not."

Bryan chuckles good-naturedly. "I see we have reached the limits of religious unity."

"Only because you're too cowardly to tackle evil head on. It's not enough to simply call out evil. You must destroy it." A murmur of agreement runs through the group on his side. "In that same chapter, verses five and six, Cyrus commands us to 'Vigilantly search for untruths that disparage The Way—and once found, attack the untruth. Those who oppose The Way are enemies of Earth and of all life upon it. Their lies cannot be tolerated by the faithful.' And that is why I say this trial is a mockery of *true* justice. You're allowing Darrow and his Prudaean friends to poison more young minds with their talk of—" The man's voice has been steadily rising. Two uniformed officers are now approaching the edge of the crowd, so he adjusts his tone. "But I suppose that's all you *can* do. Real men, men who have the strength of their faith and their convictions, have other options. We protect our families. Our faith."

"Okay, then," Clio whispers from behind me. "Even if I hadn't seen his face in the newspaper photo, I think we could have deduced that guy is itching for trouble." She's flushed and seems a bit out of breath.

"Are you all right?" I ask. "I was wondering where you'd gotten off to."

"I'm fine. It's just this humidity. It's awful—like breathing pea soup. How do southerners stand it?"

"You get used to it." Again, I think of Ida's kitchen and chuckle. "Actually, no. You don't get used to it. You just pray for cooler weather."

"Well, at least we'll have an excuse when a bunch of people hit the ground in a few minutes. This weather is enough to give anyone heatstroke. Come on, I want to show you something."

I follow, and as we walk, she says, "Did you and Tate get the trail through the woods cleared out?"

"Yeah. Tate is in a foul-ass mood, though. I mean, I know he doesn't know me, but I think if we'd given him twenty minutes, he could have ripped out all of that underbrush on his own, without the aid of the GardenGenie."

"Wish I could take one of those things back to Skaneateles. Connor and Harry would never give me sass again if I liberated them from yard work."

We round the side of the courthouse, and she points to a small tent where a bunch of kids have gathered. One of the boys slaps another on the back and says, "We found you a brother, Elmer!" Elmer shoves him, but it's clear they're joking around.

Off to the left, a girls' trio, who look like they might be sisters, is singing.

> *You can't make a monkey out of me, no, no.*
> *I am human through and through,*
> *All my aunts and uncles, too.*
> *Oh, you can't make a monkey out of me.*

As we get closer to the tent, I see what has the kids so enthralled. A small chimp in a suit is seated at a child's piano, next to a sign that says *Monkeying Around with Jo Mendi*. There's a table with little monkey dolls. Another table is selling bananas.

And through it all, the girls keep singing, over and over, *Oh, you can't make a monkey out of me.*

"It's like a carnival," Clio says. "Hard to believe three people are about to be killed."

But they are. The one saving grace is that the guys who grab Scopes and Darrow seem a little reluctant to hang them in front of the families. A newspaper account by columnist H. L. Mencken claimed seven men, four of them armed with rifles, will shove Scopes and Darrow into the back of a truck and drive them to a small Cyrist temple, where the same minister who was verbally jousting with Bryan a few minutes ago will join them with a woman he claims is Lela

Scopes. By the time the crowd arrives, the deed is done. Two police officers show up, probably the two I saw earlier. Arrests are made, and only the preacher admits to the hanging. He serves two years in the state pen. Mencken and a few others suggest the cops were in on it or they'd have stopped them at the courthouse, but I don't think that's true. I suspect they just realized they were outgunned by the four men with rifles, especially given the massive crowd, many of them kids, who could be in danger if bullets began flying.

The judge has already started speaking when we step through the back door of the courthouse, which is now empty, and sit on a bench near the cloakroom. There's no risk we won't hear them, since they've set up speakers for the overflow crowd. We don't have a specific time that they'll grab Scopes and Darrow, but we do know what will trigger the attack, and it happens pretty quickly.

I don't recognize Darrow's voice when he begins speaking, but I know it's him when he begins pointing out the banners on either side of the platform. "Off to the left of where the jury sits a little bit, and about ten feet in front of them, is a large sign about ten feet long reading *Read Your Bible*, and a hand pointing to it. On the other side, we have two Cyrist crosses and the words *Our God Made Us Men*. I move that these signs be removed."

The judge agrees, but Bryan's assistant counsel asks why. "It is their defense and stated before the court, that they do not deny the Bible or any religious text, that they expected to introduce proof to make it harmonize. Why should we remove the sign cautioning the people to read testaments of God just to satisfy the other side of this case?"

Darrow then says the signs can stay, as long as he can post signs advertising the biology text Scopes taught from and another that says *Read Your Darwin*. "I read the Bible myself on occasion," Darrow continues, "and it is pretty good reading in places. But we're making this out to be a case of either the Bible or evolution, as we have been informed by Mr. Bryan, who is himself a profound Bible student and has an essay every Sunday as to what it means. We have been informed that a Tennessee jury who are not especially educated are better judges of religious texts than all the scholars in the world, and when they see that sign, it means to them *their* understanding of scripture. It is pretty obvious it is not fair, your Honor, and we object to it."

The court gives a long-winded yes, and then there's a scuffle. Screams. Two gunshots fired, presumably into the air.

"I think that's our cue," Clio says. We step into the cloakroom and she transfers one of the stable points to me. "It's set for two minutes ahead."

She blinks out first. I hear Bryan telling the men to be reasonable. I think the judge says something, too, but it's hard to hear over the crowd.

"Stay out of this, old man," one of them shouts. "Or we'll take you, too. You have to make an example of these people. 'Those who oppose The Way are enemies of Earth and of all life upon it. Their lies cannot be tolerated by the faithful.'"

I pull up the stable point Clio gave me, which is behind a row of tall, thin fir trees next to the temple, and jump. The shadow of the building with the Cyrist cross stretches across the dirt parking lot, and just beyond that, two nooses are swinging from the lowest branches of the large oak.

Clio steps out, gives me a little finger wave, and then ducks back behind the tree. That's not exactly where I thought she'd be, but maybe she wanted to be over there in case my target gets past me. I guess she can just as easily blink out from there.

The ruddy-faced guy who was yelling at Bryan earlier throws open a door about five yards away toward the back of the building. As expected, he has the Sister with him. She's gagged and her hands are tied, and he has a rope coiled around one arm. I yank back my sleeve, pull out the little dial on the Timex device, point it toward them, and press. He slumps to the ground. The Sister, who we assume is Kappa, is protected by a CHRONOS field, so she's not affected. She stumbles when he goes down but regains her balance.

She moves toward me and looks at my key, confused. Clio has the Nauseator device, which is another reason I thought she'd be close by. We were going to grab the Sister and blink out.

Damn it, Clio. What are you up to?

But I know what she's up to. She's rescuing Darrow and Scopes. Which I get, but . . . we can't blink out with them. They don't have the gene.

The truck is here now, with seven men and four freakin' rifles. I yank Kappa back into the hedge and we watch as the truck hops the curb and barrels full speed toward the tree. It brakes and skids. They're clearly wanting to finish this before anyone following them, such as the police, can arrive, so they climb out of the truck bed before the thing is fully stopped, dragging Darrow and Scopes.

The driver and two men who were in the cab pile out. And then nine grown men drop to the ground.

"Let's go," I say to Kappa, and we begin running. Clio is already grabbing Scopes, the lighter of the two men, and trying to heave him back into the truck.

I tell Kappa to get in the cab and then take Scopes off Clio's hands. Next, I grab Darrow and the two of us load him, as well, and slam the gate.

"What's the plan? And why the hell didn't you tell me?"

Kappa holds out her hands and I realize they're still bound.

"Where are we going?" she asks when I remove the gag. "They said to grab the handle and blink, and you'd take me straight home."

"Yeah," I say. "That's pretty much what I was told, too."

Clio whips the truck onto the road that runs behind the temple. "I'm sorry, okay? If this doesn't work, I'll take her home and we can do Plan B later."

I don't even want to ask what Plan B is. "We don't have time to drive them out of the state, Clio. The clock is ticking."

"We don't *have* to get them out of the state," she says. "All we have to do is drive until they're awake and okay to take over. They can go to the nearest airport and get the hell out of here. I don't think most people will blame them for stealing the truck belonging to a lynch mob."

"It's a good plan," I tell her. "I just wish you'd trusted me enough to let me in on it."

"I *do* trust you. But I wanted to give you plausible deniability with those CHRONOS people."

"By increasing the size of the target on your own back? Whatever happened to sticking to observing?"

"Obviously, that's out the window. First, we're not playing a game. Second, even if we were, Saul swore this wasn't one of his moves. And third, he's planning to kill us all anyway. Oh, and this watch gadget is cool, but I want my laser back."

Kappa shifts to look over her shoulder. "How long before those men wake up and we can go home? This is a very bumpy transport."

I tell her I don't know and look back at Clio. "You do know CHRONOS is running the TMU checks. They're likely to send someone, maybe even Timothy and Evelyn, to reverse this, even if that means going up against us. You said before that Darrow is important, so . . . it could change something."

"It might." She lowers her voice. "But I'm going to guess it's a wash. He argues one case that furthers civil rights, and one that sets them back. And he dies thirteen years from now. Plus . . . I think they're bluffing. We hold the better hand. If they get too pious about protecting this screwed-up history, Alex will halt the research."

I don't respond. Because while I really hope it will be that simple, I suspect a lot of what Jack told Tim and Ev was bravado. Jack might *ask* Alex to stop, and Alex might even want to stop and *agree* to stop, but he's currently at the whim of Cyrist Sword, which is either connected to the military or maybe it *is* the military. I'm still not clear on that. And even with the Fifth Column in the mix, it might not be as easy as pulling the plug.

PRESIDENT LAWRENCE PATTON MCDONALD—FROM THE THIRD INAUGURAL ADDRESS (JANUARY 20, 1984)

Make no mistake, we are at war.

This is not a new conflict. We have, in fact, been at war for our entire history as a nation. In Philadelphia, in July of 1776, our founders gathered to write the Declaration of Independence not simply to break with Great Britain, but to declare war on the opponent birthed only two months prior, in Bavaria, where Adam Weishaupt urged his Illuminati to go forth and create a New World Order.

Our opponent grew strong during the last half of the 18th century, waging war against the French monarchy, elevating reason as their goddess. Those of us in the Cyrist faith recognize this false goddess as Prudence, cast out of the Garden of Eden by God and Cyrus. Other Judeo-Christian faiths may label the false spirit as Lucifer, but for us all, it is the voice that would have us question tradition, authority, and religion. And within our secular government, wise men realize this foe always marches forth under the banners of equality and democracy—the most deceptive of phrases, the sword wielded by demagogues and frauds.

In France, vast mobs waged this battle, seeking to silence opposition, using tactics of terror and lies against those who would stand up to them. But traditional beliefs, values, and institutions were strong, and they carried the day.

Our foe slithered back into its hole and waited. But not for long. In 1848, Karl Marx published his declaration, giving a new name to one arm of the vast conspiracy against our freedom to embrace tradition. It surged again in 1917, as the mobs took Russia.

Most worrisome, however, it has reached a treacherous peak in the years since World War II, as our enemy has co-opted Americans, some well-meaning, others simply weak and gullible, to do the bidding of a small, elite cabal infiltrating every operation of our economy and every activity in our daily lives. It is the voice that urges not peace through strength and manhood, but harps instead on the horror of modern warfare, urging us to accept the beauty and even the necessity of peace, with the terms of that peace always set by our enemy.

Our foe is, today, stronger than ever. It seeks to subvert tradition by removing prayer from our schools. It seeks to subvert the traditional family by taking women from the pillar upon which all God-fearing men have placed them and pull them into the most vile and degrading professions, all in the name of equality. It further threatens the family by claiming that sexual relations outside marriage, even the most perverse and unnatural variations, should be allowed or even protected by law.

Where we can work with other nations who seek the same goals, we will do so. But we will have no further part in your New World Order. We will not allow your movies and TV and music that praise the communist menace, that glorify witchcraft and demons and every sort of perversity, to flourish here. It is an insult to the

Judeo-Christian-Cyrist heritage of this great nation to lend credence to anything that supports the worldwide forces of Satan and his handmaiden. We are a vast and powerful nation. We have no need for international cabals that seek to subvert our traditions.

We are Fortress America. Your perversions of the natural order will find no home here.

∞23∞

Despite my best efforts at persuasion, I arrive at the Fifth Column without Sigma. I tried everything, even telling her I have every intention of rescuing the other victims in Salzburg once we stop Saul, which, God help me, is the truth. She simply stared back at me, her face a study in stubborn defiance.

"Do either of you have any tips for dealing with an unreasonable Prudence?" I ask Kate and Beta.

Kate shakes her head. "I generally went with avoidance."

"Depending on the age of the Prudence," Beta says with an enigmatic smile, "chocolate and wine have both been known to work. Otherwise, I can only advise patience. At some point, we usually realize we're wrong, even if we rarely admit it, and gradually work our way around to cooperation."

"But . . . what if the Prudence in question isn't wrong?"

"Oh, well, I'm afraid you're in it for the long haul, then. We Prudences can survive for weeks on righteous indignation alone."

I sigh. "I'd just assign her an out-of-the-way corner, but the cabin isn't large, and we now have ten people coming and going. I'm a little worried Tate is going to punch a hole in the cabin walls if she doesn't cut him some slack."

Beta's eyes widen. "Tate? Tate Poulsen is there?"

"*A* Tate Poulsen is there. He doesn't remember being involved with Prudence Alpha. In fact, I don't think it would have happened for him yet, even if we were in that timeline. Ugh." I drop into the armchair and rub my eyes. "Sorry. This is just frustrating. I have a monster of a headache trying to keep everything sorted, and in . . ." I glance down at the key. "And in less than twenty hours, my house is going to blow up. Although I guess it's your house, too."

Kate sighs. "I'll be long done with it by then, regardless of how this turns out. But I'll admit I don't like the idea of Saul reducing my home to a pile of rubble."

"Same. And all of that aside, whatever temporary truce Saul had with us during the game will end. Timothy and Evelyn can go back to the new and possibly not-so-improved CHRONOS. Tate, too. But a cabin in the woods in 1941 may be the only place the rest of us will be safe."

"If you need more boots on the ground . . ." Kate trails off, looking like she's reconsidering the words, and then barrels ahead. "If you need more people, go back to when I could use the key. I'm sure Kiernan and Other-Kate would also—"

"No. Oh, no. We have the boots. We're just not sure where to put them. And . . . I have no idea what sort of chaos that would cause. Even thinking about it . . ."

There's a hint of relief in Kate's eyes. "Understood. I was trying to help, but I probably made your time-travel headache worse."

"I haven't actually traveled in time," Beta says. "But . . . my head does get fuzzy on occasion. And I always find it helps to focus on the One Thing. The one thing you most need to accomplish. The one thing you can't push aside. Finish that, and then move on to the next One Thing."

I'm thinking it's really *not* helpful, especially since the Fifth Column's insistence that we save the various iterations of Prudence has made it difficult to even figure out what that One Thing might be. But is that really true? With the exception of Timothy, Evelyn, and Tate, we've all read through the files of the Fifth Column, and all of us agree that the change involving Nixon's presidency is most likely the pivot point. It's the nexus of a particularly toxic brand of Cyrisism and hypernationalism.

The two Lawrences, Dennis and McDonald, seem to be at the center of it. And, of course, Saul.

Which means there are several conversations I need to hear.

Ideally, Evelyn, Timothy, or Tate would simply jump into Dennis's office and set a local point—new and improved, now with sound. But when I mentioned this to Evelyn, I received a lengthy, unwanted lesson in bureaucracy, CHRONOS-style. Local points set on your key must be approved in advance by the jump committee. They check to see what the laws are in the area during the time period under surveillance, whether CHRONOS has classed the information that may be gained as a high priority, whether the information is still classified, and several other things. Failure to secure permission before setting a local point can result in censure or even temporary suspension. And since the TMU is the only one who can erase local points from your key, Evelyn wouldn't be able to hide the fact that she violated that rule.

I can't help wondering whether these more restrictive laws are because they added audio, making the stable points seem more intrusive. I mean, they violate privacy already. I doubt Templar Dennis would be happy to learn that I know about his personal massage habit. On the other hand, how much worse would it be with both video *and* audio?

The privacy violation sounds like a fairly minor infraction to me, and one that pales next to the other things she and Timothy are doing. But it seems to be Evelyn's line in the sand. She ticked off the list of currently approved local points—two at the Scopes trial, two at the antislavery convention, and four at Monterey Pop. The first two are moot, given that we've rescued the Sisters there, and I have serious doubts how much use the latter will be, since it's a rock concert with thousands of people. We probably won't be able to hear anything over the music and the crowds, but I sent them in anyway. The closest stable point we have is at Cannery Row, so they can deal with catching a cab and seeing if their replica tickets from CHRONOS pass muster to get them into the arena.

I considered asking Timothy or Tate, thinking one of them might be more of a risk-taker, but maybe it's time to tap my inner Little Red Hen and simply do it myself, especially since it's a task I can handle without overtaxing my ankle.

"Kate, do you still have a stable point in the closet of the Templar's office at the Sixteenth Street Temple?"

"I'm pretty sure I do. I can't remember ever deleting any local points. Never really had a need to, since I stopped using the key after President Patterson made it clear that there would be major penalties for those I loved if I didn't curtail my time-travel habit." She pulls out her key as she speaks. "Could take a minute to find, though. I can still pull up the interface, but it's not second nature like it once was. You're not planning on going in alone, are you?"

I shrug. "Not sure. If I do, Jack will be monitoring me. And it will only be for a minute. I'll pop in, hide a recording device in the closet, and then come back for it. Speaking of, do you think Charlayne has a recording device I could borrow?"

A quick call confirms that she does, and also that she doesn't think it will do me any good. "I think you'll find the signal-blocking technology at any Cyrist temple is decades, if not centuries, ahead of its time. That's true of a lot of our tech, to be honest. The only reason you and Katherine were able to jump into that office without raising an alarm is that it was timed to coincide with the security drill that I scheduled—and we still nearly got caught."

"Would that be true in 1969, as well?"

"I have no idea," Charlayne says. "But again, don't assume the tech in that place in 1969 *originated* in 1969. Several sections of the temple are under a CHRONOS field. Anything they had in previous timelines is probably still there."

I jump forward a half hour and Charlayne is in the living room with Kate, Beta, and one of the other Sisters. She hands me a tiny disk and gives me instructions for placing it. "Bring it back when you're done. I think you're mostly going to get static. But if they're using similar tech to what we had, I may be able to adjust for it."

Kate transfers the stable point to my key. It's dark, but as I scroll through, lights go on and off. I change the date to June 11, 1969, not because I'm going to use it right this instant, but because I want to find the moment when the girl we think may be Eta comes in, so that I can get Kate and Beta's opinion.

I expect the girl to head straight for the bathroom when she enters, but she doesn't. Instead, she puts the wig in a bag hanging from the coat rack. Then she locks the door behind her, and strips down to her undershirt and tights. A chill runs through me, and I'm thinking I absolutely do not like where this seems to be going. Then she crouches down next to the cot against the wall, unzips the mattress, and sticks her right arm inside a few inches. There's already a faint glow in the room from the CHRONOS field in her bracelet, but it's nowhere near as bright as the key she pulls out from the mattress.

The girl sticks her hand in again, this time all the way up to her elbow, and comes out with a wad of cloth. She shakes it out and pulls the dress over her head. I can't tell much about the color of the dress in the light of the CHRONOS key. It's a bit tight, but once she gets into it, she picks up the dreary gray tunic, slips it on without buttoning it, and begins trying to bring up the CHRONOS interface.

Every few seconds, she blinks hard. After the third time where nothing happens, she gives the door a nervous look and tries again. This goes on for about a minute. Her expression grows more and more frustrated.

And then she disappears.

Exactly thirty seconds later, she's back, wearing a white flower in her hair. She strips again and shoves the dress—which I'm now certain is lime green—to the very back of the mattress. As she's pulling her hand out, something catches her attention, and she stops. It's an envelope with three musical notes on the back. She hesitates for a moment, then opens it and pulls out a couple of tiny squares of paper. After a glance at the door, she puts all but one of the squares back in the envelope, sticks it into the mattress, then places the key back near the front and zips it up. As soon as she's dressed again in the gray suit, she slips the square of paper into her pocket and hurries into the bathroom. She wipes her shoes, which are dirty, with a few squares of tissue, yanks the flower from her hair, and flushes both the paper and the dirty tissue down the toilet. Then she runs the sink briefly, and heads back into Dennis's office.

I have so many questions. Where did the key come from? Does Dennis know what she's doing? Is that a booster patch? If so, where the hell did she get it? And how many times has she jumped from that closet? I don't think this was the first occasion. She didn't have any trouble pulling up the interface. The only problem she had was with actually jumping.

"Did you find anything?" Kate asks.

"Yeah. I was under the impression that none of the Sisters could use the key."

"We can't," Beta says. "We can operate the diaries. When we're younger we can scroll through and look at stable points on a key. Or I *guess* all of us can. I'm not sure if all of us have held one, come to think of it. Why?"

"Because someone taught Eta a new trick."

Charlayne shakes her head. "That's not something that can be taught. They were very careful to edit that trait out. In fact, it was a requirement for the exemption the Cyrist Church received from the government. But . . . hold on."

She taps her comm-band, pages Ben, and tells him what we know.

"Sure," he says. "I mean, if she was taken as an infant, it's possible. If Saul found a less-than-ethical gene therapist, that is. He's obviously a walking CHRONOS gene repository, so finding a copy of the gene wouldn't be an issue. But I don't know how much the gene changes with age. If he was in his thirties at the time the gene was harvested, and they edited based on that, I suspect her ability would be limited. And possibly short-lived."

I thought my headache was bad before. Jack is currently combing through the stable points at Monterey, trying to find the best time for one of us to jump in and rescue her. That was, however, going on the assumption that Eta was a passive pawn in all of this, under a CHRONOS field, but locked on a straightforward chronological path.

It's also another lie Saul told, although that's no surprise. He implied that grabbing the Sisters was a sideshow. A little bit of revenge for their perceived betrayal that had nothing to do with the game and didn't change history in the slightest. But he's the only one who could have carried an infant forward in time to a point where gene therapy of any sort was an option. He might have started with Eta as a pawn, but he marched her to the other side of the board and turned her into something very different. And that could complicate our plans to bring her home.

∞

Bogart, Georgia
November 5, 1941

"So that makes six." Clio closes the tablet. "Six versions of Little Miss Eta during the Friday evening set and the first hour of the Saturday afternoon set. She's roughly ages ten to fourteen, although that's a ballpark guess. Clearly a music lover, but there's something else going on, too. Her eyes are moving most of the time, like she's watching the crowd. Looking for something. Or someone."

"Why didn't she set observation points?" Jack says. "It would have been much easier."

"Maybe she doesn't realize she can," I tell him. "It took me a little while to catch on to that. Wherever she got the key from, I doubt it came with an instruction book. Mine sure didn't."

For the past fifteen minutes, Clio and I have been scrolling through the four observation points at the festival. Jack joined us after he got back from checking in with his dad and Alex. Still no new Saul sightings, so that's good. Tyson is in one of the armchairs, although I'm not sure what points he's observing. Maybe the café. I'm starting to lose track, because we've all split into different tasks and it seems like someone is popping in or out every minute or so. Timothy and Evelyn are back at CHRONOS, conferring with Angelo and TMU to make sure we haven't made the world a worse place with our latest rescues. Katherine and Rich are watching the moments leading up to Cyrist Sword's Saturday afternoon raid on the Monterey Pop Festival. Sigma is still engaged in massive passive resistance, glaring at Tate out of the side of her eye. Apparently, the stories handed down from Prudence to Prudence built the guy up to be a hero, and to be honest, Kate's diaries also suggested there was, at the very least, a selfless streak. This guy seems self-absorbed and kind of depressed.

Depressed is also the vibe I get from Eta in these tiny little snippets we see of her life. On most occasions, she's walking past, a quick flash of lime green and sometimes gray. The version we were able to watch for more than a few minutes is when she's around ten. She was just in the green dress, minus the tunic, that time, and the CHRONOS key was clearly visible in her pocket. The dress is sleeveless, and despite the fact that it was mid-June, the weather was clearly chilly judging from the clothes other people were wearing. A young couple sitting nearby saw Eta shivering against the back fence and offered to let her share their blanket. She looked absolutely terrified at first and skittered away. Eventually she came back and sat with them for about thirty minutes until they asked her something. She nodded and stayed until the song ended. Then she appeared to thank them and wandered off to the other side of the arena.

All of this was in pantomime for us, for several reasons. First, it's a music festival and the stable point is a few meters away from where she was sitting, so we wouldn't have been able to hear her speaking if we'd actually been there. But it also turns out that even though the stable points Timothy and Evelyn set technically *have* an audio track, our keys aren't equipped to pick up the signal.

The other version of Eta who was in the frame for more than a few seconds had hair just below shoulder length, worn in two low ponytails. She was in the same dress, maybe a year older, and in a typical prepubescent chubby stage. The dress was too tight around the middle and it kept riding up. She stood near the fence, clutching the gray tunic around her like a coat, and didn't stay but a few minutes.

There are other fleeting glimpses, and a few general rules emerge. She's always in the same dress, and she never seems to stay more than half an hour. She's also only there when the place is packed. Usually at night. And she never goes to the front, possibly because of the four adult members of the Process Church who are near the front, on the left side, in their black robes.

If not for the green dress, I don't think we'd have recognized the oldest version, who was still only fourteen, tops. We only got a brief glimpse of her face. She was now at least an inch taller and rail thin, the dress tight only in the chest and barely skimming mid-thigh. Her hair was long and wild, and she didn't seem to be listening to the music this time. It was one of her rare daytime appearances, and she pushed her way through the crowd at the edges of the auditorium, moving for the first time toward the front.

Clio asks if I'm going back to the temple. I look up from the key and nod. As Charlayne suspected, the device I placed in Dennis's closet yielded mostly static. They could only pick out a few words in the cleaned-up version I retrieved from her the next day. All were either Saul's voice or Eta's, both of which are higher pitched than Dennis's. Saul says something about them having an agreement, right after he smacks the desk with his fist. That's just before I see Dennis in the stable point saying something along the lines of *then you'll have nothing.* Eta says she hates flying.

"Are you going to take the key out of the mattress?" Jack asks.

"I don't know," I say. "A kid with a key is risky. And being raised by Dennis and his wife might be an improvement over Saul. But obviously she's spending time in California, too—and I don't just mean at the festival. That tunic is the gray variant of the outfit the Process Church kids wear. We don't really know what else Eta might be doing with the key."

Katherine looks up at the mention of Eta and joins us. "I think I found her. Scroll to Saturday morning around ten."

When I do, I see several thousand chairs lined up in the arena. Dozens of people in gray uniforms are wiping the morning dew off the chairs and then placing a sheet of paper on the seat. The seat closest to me has already been wiped and plastered with a flyer. I can't read all of it, but apparently the Process crew is bringing their loaves-and-fishes show here, as well. The heading is *FOOD FOR THE BODY,*

FOOD FOR THE SPIRIT. Blueberries are sketched along the margins, and in the main text is an invitation to join the Process Church of Divine Revelation in the campground for free breakfast before the afternoon concerts on Saturday and Sunday. *Come for the Pancakes, Stay for the Prophecy!*

As I zoom in on the section of the arena where the workers are, I realize they seem unusually short. I skip forward to when they're closer to the stable point, and realize they're kids, and more specifically, the kids from the Process Church. They're mostly blonds, but there are a few dark heads in the mix.

"You're right," I say. "One of those kids could be Eta."

Katherine shudders. "It makes me sick. Saul did untold damage to the original Prudence. Now he's found a way to torture another one. If we can get her at this age, when she's younger . . ."

"That's probably what we should do *eventually*," Tyson says. "But I think we need to talk to the older one first. The one who's there on Saturday."

Jack agrees. "She's pissed about something. That expression was one hundred percent girl on a mission. The only thing I'm worried about is that it's getting close to the point when Cyrist Sword shows up. Which means she could be one of the six fatalities or among the injured."

"Except we've seen a picture of an older version," Tyson says. "With Manson's crew. I'm not saying that would be a significantly better outcome, but she survives beyond this day. Assuming she doesn't change anything. Or we don't."

"So who wants to take point on trying to gain the confidence of an angry teenage girl?" Jack asks.

"Not me," Tyson says. "And not you, either. We need to be elsewhere. I've been watching the stable point in Dennis's office. I think you and I need to try to reason with an obnoxious old fascist. If nothing else, maybe he'll at least satisfy my curiosity about how he recognized me in New York. Can you get a Cyrist Sword uniform to go with that snazzy tattoo?"

"Maybe?" Jack says. "I can definitely ask."

I'm about to volunteer to approach Eta. I was never a particularly angry teen, although I had some ferocious battles of wills with my mother. But I think Eta is as much sad as she is angry, and I've had some experience with that. While I'm a little worried that chasing her around the festival could put a bit too much strain on my ankle, the shoe seems to be keeping it steady and relatively pain-free.

But Katherine says, "I'll do it. Saul has hurt her. He's also hurt me. Nothing bonds like a common enemy."

"NOT SO SWEET MARTHA LORRAINE" BY COUNTRY JOE AND THE FISH (1967)

The joy of life she dresses in black,
With celestial secrets engraved in her back
And her face keeps flashing that she's got the
knack.
But you know when you look into her eyes,
All she's learned she's had to memorize,
And the only way you'll ever get her high
Is to let her do her thing and then watch you
die.
Sweet Lorraine, aw, sweet Lorraine.

∞24∞

KATHERINE
Monterey, California
June 17, 1967

I have never much cared for late 1960s fashion. There's little structure, and the colors hurt my brain. Normally, out of the two choices in our costume stash, I'd have chosen the dress Clio brought back from Skaneateles. The cut is about right, and it's a pale blue with tiny daisies. Either Kate shares my dislike for neon shades, or she simply couldn't find fabric as atrocious as the combo Evelyn brought back from CHRONOS—a bright orange bodice with a skirt covered in large geometric shapes in every electric color imaginable. There are boots, too, and a white hat with a floppy brim.

For this jump, however, I opt for the eye-gouging outfit. It's a grown-up version of the lime-green number that Eta is wearing, and I think she'd like it. Plus, this dress literally screams that I am not an authority figure. The real question is when to show her the one thing I'm wearing that I *know* will make her sit up and take notice . . . the CHRONOS key. It's on Angelo's chain, shielded by an inside pocket sewn into the bodice of my dress.

Rich, who blinked in before me, looks completely normal. This is a typical jump costume for him, and I wonder if Evelyn didn't replicate something from the files used by the other version of Rich currently at CHRONOS. I've seen him on the platform heading out to any variety of musical events in stuff that looks almost identical. Concert garb has kind of sneaked into his personal style, as well, since he tends to bring back band T-shirts from his jumps.

Tate, however, has been ill-served by Costuming, and there's nothing in the stash Clio brought that would come even close to fitting him. They could have put him in leather. Denim. I've even seen a bit of flannel in the crowd. But, no. They had to choose a brightly colored paisley. Era-appropriate, yes, but it's a bit much even in the pale glow of the security lights. And it really doesn't match his current gloomy expression.

"Well, aren't we a motley crew?" Clio says when she pops in, completing our foursome.

Rich tells her that band is about fifteen years later, and seems rather pleased with his joke, even though none of us have the slightest clue what he's talking about.

Sending Timothy and Evelyn to set the stable points here was a bit of a bust. Not only were they useless for listening, given the loud music, but there were also too few of them to be of much use for surveillance. So we jumped in a bit before dawn to set some more, focusing on the area where the Process children were gathered before they began wiping down the chairs, and a couple up in the box stands.

In retrospect, we should probably have worn black for this and gone back to the cabin to change into our groovy getups. If any security guards come through, Tate and I are veritable beacons in the night. But they must all be busy patrolling the campgrounds, because we meet back at our rendezvous point without incident.

It's actually eerily quiet. Either the people from the Friday night concert were good citizens who carried out their debris, or they already had a cleanup crew come through after the concert ended around 1 a.m. The stage at the front of the arena is bare, aside from the huge yellow banner strung along the bottom with *Music, Love, and Flowers* above the words *Monterey International Pop Festival*.

Tate and I return to the section of the stands near our jump location, while Clio and Rich blink forward to when the backstage area is unlocked so they can set a few more, hopefully helping us to locate this Owsley Stanley guy. Despite the fact that we're not here on a pleasure trip, I think Rich is a bit psyched. There's no guarantee that Clio's friends will be there, given that they aren't on the schedule until tomorrow night. But she thinks there's a decent chance they'll be hanging out backstage, since there are several San Francisco–area bands playing today. Hopefully, she'll be able to speak to Owsley, although I'm not sure what she plans to tell him. It might work to just say the cops are coming.

I'll admit I have somewhat mixed feelings about the guy getting away entirely when he's clearly breaking the law . . . even if it is a relatively new law. People *did* have negative effects from acid use. But he doesn't deserve to be shot onstage by these Cyrist Sword people, especially when Rich and Clio are both certain there's no way sixty-some people could have died here from overdosing or getting a bad batch. Rich's certainty comes from the fact that it didn't happen that way in the past. Clio simply says Owsley has an impeccable reputation and he's not in this to hurt people.

But all of that was before we saw Saul and Owsley together at Satan's Cavern, with Mary Ann looking on from the doorway. She gives me a bad feeling, and no, it's not simply that she's involved with Saul. For that, she has my sympathy. It's not even the faint Nazi and Satanist overtones to this religion she's created. She's just creepy.

The general consensus of the group is that Saul was paying Owsley to replicate the booster patch and maybe increase the potency. Which still seems likely. We scrolled through and that's the only interaction we see between the two, at least at the café. But I can't help thinking of all those people overdosing. It's been a while since Saul wiped out a village. Maybe he hired a collaborator this time?

I begin searching through the crowd for Eta. The older, angrier version, partly because that's the one I need to find, but also because I have a field extender in my pocket, and if I see a version of her young enough to grab and blink out, I don't entirely trust myself not to take the risk.

What bothers me most is the possibility that she's in this situation because I choose not to take Saul up on his offer to forgive and forget. I have no way of knowing the age Saul was when he made that call to me in the library compared to his age when he had Eta altered. Even if he had it done when she was an infant, he could have dropped the baby off with Lawrence Dennis immediately afterward and blinked forward to when she was seven or eight, without any time passing for him. If Jack is right and Saul is aging out of his ability to use the key, the thing he wants from me might be transportation to these other timelines in case he runs out of these booster patches. He has the gene, so he could travel with me using the field-extender device. Could he use Eta the same way?

If I go back and tell him yes, would she be spared?

I'd almost forgotten that Tate was next to me when he clears his throat and says, "When did *you* figure out that Saul is a worthless, lying gox?"

"About two weeks ago. Give or take a few days. Or a lifetime ago, depending on whether you want real time or how long the past few weeks have felt. There was a twelve-hour period when Rich was dead that lasted at least a year. How about you? Tim and Ev were very vague on your circumstances, but there was another timeline where—"

"Yeah," he says. "I know. Sigma has told me all about it. In detail. Although I'm not sure how much of that is real. It's like the stories they told around the fire in Eystribyggo, the village I studied. With each telling, the narrative veered a bit further from the truth. I think maybe these tales have been told one time too many. But to answer your question, about four months ago. Saul learned something, swore to keep it in confidence, and then turned me in. And someone in Eystribyggo died because of it."

I don't get the feeling he wants to talk more about that, but since he's now in a relatively chatty mood, I shift to the question that we're all wondering. "Any idea why Timothy and Evelyn haven't come back yet?"

"They said there was something else they needed to do. Maybe they'd be back later. I mean, this isn't exactly what any of us signed up for."

"Why did you stay? Just for the pleasure of finishing what you started in the cafeteria on some version of Saul?"

Tate gives me a wry smile. "I'll admit that was a part of the equation. It was partly as a favor to Angelo. He tried to keep them from extending the suspension. And he says he'll probably be able to get them to lift it now, if we're able to prove Saul is tampering with your—um, with Kathy's—meds. It wouldn't be the first time someone has had an affair in the field. Just the first time they left behind a child."

"Depends on the timeline," I say. "I can think of several examples."

"But even if I can't go back to study in Greenland, I want to be part of the holoexperience they're building. I think it will be a good teaching tool. And, it's the closest thing to being there, I guess. So I said I'd help Angelo. But I don't know if I'd have agreed if I'd known I'd be watching a monster decapitate a boy barely as high as my knees. Sigma may exaggerate her stories a bit, but she's completely correct on that point. That's messed up and it shouldn't be allowed to stand. I may have had a bit of a falling out with Evelyn about that, but I saw her face when we were there. She thinks we should fix it, too. Timothy even more so. Trouble is, believing we should fix it calls into question everything they've been taught."

"Everything we've all been taught," I say. "I'd have told you the same thing a few weeks ago. Based on the diary of my granddaughter, another version of me, in another timeline, was making similar claims into her seventies. I don't think she entirely understood the magnitude of multiple realities. But what you just told me is why you agreed to come in the first place. Why did you stay when they didn't?"

He shrugs, something that is far from a tiny gesture with his massive, paisley-clad shoulders. "I owe a penance. I thought the *Book of Cyrus* was a joke. And I don't know if our version of Saul finished writing it after Morgen died, but before that, I contributed a few verses over beers at the OC. So we're going back to Salzburg to save those people. I haven't told Sigma yet, but she said Madi doesn't plan to let that stand, either. I thought about it, and even if it costs me the right to work on the Viking exhibit, even if it's history that happened in multiple timelines, and even if we can't fix every instance where that kind of thing happened . . . it's wrong not to fix the one we witnessed. It doesn't *have* to happen, at least not in the new timeline we'll hopefully be creating once Saul is dead and the better version of those books is delivered to the temples. Have you read it?"

"Not yet. Haven't had time." We haven't shared the fact that it was written by Jack in a DARPA on-call room. I'm a little less worried about this being discovered by CHRONOS since Madi told me Jack made a jump back to place a few copies in the hands of some Fifth Column colleagues for them to post online, and Madi herself took one back to Charlayne for them to copy and distribute.

Tate grins. "Saul would hate this version. Morgen, too. But I could actually get behind that branch of Cyrisism if I were the religious type. Too bad it never caught on."

I raise a fictitious glass to toast. "Let's see if we can fix that. Here's to better timelines ahead."

There's a flash of orange light off to the right as Rich and Clio pop in. He's holding a green booklet with what looks like a drawing of the god Pan on the front and an inset of a girl bathing in a pond. "Official program." He grins. "Got some autographs, too."

Clio sits on the bench below us. "Pretty sure Janis Joplin thinks he's crazy. And that still didn't stop her from squeezing his ass."

"She did not. Her boyfriend was right there."

Even in the dim light, I can tell he's blushing. "You're such a geek, Richard Vier." I lean over and kiss him.

"Guilty as charged. Have you found Eta yet?"

"I'm pulling that up now," I tell him, deciding not to admit I've barely had a chance to look. Even though we can't afford too many moments off task, the conversation was time well spent, because I'll feel much more confident about relying on Tate.

"Okay. I'll start, too. And . . . Janis Joplin did not squeeze my ass."

"Good. Otherwise, I'd need to go have a little chat with her, and that could get awkward."

Richard and I focus on the older girl. I have Tate concentrate on finding the younger version, and Clio watches the backstage stable points. We have the time and approximate location from the ones Tim and Ev set, so it doesn't take long to find her. The tougher part is tracking her when she moves out of one stable point and into another. Eventually, however, our task and Clio's look like they're about to merge, because Eta is making a concerted effort to get backstage.

She does not succeed. And I think she knew she wouldn't, because she pulls a note out of the pocket of her tunic and whispers something to the guy. He gives her a knowing look, then reaches into his own pocket and tries to hand her something. She shakes her head vehemently and pleads with him again. The guy sighs, tells her to wait, and disappears backstage.

She stands by the fence and waits.

And waits.

After about fifteen minutes, she tries again, clearly hoping the guy currently standing there will be more helpful. He's not. After several minutes of pleading, and clearly lacking a second note, she pulls out her key and checks the time. I can see from the stable point that it's just after 3:12 p.m. Eta definitely knows the raid is about to happen, and she knows she can't wait any longer. In fact, given the crowd she'll need to push through to get back to a spot where she can blink out unnoticed, I'm a little worried she may not make it before the first shots are fired.

But the crowd seems thinner now. Rich and I could tell even from the locations that Timothy and Evelyn set that quite a few people begin leaving early. They didn't look like they were in very good shape. Rich has watched the documentary of the event in our time-line, and he said there were plenty of people who were stoned, and lots of glassy-eyed expressions, but no one was heading for the gates while Janis Joplin was singing. Even though her career would last only a few years, this was her breakout performance. People were riveted. He said Cass Elliot from the Mamas and the Papas was staring at the stage, mouth agape, when Janis finished singing "Ball and Chain."

"I need to talk to her while she's waiting for the guy who took the note to come back," I say.

"He seems to have tried to deliver it," Clio says, looking up from her key. "The guy walks around for a couple of minutes looking for somebody or something, and then he's called off to help move equipment. If she's trying to warn Bear, though, he's out back. There's this painted bus some of them hang out in between sets."

"Furthur?" Rich says.

"Further than what?"

"Is it Ken Kesey's bus, Furthur? I saw a bus like it in the documentary, but I was never able to tell if it was the *same* bus."

Clio gives him a look like he's totally insane. "It's a *bus*. They painted it psychedelic colors. Bear was headed out that way. That's all I know. It's probably where the Cyrist Sword guys grab him. They storm the place from both directions."

"I think I found the girl," Tate says. "The younger one, I mean. She's looking down at the chairs they're wiping most of the time, but then she stops to tie a shoe for one of the littlest kids. When she looks up, there's a pretty clear shot of her face."

He gives the rest of us the location. And yes, it's her.

"Can you continue looking to see if you spot her during the show? Let me go talk to her older self first. Then we'll figure out next steps." I take a deep breath and pull out the key.

"Hey," Rich says softly. "Remember what I told you the other night. You're not alone. She needs help. We're going to help her. And we'll get her home safely."

∞

The sound is a physical shock when I blink in. A series of beeps, and boops, and electric guitars. A woman screams *Harry*. I can't see the stage from here, but this is the Big Brother and the Holding Company set, so it must be Janis Joplin, who may or may not have squeezed Rich's ass after signing his program. The beeps and boops continue, ending with a plaintive *Harry, please come home*. I guess I jumped in toward the end of the song, because the group says a few words I can't really decipher over the crowd noise around me and then launches into a more bluesy number.

I arrived at a stable point on the same side of the arena as Eta, and now find myself squeezing past the people she navigated around as I watched through the key. A couple with a baby that is, miraculously, asleep in its fur-covered back carrier. Another couple sharing what is almost certainly a joint. A guy in a stovepipe hat. Looking around, I think we could have pulled absolutely anything out of any closet at any point in time, and there would have still been someone who looked more anachronistic. Which kind of has me wondering if there are other time travelers here. Does the CHRONOS in this timeline block travelers from Europe or China the same way those countries seem to be blocking us? Or is *CHRONOS* blocking us from time traveling abroad? And . . . I don't have the time or the brain cells to waste thinking about that.

When I finally reach the spot where Eta is, I nudge the guy standing closest to her so I can squeeze in. She glances at me out of the side of her eye for a split second, then cranes her neck again, trying to see.

"I saw you trying to get backstage," I tell her. "You seem worried, and . . . um . . . I have a friend who knows one of the bands. She was backstage before the concert began. Maybe she can help you?"

Eta frowns. I'm not sure how much of what I said she could hear over Janis screaming *roadblock* over and over into the mic. She gives me a longer look now, taking in the hat, the dress, all the way down to the boots. So yeah . . . maybe the outfit was a good call. She gives the stage an imploring look and seems reluctant to leave. It's been about six minutes since she handed the guy the note, and she clearly hasn't given up yet. "Which band?"

"They're called the Grateful Dead."

Her eyebrows go up, and my first thought is *oh, she must be a fan* . . . but then I remember that Owsley Stanley is their sound technician.

"Yes!" she says. "That would be a huge help. Where is your friend?"

"Follow me."

I lead her back to the little wedge between the stands and the fence where I jumped in, and then navigate so that I'm blocking her exit. She looks at the dead end that narrows to an impassable sliver and then back at me. "Where are they?"

When I pull out the CHRONOS key, a look of complete terror fills her eyes, as I knew it would. She tries to push past me, but I grab her shoulders.

"Eta, I am *not* Cyrist. Not working with Saul, not working with Templar Dennis. I know what you're trying to do. These people aren't supposed to die. We'll help you stop it and then we'll get you home to your sisters."

The last words come out without me really thinking about them, and I wish I could pull them back. For a moment, I think she believed me. And then I blew it.

"I don't have sisters. If you mean Dennis's daughters by his first wife, I never even met them."

"No. Eta. Listen to me, please. I mean your family. Your real family. But first, we have to fix this. If you can jump, I'll give you the stable point. Or we can use this thing."

When I show her the field extender, she makes a sick face. "No. Ick." She pulls up her sleeve to show a familiar gray patch. "I have this, so I should be okay for an extra jump."

"Where did you get that?"

The question seems to trigger alarm bells, because she doesn't answer.

"Okay," I tell her. "I just need to tap my key against yours to transfer the location."

After I do, she pulls up the stable point. "It's nighttime. And there's a really big guy there."

"Yes. That's Tate. He's our . . . um . . . bodyguard. And friend."

"He looks like Thor."

∞

Eta sits about six feet away and keeps her key in her hand as she speaks. "If you're not Cyrists, where did you get your medallions?"

"They didn't originate with the Cyrists," Rich says.

"But they're at the Six Temples. They've been there forever."

"Where did you get yours?" Clio asks.

Eta stares at Clio for a moment, then shakes her head and turns back to me. "How do you know my name?"

I obviously can't tell her everything. We don't have time for that, but even if we did, it would freak her out. Hopefully, we'll have time to break it to her gradually. "Your family named you," I say. "After the seventh letter of the Greek alphabet. *E-t-a*. I guess Saul decided to keep it, but somewhere along the line the spelling got changed."

"Are you part of my family?" The question seems to be intended for all of us, but her eyes slide toward Clio.

"Katherine and I are . . . extended family," Clio says. "Madi, too, but she's back at the cabin. I guess you and I inherited the same curls."

"The curls of Prudence," Eta says.

This surprises me, and for a moment I think she's been told at least some of her origins, but then I notice her pressed lips.

"I have to wear a wig when I do jumps to the temples, and the Templar's wife made me keep my hair short so it was less obvious. I think she was superstitious. But she was nice to me for the most part." She glances down at the lime-green dress. "Do you really know the Grateful Dead?" When Clio nods, she adds, "Can you get a message to that Owsley guy?"

"I can. Are you trying to tell him the Cyrist Sword troops are coming in a few minutes?"

Eta nods. "I think that one is the easiest to stop, so people don't panic so quickly. I don't know the exact time, but Country Joe and the Fish are singing the Lorraine song. They reach the *sweet lady of death* line, and then people come crashing through the gates . . ." She shudders. "And then I have to figure out how to stop the others. We were over at the football field, the one they're using for camping, cleaning up after the pancake-breakfast service. Danny—he was one of the little kids and he was sad because he got caught breaking the rules. They said there wasn't enough of the blueberry syrup, so we had to eat maple, which Danny didn't like. He had to wait until the service was over, and then he got three hard whacks from Father Matthias. Said next time he'd have to tell *her*. So we're dancing to the music, that "Dust My Broom" song. I was trying to cheer him up. Then Danny got sick. He started drooling and shaking. One of the girls said she'd go find the *Oracle*."

I'm not sure it's possible to pack any more sarcasm into a single word than she does with that last one.

"You mean Mary Ann de Grimston?"

She nods. "No one is allowed to call her that, though. Saul used to, but not anymore. For a while, she went by Prudence, but now it's just the Oracle, even though she can't read the *Book of Prophecy*. Some Oracle. Saul has to read it to her, and he's angry most of the time now, so sometimes he lies. She says I'll have to read it to her from now on."

"If Saul is angry, why does he stay?" I'm hesitant to interrupt her, but I'm honestly curious. When Saul is angry, he leaves. Sometimes he explodes first, but he doesn't stick around. I was always the one to apologize, because otherwise, I was pretty sure he'd stay gone.

She considers my question for a minute. "I think he loves her. Or at least he did. But now, where else would he go? He can barely use the key or the Book."

I have to hold back a gasp. We expected he was having trouble using the key. But most people can use the peripheral equipment for a few decades after they lose the ability to jump.

"It won't be long, and he'll be as useless as the Oracle," Eta says. "I think he knows that. That's why he was trying to get that Owsley guy to make some of his patches that he brought back from the future. That's one reason we're here. The Or—" She takes a deep breath. "Mary Ann. Mary Ann said we should stay in San Francisco. Or maybe go back to DC for a while. But then she changed her mind all of a sudden. Said Saul could help her talk with the persp . . . I can't remember the word she used, but people who might want to join."

"Prospective members?" I suggest.

She nods. "That's what they were doing when the older girl . . . I don't remember her name . . . went to tell them about Danny. By the time they found Mary Ann, he'd stopped shaking and was staring up at the sky. He was still breathing, though, at least when I was next to him. Just barely, but she said he was dead. Said God was punishing him for breaking her rules. One of the older girls said Danny was jerking like some guy she saw outside the bad-trip tent. Then Her Holiness started ranting that one of the fucking ungrateful hippies— her words, not mine—must have given him acid. Brother Zarick said we should ask the police for help, and then while she's reminding him he doesn't make the decisions, the trucks come roaring in from all sides. She said the soldiers or whatever you want to call them would help Danny and has Saul scoop him up in his arms. Like she hadn't just told us he was dead. I waited, hoping he'd come back. She'd told us people were dead before, and then they'd show up a few months later."

"You're kidding," Tate says.

Eta rolls her eyes. "They weren't *really* dead. It's one of the ways she and Saul like to mess with your head. They said Father Robert was dead, and then I saw papers on her desk saying he's suing her. But Danny's really dead. Or at least he is after *this* day. Sometimes, I come back here and I see him. I have to keep my distance, because I'm going to leave after I fix this and save up enough of those patches, and if Mary Ann finds out I have her medallion I'll never get away."

"Whoa, back up," Clio says. "*Her* medallion? I thought she couldn't use it."

"She can't. Can't even see the light." Eta is quiet for a minute and then says, "I think Saul had a spare and she took it. Or he gave it to her. Maybe it was the one he gave Dennis a long time ago. I don't know why else it would have been in her desk. I saw the light in the drawer when I took a message to her from Brother Zachariah one day. I sneaked back in and snatched it before one of our trips to read the prophecies at the temples. I knew I couldn't take it back with me, and I wasn't even sure I could use it yet, so I hid it."

"At Dennis's office in the temple," I say.

She nods, not even asking how I know. "I don't regret taking it. She can't use it and I needed it. But she punished everybody. And I think she still suspects me, so . . . I leave the key at the temple. We visit every six months so I can do stupid publicity stuff. When I come here, I have to be sure she doesn't see me. And that I don't see myself, because that makes me feel weird. Sometimes I wear the stupid blond wig I wear when we go to the temples to change the prophecies. Mostly I stay in the trees so I can watch when we're over by the picnic shelter. Sometimes, I'm in these stands so I can watch down there." She nods toward the field. "Danny helped me put the invitations on the chairs. And I watch him dancing to the music with the rest of us on Friday night before Father Matthias took us back to the campground. Danny's still here, and I can still see him, but he's never going to get older, because this time it wasn't a lie. She actually killed him. I'm not sure if she meant to, but she did."

Rich checks the time on his key. "I think we can save him. If we work together. But that means you're going to need to trust us. And we're kind of short on time."

"Do you think that's still true?" Clio asks. "I mean if Saul really can't use the key. And if it's what do you call it . . . a dead man's switch? The house will blow up anyway. We'll have to find another way to save Alex and the others, because if Saul can't jump forward, they'll go ahead with their orders, right? Assuming he ever planned to cancel them."

"There's still the matter of a frequency scanner in the device," I say. "Alex hasn't been able to nail down why it's there or how it's connected to the countdown."

"You're right," Rich says. "It just feels . . . wrong to risk it. I can almost feel the timer ticking down. Maybe I simply need this to be over. And either way, I think we need to get her to the cabin."

"Is that the place about to blow up?" Eta says, one eyebrow raised.

"No," Rich says. "We won't take you there until we're sure it's safe. A minute ago, you said you think Mary Ann killed Danny. How?"

"Well, she's a witch."

We're all silent for a long moment, and then Tate says, "There's no such thing as a witch."

"Of course there is," Eta says. "What else do you call someone who makes potions that kill people?"

FROM THE FILES OF THE FIFTH COLUMN

SECOND RECRUITMENT INTERVIEW: [NAME REDACTED] (NOVEMBER 5, 1994)

When it was first founded, Cyrist Sword and Shield had one main target—the pacifist, anti-war left. They were linked to communism, and in the mind of Grand Templar Dennis and Larry McDonald, they were the epitome of evil. We couldn't criminalize free speech or opposition to the war, so we tried to get the public to associate hippies and the counterculture with marijuana and LSD.

Later, once McDonald was president, the sphere gradually widened to African Americans, and we made a concerted effort to connect them with heroin use. Women's groups were easy to connect to witchcraft, since Cyrists had been doing a bit of that all along. By attaching huge fines and sentences and playing up the threat, we could shut down dissent, arrest group leaders, run raids on their meetings and their homes, and smear them in the media. You didn't even have to break a law by McDonald's second term. Just being part of a suspect group was enough to land your ass in jail.

∞25∞

Under normal circumstances, I would have waited until the girl left the office. She's just doing her job, and given Dennis's age and attitude, I doubt he's one of her favorite clients. But as I watched her leaving, I caught a glimpse of the logo on her dress. It looks familiar. I'm not certain, though, and I need to be. I doubt I can count on Dennis, who is half snoozing in his chair after his massage, to tell me the truth.

I do wait until she pulls the dress back over her head, though, and as she's looking down and smoothing out her skirt, I jump into the room. The girl startles, but I don't think she actually saw me blink in. Most likely, she thinks I was hiding in the closet, since the door is slightly ajar.

She opens her mouth to speak. I shake my head, very glad I opted for the pistol rather than the pen laser. If she'd seen me pointing that at her, I doubt she'd have been frightened enough to stay silent.

I move a few steps closer so I can see the logo on her dress. It does look like a small red pinwheel from a distance, like Madi said. But she wasn't with me and Clio, so she never saw the more stylized Process logo painted on the sign outside Satan's Cavern.

The girl, who clearly thinks I'm staring at her breast and not the logo, sighs and reaches down for the hem of the dress to take it off again.

"That won't be necessary," I say, startling Dennis out of his nap. He jerks backward in the chair but recovers quickly and reaches toward the desk. I don't know if he's reaching for a gun or a panic button, but he doesn't get far, because Jack steps out of the closet, wearing the Cyrist Sword uniform he got from his dad's Fifth Column contacts. He's holding a tablet in one hand and one of the laser pens in the other.

"Hands back," he says. "And keep them where we can see them."

Dennis must recognize the pen as a weapon because he sighs and puts his hands on the arms of the chair. "Security will be here shortly anyway," he says. "This office is always under surveillance."

I glance toward the young Processean and back at him. "Even during your massage, Templar Dennis? I don't think so."

"And you don't need security," Jack says. "We're just here to talk. Miss, this should only take a few minutes, if you'd like to wait in here . . ." He nods toward the door.

She looks at me for permission, probably because I'm holding the gun and Jack just has a silver pen in his hand. I'm tempted to tell her to wait in order to see if I can get any information out of her, but I doubt she knows anything more than I was able to tell from the logo. My only question is why Dennis is buying blow jobs from the group his church is currently painting as the epitome of evil, but that's more of a question for him.

Dennis looks at me and chuckles dryly. "That pendant of yours is a mighty funny thing. You don't look like you've aged one bit since I first saw you in 1940. The other con man I know with one of those looks like he aged five years between the last two times I saw him, and those visits were only six months apart. The last time he was here, he actually had to take an *airplane*. Ain't that a hoot?"

I file away the fact that he said he first saw me in 1940. I'm pretty sure that's one of the few honest things he's ever said to me, although if that's the case, he shouldn't have known I attended that book talk in 1936. It must be something Saul told him, but I never shared that with anyone. Not even Rich. I was too embarrassed about my rookie mistake of letting my personal feelings get in the way of my research.

"You look like you've aged forty years," I tell him.

"Close to it," he says. "What happened to those bright baby blues?"

"Don't need them."

He snorts. "I wouldn't throw them away just yet, son. And who have we got playing soldier boy over here? That patch on your shoulder is pretty much the same as the one we designed a few years back, and I see you got yourself a tattoo, but if you think I'm buying you as CSS for a single damn minute, you're in for a disappointment."

"It's just Cyrist Sword in my era, sir. And with all due respect, whether you believe I'm a member or not isn't relevant. Obviously, you have access to the *Book of Prophecy*, so you're no stranger to getting information about the future. But you're about to elevate a man into office who will plunge the United States into a modern dark age. In my time, our technology and our weapons are decades behind other nations."

Dennis glances at Jack's pen. "If that thing really works, and I'm not sure I believe it does, then I'd say Cyrist Sword is doing just fine in your time."

Jack doesn't miss a beat. He aims at the potted ivy on the smaller desk next to the door and fires. The plant is obliterated, and a tiny piece of the clay pot chips off. Dennis's expression grows smug, no doubt thinking Jack illustrated his point perfectly.

"Imagine one of these that can take out a couple of square miles at a click. In the face of that, would you want to be armed with the version that can kill a single man or the occasional houseplant? Because that's the situation Cyrist Sword is facing."

I'm not sure if what Jack said is bullshit or not, but Dennis at least stops to consider it. Then he says, "As your comrade here noted, I'm old. Seventy-five years old this past Christmas. I am not well. I have hardening of the arteries, which makes walking difficult for me. And occasionally makes the job of the young lady you escorted into the closet a bit more of a challenge. Or irrelevant."

"You have your ministers and handpicked politicians out there claiming demons are real," I say. "In a few years, Larry McDonald will have you overseeing the public execution of the leaders of the group your lady friend in there belongs to. You'll actually tell the American people in the late twenty-first century that there's such a thing as witches. You were once honest enough to admit that your unwillingness to suffer fools gladly could have gotten you lynched as a young man. And now you'll close out your life as the lyncher instead of the lynched. What a depressing moral arc."

"Oh, I get it now," Dennis says. "You're trying to play on my conscience, and he's trying to play on my pride. But as I noted, I'll be checking out soon. So unless whatever group the US is fighting in your time can jump those lasers back to 1969, please tell me why I should care?"

I shrug. "You've got kids. Probably a grandkid. An adopted daughter, but you seem to have mostly abandoned her to Saul, except for when you can put her talents to use. Is she the new 'Inspired Child'?" His lips tighten slightly at the mentions of family, and again when I mention Eta. Maybe there is a tiny bit of conscience in there.

"She's better off with her father. With other children. And Saul, as you call him, brings her around to visit."

"Sure he does. Whatever helps you sleep at night, old man. I guess she's better off there as long as Saul keeps training her to read the *Book of Prophecy* and takes his little protégé around every few months when he gives you and the other Templars a new set of stock tips. But leaving typical moral concerns aside, why did you write your books? So that your ideas about the economy, about human nature, and all those other things live on. So that you have an answer to the question I asked you in 1940, and before that, too, at your book signing in 1936. The question you were asked as a child preacher. *Why are you here?*"

His eyes narrow. "Even if you were twice as smart as you think you are, you still wouldn't be worth a second of my time. I'm here in this temple because I decided it might be easier to make money and shape this fool nation from the pulpit. The guy I suspect you're really after gave me a way to do that. He's the only reason I knew about your smart-ass question at the book talk."

His comment takes me aback. I didn't tell anyone about that, so how could Saul have known? The only possibility would be if he was at the event, too. I didn't see him, but then I didn't pay much attention to the audience. There's no reason the adult Lawrence Dennis would have been on Saul's research agenda, although I suppose the child evangelist might have been. I'll have to ask Rich or Katherine if they know whether Saul was ever a field monitor, because that's the only reason I can think of that he would have been at that event.

"The only thing I believe from his truly laughable *Book of Cyrus*," Dennis says, "is that there is no heaven. Our reward is here on earth. My reward is apparently money I'm not allowed to spend on anything that truly pleases me, clogged arteries, and the occasional carbuncle on my ass. But I have the satisfaction of knowing I'll be leaving behind a leader and an apparatus that will keep the communists from taking over. The same two groups that were battling for the soul of this nation in the 1930s continue to battle today. Larry McDonald may be a religious nut, but he gets that there is no middle ground. You do what you have to do to keep *them* from winning."

Jack, who has been typing something into his tablet, gives Dennis a look of disdainful pity. "Yeah, well, you fail in the long run. Who do you think has that bigger laser I was talking about?"

That draws a full belly laugh from Dennis, but Jack has a damn good poker face. I'm certain he's lying, and I still find myself believing him.

After about thirty seconds, Dennis sobers. "Bullshit."

Jack shoves the tablet in front of him. "Flip through. The screen will work for any finger. You don't need the damn gene to read it. This is a file my CO gave my unit last week. I doubt we have three months before it's over. They've got better weapons, not just tactical and nuclear, but biological, too."

Dennis flips through a few pages, skimming them. I have no idea what he's reading. Jack is totally off script now. The file he showed me earlier dealt with McDonald using Cyrist Sword to target black leaders. There's also information about new miscegenation laws and a few other things the group decided might sway him. But this appears to be something entirely different.

Jack says, "The Soviets took over the rest of Europe a few decades back. Isolationist policies started by McDonald meant we couldn't help them. Couldn't help any of our allies. My buddy says we better start learning 'The Internationale' because barring a damn miracle, it's what they're going to be playing at ball games from here on out."

Dennis continues reading and then stops on the other file that I *did* know Jack had on the tablet. "What's this?"

Jack glances over. "Oh, that one's not from my time. That's from a couple of years from now. The girl sitting on the back step there might look familiar."

It's the article about the raid on the Manson cult. The picture is the one Clio showed us earlier, with Manson inset in a round frame in the front and several members of his "Family" seated on low wooden steps.

"That's not her," Dennis says, "she's not that old." He glances back up at the date. Three years from now. "She wouldn't even be that old in 1970."

He's right. The girl who arrived at the cabin with Katherine and Rich is even a few years younger than the girl in the photo, and no one has forced or persuaded her to shave her head. We don't know what age she'll be when she ends up with Manson. But it's a moot point because it's never happening.

"How old she is in that picture depends entirely on how old she was when Saul hands her over to them," I tell Dennis. "You just said he looked like he aged more than usual between visits. And *our* information says she won't even be born for another seven decades or so. It's her, and McDonald's thugs kill her during that raid."

Dennis pales slightly at that. Does he actually care about the girl? Or is he only thinking about the fact that her death could mean there's no one to read his *Book of Prophecy*? Does he know what Mary Ann and, I assume, Saul are planning? He's the only link between them and Larry McDonald that we know of, but it's possible he doesn't know everything they're up to.

"You're lying," he says, pushing the tablet away.

"Not lying," Jack says. "But we don't intend to let it happen. You could make things a whole lot easier by picking up the phone and telling McDonald to call off the CSS operation scheduled for Saturday."

Dennis shakes his head. "Can't. The *Book of Prophecy* predicted that the hippie love fest they've got going in San Francisco is only going to get worse over the summer. We've promised the governor some assistance."

"You're telling me the governor of California is okay with you killing nearly seventy innocent people?" Jack says. "Do you realize how many of them are kids?"

"Your buddy over there played the kiddie card last time, soldier boy. And I don't know what you're talking about. All we're doing is making an example of a known drug dealer and ending the concert." He sighs heavily. "And we're done here. This gig got old years ago. Either shoot me or get the hell out of my office."

We could show him the newspaper articles. He might believe them, or he might not. But he's at the point where I think he might push the panic button or call for security rather than listen to us any longer. So I simply move a few steps away and give a thumbs-up to Katherine, who's watching so she can jump in with Eta.

For a moment, there's complete silence, partly because both of them are fighting off the nauseating effects of joint travel. It's the first time I've noticed any resemblance between mother and daughter. It's faint. The girl looks more like Saul. But Katherine is definitely in the mix, too.

Dennis watches her for a moment. Then he gives her a sad smile and holds out the candy jar. "Need a peppermint?"

She shakes her head. "No. I need you to call off your soldiers."

∞26∞

Jack spreads out the blanket and we park ourselves in front of an oak tree with a clear view of the picnic shelter on the other side of the football field. I pour some coffee from our picnic basket into two small mugs, and we settle into our cover as a young couple relaxing before the concert.

He leans back and looks up at the tree branches spreading out above us. Tiny dots of sunshine make their way through the leaves and dance across his sunglasses, which were pretty much the only disguise we could come up with aside from hats. "Do you think there's a timeline, somewhere and somewhen, in which the Lawrence Dennises of the world cave in response to the heartfelt pleas of teary-eyed girls and repent of their evil deeds?"

"I hope so," I say. "If there are as many variants as Alex seems to think there are, then there should be, right?"

"Should be," he agrees. "Unfortunately, this one ain't it, love."

He's right, but from what he's told me, Eta made more progress in ten minutes with Lawrence Dennis than Jack and Tyson could have made in ten years, even with the five different choose-your-own-adventure scenarios Jack had stored on his tablet. The *Red Dawn* scenario seemed to make some headway, but not nearly as much as Eta telling him about the little boy she knows who will die if nothing changes.

Dennis wouldn't agree to completely scrap the raid, but he promised that the death toll will be limited to a drug dealer and a poisoner. Although I think Clio will do her best to ensure that Owsley Stanley is long gone by the time the Cyrist jackboots arrive.

We're not inclined to take Dennis's assurances on faith, however. *Trust, but verify*, as the current governor of this state will eventually say in some timelines, when he's the staunch anti-communist in the White House, rather than Larry McDonald. And that verification is the reason the whole gang is here bright and early on this chilly Saturday morning, with the exception of Sigma, who is still essentially on sit-down strike, and Tate, who Saul would be able to pick out of the crowd even across a packed arena. He'll be monitoring stable points in case he's needed. And, of course, Timothy and Evelyn aren't here, since they've apparently quit our little band.

Eta is with Katherine and Rich, dressed in the flowered jumper that Clio wore on her trip to San Francisco, with her hair piled under Katherine's floppy white hat. The dress is a bit too large, but I don't think I've ever seen anyone so happy with new clothes. Eta says Saul stayed close to the shelter where their vehicles were set up, saying the music was so loud closer to the arena that he could barely hear himself think. He'd recognize all three of them, so they will be giving a wide berth to the picnic shelter near the football field where the Process Church is currently prepping for their pancakes and prophecy recruitment soiree.

Katherine tried to get Eta to stay behind at the cabin. There was a heated debate, which I suspect could be the first of many. She could have forced the issue, because if Eta believed she could make the jump on her own, she would have threatened to leave. But I think Katherine realized the girl needs to see what happens here for herself, one way or the other. She barely knows us, and she's been raised by liars, murderers, and con artists. Trust will not be her default mode.

Also, it's a tiny cabin, and we haven't introduced her to Sigma yet. It's not like looking in a mirror—Eta is extremely thin and nearly seven years younger. But the resemblance is close enough that she's going to have questions that will take time to answer. And maybe an introductory-level article on cloning, although God only knows what her education has been like in that place. She may need some basic science before it would make any sense.

Clio and Tyson jumped ahead. Most of the crowd this early is people who camped in the woods and vendors arranging their wares in booths outside the arena, waiting on the crew that actually has money to show up in a few hours, about the same time that the first performers start arriving. Clio's goal is to find Owsley. We debated this one long and hard. The issue for me wasn't so much that the guy is breaking the law. The stuff is legal in some states in my time, but expensive as hell, because it's only allowed in licensed parlors. Even if I wanted to try it, I would have balked at the price tag, and that was back when I wasn't particularly concerned about finances. My worry is more that this seems to violate the spirit of our agreement with Dennis. No, he didn't say we couldn't warn the guy, but then he probably didn't know Clio had partied with him. And here I was thinking she was old-fashioned because she gave me weird looks for the blue streak I like to wear in my hair.

If they can't find Owsley, she'll spread the word that they've heard the event is about to be raided. Which could easily result in a number of canceled performances, because the bands aren't being paid for this, and jail time would get in the way of the gigs that do pay the bills. At the very least, Rich noted that the warning will change the concert, because a few of the singers will be much more subdued than usual. And after that, just in case they're unsuccessful, Clio and Tyson are going to try to locate the two audience members who were trampled and/or shot to see if they can get them out of the arena.

Jack and I are the two people Saul is least likely to recognize, so we're on a nearby hill above the picnic area, where I can already see several worker bees gathering. Most are in gray tunics, but some wear the black variant. I'm guessing it denotes some sort of rank.

If Lawrence Dennis keeps his agreement, a van will pull up in a few minutes, before the Processeans are supposed to begin serving breakfast. They will claim to be health inspectors and will confiscate anything with the slightest hint of blueberry. Jack said Dennis didn't seem to think Mary Ann would agree to go in for questioning, which seems like a reasonable guess to me, but he didn't exactly elaborate on what would happen to her after that.

He simply told them he would handle Mary Ann, but Saul was our problem to deal with, and that is, no doubt, the other reason Katherine wanted Eta to remain at the cabin. The man is a monster, but she knows he's her father. We can't risk leaving him alive if there's even a remote chance he can use the key, but seeing him killed would only add to everything else the kid has been through. Even if the timeline is reset and I know the men I killed on Hatteras Island are alive, I'm guessing I'll still have nightmares. And even though he's no longer dead, I'll probably have nightmares about pulling Rich out of the pool. It's not the kind of thing you shrug off easily.

I pull up the stable point inside the arena where Tate said he'd spotted the younger version of Eta and watch for a few minutes, but I can't find her.

"Maybe she joins them later," Jack says. "Although I guess rescuing the younger one isn't even an option anymore. Unless Eta wants it."

"It may work the other way around," I say. "Rich seems to think so. But . . . how would you broach that subject? If the Sisters or Katherine even suggested it, it could come off sounding like they'd rather deal with the cute eight-year-old who has fewer traumatic memories and, probably, less attitude. On the one hand, there's a good chance she'd be a happier person in the long run if some responsible adult stepped in and simply made that decision for her. On the other hand, it's kind of like erasing half of her life."

"She'd have double memories, too," Jack says. "So how much would you really be saving her from if Saul and Mary Ann haunt her . . . dreams." He nods toward the football field. "Showtime."

I follow his gaze and see a white van working its way across the lawn toward the picnic shelter. We continue to watch, although our view is blocked occasionally by a group of people making a rug of some sort on a giant loom in the foreground. Off in the distance, though, the worker bees in gray and black are soon in a frenzy because two men in suits have grabbed a jug from the prep table.

As we're watching them carry it back to their van, a man in a black robe steps into our field of vision. He's clearly trying to look menacing, but all I can think of is that he looks like this dorky guy who used to get pissed about people coming in late for a photography club I was in as a teenager.

"Can I help you?" Jack says.

"You can start by telling your girlfriend to take her finger off the button of that watch. Father Cyrus told me what it does. Gimme."

He holds out his hand. I look around at all of the places where someone with a gun could be hiding and am tempted to give the guy the watch, but Jack cheerfully tells him to go fuck himself.

"You might want to worry more about what *I've* got in my pocket," he adds, "because I can assure you this is not because I'm happy to see you."

The guy glares down at us. "Father Cyrus said to tell you you're not the only ones who can spy with the mystical medallions. He's watching you right now. Has been watching since you sat down and poured the coffee. You think you found all of his pawns, but . . . he decided to take the little one to the playground. If you want her to stay safe, give this to Cassie."

He drops a folded note that flutters down like a tiny butterfly. By the time it lands in my lap, he's scurrying back to help the other bees defend the hive.

There's no salutation and no signature. Just four sentences. But it's obvious the goth-dork meant Kathy.

> *Guess we're doing this the hard way. Be a good mommy and meet us at the playground in ten minutes at 3:30. Don't be late and don't bring any friends. This is family playtime!*

It's not even eleven, but I'm sure he has people watching who can enact a penalty if she doesn't jump forward to meet him within ten minutes. I ask Jack if he knows where the playground is as I tap the disk behind my ear to ping Katherine. He doesn't, but heads toward a group with kids to see if they know. Down at the picnic shelter, another woman has joined the workers. This one is wearing a red clerical stole over her black pants and tunic, the only splash of color under the shelter's awning.

When Katherine responds, I tell her to meet me at my current location and suggest that she come alone. I'm fairly certain Rich won't stand for that, and sure enough, by the time Jack is back with directions to the playground, I see Katherine, Rich, and Eta trudging up the hill toward us.

Beyond them, down at the picnic breakfast, the two agents are now surrounded by at least a dozen men and women in shades of black and gray. A bit of sunlight glints off something in the hand of one of the women. It could be a ladle, but from the way she's waving it around, I'm guessing it's a knife.

Then one of the other women's knees fold and she drops to the ground. I didn't hear gunfire, though, and she definitely wasn't stabbed, since she was behind the one with the knife. In fact, the one with the knife forgets about protecting Mary Ann and kneels down to check on the other woman, who looks like she's vomiting.

Mary Ann takes full advantage of the distraction. She turns and bolts for the fence.

Katherine gives me a nervous smile as they approach. She knows I wouldn't have called her up here, out in the open, if it wasn't absolutely necessary. I hand her the note and she grimaces.

Eta is already watching the scene at the bottom of the hill. "Is that the Orac . . ." She curses under her breath. "Is that *Mary Ann* trying to go over the fence?"

"I believe it is," Katherine says. "Can you guys wait here with Madi and Jack for a couple of minutes? I need to take care of something."

Rich, who read the note over her shoulder, says, "I have something to take care of, as well."

"It's of a *personal nature*," Katherine says.

"Yep. So is mine. Eta, we'll be right back."

Eta doesn't seem to hear any of this. She's focused intently on the scene below.

Jack sighs. "And I'm going to go see if I can help those guys before Mary Ann's people rip them to shreds. Where the hell are the cops?"

By the time Jack gets down there, the police have joined the fracas at the fence, and seem to be trying to decide which group to assist. The two agents posing as health inspectors must say some magic word or give a secret handshake, however, because it's only a few seconds before the police join in pulling away the workers so that they're able to get Mary Ann off the fence and in cuffs.

"Look," Eta says. "That's our group coming around the side of the arena. We just finished getting the chairs ready. Danny will be almost at the back of the line, because the rules say line up by age except for second oldest, who takes the back as line monitor. I'm near the middle. If I was still there at this age, I'd probably be line monitor. Maybe even front."

"Where are you now?"

"Mostly at the house in New Orleans. That's how I knew about those pretty lady plants. Father Matthias said having me leaving the group every few months to do things for the Cyrists is disruptive. He said the other kids were jealous and that I bragged. I don't think that's true. They just asked about the plane ride and I told them. But the Oracle . . ." She whacks the side of her head with the heel of her palm. "*Mary. Ann.* This is starting to piss me off. I know her name, but it's like I can't break the rule without forcing the words to come out of my mouth. If I can say *Saul* instead of *Father Cyrus*, I should be able to say hers, too. It's like she put one of her spells on me."

"It's not a spell, hon." I try to think of a way to explain it that doesn't involve the word *brainwashing*. "Mary Ann knows how to condition minds, and you were pretty young when you started there. When new kids come in, it probably takes a while for them to learn the rules, right? It will take you a while to learn to forget them."

I watch the little kids marching in line and all I can think of is Fort Ord a few minutes up the coast, training boys just a few years older than the one at the very front of the line to march off to war. Drill instructors screaming in their faces, because you have to break the man to build the soldier. I guess if you get kids early enough, you don't even have to break them before you start molding them.

The group has completely rounded the corner, and the front of the line is now obscured by the small crowd that has gathered to watch the drama of the cops trying to keep the Process members back so the other guys can cuff Mary Ann. Maybe they told the Monterey police some version of the truth, because you'd think they'd be a little curious about why health inspectors carry handcuffs.

Eta is staring intently, almost certainly looking for her younger version. To distract her, I go back to something she said about New Orleans.

"What was the pretty lady plant you mentioned?"

"That's what . . . *she* . . . calls this plant with dark purple flowers she grows in the garden outside the house in New Orleans. The berries actually do look a little like blueberries. She got pissed when one of the neighbors asked her to put chicken wire around it so no one would be tempted. Said anyone stealing from our garden deserved whatever they got. I looked through plant books when we went to the library each month, and it's really called nightshade. Or belladonna, which is Italian for *pretty lady*. She told one of the older girls they used to put drops of it in women's eyes to make them look prettier, although I don't know how eye drops could do that. If they used it too often, though, they went blind. The berries are sweet, like blueberries, but it doesn't take many to kill you. Especially a little kid like Danny." She sighs and pulls out her key. "I don't see me down there. And he just tripped on his shoelace, even after I tucked the edges into the side. Something is wrong. I need to go see."

"Wait. Let's watch through the key, okay? Here. Let me give you the stable point near the picnic tables. You can make sure Danny is okay."

"But you can't hear anything."

"Yeah. I think we can blame future lawyers for that. But we don't really need to hear, do we?"

She shakes her head, still looking a little uneasy about it. I think she may realize I'm trying to distract her, but she lets me transfer the stable point, possibly because she's already somewhat diverted by the sight of the two agents trying to get Mary Ann and the woman who was vomiting into the van. It's attracting a small crowd, a few of whom are booing the cops.

The van pulls away. One of the local police announces that the pancake breakfast has been canceled due to health-code violations. More boos, but they seem good-natured. The cop laughs, saying he was looking forward to it, too. The workers, who are pissed, begin packing up the items they'd just unpacked.

We scan forward fifteen minutes. I'm a little worried they're going to feed the kids anyway, and who knows if the agents in the van got all of the blueberry variety?

"What time did you guys eat? Before, I mean, when Danny used the wrong syrup?"

Eta continues staring at the stable point. In one corner of the shelter, the kids are still sitting quietly in neat little rows. "They said we could eat after. Once they knew what was left. Danny got in trouble for licking the blueberry off the ladle. Well, not with his tongue, but scooping it off and licking his fingers. And then one of the boys said they also saw him licking one of the paper plates someone left on the table. Which was true, but he didn't need to tattle." She breaks away from the stable point and looks over at me. "He's okay, though. We did it." There are tears in her eyes, but she's smiling. "I just hope Clio can save the guy they're planning to shoot. He's a little grouchy, but the older girls say he's a very good tipper. I clean the tables sometimes, and he'll order meals with French fries or toast. He never touches them, just the meat. One time I got a *whole* baked potato, with sour cream *and* butter."

I return her smile, hoping she thinks the tears that begin stinging my eyes are only for Danny. She clearly considered that potato a great bit of fortune, and I'm now wondering if her thinness isn't more than just the willowy phase a lot of girls go through.

"And Owsley did me a really, really big favor a few years ago. I'm not sure I'd be here if he hadn't."

I'm about to follow up on that, but Jack drops down on the blanket next to me, and this seems to remind Eta that Katherine and Rich still aren't back.

"Do you think they're okay?" she asks.

"They're okay," he says. "Probably making out in the bushes again. You'd think they'd know better after that poison-ivy incident, but some people never learn."

Eta snorts, and I give Jack a look that I seriously hope telegraphs the words *shut the fuck up*. At some point, Eta's probably going to find out Katherine is, more or less, her mother, so I really don't think we need to foster the image of her fooling around in the foliage at a rock concert.

"And . . ." he says with an impish grin, "I'm going to go rattle the bushes to see if I can find them. *Very discreetly*. What time was our appointment again?"

"Two-thirty."

"Eta," he says, "can you keep an eye on Madi and make sure she doesn't go running around on that ankle? She's kind of hyper."

She rolls her eyes. I doubt *hyper* is even a word in the 1960s. But he's right. I don't care what the note said. Katherine needs backup, and Rich probably shouldn't be it, since Saul may still think he's dead in the basement. If we're going on the assumption that breaking the rules can result in danger to Alex and the others, then he needs to be watching from a distance.

Eta must be sharp enough to realize that the look I gave Jack meant something, although I don't think she's sure what. She watches me for a moment and then says, "Clio and Katherine said you're also part of my extended family."

"Yep. We're something like second cousins six times removed."

"What does that even mean?"

"It means you have a big and very . . . *multigenerational* family."

"That seems so weird," she says. "We're not supposed to talk about family in the Process. The leaders said some people don't have family, so it would be cruel. Like bragging. So everyone is your family in a way, which I guess is okay, and kind of true. But in another way, it feels like you don't have family at all."

"So you don't live . . ." I start to say *with Saul* but switch at the last minute. "I mean, kids don't live with parents?"

"Nope. We bunk with the new acolytes who are also still learning the rules. Shouldn't Clio and her boyfriend be back?"

"Tyson's not her boyfriend."

She smiles knowingly. "Are you sure about that?"

I'm actually *not* sure, come to think of it, so I just say they should be back soon. But she's definitely right on one account. They *should* already be back. *Would* already be back unless something went wrong.

Eta begins looking at a stable point on her key. "Clio should already be here. That's bad."

Apparently, Eta has already learned the fundamental rule of time-travel on-time arrival.

"I'm gonna go forward and check," she says. "If I'm not back in a minute, I got stuck and you need to come get me."

"No! We should watch through the key."

"I need to *hear* it. So I'll know what's changed. And you'll slow me down. No one else will see me. I promise."

There's no way I'm going to let her see—or hear—anything from the last few minutes of that concert alone. But I can tell from the very Thea-like set of her jaw that nothing is going to persuade her.

"Fine. But at least give me the stable point you're using so that I *can* come get you."

She transfers the point once I show her how, then takes a few steps into the bushes and squats down. It takes two, maybe even three, tries before she blinks out. Which means I absolutely have to follow, because her getting stuck now seems less like a remote possibility than a very real probability. And so I, too, step into the bushes and pull up the stable point.

At first, I think it must be the wrong location, because it's dark, although not pitch black like some I've seen. There are slats of light and a few other brighter areas in what looks like a massive room.

I have to scroll forward a bit because Eta is still in the stable point. It doesn't work the first time, and I realize I'm standing up. So I squat and blink.

She startles when I arrive. "Damn it," she hisses next to my ear. "I told you to wait."

"I don't take orders well. It's a family trait. Where are we?"

"Under the box stands."

The music is so loud I can feel the vibration of the music beneath my knees. It builds, then trails off and is replaced by applause, a huge drum crescendo, and more applause. As my eyes adjust, I realize the slightly lighter areas I saw through the stable points are other keys. More specifically, other versions of Eta's key, held by other versions of Eta. At least six of them.

"There's a clear spot over here," she says. "Come on. It's only a couple of minutes now."

I sigh and crawl along next to her. Apparently, my concern that she'd have to watch Owsley's execution alone was unwarranted, but I think this may be even worse.

Eta tugs my sleeve. "Don't look at them and they won't look at you. We have a rule."

The next band is already setting up by the time we reach the front. "This spot is open because you can see from here. I just listen. I saw it once and I don't want to see it again. One time, something I did made it quicker by almost a whole line of the song, so then I knew I could change it if I kept trying. So I'd make a change, blink under here, and wait."

"How did you come here so many times if you left the key in Dennis's office?"

"I sleep on the cot when we're in DC. Saul's fine with that because he can get a hotel and do whatever he wants. Most of these were in the past few days. They're changing it so the Templars come to us in DC instead of us traveling to the other—"

Whatever else she says is drowned out when the music begins. Then she leans closer and says, "The first verse is safe. It happens in the second."

I move a little closer to the gap she pointed out. She's right. You can see the stage if you look upward and tilt your head to the side. The lead singer, Country Joe, has on a shirt that's almost as loud as the one CHRONOS Costuming sent for Tate. There's a large flower painted on his cheek, and he has a small American flag in his pocket.

Eta begins to tense up as the lead singer belts out the words, *aw, sweet Lorraine.* She holds her breath, and he continues. "Sweet lady of death wants me to die, so she can come sit by my bedside and sigh, and wipe away . . ."

She squeezes my arm. "They made it past the line. They made it—"

And then the instruments screech to a halt as I look through the gap and see the singer backing away, holding his guitar slightly higher on his body like a shield. Some people in the audience are frozen, while others are tearing toward the exit.

Three people—Mary Ann de Grimston, Clio, and Tyson—are kneeling on the stage with their hands apparently cuffed behind their backs. Six men in uniform surround them. Two have guns pointed out at the crowd. Three more, each carrying a pistol, stand behind their prisoners. One steps up to the microphone the singer abandoned. "No one leave. Close the gate. This woman deals in drugs and deadly poison. She is a witch, and thou shalt not suffer a witch to live."

The man directly behind Mary Ann de Grimston fires his gun at the base of her neck, and her body slumps to the side. There are screams from the audience, mixed with identical gasps of horror from all corners of the crawl space. The Eta beside me clutches her head. I have a fleeting second to wonder how many different memories she's reconciling right now before the man says, "This woman deals in drugs and defies the law. She is a witch, and—"

Tyson's scream of *No!* combines with the man's voice. I'm about to turn away because like Eta, I cannot watch this. But there's no gunshot. Just the sound of bodies hitting the ground. And at the front of the stage, I see a bright blue paisley shirt even more garish than Country Joe's.

Tate's voice comes over the microphone. "Everything is under control. These people will be fine. Proceed in an orderly fashion toward the exits so that no one else gets hurt."

I don't think he intended the words as a threat, but I'm certain there were plenty of people who took it that way. On the plus side, they listen. People stop shoving and move along, almost as orderly as the Process kids in their line this morning. I can see the change in behavior through the gap and hear it from the footsteps above us. When I look back at the microphone, Tate is practically carrying Tyson and Clio offstage. I see three blips of orange light in the wings, and then they're gone.

"What . . . *was* that?" Eta whispers.

"Yeah," another voice says from a few feet away. "Are all those people dead?"

I sigh, trying to figure out what to say. Would they be sad if I said Mary Ann is really gone? Or would they cheer? I'm not sure I can handle a rousing chorus of "Ding, Dong, the Witch Is Dead," and it would probably confuse the hell out of the people above us trying to exit the arena, so I sidestep the implied question and simply say, "The soldiers and the people in the audience who fell to the ground will be okay in a few minutes. It's like they're asleep for a bit. And *Danny is alive*. So you can all go home. It's over."

Only, it's not over. I'm almost certain that another Eta, younger than any of those down here with me in the dark, is still in the hands of a monster.

∞27∞

I'm surprised there's no noise as I approach the playground. Just a whisper of wind. It's a pretty day, and I've seen several young families who camped overnight. But as I get closer, I spot a handwritten sign on the gate. *Playground Closed. Sewage Leak.*

It's possible the sign is even true. I just passed the bathrooms and am seriously concerned that Rich's research proposal is based on a false premise. Either that, or the situation was truly bleak at Woodstock and Altamont. The concert hasn't started and there's already a line, because they'd much rather wait than use the porta-potties.

The chain-link fence surrounds what seems to be the classic playground quartet of this era—swings, merry-go-round, monkey bars, and the ubiquitous metal slide that is almost blindingly bright in the summer sun. No sign of Eta. No sign of Saul. But there are woods on two sides and the bathrooms on the third.

I really hope Saul doesn't make me wait. Or simply not show. Either would be in character. The only thing I can be fairly certain of, unless he's had a complete personality overhaul, is that he won't shoot me before boring me with a long diatribe on how very clever he is.

Or maybe he will. I've been wrong about plenty in the past few days.

I sit on the edge of the merry-go-round, facing the gate, and wait. About three minutes later, I hear another gate squeak open. I really should have checked to see if there was a second one. Turning to the left, I see Saul. His hair is now nearly as long as mine, and he has a neatly trimmed beard. It's black, but there are specks of gray. He's abandoned the black robe for the jeans and white shirt he so often wore when we were off duty. He holds Eta with one arm. She's seven or maybe eight. A little too old to carry around on his hip. She's wearing the same drab gray outfit I saw her working in earlier.

"See, Eta. I didn't lie at all. There she is. That's your mommy. Isn't she pretty?"

Eta doesn't answer. She just looks at me and then back at him. "Put me down, please. You're hurting my leg."

He does. "Go swing, *sweetness*. Be careful on the monkey bars, okay?"

She gives him a look of extreme wariness when he calls her *sweetness*. Does Saul even know he's riffing on his now-dead enemy? Or, at least, dead back in our time.

"I see you're channeling Morgen Campbell as your example for a sterling father-daughter relationship," I say in a low voice once she heads over to the swings. "Do you think he ever called Alisa *sweetness* when he wasn't trying to piss her off?"

"Doesn't matter," he says. "Eta won't be coming with me. And apparently, neither will you. Too bad you didn't take my offer."

"Are you flying somewhere? Because I've been told you can barely use the key."

He pulls an envelope out of his back pocket and opens it, taking out a tiny gray patch. "I actually need to thank your friends for this. Lawrence Dennis is an ungrateful fuck, and his toy soldiers were about to shoot my dealer. The first batch he made me was at least as good as the crap your friend in 2136 cooked up. I'm on my very last dose of the previous batch, and I'm not quite sure what I'd have done. But your friends gave him a heads-up—something I think went poorly for them—and I found him out back by the buses."

"Boosters can only help so much, Saul."

He shrugs and again holds up the envelope, which I can now see has musical notes printed on the back. "I've got fifty of these. Might have to take it slow getting back to the time where our game began, but that's okay. A few decades at a time. But I will get back to Cyrist Sword in 2136 or 2146 or whenever your friend finishes his little project. He's close, Kathy. The poor sap was reluctant to help at first, and he's riddled with guilt that he's letting all of you down by helping me, but he keeps muttering that this would be such a big breakthrough. Science is like a drug for him. Like those buzz bean things he's popping all the time. He can't give up the thrill. Can't deny it. And he says it doesn't take nearly as much ability with the key to move from one reality to the next. Moving through time is the tough part."

I'm not sure how much, if any, of that is true. But it doesn't matter. I just need to end this. We're running out of time. I'd rather not do it with Eta watching, but I may not have a choice.

"I'll shop around," he continues. "Find a timeline I like. Settle down. Maybe get a dog."

"You could name him Cyrus," I say. "Maybe start a club. You'd need a name for that, too. Oh, I know. The Objectivist Club."

"Funny, Kathy."

As this Saul is speaking, another Saul opens the gate. He's carrying one of the tiny laser pistols he likes that looks a bit like a derringer, and it's pointed at Eta. She's still swinging, facing this way.

"Didn't think I had enough oomph to spin off a splinter, did you? I've been saving up especially for you. And here's the thing. I'm going to let you choose. I have an even dozen people in these woods who are armed and more than a little pissed that their Oracle has been falsely arrested. They spotted Merrick. They also spotted Rich. And yes, I know you cheated and rescued him early. I hope you at least gave him one night of . . . passable sex. He's been panting after you since you met."

Eta pumps her legs and points her toes at the sky. I don't know how much she can hear of what we're saying, but she's watching us.

"Like I said, things didn't go so well for two of your friends, and my people literally have the others in their sights. You can't flip the timeline. It's well and thoroughly screwed. But things are only marginally different. A few more whack jobs in charge. A little less reason. A little more acceptance of the superstitious claptrap about witches and demons that makes you so righteously indignant. But you could go off and live a decent life in 1967. You did it once before. You could even live that life with Vier if you can't find anyone better. You can still save all of your friends."

He didn't mention everyone who's here with me, however, which gives me some hope. It could be an oversight on his part, but I obviously can't bank on it either way.

The other Saul yanks Eta out of the swing when it comes close to him. She screams until he shushes her, and then she looks back and forth between the two Sauls. It seems more like annoyance than confusion, so I think she's seen something like this before.

"Here's the deal," he says. "Go over and pull the armband from that clone. It's not even a real live girl. Just a carbon copy. Poof. She blinks out and you and your friends live happily ever after. More or less. Or I can pull your key. Kathy's choice. No tricks. Witches' honor." He forks his fingers and makes a V on his cheeks, pointing at his eyes. It's clearly a joke, but I don't get it. And I see someone now, a flash of blond hair in the narrow strip of woods between here and the bathrooms.

"If any of your friends manage to outsmart my Process ninjas, I'll even let them rescue her. Otherwise, she can go back with Father

Matthias. They'll feed her, clothe her, and eventually she can become a groupie for one of those bands playing at the arena. Oh . . ." Saul cups his ear. "Is that the sound of silence? Guess they had to cancel."

It *is* largely silent now. The fact that the concert isn't still going on is worrying, since he said Owsley got away, and his death is what stopped it last time, at least in part. The only thing I hear is a door closing on one of the porta-potties.

"Or," I say, "I could just shoot you."

He gasps. "In front of our darling daughter! For one thing, I'm not sure how the guy with the gun over there would take it. And . . . I don't think you have the nerve. Am I him, or is he me? Am I live, or is it Memorex?"

He knows I won't erase Eta. We might as well get this over with, so I say the words. "You're crazy." He takes a step toward me and I pull the laser from my skirt. "Always have been. Mommy and Daddy screwed you over with that extra genetic tweak. *You. Are. Crazy.*"

This is probably a splinter. I know that. But I fire the laser at his chest a split second after he grabs the chain that holds my key, the chain that Angelo gave me, and twists.

Guess the chain isn't as strong as I—

∞

The Saul holding the girl puts her on the ground. She scuttles like a crab until she's a few feet away from him. "Well, Eta. That was kind of messy, but that's a problem with a lot of families. Sorry about your mom. Hopefully, you'll make wiser choices when you're all grown up."

Dear God, I hope she does, too.

I think she saw me as I approached. But she's pointedly staring at her shoes. Squeezing her eyes shut.

The gate creaks when I open it, but that's okay. I want him to be looking at me.

He opens his mouth, but I shoot before he can speak. No point in giving him a chance to get started. No last words for you, Saul Rand. Silence will be your epitaph.

I sit down in the dirt next to Eta. What can I even say? Should I echo what Saul said? *Sorry about your dad. Hopefully, you'll make wiser choices when you're all grown up.*

In the end, I just tell her, "I'm sorry. You don't know me, and there's no reason for you to believe me, but I won't let anyone hurt you again."

And that's true. But what will happen once we deposit the new and improved *Book of Cyrus* and the timeline flips? Both Etas can't continue. Rich says it's this little girl right here who will go forward. And I'm glad, but also heartsick for the older version.

The gate creaks again. Eta looks up, but I don't. If this is another Saul splinter, I'll know soon enough.

"He's still breathing." A quick blast from her pen laser takes care of that, and then the second Other-Me sits in the dirt beside us. She holds out the laser, which is the one we took from Sutter, and runs her finger over the words *Objectivist Club* engraved on the side. "Guess this means Morgen wins. I thought Saul might have more than one splinter."

I still don't look at her. "He might still. It's been about five minutes, and Jack said his last splinter didn't survive much longer than that. But I think we wait the full fifteen minutes. Maybe longer."

"Someone could see us, though," Eta says. "Even the police."

It's a valid point, and it says something about the state of my mind . . . both of them . . . that it took an eight-year-old to point it out.

Other-Me says, "We could hide his bodies in the porta-potty. It smells horrible. Don't think I could have held out in there much longer."

The Saul who yanked my key vanishes.

We don't make it to the porta-potty with the other one. The two of us drag him a few steps into the woods, leaving a thin trail of blood in the sand. I tell Eta not to watch, but she's already one step ahead of me on that front, with eyes squeezed tight as she sits on the edge of the merry-go-round. But after a moment, she joins us in the woods, still not looking at the body.

"I'm pretty sure I'll blink out in a few minutes," Other-Me tells Eta. "Like the other Saul. Just so you're not surprised."

"Where will you go?"

Other-Me smiles sadly. "No one knows. But you'll have people to take care of you."

Brave words from the one about to blink out. Does Eta have *people*? If what Saul said about the Processeans having a gun on Rich is true, it's possible that she'll only have a *person*—just me—to take care of her. Which scares the holy hell out of me. Almost enough that I hope it's one of those fluke situations and I'm the splinter.

We wait in silence for about a minute. Then I hear a rustle in the woods on the other side of the playground. The three of us freeze, but then I see a block of bright blue paisley burst into the open.

I stand up and wave my arms, ridiculously happy to see someone, anyone, who won't blink out.

Eta stares as he runs toward us. "Who is that?"

"That's Tate. And yes, he looks like Thor."

"Who's Thor?" she asks.

Then Richard steps out of the woods and the tears flood over. I risk a look and see that Other-Me is having the same reaction.

Tate stares down at Saul's body. I can't read his expression, though. Is he a little sad? Or just sad that he didn't get to kill him? Or that he can't shoot him again for good measure, since there's a little girl watching?

Other-Me is gone before Rich reaches us. I'm relieved for him because he doesn't have to decide which one to hug. And glad for her because she had the chance to see that he was okay.

"Have you seen the others?" I ask him. "Saul said Tyson and Clio—"

"They're okay." He glances at Eta and says, "The *poisoner*, not so much. We'll meet them at the cabin."

"How long has it been?" Rich asks, glancing down at Saul.

"I spun off Other-Me in the port-a-potty fourteen minutes ago. I don't know how long my other one lasted, because he pulled her key. And the splinter she shot vanished about six minutes back. Let's give it a few more minutes. I'm just scared we could yank it not knowing whether it's another splinter . . . and we end up with another time shift before we can fully repair this one."

And so we wait. At eighteen minutes, I look up at Tate. "Do you want to do it?"

He actually looks torn. Angry, but also hurt. Not at my words, or at least I don't think so. It seems to be directed at Saul.

"I'll do it," Rich says.

And as soon as the key is yanked over Saul Rand's head, everything shifts.

EPILOGUE

KATHERINE
BOGART, GEORGIA
NOVEMBER 5, 1941

Even though the morning is chilly, the front porch calls me. So I grab a blanket from the couch and take my cup of tea out to one of the rocking chairs, closing the door gently to avoid waking the others.

Correction. The morning is cold. But I need to feel the frigid air against my face. I need to watch the sun inching slowly upward into the sky. I need to be reminded that some things are constants, regardless of the timeline. The sun continues to rise in the east. When this day is done, it will set in the west. Whatever changes we discover when the Temporal Avengers meet inside after breakfast, those things will remain the same.

Another constant is the fact that tea will be weak and tepid if you pour the water too soon and carry it outside on a cold morning. Having a wide variety of teas available in an instant is one thing I'm going to miss. From here on out, my morning tea will require a bit of forethought in buying the various kinds I like and a bit of patience waiting for the kettle to boil. In this case, it wasn't impatience on my part that made me yank it off the burner, but the fact that the darn thing was starting to whistle and there are ten other people in this tiny cabin, all of whom are smart enough to sleep in after several exhausting days. Several exhausting weeks, to be honest.

After Jarvis yelled at me for trying to smash the game console, which would apparently have blown the house in Bethesda to bits, we all agreed this cabin should be our post–time shift rendezvous point. Any changes would probably be less noticeable further back in time, and Clio said this cabin would still be safe. As long as Kiernan Dunne is under a key, she said, this house will be in his name in November of 1941.

As usual, she was right. The cabin was not only here but stocked with even more food. Two double mattresses and a twin had been delivered and were made up in the main room of the cabin, and an extra twin mattress was squeezed into the bedroom where Rich and I slept. That one had a brightly colored blanket, and there was a small pink suitcase with pajamas, clothes, and a toothbrush for Eta. All of which means Clio made a jump back to Skaneateles to put in a request before meeting us here.

We hadn't yet heard the details of Clio and Tyson's close call when we arrived at the cabin. Rich had looked around at the extra beds and joked that Clio had twitched her nose and made room for everyone. Eta smiled and said Clio looked more like Serena than Samantha. Rich said at least she wasn't Endora. I didn't get any of those references. I'm really wishing I'd taken the late 20th-century cultural literacy subliminal training.

The only reason I realized it was a witch reference was that Tyson seemed a little unnerved by the comment, and I'm certain he *did* get that subliminal training. He shot Clio a concerned look, and she mouthed *I'm okay*. Then she said if she were really a witch, she'd have conjured up beds for all eleven of us, because by that time, Timothy and Evelyn were here as well, with several oversized suitcases.

I tuck the blanket beneath my feet and curl my fingers around the mug, still trying to process everything. Feeling the shift happen as I watched Saul's body disappear was surreal. Rich and Alex did consider the possibility it might cause the shift, since it was Saul alone who set things in motion, but they ultimately dismissed it. All copies of the *Book of Prophecy* are under their own CHRONOS field and would, therefore, have survived even if he were erased. And Lawrence Dennis is, to the best of our knowledge, still under a CHRONOS key. If Saul was ever actually planning to run all of this as a game of Temporal Dilemma, I'm certain that would have been one of the moves he entered.

Eta came with us to the cabin without question, even smiled at a few of Rich and Jack's jokes. As tired as I was, I still lay in bed for a long time last night, looking at her face in the light of the full moon shining through the window and wondering how she could fall asleep so easily after the things she saw yesterday. Was that a testament to the resilience of a child's mind or simply a sign that she hasn't processed any of it? Or maybe evidence that yesterday wasn't one of the worst experiences she's had? The last possibility worries me most of all, because no matter where we decide to settle, therapy will never really be an option for Eta. Or any of us, I guess.

As I lay there, all I could think was how very lucky I am. Rich is alive. Eta is safe. But I couldn't help wishing there was a second mattress on the floor for Eta's older self.

What baffles me most is that Madi says she didn't vanish immediately. The shift happened right after they blinked back to the stable point they'd set near the blanket beneath the tree. They could hear the music playing again. Families were gathered near the picnic shelter the Processeans had commandeered, and there was no sign of the group anywhere. No sign of the Cyrist Sword vehicles, either. Madi considered jumping straight back to the cabin with Eta, but Eta pointed out that one or more of us might be hurt and unable to travel. So they grabbed the blanket, asked someone for directions to the playground, and met Jack heading back toward them. Once he knew they were safe, Jack reversed course and ran to the playground to check on us, since he could move faster than either of them, especially Madi with her sore ankle.

We had moved back to the playground to make sure there were no tracks to cover up, but the thin line of blood from where Other-Me #2 and I dragged Saul across the ground vanished along with his body when we pulled his key. Richard was in the process of checking the stable point at the cabin. He could see Clio and Tyson sitting on the couch, but not the others who were with us at the festival. Rich and Tate were about to circle back around to the arena to check on them when we heard Jack call out to us.

Madi said she was lagging a few steps behind when the girl stopped and ran back to her. There were tears in her eyes, but she was smiling. She said, "They found me!" Madi walked ahead to the point where she could see the playground, where the younger Eta was sitting on the merry-go-round running her shoe back and forth in the sand.

And when Madi looked back, older Eta was gone.

My first thought was that she'd used the key to jump away. That she felt like there would be no place for her. Or worse yet, that she tossed her key aside on purpose, for that same reason, knowing she'd vanish outside the CHRONOS field. Madi didn't find the key, but I think it would have disappeared once it was no longer activated.

Rich, however, says he's pretty sure the time shift simply turned that version of Eta into an odd version of a splinter, because there was no question that her younger self was coming with us. If there's a Saul in this timeline, he wasn't in 1967 Monterey. And if there's a Mary Ann de Grimston running a cult in this timeline, Eta will not be among her young recruits. The time shift changed her path.

I *guess* that makes sense, although it's also the sort of comforting explanation you might give a parent who was worried that her child was out there, somewhere, in pain. And it's a comfort that Madi says

Eta was happy in that final moment. We'd only just met her, and the rational side of my mind says it shouldn't hurt this much to lose her. But it does.

Because it still feels like a death. That girl will never exist. This Eta will have different experiences. She will grow up knowing love. She will grow up with a mother and a father.

Any time I have a moment of doubt, I think about the video Kate made the day after my funeral—well, not mine, but the me I was in that other reality. This me won't have the constant dread that Saul will find us. This me won't be keeping secrets about my past from my family. Maybe without those worries, I can relax and simply be a mom.

There may be objections from the Sisters on this point, given what Prudence apparently told them about my parenting skills. And five or six years from now, if I've totally screwed up the job of mom in this timeline, too, I may wish I'd listened. But it's not negotiable.

I'm so deep into my mental rehearsal of the argument I plan to submit to Beta and any other Sister who objects that I don't even see the truck until it's pulling into the yard. I tense up automatically, because I still don't know much about 1941 or really any year in this timeline. But I suspect the woman getting out of the truck is one of the caretakers, since she came down the road that runs across the fields from the farmhouse to this cabin, and there's no escaping because she's already seen me.

She comes a few steps closer and peers through the porch screen. "I'm Alice Owens, one of the caretakers. I hate to ask you for a favor when I don't even know your name yet, sweetie, but would you mind helping me get these pans out of the truck? Mr. Dunne called and said a bunch of you were heading into town for a funeral over in Athens this afternoon so I shouldn't bother you, and I really wasn't going to, but . . . there's no way I could ever let people in grief do their own cooking on the day of a funeral. That's not how we do things down here, and my mama would come back and haunt me if I even thought about it."

"That's really sweet of you, Mrs. Owens."

"No trouble at all. Mr. Dunne has always treated us so well. Anyway, I've got eggs, some country ham, and all the fixin's here. I'm guessing there's ten of you judging from the mattresses Bill bought yesterday. Just hope I cooked enough."

I'm in sock feet, so I wait on the steps, and Mrs. Owens hands me three huge pans wrapped in foil and a large jug.

"That's fresh-squeezed," she says. "Now I'll get out of your hair like I promised. Hope y'all enjoy it."

My stomach growls and I realize we haven't had a real meal in ages. Last night, we were so tired we grabbed a bowl of something called Kix before we crashed. Naturally, that thought triggers Saul's voice in my head. *You really do suck at this mom gig, Kathy.*

Did the other Katherine hear that voice, too? I think she probably did. And he can fuck off. There's nothing wrong with cereal for dinner on occasion. It says fortified with vitamins right there on the box.

Once the others are awake and we've all eaten, Sigma and Tate offer to take Eta on a walk.

Sigma must notice that I tense up, because she squeezes my arm. "We're not going to take her anywhere without your permission. I'm still not leaving anyway, because my conditions have not yet been met. Tate simply pointed out that this is probably not a discussion you want Eta to overhear."

"Not that it's horrible stuff they're going to tell you," Tate adds quickly. "I got the overview of our situation from Angelo last night when I went to pick up my belongings. The aliens still don't attack until 2092, and it's a lower-casualty version than we had, so that's good. I just thought that if you're planning for Eta to stay with you, she's going to have to keep enough secrets as it is. No need to add more."

He's right, and I didn't think of it, which triggers the snarky comment from Saul's ghost again. I push it away, thank Tate and Sigma, and they go off to find Eta.

When I sit down next to Rich, he hands me a printed packet Evelyn made for each of us. It's about thirty pages, total, secured with a binder clip.

"Yes," she says, noting my expression. "It's old-school. Typewritten, even. I need to get used to it. I'm not sure when and where each of you will be going, but Timo and I have decided on 1963, so we won't have computer tablets and comm-bands. But before we get into all of that, I'll give you one of these." She hands each of us a paperback version of the *Book of Cyrus*. There are a couple of different covers. Richard's looks like it was read several times. There's a brown ring on the cover of mine that suggests it was used as a coaster for someone's morning coffee, so maybe it was read, too.

"They're not the ones we deposited at the temples," she says. "We bought these in a bookstore."

"Well, several bookstores," Timothy amends. "Cyrisism never really caught on. There are a few congregations, and it's taught in some world-religion courses, partly because it has a bit of a resurgence in the late 1990s when someone started making motivational posters based on the verses. But then it promptly died out again. The three new copies are from a bookstore in 2003, and the guy seemed glad to unload them."

Madi, who's sitting on the edge of the armchair next to Jack, says, "Well, pooh. I really thought you had a bestseller there, babe."

He grins. "I'm actually not surprised about the motivational posters. I cribbed liberally from an old archive at DARPA. There was a folder labeled Training PowerPoints that had some great ones."

"Glad to see they kept the classic Cyrist symbol," Tyson says. "The infinity sign is a nice touch. I have to admit I'm a little confused, though. We thought you guys quit."

"We sort of did," Evelyn says. "I had a . . . tough time after the trip to Salzburg. Not blaming any of you. We had the file right there in front of us. We read it. And . . ."

"And we ignored it," Timothy says. "Because they were already dead, right? Centuries and centuries ago when ignorance was rampant. When people didn't know any better. We just kept thinking . . . what would Rose do? But when you come face-to-face with a man who has beheaded a bunch of kids, it doesn't seem so simple."

"You might want to hunt Rose down and ask if she's willing to share the reason the jump committee gave her that assignment," I say. "Or ask Angelo. I don't know if it's the same in your time, but either way, it's not my story to tell."

"That's not really going to be an option for any of us, but I'll get to that in a moment," Evelyn says. "We kept thinking about all of the other events that happened in our history. Things eventually got better, but there are still pockets of ignorance. People still demonize the things they don't understand. Good people watch and do nothing while innocent people die. And we knew the *Book of Cyrus*—the old version, I mean—made that worse."

Timothy says, "In the end, we couldn't shake the feeling that being a good historian, just standing by and watching that shit happen, was in direct conflict with being a good person. So, we went back and picked up the file that Archives had put together about the *Book of Cyrus* and jumped to the original locations of the Six Great Temples, which were closer to the Six Great Shacks at first." He rubs his right leg. "Extraordinarily well-guarded shacks. Their penchant for Dobermans goes way back, although they looked a little different in the early days. The ones in sixteenth-century Madrid had *dientes gigantes*, and I have the scar to prove it. Or at least I did. CHRONOS Med took care of it during our out-processing."

"So, CHRONOS is still there?" Rich asks.

They nod, but judging from their expressions, it's clearly a quali-fied *yes*, and they're just trying to figure out the best way to explain it.

"It's still called CHRONOS," Timothy says. "But if you remember the first part of *A Brief History of Time Travel*, there was a group called the Chrono-Historical Research Organization, aka CHRO?" We all nod, and he says, "Well, that's pretty much what exists today. The book would be more aptly titled *A Very Brief History of Time Travel*. Madi and Jack are in there, but more as a cautionary tale, and I'm pretty sure there were some fictional elements added. Either that, or you haven't told us about the dinosaurs yet."

Jack snorts. "Alex and I had a little fun with that one. Do they actually teach the book at CHRONOS?"

"Don't know," Evelyn says. "Archives had a copy, though. Aside from Jack's creative writing sample at the beginning, it mostly says there was some wild experimentation in the early days and then ITOC was formed, and the world decided to step back from the prec-ipice. There is no in-person time travel. Never has been. Stable points are viewed in the classroom only. Some have sound, but that's still a point of contention."

We all take a moment to digest this, and then Clio says, "So, if there's no in-person travel, does that mean . . ."

"Right," Timothy says. "Angelo is currently the only person in our time with the CHRONOS gene. There are a few others without the gene who were under a CHRONOS field, mostly government leaders, and they are under the impression this was an incursion from another timeline. Which it was, technically."

I exchange a look with Rich and Tyson, and then ask the question I'm sure we're all thinking. "Do any of us even exist?"

"Sort of? Your mom still works at CHRONOS, and you're still a historian, but you look a lot more like your mom these days, since you didn't get the extra genetic alterations. Tyson might exist, but he's not at CHRONOS. Ev and I never met. Saul does exist, but Angelo said he went into finance with his father. Tate and Rich exist. Tate's even at CHRONOS. But neither of them look anything at all like they do now."

I don't have to imagine what Rich looks like. We saw a picture of his non-CHRONOS self in Sutter's office a week or so back. The same gray eyes, but otherwise, little similarity to my version of Rich or to Peter Parker, the character Tyson is convinced was the inspiration for Rich's genetic designer. It's really hard to imagine, however, what Tate might look like if his DNA was never tweaked by a designer who was apparently fixated on ancient comics.

Tyson frowns. "So you're telling me they think there was an incursion from an alternate time and they're doing nothing about it?"

"I think I can field this one," Jack says. "I'm guessing they decided to implement a program that this theoretical physicist named Ian Alexander began back in 2136, but ultimately abandoned because world governments decided not to allow human time travel."

"Ding, ding, ding," Timothy says. "Give that man a prize. That was, indeed, one element in the defense plan that was developed in the early days of time travel." He gives Jack a slightly annoyed smirk. "Back when the team of Jack and 'Mad Max' Merrick were nearly eaten by dinosaurs."

"Chosen only for the purposes of alliteration," Jack tells Madi. "I fully expect you to keep your last name. And we're not honeymooning in the Mesozoic era."

"The other part of the defense plan," Evelyn says, "is a small strike force that can deal with any incursions that get past our shield. I'm guessing Katherine and Rich will be looking for a slightly less dangerous occupation, and Timo and I are close enough to retirement that we wouldn't be good candidates, even if we were interested. And we're not. We have plans. But if any of you are so inclined, the goal of that project isn't simply to protect our timeline from incursions, but to share the technology with other, similar timelines in the hope of eventually preventing rapid and uncontrolled proliferation of new realities. The contact's name is on the list, along with a brief historical timeline with relevant changes. I've organized it with a quarter-century per page, personalized a bit to your own individual fields of study. If you'd rather not know what's coming up beyond your time, feel free to discard those pages.

"There's also a page with specific details about what is and is not allowed. Obviously, there's no way any of this can be enforced, but common sense suggests that passing along the gene would be ill-advised. There are always kids who need homes if you want a family. Aside from that, those of us who opt not to join this CHRONOS defense squad, or whatever they'll call it, are directed to pick a place and a time, and stay put. The standard emergency protocol is in place. Find the nearest safety-box location to the time and place you plan to settle down and pick up an ID and information on accessing a bank account with a starter allowance. Thumb through the packet, and if you have any questions, let me know before we leave. And if any of you wind up in or around 1963, we'll be in Dallas for at least a few years, so feel free to look us up. We'll be in the phone book."

"I have a question," Madi says. "What about the Zaubererjackl trials and the executions in Salzburg? The timeline doesn't mention them, and that's an issue for Sigma. For me, too."

Tim and Evelyn exchange a look. "It still happens," he says. "No *Hexenpest*, which shouldn't surprise you, since you noted the virus was Saul's doing. We were only cleared to travel to the Six Temples and a few libraries."

"It's interesting that you mention Salzburg," Evelyn continues in a measured voice. "Timothy and I were just telling Tate that we played one last game of Temporal Dilemma before leaving CHRONOS . . . Yes, The Game still exists and it's more popular than ever. We ran a scenario in which we gave a tiny bit of seed money to an enterprising young man in Salzburg—perhaps someone like this Jakob Koller who becomes known as the Zaubererjackl—so that he might start an orphanage in the mountains outside of Salzburg rather than organizing children as a band of thieves and beggars in the city. Once the children were no longer begging the townspeople, the witch frenzy died down. It wasn't a successful strategy for flipping the timeline, though. Admittedly, we ran it on our small game console in our quarters, but . . . it didn't budge the timeline in the slightest." She raises her eyebrows and gives Madi a little smile. "What a funny coincidence that you bring it up."

This is clearly as far as she and Timothy are willing to go beyond their explicit orders. But it sounds like an excellent plan. Simply freeing the children wouldn't work. The prince-archbishop would have them rounded back up and they'd be on the gallows again the next week.

After Timothy and Evelyn leave, Rich and I head out to the rockers on the porch again to discuss our options.

"I'm thinking 1967," he says. "You didn't have trouble getting a teaching job in the sixties in the other timeline. I probably won't, either. Or maybe . . . I could be a music critic. *Rolling Stone* publishes its first issue in 1967. I could probably get in on the ground floor. And . . . I know it's a pretty volatile time. Lots of social turmoil. But it's the era Eta knows. She's going to have a hard enough time adjusting without us taking her out of her comfort zone."

"It sounds good to me. As long as you give me a catch-up course on pop culture. So that's the when. Now we need to pick where. I'm a little worried California might hold some bad memories for her."

"We could let her help us pick a place," he says. "It might give her a sense that she has some degree of control over her life. I don't think she had much of that before."

I spot Eta coming through the woods with Tate and Sigma. She's chatting with Sigma about something, and I realize I never asked the girl to keep her relationship to Eta secret. And maybe I shouldn't keep it secret. Maybe she should know she has choices. Rich should know that he does, too.

So even though it kind of makes my stomach churn, I say, "You're not even tempted by the defense-squad thing that Tim and Ev mentioned? You probably have ten more years where you could use the key. That's a lot to give up."

He reaches across the arm of his rocker and takes my hand.

"I'm not tempted. Are you?"

"No."

We sit there for a moment in silence, and I flash forward to some point in the future when we'll have our own porch and our own rockers. Gray hair, creaky joints. And memories. The idea of building those memories, of growing old with Rich next to me, is all the future I want or need. There are things I'll miss about our time. My parents. Angelo. But that future is for another, apparently very different version of me.

"I'm still a little worried that I'm not up to it," I tell him. "That I'll let her down and she'll grow up to be the angry young woman that Prudence was. But I'm committed to giving it my best shot."

He smiles. "Even if you're not the world's best mom, even if you screw up royally on occasion, Eta will turn out just fine."

"Really. And how can you be so certain?"

"Simple. I'm going to make sure she has the world's best dad."

$$\infty$$

TYSON
FIFTH COLUMN HEADQUARTERS
JULY 16, 2058

"I'm nervous," Clio whispers when we jump in. "I hate job interviews. I always stick my foot in my mouth."

"You'll be fine. You're literally one of the only people on earth who can fill the job description. At least, one of the only people in this timeline."

She gives me a nervous smile. "I'm just glad Other-Mom won't be here. I will never stop being weirded out by that."

Her discomfort around Kate Pierce-Keller is a little amusing, given that we have been literally surrounded by people of varying ages over the past few weeks who look almost as much like Kate Dunne. Clio says it's more the mannerisms. Something about the smile. I suspect it's like the robotics uncanny-valley idea.

This is our second jump to the headquarters of the Fifth Column, although this is a different stable point. Last time, there was a lot of catching up to do. They're apparently debating whether to have all the Sisters of Prudence in the same time period, now that there's no role for them, and we may need to help with transportation once they make up their minds. Clio and Madi were also relieved to see that Kate was no longer in a wheelchair, and her husband and son were fine after the time shift.

We're also in a different location this time. On the previous visit, we were in a library at the main house. This is a waiting room of some sort in one of the other buildings. There's not much here aside from a couple of chairs and the door to an inner office. I hear voices inside, so we take a seat and wait.

On that first trip, we came with Madi, Jack, Tate, and Sigma, after Sigma's condition was sufficiently met. We couldn't guarantee that no child would ever die on the gallows in Salzburg, but no child died there in 1678. The only change to the timeline, as best we can tell, is that there is no legend of the Zaubererjackl.

We were a bit surprised to find that the Fifth Column still existed as an organization. Richard's best guess when we discussed it before they headed off to 1967 was that the organization would now be only the handful of people who were under a CHRONOS field. He was even a little concerned that we might need to track them down, because there would be no need for a compound. Cyrist International does exist, but it's a firm that produces metaphysical books and multimedia. There's never been an organization large enough to require four columns, let alone a fifth.

The Cyrist Fifth Column in this timeline was less organized, but it still existed as a small group of Cyrists within the government and major corporations who endeavored to bring the positivity of their faith into their respective institutions and push for ethics guidelines. As with most such groups, they had a few successes and a lot of failures.

Cyrist Sword and Shield was never created. Lawrence Dennis was still a preacher, but that's because he returned to his traveling ministry instead of attending Harvard. While the historical record is a bit vague on how it happened, I think I know. All it would have taken in that era was a hint about his race to the college registrar to remove him as a threat. On one level, it bothers me. But his policies hurt so many people of every race, especially his own. The hypocrisy makes it hard to have much pity. I can't really blame Tim and Ev if that is, in fact, what they did. After all, I thought about doing the exact same thing. If it kept him from being a tool of Saul Rand, it was clearly for the best. And maybe he managed to actually find the happiness that seemed to elude him in his other lives.

"I'd think you'd be more at ease around Other-Mom than you are around your actual mom right now," I tell Clio.

Clio twists her mouth. "Point taken."

Kate and Kiernan Dunne are less than happy with the fact that Clio is considering this job. Fixing your own timeline is one thing. It's a bit hard to avoid that danger, although Clio always had the option of hiding in the past. Fixing other timelines, though? They told her that was just courting trouble.

But I'm not sure we're looking for trouble so much as heading it off. This Stanford Fuller guy is worried that the equilibrium is shifting. Fuller is one of the two people we'll be talking to today, along with a man named Daniel Quinn, who is some sort of liaison between the government and a group of people with gifts similar to Fuller's.

I wouldn't necessarily believe this, but Alex agrees. His upgrade to the medallion currently allows us to view a limited number of geographical and chronological points in about thirty different timelines, which he says is just a fraction of the realities he's been able to identify. Stan Fuller says the thirty we can view would have been pretty much all there were back in the early 2020s when he started trying to codify them.

Clio slips her hand into mine. "My parents will come around. They always do. The one condition I promised them I'd say was non-negotiable if I take the job is that we have permission to travel to whenever they are at least a few times a year."

My eyebrows go up at the word *we*. "So . . . you told them that we're . . . um . . .?" I'm really not sure how to finish the statement. This is still new, and it feels fragile. All I know is that my world stopped spinning in that second between the guard pointing his gun at Clio's head and the one when he fell to the ground and she was safe. Tate had to practically lift both of us off the stage. As soon as he found a key to remove our cuffs, my arms went around her. I was still holding her when the timeline flipped.

"Of course. I told them on our first trip to Skaneateles. Why do you think they didn't shoot you?"

I laugh. "You told them, but not me?"

She shrugs. "I was a little worried that you might be planning to go back to Memphis."

It takes me a second to realize that she's talking about Antoinette Robinson. "Oh. No. I mean, yes, I was attracted to her. I'll admit I checked the stable point you gave me to see if she's still there, leaning against the drugstore wall. Because it means we're close to that timeline. Somewhere in the ballpark. And yes, she's there. Different color dress, though, which strikes me as weird. Did you check for the white-picket-fence guy?"

Clio nods. "He's fine. Different wife. By which I mean different from both of the other timelines. Five kids. Did you check the drugstore wall in the adjacent timelines?"

I actually hadn't thought of that, so I shake my head. "Is your ex-fiancé there in all of them?"

"He's missing in two of the thirty. Still exists, just not in Chicago. Which is a pretty decent ratio of frog-tongue universes to not."

The door opens and Tate Poulsen steps out, looking a little stunned.

"Your turn," he says. "And as a heads up, this may be a slightly more unusual timeline than we thought."

∞

MADI
Bethesda, Maryland
April 7, 2137

"Eck." Yun Hee toddles toward us, holding the brightly colored fake egg in her chubby hand.

"That's right!" RJ says. "June Bug found an egg! Give it to Mommy so she can put it in the basket, and let's go see if we can find another one."

Lorena takes the egg and puts it next to the other two in the basket. "There are three more," she says, holding up the requisite number of fingers. "How many is three?"

Yun Hee grins and ignores her, saying "More eck!" as she goes back to RJ.

"I can't believe how much she's grown."

"Nearly four months," Lorena tells me with a grim smile. "Kids change a lot in that time."

I nod, thinking that Lorena may also have missed a lot during those months, given the schedule Jack said she was forced to keep by the commander who was working for Saul. Did she miss Yun Hee's first steps?

My thoughts must show in my expression because she says, "Oh, stop. It wasn't an easy couple of months, especially when they had us in those cramped quarters. But I was in the middle of a pretty time-consuming project at work before all of this began, and my supervisor had never heard of the concept of work-life balance. I probably saw as much of Yun Hee as I would have if you'd never found that key. The project Saul's guy forced me to work on wasn't technically challenging in the conventional sense. I'd already developed the serum for Jack. But at least I was in a lab and there was some challenge to figuring out how to give Saul a patch that was just strong enough to make him think I was actually trying. And I'm happy with my new job at DARPA. The hours and pay are better, and I think I'll get some interesting projects. I wish Alex wasn't taking a leave of absence, though. The office is too far to go home for lunch, and I hate eating alone."

"Yeah, but . . . I'm glad to see him taking a break. Picking up a hobby if nothing else." I glance over at the picnic table where Alex is, as usual, at his tablet. Instead of the typical numbers and graphs, however, he's working on a 3-D sketch of Yun Hee. He has another month at DARPA, and then he's going to take the summer off and take a few art classes while he decides whether he wants to continue in temporal physics or begin a holoportraiture program in the fall.

Once Yun Hee finds the last *eck*, she needs another distraction to keep us from having to hide them again. So Jack, who was overseeing the barbecue, steps inside to grab Daphne, the whirling dervish of auburn fur that he bought me last week as a late Christmas gift, since we skipped past Christmas and New Year's so that we could catch up with the others.

Aside from our jump to the Fifth Column with Sigma after we left the cabin, we've mostly been here at the house. The sense of relief I felt seeing it whole makes me feel a little guilty. Ultimately, it's just a place. Just a thing. I'd obviously have let it blow sky-high rather than trade a single life we saved. I'd have traded it to save the older Eta, even seeing, as she did, that tableau on the playground and knowing the child sitting next to Rich and Katherine would never suffer any of the pain or indignity that the other one did.

But it's still nice to be home. And it is my home, willed to me by James Lawrence Coleman himself at his mother's direction. I'm no longer registered in the master's program at Georgetown, but I could be. I could even pick up the thesis again. But what would I write? There's no way I can say that Coleman rescued books from alternate timelines that would never have seen the light of day if he hadn't published them under his name. I can only answer the question of whether he was a plagiarist or not. The question is black or white, and the answer is decidedly gray.

I look back over at Alex. Does it feel strange to him to be contemplating giving up what I'm sure he viewed as his life's work? I've had a chance to watch him for the last week, since he took me up on my offer to stay here while he's taking classes. The same offer was given to Lorena and RJ. We have plenty of room. But I think they're happier in their apartment, and I'm sure this place holds more negative than positive memories for both of them, although Yun Hee probably misses the yard.

Alex, on the other hand, is just happy as long as he can learn. He could be in a capsule on the dark side of the moon, as long as he had caffeine, some sort of nutrition, information to be absorbed, and a problem to solve. He throws his entire heart and soul into any project, and I see the same look of concentration on his face now, as he stares at the portrait, as I saw when he was poring over charts and graphs and timelines.

I think he's also able to have some closure because of the medallion I hold in my hand. There was no point repeating what he'd done in the other timeline, and while he fed Saul partial results, he made the multiple-timeline breakthrough a few weeks before the combination of Saul's death and the new and improved *Book of Cyrus* flipped the timeline. This medallion is version 2.0. It's the same casing as before, and it has the same amber glow. But it has been given a more limited version of the upgrade that Tyson and Clio will use in the field. Tate, too, if he decides to join them.

The new stable points are grayed out, so I can't jump to other timelines. Unless Jack and I change our minds about joining this defense force, that will never be an option. But I can see those other realities, and it's a bit addicting.

For the most part, I only watch the location here in the backyard. That's relatively safe, with little risk that I'll encounter a naked ancestor. Occasionally, this yard is occupied by people I don't know, even if I stick to adjacent timelines. Occasionally, the stable point is inside the lobby of an apartment building that looks a lot like the one currently on my left. Two timelines show Kate and Kiernan Dunne in this house. A girl who looks a bit like Clio plays with her aging Irish setter, who I'm pretty sure is also named Daphne, and a brother who's nearly the same age. That girl's name is Clio, too . . . I can tell from watching Kate call to her to come inside. But I'm pretty sure it's not the Clio I know.

Most of the time, however, some variant of the descendants of Kate Pierce-Keller and Trey Coleman live in this house. A boy I assume is Grandpa James often sits beneath a willow reading a book. Sometimes, his younger brother coaxes him over to the basketball hoop that hung for several decades on the back of the garage.

If I scan forward in some of those timelines, Nora appears. I watch her on a tree swing, being pushed by her father, before the drama of James's plagiarism trial came between them. He helps her out of the rubber ring, then swoops her up and spins her around. Her hair flies out in golden wisps against a pink-and-blue twilight sky. Even as a little girl, Nora's smile was the same as the one I remember . . . and it always makes me rethink Kate's standing offer to arrange an introduction. Kate had several different ideas for a story that she could pass down to connect us. It's tempting, and I may yet decide to take her up on it. She would still be Nora. The odds are very good that she'd still call her local mayor a chucklefuck. And I think we'd be friends. But it wouldn't be the same, and I'm worried the new relationship would push aside memories of when I was actually her granddaughter.

One restriction I keep when using this key: I do not look at any variant of the future. I'm curious, of course, as anyone would be. Do Jack and I have children? Do we stay here, or move somewhere with fewer disturbing memories? I've already reached the point where I can go into the living room without my memory automatically dredging up Thea's last moments. And I think I'll eventually be able to dive into the pool in the basement without thinking of a timeline where I swam through Rich's blood, hoping I wasn't too late to save him.

I'm pretty sure memories like that would have kept Katherine from ever wanting to live here. I now have a second photo album on my shelf, next to the one from Clio's family. Katherine's first entry is a road trip from the East Coast back to San Francisco in late August of 1967, with a short stop in Dallas to visit the Winslows. Two weeks later, they headed back to DC with a second child in the back of the station wagon. There's no way they could have found the boy and cleared his adoption in two short weeks, but surely they're allowed one cheat? The album that was waiting on my doorstep the day after we returned is filled with holiday photos, vacation snapshots, and every detail of Eta and Danny's accomplishments.

Jack drops down on the grass next to me. "What are you thinking about, Mrs. Merrick?"

This is merely stage two of our running joke. We haven't gotten around to formalizing anything or even found that boring afternoon where one of us will officially propose. Jack even has Jarvis in on the game. Earlier today, when we were trying to coax the food unit into spitting out a palatable pasta salad for this cookout, Jarvis chimed in to ask me if I was preparing for another boring afternoon.

I lean back against Jack and look out at the lawn. My garden is still missing, but we'll be fixing that bright and early tomorrow morning. Assuming the puppy doesn't dig it up.

"I was thinking about Katherine and Rich. How they led a happy life. *Are* leading a happy life. *Will* lead a happy life. It's hard to separate the past, the present, and the future when thinking about them."

He presses a kiss against my temple. "For the wise soul does not dwell in the past, does not dream of the future, but concentrates the mind on the present moment. Therefore do not worry about tomorrow, for tomorrow will worry about itself."

"You're quoting your book again, aren't you?"

"I am indeed, although I have no clue what verse it is. And it's stolen shamelessly from both the Buddha and the Bible. This place is apparently destined to house plagiarists for a noble cause. But you should heed my wise words and concentrate on *this* present moment, because our burgers are getting cold."

And so I follow him to the picnic table where our friends are waiting, to share the most precious thing we have—time together.

∞Acknowledgments∞

Ending a series always feels a bit like moving to a new house. You take some things with you, but you leave a lot of memories between the walls of the old place. The new house you're heading to might be in the same general area, and you might end up loving it just as much, but it will never be quite the *same* vibe. And as you walk out that door for the last time, you know you're leaving a chunk of your life behind.

There are more stories I want to tell in the CHRONOS universe (once I untangle my brain a bit), but several characters who have been with me since *Timebound* take their final bow in this book. I'll miss them, yes . . . even Saul. So it's definitely a bittersweet feeling.

Okay, enough of that. Here at the end, I always like to take a few minutes to sort out fact from fiction. There are numerous historical figures in this book, and I've retained their words and opinions as suggested in interviews and biographies when possible, at least before the timeline goes off the rails. And even after that, I made an effort to take their published words and adapt them to the new reality. So here's a partial breakdown:

- Excerpts from fictional newspapers appear between chapters. These are based to varying degrees on articles from the time period, although they diverge a bit from actual history once alterations to the timeline begin.

- Verses from the *Book of Cyrus* are sprinkled throughout the manuscript. This is obviously a work of fiction, but Saul Rand stole liberally from the Bible and other religious texts, so you may get Sunday-school flashbacks.

- Aside from the conversion to Cyrism, the sections dealing with Jemima Wilkinson, also known as the Publick Universal Friend, and the family of Judge William Potter are based on fact, including Susannah Potter's death on New England's Dark Day in 1780.

- The Cora Tree can be seen on Hatteras Island, near the town of Frisco. I took some liberties with the dates, but no one knows for certain when lightning struck the tree or when the letters were burned into the bark. Pea Island Life Saving Station was the first all-black Coast Guard unit, and Maloyd Scarborough was one of the lifesavers stationed there. And if you travel to Ocracoke, you can still hear traces of the Hoi Toider (High Tider) accent, also known as the Ocracoke Brogue.

- Details pertaining to the Zaubererjackl witch hunt and executions are accurate. With the exception of Sigma Schwester, all of the people listed were executed on that day. The witch frenzy was unusual in that most of the victims were male, most likely to cut the number of beggars in the town of Salzburg during a sparse winter.

- Accounts of the Harwich Mob can be found online in William Lloyd Garrison's abolitionist paper, *The Liberator*.

- Aside from the addition of Cyrists intent on hanging Scopes, the events of the famed "Monkey Trial" are historical, including the media circus that the town of Dayton put on for tourists. John Scopes did have a sister named Lela who lost a job teaching math when the school board asked whether she agreed with her brother's position on evolution—a subject that would never have even come up in her classes.

- Lawrence Patton McDonald was never elected president, but most of the other details are factual, and the speeches included between various chapters are based on ones that he gave before his death in an airplane crash in 1983, when the Korean passenger plane he was aboard was shot down after it entered Soviet airspace. A fervent anti-communist, McDonald was an officer in the John Birch Society and ran a private intelligence agency called Western Goals while serving in Congress.

- Mary Ann MacLean and Robert de Grimston met when they were working with the Church of Scientology in London, and formed their own group, the Process Church of the Final Judgment. I changed a few bits to incorporate Cyrist beliefs, but most of the information is factual. After the cult disbanded, several of the leaders (including Mary Ann) went on to form Best Friends Animal Sanctuary. The group struggled after several reports suggested a tie to Charles Manson, although this was probably circumstantial.

- Sections dealing with the Diggers, Owsley Stanley, and other Haight-Ashbury residents during the Summer of Love are, for the most part, historical. To the best of my knowledge, Bobby Weir didn't have a fling with a time traveler, but based on his comments in various interviews I've watched, he probably can't rule it out, either.

- I stuck as closely as possible to the set list at Monterey Pop, mostly so I'd have an excuse to listen to the playlist I set up at Spotify (https://bit.ly/BellBookAndKey). And Richard's project on the availability of bathrooms and violence at concerts definitely merits further study.

I'm certain I've left something out, but if you have a question about what's real and what isn't, give me a shout on Twitter.

Okay, on to the acknowledgments. Huge thanks, as always, to my publishing team at 47North, including Adrienne Procaccini and Megha Parekh, who stepped in while Adrienne was out working on an adorable personal project. Mike Corley created a wonderful cover, and the ever-talented Kate Rudd and Eric G. Dove breathed life into my characters in the audio version. Many thanks to Tegan Tigani for helping me untangle conundrums and kerfuffles in the developmental edit, and to the dedicated group of copyeditors and proofreaders who caught my goofs and typos.

Special thanks to my CHRONOS Repo Agents, beta readers, and assorted friends and family for their feedback and support: Cale Madewell, Chris Fried, Karen Stansbury, Ian Walniuk, Mary Freeman, Meg A. Watt, Alexa Huggins, Alexis Young, Allie B. Holycross, Amelia Elisa Diaz, Angela Careful, Angela Fossett, Ann Davis, Antigone Trowbridge, Becca Levite, Bianca Najjar, Billy Thomas, Brandi Reyna, Chantelle Michelle Kieser, Chaz Martin, Chelsea Hawk, Cheyenne Chambers, Chris Fried, Chris Schraff Morton, Christina Kmetz, Claudia Gonzaga-Jauregui, Cody Jones, Dan Wilson, Dawn Lovelly, Devi Reynolds, Donna Harrison Green, Dori Gray, Emiliy Marino, Erin Flynn, Fred Douglis, Hailey Mulconrey Theile, Heather Jones, Hope Bates, Jen Gonzales, Jen Wesner, Jennifer Kile, Jenny Griffin, Jenny Lawrence, Jenny MacRunnel, Jessica Wolfsohn, John Scafidi, Karen Benson, Katie Lynn Stripling, Kristin Ashenfelter, Kristin Rydstedt, Kyla Michelle Lacey Waits, Laura-Dawn Francesca MacGregor-Portlock, Lindsay Nichole Leckner, Margarida Azevedo Veloz, Mark Chappell, Meg Griffin, Meredith Winters Patten, Mikka McClain, Nguyen Quynh Trang, Nooce Miller, Pham Hai Yen, Roseann Calabritto, Sarada Spivey, Sarah Ann Diaz, Sarah Kate Fisher, Shari Hearn, Shell Bryce, Sigrun Murr, Stefanie Diegel, Stephanie Kmetz, Stephanie Johns-Bragg, Steve Buck, Summer

Nettleman, Susan Helliesen, Tina Kennedy, Tracy Denison Johnson, Trisha Davis Perry, Valerie Arlene Alcaraz, and the person (or, much more likely, persons) I've forgotten, at least in this timeline.

Extra special thanks to Pete for talking me through the inevitable panic attack as my deadline approached. Ian and Ryan brought me coffee and tea and made me laugh. Griffin kept me company during midnight writing sessions and reminded me that even when deadlines loom, I still need to get out of the chair and attend to important priorities like his dinner.

And finally, a multitude of thanks to you—the readers who took this journey with me. The past few years have been strange beyond measure, and it was a pleasure to hide out for a bit each day in my fictional world. I hope that these books gave you a small break from the chaos and that you'll come along on whatever journey I begin next. Stay safe, and happy time travels!

∞About the Author∞

Rysa Walker is the bestselling author of The Delphi Trilogy (*The Delphi Effect, The Delphi Resistance,* and *The Delphi Revolution*); the CHRONOS Files series (*Timebound,* winner of the grand prize in the 2013 Amazon Breakthrough Novel Awards, *Time's Echo, Time's Edge, Time's Mirror, Time's Divide,* and *Simon Says: Tips for the Intrepid Time Traveler*); and *Now, Then, and Everywhen* and *Red, White, and the Blues* in the CHRONOS Origins series. Her career had its beginnings in a childhood on a cattle ranch, where she read every book she could find, watched *Star Trek* and *The Twilight Zone,* and let her imagination soar into the future and to distant worlds. Her diverse path has spanned roles such as lifeguard, waitress, actress, digital developer, and professor. Through it all, she has pursued her passion for writing the sorts of stories she imagined in her youth. She lives in North Carolina with her husband, her two youngest sons, and a hyperactive golden retriever. Discover more about Rysa and her work at www.rysa.com.